Lovecraft's
Monsters

HAUNTINGS

"That delicious sense of tantalization, of maybe and what if, impelled me through page after page, encountering intriguing characters, spine-shivering settings, and bits and pieces (sometimes literally…of corpses)…."—*Hellnotes*

"Datlow once again proves herself as a master editor. Her mission to broaden readers' concepts of what a haunting can be is nothing short of a success, and the twenty-four stories on display run the gamut from explicitly terrifying to eerily familiar. Readers who wish to be haunted themselves should not miss this one. Highly recommended."—*Arkham Digest*

"[Ellen Datlow] has this crazy knack of consistently putting together stellar anthologies and *Hauntings* is no different."—*Horror Talk*

"Take a gander at Ellen Datlow's stellar collection *Hauntings* and learn what being haunted really means…."—*Revolution SF*

DARKNESS: TWO DECADES OF MODERN HORROR

"This diverse 25-story anthology is a superb sampling of some of the most significant short horror works published between 1985 and 2005. Editor extraordinaire Datlow (*Poe*) includes classic stories from horror icons Clive Barker, Peter Straub, and Stephen King as well as SF and fantasy luminaries Gene Wolfe, Dan Simmons, Neil Gaiman, and Lucius Shepard… This is an anthology to be cherished and an invaluable reference for horror aficionados."—*Publishers Weekly*, starred review

"Make sure you are in a safe place before you open it up."
—*New York Journal of Books*

"Eclectic…a complete overview of some of the best horror stories published in the last twenty years."—*SF Site*

EDITED BY ELLEN DATLOW

LOVECRAFT'S MONSTERS

TACHYON

Tachyon Publications
1459 18th Street #139
San Francisco, CA 94107
www.tachyonpublications.com
tachyon@tachyonpublications.com

Series Editor: Jacob Weisman
Project Editor: Jill Roberts

ISBN 13: 978-1-61696-121-3

Printed in the
United States
by Worzalla
First Edition: 2014

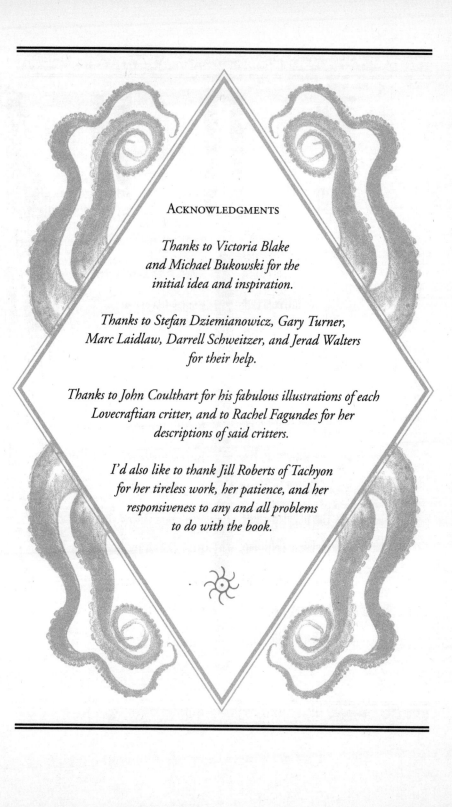

ACKNOWLEDGMENTS

*Thanks to Victoria Blake
and Michael Bukowski for the
initial idea and inspiration.*

*Thanks to Stefan Dziemianowicz, Gary Turner,
Marc Laidlaw, Darrell Schweitzer, and Jerad Walters
for their help.*

*Thanks to John Coulthart for his fabulous illustrations of each
Lovecraftian critter, and to Rachel Fagundes for her
descriptions of said critters.*

*I'd also like to thank Jill Roberts of Tachyon
for her tireless work, her patience, and her
responsiveness to any and all problems
to do with the book.*

#

Foreword

Stefan Dziemianowicz

CTHULHU! YOG-SOTHOTH! AZATHOTH! Shub-Niggurath! Nyarlathotep! Are there any more provocatively named beings in horror fiction? The very spelling of their names suggests the alien and the outré. The tortuous phonetics required to say them out loud equates the unpronounceable with the unspeakable.

These are the monsters of H. P. Lovecraft, some of the most fabulous and horrifying creations in all supernatural fiction. Titanic, biologically impossible beings from dimensions outside our own, they appear only infrequently in Lovecraft's stories, but when they do they sweep aside human beings like so many pesky gnats, leaving a trail of destruction and chaos in their wake. And these five are just Lovecraft's best-known monsters. His complete bestiary includes abominable snowmen, human-amphibian hybrids, lumpen mountains of protoplasm called shoggoths, gore-gulping ghouls, bat-winged night gaunts, sentient fungi, and more. Some of his monsters exist only as consciousnesses in the human bodies that they serially appropriate and discard. Others have no fixed form or substance, and are known only by their malign influence on organic and inorganic matter in their vicinity.

Lovecraft's monsters are the trademark by which most readers, both within and without the genre, recognize his stories today. But there is much more to them, and what Lovecraft hoped to express through them, than there is to other monsters in supernatural fiction. Writing to his friend Frank Belknap Long in 1931, Lovecraft referred to the monster-based pseudo-mythology he was elaborating through his fiction as "Yog-Sothothery," and described it as a tool for overcoming "personal limitation regarding the sense of outsideness" that he hoped to evoke in his stories. Lovecraft disdained traditional folk-myth-based weird tales for their "many blatant puerilities & contradictions of experience which could be subtilised or smoothed over if the supernaturalism were modelled to order for the given case." For Lovecraft, the "new artificial myths" of Yog-Sothothery represented a possible "aesthetic crystallization of that burning & inextinguishable feeling of mixed wonder & oppression which the sensitive imagination experiences upon scaling itself & its restrictions against the vast & provocative abyss of the unknown."

The challenge in writing weird fiction, as Lovecraft saw it, was to give shape to the unknown but in a way that didn't diminish it and, literally, bring it down to earth. In his essay "Supernatural Horror in Literature," he outlined the prerequisites for "the true weird tale" as he saw it: "A certain atmosphere of breathless and unexplainable dread of outer, unknown forces must be present; and there must be a hint, expressed with a seriousness and portentousness becoming its subject, of that most terrible conception of the human brain—a malign and particular suspension or defeat of those fixed laws of Nature which are our only safeguard against the assaults of chaos and the daemons of unplumbed space." What better way to suggest a "defeat of those fixed laws of Nature" than to introduce monstrous beings whose very existence mocked them?

Lovecraft began conjuring monsters virtually from the start of his career. In his first professionally published story, "Dagon," a shipwrecked sailor washed up on a deserted island stumbles upon a monolith whose bas-reliefs depict grotesque aquatic creatures: "They were damnably human in general outline despite webbed hands and feet, shockingly wide and flabby lips, glassy, bulging eyes, and other features less pleasant to recall." The man mistakes them for depictions of a god worshipped by a prehistoric seafaring tribe—then watches in horror as a living representation of the monstrous being emerges from the ocean.

Five years later, Lovecraft published "The Call of Cthulhu," the story that best expressed his aesthetic for the true weird tale. The plot develops from a series of seemingly disassociated events that the narrator pieces together to establish the existence of Cthulhu, a monstrous being from an alien dimension whose existence is so beyond human ken that it is perceived by humans to have the attributes of a god. A totem of Cthulhu reveals it to be a creature not of our earth:

> It seemed to be a sort of monster, or symbol representing a monster, of a form which only a diseased fancy could conceive. If I say that my somewhat extravagant imagination yielded simultaneous pictures of an octopus, a dragon, and a human caricature, I shall not be unfaithful to the spirit of the thing. A pulpy, tentacled head surmounted a grotesque and scaly body with rudimentary wings; but it was the general outline of the whole which made it most shockingly frightful.

But this miniature effigy can hardly do justice to the reality of the monster it depicts, and when the behemoth Cthulhu emerges in the flesh (so to speak) at the story's end, Lovecraft pours on the su-purple-atives to make his point:

> The Thing cannot be described—there is no language for such abysms of shrieking and immemorial lunacy, such eldritch contradictions of all matter, force, and cosmic order. A mountain walked or stumbled.

"The Call of Cthulhu" is the story that laid the foundations for Lovecraft's brand of cosmic horror fiction. When editor Farnsworth Wright accepted it for *Weird Tales* (having already rejected it once), it prompted Lovecraft's now famous proclamation "all of my tales are based on the fundamental premise that common human laws and interests and emotions have no validity or significance in the vast cosmos-at-large."

If "The Call of Cthulhu" was the first of Lovecraft's tales to incarnate cosmic horror in an alien monster, it was by no means his most graphic. That honor goes to "The Dunwich Horror," published in *Weird Tales* in 1929. In this story young Wilbur Whateley is born to the enfeebled daughter of Wizard Whateley, descendant of a degenerated New England bloodline and a dabbler in the occult. No one knows the identity of Wilbur's father but from an early age he shows abnormally advanced physical development, growing to a height and size much greater than one would expect for someone of his youth. One evening, while attempting to pilfer a copy of the *Necronomicon* (that ancient book of forbidden knowledge cited in a number of Lovecraft's stories) from local Miskatonic University, he is mauled to death by a guard dog that rips away most of his clothing. The revelation of Wilbur's savaged remains makes for one of the most spectacularly gruesome scenes in all of Lovecraft's fiction:

It would be trite and not wholly accurate to say that no human pen could describe it, but one may properly say that it could not be vividly visualised by anyone whose ideas of aspect and contour are too closely bound up with the common life-forms of this planet and of the three known dimensions.... Above the waist it was semi-anthropomorphic; though its chest, where the dog's rending paws still rested watchfully, had the leathery, reticulated hide of a crocodile or alligator. The back was piebald with yellow and black, and dimly suggested the squamous covering of certain snakes. Below the waist, though, it was the worst; for here all human resemblance left off and sheer phantasy began. The skin was thickly covered with coarse black fur, and from the abdomen a score of long greenish-grey tentacles with red sucking mouths protruded limply. Their arrangement was odd, and seemed to follow the symmetries of some cosmic geometry unknown to earth or the solar system. On each of the hips, deep set in a kind of pinkish, ciliated orbit, was what seemed to be a rudimentary eye; whilst in lieu of a tail there depended a kind of trunk or feeler with purple annular markings, and with many evidences of being an undeveloped mouth or throat. The limbs, save for their black fur, roughly resembled the hind legs of prehistoric earth's giant saurians; and terminated in ridgy-veined pads that were neither hooves nor claws. When the thing breathed, its tail and tentacles rhythmically changed colour, as if from some circulatory cause normal to the non-human side of its ancestry. In the tentacles this was observable as a deepening of the greenish tinge, whilst in the tail it was manifest as a yellowish appearance which alternated with a sickly greyish-white in the spaces between the purple rings. Of genuine blood there was none; only the foetid greenish-yellow ichor which trickled along the painted floor beyond the radius of the stickiness, and left a curious discolouration behind it.

But leave it Lovecraft to imagine a horror even *worse* than this travesty of organic life. A short time after Wilbur's death, an invisible monster begins rampaging across the New England countryside, mowing down homes, gobbling up the locals, and stomping enormous footprints into the ground. Only after this, the true Dunwich horror, has been dispatched is it revealed that Wilbur and the invisible monster were twins, born of a human mother and the monster Yog-Sothoth—and that, incredibly, of the three, Wilbur was the one who looked the *most human*.

As memorable as the monsters in these stories are, and as vividly as they convey the sense of outsideness Lovecraft hoped to express through his weird fiction, they are not as typical of Lovecraft's fiction as they might seem. Many of the so-called monsters in Lovecraft's stories are more subtle and insidious, and manifest their horrors on a more intimate level. In "The Colour Out of Space," an invisible alien influence in a meteorite that crashes to earth taints the surrounding countryside, bringing a slow and inescapable corruption to the flora, fauna, and humans on the farm where it lands. "The Shadow over Innsmouth" features a town whose peculiar-looking residents are revealed to be the hybrid spawn of human beings and an amphibious deep-sea race. In a number of Lovecraft's best stories—among them "The Thing on the Doorstep," "The Shadow Out of Time," and "The Haunter of the Dark"—the monstrous is expressed in terms of a force or influence that takes possession of a human consciousness or dispossesses a person of his body.

Lovecraft was fond not only of mentioning his monsters from story to story, but also those conceived in the spirit of his writing by Clark Ashton Smith, Robert E. Howard, Frank Belknap Long, Robert Bloch, August Derleth, Henry Kuttner, and other contemporaries. The shared world of monsters, books of forbidden lore, and eerie locales that they created has, since Lovecraft's death, been dubbed the Cthulhu Mythos, a loose and inclusive subgenre of Lovecraft homages and pastiches that varies in its fidelity to Lovecraft's ideas and continues to grow through the contributions of successive generations of writers. *Lovecraft's Monsters* is itself a collection of tributes to Lovecraft, all of whose selections either explicitly or implicitly reference Lovecraft's most monstrous creations and the tales of cosmic horror that gave them birth. Howard Waldrop and Steven Utley's "Black as the Pit, from Pole to Pole" appropriates elements of Lovecraft's "At the Mountains of Madness" for its monsterfest inside a hollow earth. Neil Gaiman contributes to Lovecraft's Innsmouth mythology with "Only the End of the World Again," a tale that pits folk-myth-based horrors against Lovecraftian horrors. Kim Newman's "A Quarter to Three" turns

Lovecraft's Innsmouth inside out for a comic pop culture riff. Thomas Ligotti's "The Sect of the Idiot" evokes Lovecraftian cosmicism in its most abstract form, while Laird Barron's "Bulldozer" gives it an earthy physicality. John Langan's "Children of the Fang" writes a new chapter for Lovecraft's tale "The Nameless City." And Fred Chappell's "Remnants" conveys through the "wrongness" that humans sense in the alien architecture overwhelming their occupied earth the sense of outsideness that Lovecraft considered crucial to weird fiction. The variety and eclecticism of the stories collected in this volume surely would have pleased Lovecraft, who no doubt would have been surprised to find that his tales of monsters and the monstrous had inspired so many writers of today to scale the imaginative heights cleared here.

Stefan Dziemianowicz
New York, 2013

Introduction

Ellen Datlow

I NTEREST IN H. P. LOVECRAFT's fiction never seems to wane. His influence on his contemporaries and on so many writers since he died is a testament to the power of his imagination. Why might this be? Possibly it's the richness of the mythos he created. The monsters, the unseen world behind the screen of normality in *our* world.

My initial exposure to the mythos was during my early teens, when I was reading lots of science fiction, so my experience with Lovecraft strongly contrasted with the sense of wonder and embrace of the unknown in science fiction. H. P. Lovecraft's hidden worlds and the mythos he created seemed inspired by and in turn promoted a sense of fear and dread of the unknown.

Over time, I've read numerous pastiches of Lovecraft, but most—for me, at least—are too obvious, and bring little new to the table. I'm far more impressed and often surprised by writers who use the mythos in ways that its creator never dreamed of (and might indeed have him spinning in his grave).

This is the second time I've edited a Lovecraftian anthology. My first was *Lovecraft Unbound*, containing mostly new stories inspired by Lovecraft. As readers familiar with my theme anthologies know, I always attempt to push thematic boundaries to the breaking point: that is, if I can justify to myself that a story I encounter (by commissioning originals, or by researching and listening to suggestions for reprints) fits within the theme of my book, and I love that story, I'll acquire and publish it.

For *Lovecraft's Monsters*, I had three goals in choosing stories: the first, as usual, was to avoid pastiches; the second was to use stories that have not been overly reprinted in the many recent mythos anthologies; third, I wanted to showcase Lovecraftian-influenced stories by at least some authors not known for that kind of story. So in this case there are poems by Gemma Files, and stories by Steve Rasnic Tem, Karl Edward Wagner, Joe R. Lansdale, Brian Hodge, Nadia Bulkin, and a collaboration by Howard Waldrop and Steven Utley.

I believe I've succeeded in all three goals and hope that you'll enjoy reading *Lovecraft's Monsters* as much as I did working on it.

THE DEEP ONE

Only the End of the World Again

Neil Gaiman

IT WAS A bad day: I woke up naked in the bed, with a cramp in my stomach, feeling more or less like hell. Something about the quality of the light, stretched and metallic, like the colour of a migraine, told me it was afternoon.

The room was freezing—literally: there was a thin crust of ice on the inside of the windows. The sheets on the bed around me were ripped and clawed, and there was animal hair in the bed. It itched.

I was thinking about staying in bed for the next week—I'm always tired after a change—but a wave of nausea forced me to disentangle myself from the bedding, and to stumble, hurriedly, into the apartment's tiny bathroom.

The cramps hit me again as I got to the bathroom door. I held on to the door-frame and I started to sweat. Maybe it was a fever; I hoped I wasn't coming down with something.

The cramping was sharp in my guts. My head felt swimmy. I crumpled to the floor, and, before I could manage to raise my head enough to find the toilet bowl, I began to spew.

I vomited a foul-smelling thin yellow liquid; in it was a dog's paw—my guess was a Doberman's, but I'm not really a dog person; a tomato peel; some diced carrots and sweet corn; some lumps of half-chewed meat, raw; and some fingers. They were fairly small, pale fingers, obviously a child's.

"Shit."

The cramps eased up, and the nausea subsided. I lay on the floor, with stinking drool coming out of my mouth and nose, with the tears you cry when you're being sick drying on my cheeks.

When I felt a little better I picked up the paw and the fingers from the pool of spew and threw them into the toilet bowl, flushed them away.

I turned on the tap, rinsed out my mouth with the briny Innsmouth water, and spat it into the sink. I mopped up the rest of the sick as best I could with washcloth and toilet paper. Then I turned on the shower, and stood in the bathtub like a zombie as the hot water sluiced over me.

I soaped myself down, body and hair. The meagre lather turned grey; I must have been filthy. My hair was matted with something that felt like dried blood, and I worked at it with the bar of soap until it was gone. Then I stood under the shower until the water turned icy.

There was a note under the door from my landlady. It said that I owed her for two weeks' rent. It said that all the answers were in the Book of Revelations. It said that I made a lot of noise coming home in the early hours of this morning, and she'd thank me to be quieter in future. It said that when the Elder Gods rose up from the ocean, all the scum of the Earth, all the non-believers, all the human garbage and the wastrels and deadbeats would be swept away, and the world would be cleansed by ice and deep water. It said that she felt she ought to remind me that she had assigned me a shelf in the refrigerator when I arrived and she'd thank me if in the future I'd keep to it.

I crumpled the note, dropped it on the floor, where it lay alongside the Big Mac cartons and the empty pizza cartons, and the long-dead dried slices of pizza.

It was time to go to work.

I'd been in Innsmouth for two weeks, and I disliked it. It smelled fishy. It was a claustrophobic little town: marshland to the east, cliffs to the west, and, in the centre, a harbour that held a few rotting fishing boats, and was not even scenic at sunset. The yuppies had come to Innsmouth in the 80s anyway, bought their picturesque fisherman's cottages overlooking the harbour. The yuppies had been gone for some years, now, and the cottages by the bay were crumbling, abandoned.

The inhabitants of Innsmouth lived here and there in and around the town, and in the trailer parks that ringed it, filled with dank mobile homes that were never going anywhere.

I got dressed, pulled on my boots and put on my coat and left my room. My landlady was nowhere to be seen. She was a short, pop-eyed woman, who spoke little, although she left extensive notes for me pinned to doors and placed where

I might see them; she kept the house filled with the smell of boiling seafood: huge pots were always simmering on the kitchen stove, filled with things with too many legs and other things with no legs at all.

There were other rooms in the house, but no-one else rented them. No-one in their right mind would come to Innsmouth in winter.

Outside the house it didn't smell much better. It was colder, though, and my breath steamed in the sea air. The snow on the streets was crusty and filthy; the clouds promised more snow.

A cold, salty wind came up off the bay. The gulls were screaming miserably. I felt shitty. My office would be freezing, too. On the corner of Marsh Street and Leng Avenue was a bar, "The Opener," a squat building with small, dark windows that I'd passed two dozen times in the last couple of weeks. I hadn't been in before, but I really needed a drink, and besides, it might be warmer in there. I pushed open the door.

The bar was indeed warm. I stamped the snow off my boots and went inside. It was almost empty and smelled of old ashtrays and stale beer. A couple of elderly men were playing chess by the bar. The barman was reading a battered old gilt-and-green-leather edition of the poetical works of Alfred, Lord Tennyson.

"Hey. How about a Jack Daniel's straight up?"

"Sure thing. You're new in town," he told me, putting his book face down on the bar, pouring the drink into a glass.

"Does it show?"

He smiled, passed me the Jack Daniel's. The glass was filthy, with a greasy thumb-print on the side, and I shrugged and knocked back the drink anyway. I could barely taste it.

"Hair of the dog?" he said.

"In a manner of speaking."

"There is a belief," said the barman, whose fox-red hair was tightly greased back, "that the *lykanthropoi* can be returned to their natural forms by thanking them, while they're in wolf form, or by calling them by their given names."

"Yeah? Well, thanks."

He poured another shot for me, unasked. He looked a little like Peter Lorre, but then, most of the folk in Innsmouth look a little like Peter Lorre, including my landlady.

I sank the Jack Daniel's, this time felt it burning down into my stomach, the way it should.

"It's what they say. I never said I believed it."

"What *do* you believe?"

"Burn the girdle."

"Pardon?"

"The *lykanthropoi* have girdles of human skin, given to them at their first transformation, by their masters in hell. Burn the girdle."

One of the old chess-players turned to me then, his eyes huge and blind and protruding. "If you drink rain-water out of warg-wolf's paw-print, that'll make a wolf of you, when the moon is full," he said. "The only cure is to hunt down the wolf that made the print in the first place and cut off its head with a knife forged of virgin silver."

"Virgin, huh?" I smiled.

His chess partner, bald and wrinkled, shook his head and croaked a single sad sound. Then he moved his queen, and croaked again.

There are people like him all over Innsmouth.

I paid for the drinks, and left a dollar tip on the bar. The barman was reading his book once more, and ignored it.

Outside the bar big wet kissy flakes of snow had begun to fall, settling in my hair and eyelashes. I hate snow. I hate New England. I hate Innsmouth: it's no place to be alone, but if there's a good place to be alone I've not found it yet. Still, business has kept me on the move for more moons than I like to think about. Business, and other things.

I walked a couple of blocks down Marsh Street—like most of Innsmouth, an unattractive mixture of eighteenth-century American Gothic houses, late nineteenth-century stunted brownstones, and late twentieth prefab grey-brick boxes—until I got to a boarded-up fried chicken joint, and I went up the stone steps next to the store and unlocked the rusting metal security door.

There was a liquor store across the street; a palmist was operating on the second floor.

Someone had scrawled graffiti in black marker on the metal: *just die,* it said. Like it was easy.

The stairs were bare wood; the plaster was stained and peeling. My one-room office was at the top of the stairs.

I don't stay anywhere long enough to bother with my name in gilt on glass. It was handwritten in block letters on a piece of ripped cardboard that I'd thumbtacked to the door.

LAWRENCE TALBOT.
ADJUSTOR.

I unlocked the door to my office and went in.

I inspected my office, while adjectives like *seedy* and *rancid* and *squalid* wandered through my head, then gave up, outclassed. It was fairly unprepossessing—a desk, an office chair, an empty filing cabinet; a window, which gave you a terrific view of the liquor store and the empty palmist's. The smell of old cooking grease permeated from the store below. I wondered how long the fried chicken joint had been boarded up; I imagined a multitude of black cockroaches swarming over every surface in the darkness beneath me.

"That's the shape of the world that you're thinking of there," said a deep, dark voice, deep enough that I felt it in the pit of my stomach.

There was an old armchair in one corner of the office. The remains of a pattern showed through the patina of age and grease the years had given it. It was the colour of dust.

The fat man sitting in the armchair, his eyes still tightly closed, continued, "We look about in puzzlement at our world, with a sense of unease and disquiet. We think of ourselves as scholars in arcane liturgies, single men trapped in worlds beyond our devising. The truth is far simpler: there are things in the darkness beneath us that wish us harm."

His head was lolled back on the armchair, and the tip of his tongue poked out of the corner of his mouth.

"You read my mind?"

The man in the armchair took a slow deep breath that rattled in the back of his throat. He really was immensely fat, with stubby fingers like discoloured sausages. He wore a thick old coat, once black, now an indeterminate grey. The snow on his boots had not entirely melted.

"Perhaps. The end of the world is a strange concept. The world is always ending, and the end is always being averted, by love or foolishness or just plain old dumb luck.

"Ah well. It's too late now: the Elder Gods have chosen their vessels. When the moon rises…"

A thin trickle of drool came from one corner of his mouth, trickled down in a thread of silver to his collar. Something scuttled down into the shadows of his coat.

"Yeah? What happens when the moon rises?"

The man in the armchair stirred, opened two little eyes, red and swollen, and blinked them in waking.

"I dreamed I had many mouths," he said, his new voice oddly small and breathy for such a huge man. "I dreamed every mouth was opening and closing independently. Some mouths were talking, some whispering, some eating, some waiting in silence."

He looked around, wiped the spittle from the corner of his mouth, sat back in the chair, blinking puzzledly. "Who are you?"

"I'm the guy that rents this office," I told him.

He belched suddenly, loudly. "I'm sorry," he said, in his breathy voice, and lifted himself heavily from the armchair. He was shorter than I was, when he was standing. He looked me up and down blearily. "Silver bullets," he pronounced, after a short pause. "Old-fashioned remedy."

"Yeah," I told him. "That's so obvious—must be why I didn't think of it. Gee, I could just kick myself. I really could."

"You're making fun of an old man," he told me.

"Not really. I'm sorry. Now, out of here. Some of us have work to do."

He shambled out. I sat down in the swivel chair at the desk by the window, and discovered, after some minutes, through trial and error, that if I swiveled the chair to the left it fell off its base.

So I sat still and waited for the dusty black telephone on my desk to ring, while the light slowly leaked away from the winter sky.

Ring.

A man's voice: *Had I thought about aluminum siding?* I put down the phone.

There was no heating in the office. I wondered how long the fat man had been asleep in the armchair.

Twenty minutes later the phone rang again. A crying woman implored me to help her find her five-year-old daughter, missing since last night, stolen from her bed. The family dog had vanished too.

I don't do missing children, I told her. *I'm sorry: too many bad memories.* I put down the telephone, feeling sick again.

It was getting dark now, and, for the first time since I had been in Innsmouth, the neon sign across the street flicked on. It told me that Madame Ezekiel performed Tarot Readings and Palmistry. Red neon stained the falling snow the colour of new blood.

Armageddon is averted by small actions. That's the way it was. That's the way it always has to be.

The phone rang a third time. I recognised the voice; it was the aluminum-siding man again. "You know," he said, chattily, "transformation from man to animal and back being, by definition, impossible, we need to look for other solutions. Depersonalisation, obviously, and likewise some form of projection. Brain damage? Perhaps. Pseudoneurotic schizophrenia? Laughably so. Some cases have been treated with intravenous thioridazine hydrochloride."

"Successfully?"

He chuckled. "That's what I like. A man with a sense of humour. I'm sure we can do business."

"I told you already. I don't need aluminum siding."

"Our business is more remarkable than that, and of far greater importance. You're new in town, Mr. Talbot. It would be a pity if we found ourselves at, shall we say, loggerheads?"

"You can say whatever you like, pal. In my book you're just another adjustment, waiting to be made."

"We're ending the world, Mr. Talbot. The Deep Ones will rise out of their ocean graves and eat the moon like a ripe plum."

"Then I won't ever have to worry about full moons anymore, will I?"

"Don't try and cross us," he began, but I growled at him, and he fell silent.

Outside my window the snow was still falling.

Across Marsh Street, in the window directly opposite mine, the most beautiful woman I had ever seen stood in the ruby glare of her neon sign, and she stared at me.

She beckoned, with one finger.

I put down the phone on the aluminum-siding man for the second time that afternoon, and went downstairs, and crossed the street at something close to a run; but I looked both ways before I crossed.

She was dressed in silks. The room was lit only by candles, and stank of incense and patchouli oil.

She smiled at me as I walked in, beckoned me over to her seat by the window. She was playing a card game with a tarot deck, some version of solitaire. As I reached her, one elegant hand swept up the cards, wrapped them in a silk scarf, placed them gently in a wooden box.

The scents of the room made my head pound. I hadn't eaten anything today, I realised; perhaps that was what was making me lightheaded. I sat down, across the table from her, in the candle-light.

She extended her hand, and took my hand in hers.

She stared at my palm, touched it, softly, with her forefinger.

"Hair?" She was puzzled.

"Yeah, well. I'm on my own a lot." I grinned. I had hoped it was a friendly grin, but she raised an eyebrow at me anyway.

"When I look at you," said Madame Ezekiel, "this is what I see. I see the eye of a man. Also I see the eye of a wolf. In the eye of a man I see honesty, decency, innocence. I see an upright man who walks on the square. And in the eye of wolf I see a groaning and a growling, night howls and cries, I see a monster running with blood-flecked spittle in the darkness of the borders of the town."

"How can you see a growl or a cry?"

She smiled. "It is not hard," she said. Her accent was not American. It was Russian, or Maltese, or Egyptian perhaps. "In the eye of the mind we see many things."

Madame Ezekiel closed her green eyes. She had remarkably long eyelashes; her skin was pale, and her black hair was never still—it drifted gently around her head, in the silks, as if it were floating on distant tides.

"There is a traditional way," she told me. "A way to wash off a bad shape. You stand in running water, in clear spring water, while eating white rose petals."

"And then?"

"The shape of darkness will be washed from you."

"It will return," I told her, "with the next full of the moon."

"So," said Madame Ezekiel, "once the shape is washed from you, you open your veins in the running water. It will sting mightily, of course. But the river will carry the blood away."

She was dressed in silks, in scarves and cloths of a hundred different colours, each bright and vivid, even in the muted light of the candles.

Her eyes opened.

"Now," she said. "The Tarot." She unwrapped her deck from the black silk scarf that held it, passed me the cards to shuffle. I fanned them, riffed and bridged them.

"Slower, slower," she said. "Let them get to know you. Let them love you, like…like a woman would love you."

I held them tightly, then passed them back to her.

She turned over the first card. It was called *The Warwolf.* It showed darkness and amber eyes, a smile in white and red.

Her green eyes showed confusion. They were the green of emeralds. "This is not a card from my deck," she said, and turned over the next card. "What did you do to my cards?"

"Nothing, ma'am. I just held them. That's all."

The card she had turned over was *The Deep One.* It showed something green and faintly octopoid. The thing's mouths —if they were indeed mouths and not tentacles—began to writhe on the card as I watched.

She covered it with another card, and then another, and another. The rest of the cards were blank pasteboard.

"Did you do that?" She sounded on the verge of tears.

"No."

"Go now," she said.

"But—"

"Go." She looked down, as if trying to convince herself I no longer existed.

I stood up, in the room that smelled of incense and candle-wax, and looked out of her window, across the street. A light flashed, briefly, in my office window. Two men, with flashlights, were walking around. They opened the empty filing cabinet, peered around, then took up their positions, one in the armchair, the other behind the door, waiting for me to return. I smiled to myself. It was cold and inhospitable in my office, and with any luck they would wait there for hours until they finally decided I wasn't coming back.

So I left Madame Ezekiel turning over her cards, one by one, staring at them as if that would make the pictures return; and I went downstairs, and walked back down Marsh Street until I reached the bar.

The place was empty, now; the barman was smoking a cigarette, which he stubbed out as I came in.

"Where are the chess-fiends?"

"It's a big night for them tonight. They'll be down at the bay. Let's see: you're a Jack Daniel's? Right?"

"Sounds good."

He poured it for me. I recognised the thumb-print from the last time I had the glass. I picked up the volume of Tennyson poems from the bar-top.

"Good book?"

The fox-haired barman took his book from me, opened it and read:

"Below the thunders of the upper deep;
Far, far beneath in the abysmal sea,
His ancient dreamless, uninvaded sleep
The Kraken sleepeth…"

I'd finished my drink. "So? What's your point?"

He walked around the bar, took me over to the window. "See? Out there?"

He pointed toward the west of the town, toward the cliffs. As I stared a bonfire was kindled on the cliff-tops; it flared and began to burn with a copper-green flame.

"They're going to wake the Deep Ones," said the barman. "The stars and the planets and the moon are all in the right places. It's time. The dry lands will sink, and the seas shall rise…"

"For the world shall be cleansed with ice and floods and I'll thank you to keep to your own shelf in the refrigerator," I said.

"Sorry?"

"Nothing. What's the quickest way to get up to those cliffs?"

"Back up Marsh Street. Hang a left at the Church of Dagon, till you reach Manuxet Way and then just keep on going." He pulled a coat off the back of the door, and put it on. "C'mon. I'll walk you up there. I'd hate to miss any of the fun."

"You sure?"

"No-one in town's going to be drinking tonight." We stepped out, and he locked the door to the bar behind us.

It was chilly in the street, and fallen snow blew about the ground, like white mists. From street level I could no longer tell if Madame Ezekiel was in her den above her neon sign, or if my guests were still waiting for me in my office.

We put our heads down against the wind, and we walked.

Over the noise of the wind I heard the barman talking to himself:

"Winnow with giant arms the slumbering green," he was saying.
"There hath he lain for ages and will lie
Battening upon huge seaworms in his sleep,
Until the latter fire shall heat the deep;
Then once by men and angels to be seen,
In roaring he shall rise…"

He stopped there, and we walked on together in silence, with blown snow stinging our faces.

And on the surface die, I thought, but said nothing out loud.

Twenty minutes' walking and we were out of Innsmouth. The Manuxet Way stopped when we left the town, and it became a narrow dirt path, partly covered with snow and ice, and we slipped and slid our way up it in the darkness.

The moon was not yet up, but the stars had already begun to come out. There were so many of them. They were sprinkled like diamond dust and crushed sapphires across the night sky. You can see so many stars from the seashore, more than you could ever see back in the city.

At the top of the cliff, behind the bonfire, two people were waiting—one huge and fat, one much smaller. The barman left my side and walked over to stand beside them, facing me.

"Behold," he said, "the sacrificial wolf." There was now an oddly familiar quality to his voice.

I didn't say anything. The fire was burning with green flames, and it lit the three of them from below; classic spook lighting.

"Do you know why I brought you up here?" asked the barman, and I knew then why his voice was familiar: it was the voice of the man who had attempted to sell me aluminum-siding.

"To stop the world ending?"

He laughed at me, then.

The second figure was the fat man I had found asleep in my office chair. "Well, if you're going to get eschatological about it…" he murmured, in a voice deep enough to rattle walls. His eyes were closed. He was fast asleep.

The third figure was shrouded in dark silks and smelled of patchouli oil. It held a knife. It said nothing.

"This night," said the barman, "the moon is the moon of the Deep Ones. This night are the stars configured in the shapes and patterns of the dark, old times. This night, if we call them, they will come. If our sacrifice is worthy. If our cries are heard."

The moon rose, huge and amber and heavy, on the other side of the bay, and a chorus of low croaking rose with it from the ocean far beneath us.

Moonlight on snow and ice is not daylight, but it will do. And my eyes were getting sharper with the moon: in the cold waters men like frogs were surfacing and submerging in a slow water-dance. Men like frogs, and women, too: it seemed to me that I could see my landlady down there, writhing and croaking in the bay with the rest of them.

It was too soon for another change; I was still exhausted from the night before; but I felt strange under that amber moon.

"Poor wolf-man," came a whisper from the silks. "All his dreams have come to this; a lonely death upon a distant cliff."

I will dream if I want to, I said, *and my death is my own affair.* But I was unsure if I had said it out loud.

Senses heighten in the moon's light; I heard the roar of the ocean still, but now, overlaid on top of it, I could hear each wave rise and crash; I heard the splash of the frog people; I heard the drowned whispers of the dead in the bay; I heard the creak of green wrecks far beneath the ocean.

Smell improves, too. The aluminum-siding man was human, while the fat man had other blood in him.

And the figure in the silks...

I had smelled her perfume when I wore man-shape. Now I could smell something else, less heady, beneath it. A smell of decay, of putrefying meat, and rotten flesh.

The silks fluttered. She was moving toward me. She held the knife.

"Madame Ezekiel?" My voice was roughening and coarsening. Soon I would lose it all. I didn't understand what was happening, but the moon was rising higher and higher, losing its amber colour, and filling my mind with its pale light.

"Madame Ezekiel?"

"You deserve to die," she said, her voice cold and low. "If only for what you did to my cards. They were old."

"I don't die," I told her. *"Even a man who is pure in heart, and says his prayers by night.* Remember?"

"It's bullshit," she said. "You know what the oldest way to end the curse of the werewolf is?"

"No."

The bonfire burned brighter now, burned with the green of the world beneath the sea, the green of algae, and of slowly drifting weed; burned with the colour of emeralds.

"You simply wait till they're in human shape, a whole month away from another change; then you take the sacrificial knife, and you kill them. That's all."

I turned to run, but the barman was behind me, pulling my arms, twisting my wrists up into the small of my back. The knife glinted pale silver in the moonlight. Madame Ezekiel smiled.

She sliced across my throat.

Blood began to gush, and then to flow. And then it slowed, and stopped...

—The pounding in the front of my head, the pressure in the back. All a roiling change a how-wow-row-now change a red wall coming towards me from the night

—i tasted stars dissolved in brine, fizzy and distant and salt

—my fingers prickled with pins and my skin was lashed with tongues of flame my eyes were topaz I could taste the night

My breath steamed and billowed in the icy air. I growled involuntarily, low in my throat. My forepaws were touching the snow. I pulled back, tensed, and sprang at her. There was a sense of corruption that hung in the air, like a mist, surrounding me. High in my leap I seemed to pause, and something burst like a soapbubble...

I was deep, deep in the darkness under the sea, standing on all fours on a slimy rock floor, at the entrance of some kind of citadel, built of enormous, rough-hewn stones. The stones gave off a pale glow-in-the-dark light; a ghostly luminescence, like the hands of a watch.

A cloud of black blood trickled from my neck.

She was standing in the doorway, in front of me. She was now six, maybe seven feet high. There was flesh on her skeletal bones, pitted and gnawed, but the silks were weeds, drifting in the cold water, down there in the dreamless deeps. They hid her face like a slow green veil.

There were limpets growing on the upper surfaces of her arms, and on the flesh that hung from her ribcage.

I felt like I was being crushed. I couldn't think any more.

She moved towards me. The weed that surrounded her head shifted. She had a face like the stuff you don't want to eat in a sushi counter, all suckers and spines and drifting anemone fronds; and somewhere in all that I knew she was smiling.

I pushed with my hind-legs. We met there, in the deep, and we struggled. It was so cold, so dark. I closed my jaws on her face, and felt something rend and tear.

It was almost a kiss, down there in the abysmal deep...

I landed softly on the snow, a silk scarf locked between my jaws.

The other scarves were fluttering to the ground. Madame Ezekiel was nowhere to be seen.

The silver knife lay on the ground, in the snow. I waited on all fours, in the moonlight, soaking wet. I shook myself, spraying the brine about. I heard it hiss and spit when it hit the fire.

I was dizzy, and weak. I pulled the air deep into my lungs.

Down, far below, in the bay, I could see the frog people hanging on the surface of the sea like dead things; for a handful of seconds they drifted back and forth on the tide, then they twisted and leapt, and each by each they *plop-plopped* down into the bay and vanished beneath the sea.

There was a scream. It was the fox-haired bartender, the pop-eyed aluminum-siding salesman, and he was staring at the night sky, at the clouds that were drifting in, covering the stars, and he was screaming. There was rage and there was frustration in that cry, and it scared me.

He picked up the knife from the ground, wiped the snow from the handle with his fingers, wiped the blood from the blade with his coat. Then he looked across at me. He was crying. "You bastard," he said. "What did you do to her?"

I would have told him I didn't do anything to her, that she was still on guard far beneath the ocean, but I couldn't talk any more, only growl and whine and howl.

He was crying. He stank of insanity, and of disappointment. He raised the knife and ran at me, and I moved to one side.

Some people just can't adjust even to tiny changes. The barman stumbled past me, off the cliff, into nothing.

In the moonlight blood is black, not red, and the marks he left on the cliff-side as he fell and bounced and fell were smudges of black and dark grey. Then, finally, he lay still on the icy rocks at the base of the cliff, until an arm reached out from the sea and dragged him, with a slowness that was almost painful to watch, under the dark water.

A hand scratched the back of my head. It felt good.

"What was she? Just an avatar of the Deep Ones, sir. An eidolon, a manifestation, if you will, sent up to us from the uttermost deeps to bring about the end of the world."

I bristled.

"No, it's over, for now. You disrupted her, sir. And the ritual is most spe-cific. Three of us must stand together and call the sacred names, while in-nocent blood pools and pulses at our feet."

I looked up at the fat man, and whined a query. He patted me on the back of the neck, sleepily.

"Of course she doesn't love you, boy. She hardly even exists on this plane, in any material sense."

The snow began to fall once more. The bonfire was going out.

"Your change tonight, incidentally, I would opine, is a direct result of the self-same celestial configurations and lunar forces that made tonight such a perfect night to bring back my old friends from Underneath..."

He continued talking, in his deep voice, and perhaps he was telling me important things. I'll never know, for the appetite was growing inside me, and his words had lost all but the shadow of any meaning; I had no further interest in the sea or the cliff-top or the fat man.

There were deer running in the woods beyond the meadow: I could smell them on the winter's night's air.

And I was, above all things, hungry.

I was naked when I came to myself again, early the next morning, a half-eaten deer next to me in the snow. A fly crawled across its eye, and its tongue lolled out of its dead mouth, making it look comical and pathetic, like an animal in a newspaper cartoon.

The snow was stained a fluorescent crimson where the deer's belly had been torn out.

My face and chest were sticky and red with the stuff. My throat was scabbed and scarred, and it stung; by the next full moon it would be whole once more.

The sun was a long way away, small and yellow, but the sky was blue and cloudless, and there was no breeze. I could hear the roar of the sea some dis-tance away.

I was cold and naked and bloody and alone; ah well, I thought: it happens to all of us, in the beginning. I just get it once a month.

I was painfully exhausted, but I would hold out until I found a deserted barn, or a cave; and then I was going to sleep for a couple of weeks.

A hawk flew low over the snow toward me, with something dangling from its talons. It hovered above me for a heartbeat, then dropped a small grey squid in the snow at my feet, and flew upward. The flaccid thing lay there, still and silent and tentacled in the bloody snow.

I took it as an omen, but whether good or bad I couldn't say and I didn't really care any more; I turned my back to the sea, and on the shadowy town of Innsmouth, and began to make my way toward the city.

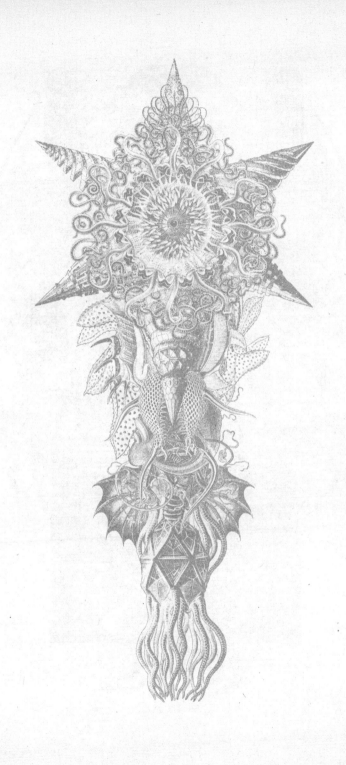

Bulldozer
Laird Barron

I.

—Then He bites off my shooting hand.

Christ on a pony, here's a new dimension of pain.

The universe flares white. A storm of dandelion seeds, a cyclone of fire. That's the Coliseum on its feet, a full-blown German orchestra, a cannon blast inside my skull, the top of my skull coming off.

I better suck it up or I'm done for.

I'm a Pinkerton man. That means something. I've got the gun, a cold blue Colt, and a card with my name engraved beneath the unblinking eye. I'm the genuine article. I'm a dead shot, a deadeye Dick. I was on the mark in Baltimore when assassins went for Honest Abe. I skinned my iron and plugged them varmints. Abe should've treated me to the theater. Might still be here. Might be in a rocker scribbling how the South was won.

Can't squeeze no trigger now can I? I can squirt my initials on the ceiling.

I'm a Pinkerton I'm a Pinkerton a goddamned Pinkerton.

That's right you sorry sonofabitch you chew on that you swallow like a python and I'll keep on chanting it while I paint these walls.

Belphegor ain't my FatherMother Father thou art in Heaven Jesus loves me. Jesus Christ.

My balls clank when I walk.

I'm walking to the window.

Well I'm crawling.

If I make it to the window I'll smash the glass and do a stiff drop.

I've got to hustle the shades are dropping from left to right.

Earth on its axis tilting to the black black black iris rolling back inside a socket.

I'm glad the girl hopped the last train. Hope she's in Frisco selling it for more money than she's ever seen here in the sticks.

I taste hard Irish whiskey sweet inside her navel. She's whip smart she's got gams to run she's got blue eyes like the barrel of the gun on the floor under the dresser I can't believe how much blood can spurt from a stump I can't believe it's come to this I hear Him coming heavy on the floorboards buckling He's had a bite He wants more meat.

Pick up the iron southpaw Pinkerton pick it up and point like a man with grit in his liver not a drunk seeing double.

Hallelujah.

Who's laughing now you slack-jawed motherfucker I told you I'm a dead shot now you know now that it's too late.

Let me just say kapow-kapow.

I rest my case, ladies and gennulmen of the jury. I'm

2.

"A Pinkerton man. Well, shit my drawers." The engineer, a greasy brute in striped coveralls, gave me the once-over. Then he spat a stream of chaw and bent his back to feeding the furnace. Never heard of my man Rueben Hicks, so he said. He didn't utter another word until the narrow gauge spur rolled up to the wretched outskirts of Purdon.

Ugly as rot in a molar, here we were after miles of pasture and hill stitched with barbwire.

Rude frame boxes squatted in the stinking alkaline mud beside the river. Rain pounded like God's own darning needles, stood in orange puddles along the banks, pooled in ruts beneath the awnings. Dull lamplight warmed coke-rimed windows. Shadows fluttered, moths against glass. Already, above the hiss and drum of the rain came faint screams, shouts, piano music.

Just another wild and wooly California mining town that sprang from the ground fast and would fall to ruin faster when the gold played out. Three decades was as the day of a mayfly in the scope of the great dim geography of an ancient continent freshly opened to white men.

Industry crowded in on the main street: Bank. Hotel. Whorehouse. Feed & Tack. Dry Goods. Sawbones. Sheriff's Office. A whole bunch of barrelhouses. Light of the Lord Baptist Temple up the lane and yonder. Purdon Cemetery. A-frame houses, cottages, shanties galore. Lanky men in flannels. Scrawny sows with litters of squalling brats. A rat warren.

The bruised mist held back a wilderness of pines and crooked hills. End of the world for all intents and purposes.

I stood on the leaking platform and decided this was a raw deal. I didn't care if the circus strongman was behind one of the piss-burned saloon facades, swilling whiskey, feeling up the thigh of a horse-toothed showgirl. I'd temporarily lost my hard-on for his scalp with the first rancid-sweet whiff of gunsmoke and open sewage. Suddenly, I'd had a bellyful.

Nothing for it but to do it. I slung my rifle, picked up my bags, and began the slog.

3.

I signed *Jonah Koenig* on the ledger at the Riverfront Hotel, a rambling colonial monolith with oil paintings of Andrew Jackson, Ulysses S. Grant, and the newly anointed Grover Cleveland hanging large as doom in the lobby. This wasn't the first time I'd used my real name on a job since the affair in Schuyllkill, just the first time it felt natural. A sense of finality had settled into my bones.

Hicks surely knew I was closing in. Frankly, I didn't much care after eleven months of eating coal dust from Boston to San Francisco. I cared about securing a whiskey, a bath, and a lay. Not in any particular order.

The clerk, a veteran of the trade, understood perfectly. He set me up on the third floor in a room with a liquor cabinet, a poster bed, and a view of the mountains. The presidential suite. Some kid drew a washtub of lukewarm water and took my travel clothes to get cleaned. Shortly, a winsome, blue-eyed girl in a low-cut dress arrived without knocking. She unlocked a bottle of bourbon, two glasses, and offered to scrub my back.

She told me to call her Violet and didn't seem fazed that I was buck-naked or that I'd almost blown her head off. I grinned and hung gun and belt on the back of a chair. Tomorrow was more than soon enough to brace the sheriff.

Violet sidled over, got a handle on the situation without preamble. She had enough sense not to mention the brand on my left shoulder, the old needle tracks, or the field of puckered scars uncoiling on my back.

We got so busy I completely forgot to ask if she'd ever happened to screw a dear chum of mine as went by Rueben Hicks. Or Tom Mullen, or Ezra Slade. Later I was half-seas over, and when I awoke she was gone.

I noticed a crack in the plaster. A bleeding fault line.

4.

"Business or pleasure, Mr. Koenig?" Sheriff Murtaugh was a stout Irishman of my generation who'd lost most of his brogue and all of his hair. His right leg was propped on the filthy desk, foot encased in bandages gone the shade of rotten fruit. It reeked of gangrene. "Chink stabbed it with a pickaxe, can y' beat that? Be gone to hell before I let Doc Campion have a peek—he'll want to chop the fucker at the ankle." He'd laughed, polishing his tarnished lawman's star with his sleeve. Supposedly there was a camp full of Chinese nearby; the ones who'd stayed on and fallen into mining after the railroad pushed west. Bad sorts, according to the sheriff and his perforated foot.

We sat in his cramped office, sharing evil coffee from a pot that had probably been bubbling on the stove for several days. At the end of the room was the lockup, dingy as a Roman catacomb and vacant but for a deputy named Levi sleeping off a bender in an open cell.

I showed Murtaugh a creased photograph of Hicks taken during a P. T. Barnum extravaganza in Philadelphia. Hicks was lifting a grand piano on his back while ladies in tights applauded before a pyramid of elephants. "Recognize this fellow? I got a lead off a wanted poster in Frisco. Miner thought he'd seen him in town. Wasn't positive." The miner was a nice break—the trail was nearly three months cold, and I'd combed every two-bit backwater within six hundred miles before the man and I bumped into each other at the Gold Digger Saloon and started swapping tales.

"Who wants to know?"

"The Man himself."

"Barnum? Really?"

"Oh, yes indeed." I began rolling a cigarette.

Murtaugh whistled through mismatched teeth. "Holy shit, that's Iron Man Hicks. Yuh, I seen him around. Came in 'bout June. Calls hisself Mullen, says he's from Philly. Gotta admit he looks different from his pictures. Don't stack up to much in person. So what's he done to bring a Pinkerton to the ass-end o' the mule?"

I struck a match on the desk, took a few moments to get the cigarette smoldering nicely. There was a trace of hash mixed with the tobacco. Ah, that was better. "Year and a half back, some murders along the East Coast were connected to the presence of the circus. Ritual slayings—pentagrams, black candles, possible cannibalism. Nasty stuff. The investigation pointed to the strongman. Cops hauled him in, nothing stuck. Barnum doesn't take chances; fires the old boy and has him committed. Cedar Grove may not be pleasant, but it beats getting lynched, right? Iron Man didn't think so. He repaid his boss by ripping off some trinkets Barnum collected and skipping town."

"Real important cultural artifacts, I bet," Murtaugh said.

"Each to his own. Most of the junk turned up with local pawn dealers, antiquarians' shelves, spooky shops, and you get the idea. We recovered everything except the original translation of the *Dictionnaire Infernal* by a dead Frenchman, Collin de Plancy."

"What's that?"

"A book about demons and devils. Something to talk about at church."

"The hell y'say. Lord have mercy. Well, I ain't seen Mullen, uh, Hicks, in weeks, though y'might want to check with the Honeybee Ranch. And Trosper over to the Longrifle. Be advised—Trosper hates lawmen. Did a stretch in the pokey, I reckon. We got us an understandin', o' course."

"Good thing I'm not really a lawman, isn't it?"

"What's the guy's story?" Murtaugh stared at the photo, shifting it in his blunt hands.

I said, "Hicks was born in Plymouth. His father was a minister, did missionary work here in California—tried to save the Gold Rush crowd. Guess the minister beat him something fierce. Kid runs off and joins the circus. Turns out he's a freak of nature and a natural showman. P. T. squires him to every city in the Union. One day, Iron Man Hicks decides to start cutting the throats of rag pickers and whores. At least, that's my theory. According to the docs at Cedar Grove, there's medical problems—might be consumption or syph or something completely foreign. Because of this disease maybe he hears voices, wants to be America's Jack the Ripper. Thinks God has a plan for him. Who knows for sure? He's got a stash of dubious bedside material on the order of the crap he stole from Barnum, which was confiscated; he'd filled the margins with notes the agency eggs still haven't deciphered. Somebody introduced him to the lovely hobby of demonology—probably his own dear dad. I can't check that because Hicks senior died in '67 and all his possessions were auctioned. Anyway, Junior gets slapped into a cozy asylum with the help of Barnum's legal team. Hicks escapes and, well, I've told you the rest."

"Jesus H., what a charmin' tale."

We drank our coffee, listened to rain thud on tin. Eventually Murtaugh got around to what had probably been ticking in his brain the minute he recognized my name. "You're the fellow who did for the Molly Maguires."

"Afraid so."

He smirked. "Yeah, I thought it was you. Dirty business that, eh?"

"Nothing pretty about it, Sheriff." Sixteen years and the legend kept growing, a cattle carcass bloating in the sun.

"I expect not. We don't get the paper up here, 'cept when the mail train comes in. I do recall mention that some folks are thinkin' yer Mollys weren't really the bad guys. Maybe the railroad lads had a hand in them killin's."

"That's true. It's also true that sometimes a horsethief gets hanged for another scoundrel's misdeed. The books get balanced either way, don't they? Everybody in Schuyllkill got what they wanted."

Murtaugh said, "Might put that theory to the twenty sods as got hung up to dry."

I sucked on my cigarette, studied the ash drifting towards my knees. "Sheriff, did you ever talk to Hicks?"

"Bumped into him at one of the saloons durin' a faro game. Said howdy. No occasion for a philosophical debate."

"Anything he do or say seem odd?" I proffered my smoke.

"Sure. He smelled right foul, and he wasn't winnin' any blue ribbons on account o' his handsome looks. He had fits—somethin' to do with his nerves, accordin' to Doc Campion." Murtaugh extended his hand and accepted the cigarette. He dragged, made an appreciative expression, and closed his eyes. "I dunno, I myself ain't ever seen Hicks foamin' at the mouth. Others did, I allow."

"And that's it?"

"Y'mean, did the lad strike me as a thief and a murderer? I'm bound to say no more'n the rest o' the cowpunchers and prospectors that drift here. I allow most of 'em would plug you for a sawbuck…or a smoke." He grinned, rubbed ashes from his fingers. "Y' mentioned nothing stuck to our lad. Has that changed?"

"The evidence is pending."

"Think he did it?"

"I think he's doing it now."

"But you can't prove it."

"Nope."

"So, officially you're here to collect P. T.'s long-lost valuables. I imagine Hicks is mighty attached to that book by now. Probbly won't part with it without a fight."

"Probably not."

"Billy Cullins might be fittin' him for a pine box, I suppose."

I pulled out a roll of wrinkled bills, subtracted a significant number, and tossed them on the desk. Plenty more where that came from, hidden under a floorboard at the hotel. I always travel flush. "The agency's contribution to the Purdon widows and orphans fund."

"Much obliged, Mr. K. Whole lotta widows and orphans in these parts."

"More every day," I said.

5.

BELPHEGOR IS YOUR FATHERMOTHER. This carmine missive scrawled in a New Orleans hotel room. In the unmade bed, a phallus sculpted from human excrement. Flies crawled upon the sheets, buzzing and sluggish.

In Lubbock, a partially burned letter—"O FatherMother, may the blood of the-(indecipherable)-erate urchin be pleasing in thy throat. I am of the tradition."

Come Albuquerque, the deterioration had accelerated. Hicks did not bother to destroy this particular letter, rather scattered its befouled pages on the floor among vermiculate designs scriven in blood—"worms, godawful! i am changed! Blessed the sacrament of decay! Glut Obloodyhole O bloodymaggots Obloodybowels O Lordof shite! Fearthegash! iamcomeiamcome"

Finally, Bakersfield in script writ large upon a flophouse wall—

EATEATEATEATEAT! Found wedged under a mattress, the severed hand and arm of an unidentified person. Doubtless a young female. The authorities figured these remains belonged to a prostitute. Unfortunately, a few of them were always missing.

The locket in the delicate fist was inscribed, For my little girl. I recalled the bulls that stripped the room laughing when they read that. I also recalled busting one guy's jaw later that evening after we all got a snoot-full at the watering hole. I think it was a dispute over poker.

6.

Trosper didn't enjoy seeing me at the bar. He knew what I was and what it meant from a mile off. First words out of his egg-sucker's mouth, "Lookit here, mister, I don't want no bullshit from you. You're buyin' or you're walkin'. Or Jake might have somethin' else for you."

I couldn't restrain my smile. The banty roosters always got me. "Easy, friend. Gimme two fingers of coffin varnish. Hell, make it a round for the house."

The Longrifle was a murky barn devoid of all pretense to grandeur. This was the trough of the hard-working, harder-drinking peasantry. It was presently dead as three o'clock. Only me, Trosper, and a wiry cowboy with a crimped, sullen face who nursed a beer down the line. Jake, I presumed.

Trosper made quick work of getting the whiskey into our glasses. He corked the bottle and left it in front of me.

I swallowed fast, smacked the glass onto the counter. "Ugh. I think my left eye just went blind."

"Give the Chinaman a music lesson or shove off, pig. You ain't got no jurydiction here."

"Happy to oblige." I did the honors and gulped down another. Flames crackled in my belly, spread to my chest and face. Big granddad clock behind the bar ticked too loudly.

Good old Jake had tipped back his hat and shifted in his chair to affright me with what I'm sure was his darkest glare. Bastard had a profile sharp as a hatchet. A regulator, a bullyboy. He was heeled with a fair-sized peashooter in a shoulder rig.

I belted another swig to fix my nerves, banged the glass hard enough to raise dust. Motes drifted lazily, planetoids orbiting streams of light from the rain-blurred panes. I said to Trosper, "I hear tell you're chummy with a bad man goes by Tom Mullen."

Jake said, soft and deadly, "He told you to drink or get on shank's mare." Goddamned if the cowboy didn't possess the meanest drawl I'd heard since ever. First mistake was resting a rawboned hand on the butt of his pistola. Second mistake was not skinning said iron.

So I shot him twice. Once in the belly, through the buckle; once near the collar of his vest. Jake fell off his stool and squirmed in the sawdust. His hat tumbled away. He had a thick mane of blond hair with a perfect pink circle at the crown. That's what you got for wearing cowboy hats all the fucking time.

Making conversation with Trosper, who was currently frozen into a homely statue, I said, "Don't twitch or I'll nail your pecker to the floor." I walked over to Jake. The cowpoke was game; by then he almost had his gun free with the off hand. I stamped on his wrist until it cracked. He hissed. I smashed in his front teeth with a couple swipes from the heel of my boot. That settled him down.

I resumed my seat, poured another drink. "Hey, what's the matter? You haven't seen a man get plugged before? What kind of gin mill you running?" My glance swung to the dim ceiling and its mosaic of bullet holes and grease stains. "Oh, they usually shoot the hell out of your property, not each other. Tough luck the assholes got it all backwards. Come on, Trosper. Take a snort. This hooch you sling the shit-kickers kinda grows on a fellow."

Trosper was gray as his apron and sweating. His hands jerked. "H-he, uh, he's got a lotta friends, mister."

"I have lots of bullets. Drink, amigo." After he'd gulped his medicine, I said, "All right. Where were we? Oh, yes. Mr. Mullen. I'm interested in meeting him. Any notions?"

"Used to come in here every couple weeks; whenever he had dust in his poke. Drank. Played cards with some of the boys from the Bar-H. Humped the girls pretty regular over to the Honeybee."

"Uh-huh. A particular girl?"

"No. He din't have no sweetheart."

"When's the last time you saw him?"

Trosper thought about that. "Dunno. Been a spell. Christ, is Jake dead? He ain't movin'."

"I'll be damned. He isn't. Pay attention. Tommy's gone a-prospecting, you say?"

"Wha-yeah. Mister, I dunno. He came in with dust is all I'm sayin'." Trosper's eyes were glassy. "I dunno shit, mister. Could be he moved on. I ain't his keeper."

"The sheriff mentioned Mullen had a condition."

"He's got the Saint Vitus dance. You know, he trembles like a drunk ain't had his eye-opener. Saw him fall down once; twitched and scratched at his face somethin' awful. When it was over, he just grinned real pasty like and made a joke about it."

I got the names and descriptions of the Bar-H riders, not that I'd likely interview them. As I turned to leave, I said, "Okay, Trosper. I'll be around, maybe stop in for a visit, see if your memory clears up. Here's a twenty. That should cover a box."

7.

I was riding a terrific buzz, equal parts whiskey and adrenaline, when I flopped on a plush divan in the parlor of the Honeybee Ranch. A not-too-uncomely lady-of-the-house pried off my muddy boots and rubbed oil on my feet. The Madame, a frigate in purple who styled herself as Octavia Plantagenet, provided me a Cuban cigar from a velvet humidor. She expertly lopped the tip with a fancy silver-chased cutter and got it burning, quirking suggestively as she worked the barrel between her fat red lips. The roses painted on her cheeks swelled like bellows.

The Honeybee swam in the exhaust of chortling hookahs and joints of Kentucky bluegrass. A swarthy fellow plucked his sitar in accompany to the pianist, cementing the union of Old World decadence and frontier excess. Here was a refined wilderness of thick Persian carpet and cool brass; no plywood, but polished mahogany; no cheap glass, but exquisite crystal. The girls wore elaborate gowns and mink-slick hair piled high, batted glitzy lashes over eyes twinkly as gemstones. Rouge, perfume, sequins, and charms, the whole swarming mess an intoxicating collaboration of artifice and lust.

Madame Octavia recalled Hicks. "Tommy Mullen? Sorry-lookin' fella, what with the nerve disorder. Paid his tab. Not too rough on the merchandise, if he did have breath to gag a maggot. Only Lydia and Connie could stomach that, but he didn't complain. Lord, he hasn't been by in a coon's age. I think he headed back east."

I inquired after Violet and was told she'd be available later. Perhaps another girl? I said I'd wait and accepted four-fingers of cognac in King George's own snifter. The brandy was smooth, and I didn't notice the wallop it packed until maroon lampshades magnified the crowd of genteel gamblers, businessmen and blue-collar stiffs on their best behavior, distorted them in kaleidoscopic fashion. Tinkling notes from Brahms reverberated in my brain long after the short, thick Austrian player in the silk vest retired for a nip at the bar.

Fame preceded me. Seemed everybody who could decipher newsprint had read about my exploits in Pennsylvania. They knew all there was to know about how I infiltrated the Workers Benevolent Association and sent a score of murderous union extremists to the gallows with my testimony. Depending upon one's social inclinations, I was a champion of commerce and justice, or a no-good, yellow-bellied skunk. It was easy to tell who was who from the assorted smiles and sneers. The fact I'd recently ventilated a drover at the Longrifle was also a neat conversation starter.

Octavia encouraged a muddled procession of counterfeit gentry to ogle the infamous Pinkerton, a bulldozer of the first water from the Old States. Deduction was for the highbrows in top hats and great coats; I performed my detecting with a boot and a six-gun. I'd bust your brother's head or bribe your mother if that's what it took to hunt you to ground and collect my iron men. Rumor had it I'd strong-arm the Pope himself. Not much of a stretch as I never was impressed with that brand of idolatry.

Introductions came in waves—Taylor Hackett, bespectacled owner of the Bar-H cattle ranch; Norton Smythe, his stuffed-suit counterpart in the realm of gold mining; Ned Cates, Bob Tunny, and Harry Edwards, esteemed investors of the Smythe & Ruth Mining Company; each beaming and guffawing, too many teeth bared. An Eastern Triad. I asked them if they ate of The Master's sacrifice, but nobody appeared to understand and I relented while their waxy grins were yet in place. Blowsy as a poleaxed mule, I hadn't truly allowed for the possibility of my quarry snuggled in the fold of a nasty little cult. Hicks was a loner. I hoped.

After the contents of the snifter evaporated and got replenished like an iniquitous cousin to the Horn of Plenty, the lower caste made its rounds in the persons of Philmore Kavanaugh, journalist for some small-town rag that recently folded and sent him penniless to the ends of creation; Dalton Beaumont, chief deputy and unloved cousin of Sheriff Murtaugh; John Brown, a wrinkled alderman who enjoyed having his toes sucked and daubed mother of pearl right there before God and everyone; Michael Piers, the formerly acclaimed French poet, now sunk into obscurity and bound for an early grave judging from the violence of his cough and the bloody spackle on his embroidered handkerchief. And others and others and others. I gave up on even trying to focus and concentrated on swilling without spilling.

There wasn't any sort of conversation, precisely. More the noise of an aroused hive. I waded through streams and tributaries from the great lake of communal thrum—

"—let some daylight into poor Jake. There'll be the devil to pay, mark me!"

"Langston gone to seed in Chinatown. A bloody shame—"

"First Holmes, now Stevenson. Wretched, wretched—"

"—the Ancient Order of Hibernia gets you your goddamned Molly Maguires and that's a fact. Shoulda hung a few more o' them Yankee bastards if you ask me—"

"—Welsh thick as ticks, doped out of their faculties on coolie mud. They've still got the savage in them. Worse than the red plague—"

"Two years, Ned. Oh, all right. Three years. The railroad gobbles up its share and I get the pieces with promising glint. California is weighed and measured, my friend. We'll run the independent operations into the dirt. Moonlighters don't have a prayer—"

"—Barnum, for gawd's sake! Anybody tell him—"

"I hate the circus. Stinks to high heaven. I hate those damned clowns too—"

"No. Langston's dead—"

"—poked her for fun. Dry hump and the bitch took my folding—"

"—Mullen? Hicks? Dunno an don' care. Long gone, long gone—"

"The hell, you say! He's bangin' the gong at the Forty-Mile Camp, last I heard—"

"—the professor's on the hip? I thought he sailed across the pond—"

"My dear, sweet woman-child. As quoth Lord Baudelaire:

'Madonna, mistress I shall build for you
An altar of misery and hew'"

"It wasn't enough the cunt sacked me. 'E bloody spit in my face, the bloody wanker—"

"—stones to *kill* a man—"

"Ah, I could do the job real nice—"

"—'*Et creuser dans le coin*'—"

"—I mean, look at 'im. He's a facking mechanical—"

"So, I says, lookee here, bitch, I'll cut your—"

"—'*Une niche, d'azur et d'or tout*'—"

"—suck my cock or die! There's your goddamned—! Whoopie! I'm on a hellbender, fellas!"

"—don't care. Murtaugh should string his ass from the welcome sign—"

"I met your Hicks. He was nothing really special." Piers blew a cloud of pungent clove exhaust, watched it eddy in the currents. "Thees circus freak of yours. He had a beeg mouth."

My head wobbled. "Always pegged him for the strong silent type. Ha, ha."

"No." Piers waved impatiently. "He had a beeg mouth. Drooled, how do you say?—Like an eediot. A fuck-ing eediot."

"Where?" I wheezed.

"Where? How do I know where? Ask the fuck-ing professor. Maybe he knows where. The professor knows everyone."

"There you are, darling," crooned Madame Octavia as if I had suddenly rematerialized. Her ponderous breasts pressed against my ribs. Her choice of scent brought tears to my eyes. "This gig is drying up, baby. It's a tourist trap. Ooh, Chi-Town is where the action is. Isn't Little Egypt a pistol? Hoochie-Koochie baby!"

Red lights. White faces. Shadows spreading cracks.

I dropped the snifter from disconnected fingers. Thank goodness Octavia was there with a perfumed cloth to blot the splash. I was thinking, yes, indeed, a tragedy about Robert Louis; a step above the penny dreadfuls, but my hero nonetheless.

Where was Violet? Coupled to a banker? A sodbuster? Hoochie-Koochie all night long.

"Excuse, me, Mr. Koenig." An unfamiliar voice, a visage in silhouette.

"Ah, Frankie, he's just laying about waiting for one of my girls—"

"Sheriff's business, Miss Octavia. Please, sir. We've been sent to escort you to the office. Levi, he's dead weight, get his other arm. You too, Dalton. There's a lad." The sheriff's boys each grabbed a limb and hoisted me up as if on angels' wings.

"The cavalry," I said.

Scattered applause. A bawdy ragtime tune. Hungry mouths hanging slack. And the muzzy lamps. Red. Black.

8.

"What do you call him?"

"Chemosh. Baal-Peeor. Belphegor. No big deal, the Moabites are dust. They won't mind if the title gits slaughtered by civilized folks."

"We're a fair piece from Moab."

"Belphegor speaks many tongues in many lands."

"A world traveler, eh?"

"That's right, Pinky."

"This friend of yours, he speaks to you through the shitter?"

"Yeah."

"Interesting. Seems a tad inelegant."

"Corruption begets corruption, Pinky," says Hicks. His eyes are brown, hard as

baked earth. Gila monster's eyes. He once raised a four-hundred-pound stone above his head, balanced it in his palm to the cheers of mobs. Could reach across the table and crush my throat, even with the chains. Calcium deposits mar his fingers, distend from his elbows not unlike spurs. There is a suspicious lump under his limp hair, near the brow. He's sinewy and passive in the Chair of Questions. "What's more lunatic than fallin' down before the image of a man tacked to a cross? Nothin'. You don't even git nothin' fun. I aim to have fun."

I'm fascinated by the wet mouth in the bronzed face. It works, yes indeed it articulates most functionally. Yet it yawns, slightly yawns, as if my captive strongman was victim of a palsy, or the reverse of lockjaw. Saliva beads and dangles on viscous threads. I gag on the carnivore's stench gusting from the wound. His teeth are chipped and dark as flint. Long. I ask, "What are you?"

"Holes close. Holes open. I'm an Opener. They Who Wait live through me. What about you?"

"I'm an atheist." That was a half truth, but close enough for government work.

"Good on you, Pinky. You're on your way. And here's Tuttle." He indicated a prim lawyer in a crisp suit. "P. T. only hires the best. Adios, pal."

Three weeks later, when Hicks strolls out of Cedar Grove Sanitarium, I'm not surprised at the message he leaves—CLOSE A HOLE AND ANOTHER OPENS.

Funny, funny world. It's Tuttle who pays the freight for my hunting expedition into the American West.

9.

Deputy Levi called it protective custody. They dumped me on a cot in a cell. Murtaugh's orders to keep me from getting lynched by some of Jake's confederates. These confederates had been tying one on down at the Longrifle, scene of the late, lamented Jake's demise. Murtaugh wasn't sorry to see a "cockeyed snake like that little sonofabitch" get planted. The sheriff promised to chat with Trosper regarding the details of our interview. It'd be straightened out by breakfast.

I fell into the amber and drowned.

Things clumped together in a sticky collage—

Hicks leering through the bars, his grin as prodigious as a train tunnel.

Violet's wheat-blonde head bowed at my groin and me so whiskey-flaccid I can only sweat and watch a cockroach cast a juggernaut shadow beneath a kerosene lamp while the sheriff farts and snores at his desk.

Jake shits himself, screams soundlessly as my boot descends, hammer of the gods.

Lincoln waves to the people in the balconies. His eyes pass directly over me. I'm twenty-two, I'm hell on wheels. In three minutes I'll make my first kill. Late bloomer.

"I once was lost. Now I'm found. The Soldier's Friend, Sister M, had a hold on me, yes sir, yesiree."

"I give up the needle and took to the bottle like a babe at his mama's nipple."

"Never had a wife, never needed one. I took up the traveling life, got married to my gun."

A man in a suit doffs his top hat and places his head into the jaws of a bored lion. The jaws close.

A glossy pink labium quakes and begins to yield, an orchid brimming with ancient stars.

"How many men you killed, Jonah?" Violet strokes my superheated brow. "Today?"

"No, silly! I mean, in all. The grand total."

"More than twenty. More every day."

Sun eats stars. Moon eats sun. Black hole eats Earth.

Hicks winks a gory eye, an idiot lizard, gives the sheriff a languid, slobbery kiss that glistens snail slime. When the sackcloth of ashes floats to oblivion and I can see again, the beast is gone, if he ever was.

The door creaks with the storm. Open. Shut.

Violet sighs against my sweaty chest, sleeps in reinvented innocence.

There's a crack in the ceiling, and it's dripping.

10.

I did the expedient thing—holed up in my hotel room for a week, drinking the hair of the dog that bit me and screwing Violet senseless.

I learned her daddy was a miner who was blown to smithereens. No mother; no kin as would take in a coattail relation from the boondocks. But she had great teeth and a nice ass. Fresh meat for Madame Octavia's stable. She was eighteen and real popular with the gentlemen, Miss Violet was. Kept her earnings tucked in a sock, was gonna hop the mail train to San Francisco one of these fine days, work as a showgirl in an upscale dance hall. Heck, she might even ride the rail to Chicago, meet this Little Egypt who was the apple of the city's eye. Yeah.

She finally asked me if I'd ever been married—it was damned obvious I wasn't at present—and I said no. Why not? Lucky, I guessed.

"Mercy, Jonah, you got some mighty peculiar readin' here." Violet was lying on her belly, thumbing through my Latin version of the *Pseudomonarchia Daemonum*. Her hair was tangled; perspiration glowed on her ivory flanks.

I sprawled naked, propped against the headboard, smoking while I cleaned and oiled my Winchester Model 1886. Best rifle I'd ever owned; heavy enough to drop a buffalo, but perfect for men. It made me a tad wistful to consider that I wasn't likely to use it on Hicks. I figured him for close quarters.

Gray and yellow out the window. Streets were a quagmire. I watched figures mucking about, dropping planks to make corduroy for the wagons. Occasionally a gun popped.

For ten dollars and an autograph, Deputy Levi had compiled a list of deaths and disappearances in Purdon and environs over the past four months, hand delivered it to my doorstep. Two pages long. Mostly unhelpful—routine shootings and stabbings, claim-jumping and bar brawls, a whole slew of accidents. I did mark the names of three prospectors who'd vanished. They worked claims separated by many miles of inhospitable terrain. Each had left a legacy of food, equipment, and personal items—no money, though. No hard cash. No gold dust.

Violet gasped when she came to some unpleasant and rather florid illustrations. "Lordy! That's...awful. You believe in demons and such, Jonah?" Curiosity and suspicion struggled to reconcile her tone.

"Nope. But other folks do."

"Tommy Mullen—he does?" Her eyes widened. I glimpsed Hicks, a gaunt satyr loitering in the Honeybee parlor while the girls drew lots to seal a fate.

"I expect he does." I slapped her pale haunch. "Come on over here, sweetness. It isn't for you to fret about." And to mitigate the dread transmitted through her trembling flesh, I said, "He's hightailed to the next territory. I'm wasting daylight in this burg." Her grateful mouth closed on me and her tongue moved, rough and supple. I grabbed the bed post. "Pardon me, not completely wasting it."

Three miners. Picture-clear, the cabins, lonely, isolated. A black shape sauntering from an open door left swinging in its wake. Crows chattering in poplar branches, throaty chuckle of a stream.

I drowsed. The hotel boy knocked and reported a Chinaman was waiting in the lobby. The man bore me an invitation from Langston Butler. Professor Butler, to his friends. The note, in handsome script, read:

Sashay on out to Forty-Mile Camp and I'll tell you how to snare the Iron Man. Cordially, L. Butler.

I dressed in a hurry. Violet groaned, started to rise, but I kissed her on the mouth and said to take the afternoon off. Indulging a bout of prescience, I left some money on the dresser. A lot of money. The money basically said, "If you're smart you'll be on the next train to San Francisco; next stop the Windy City."

I hoped Murtaugh had successfully smoothed all the feathers I'd ruffled.

This was my best suit and I sure didn't want to get any holes in it.

II.

Forty-Mile Camp was not, as its appellation suggested, forty miles from Purdon. The jolting ride in Hung Chan's supply wagon lasted under three hours by my pocket watch. Hung didn't speak to me at all. I rode shotgun, riveted by the payload of flour, sugar, and sundries, not the least of which happened to include a case of weathered, leaky dynamite.

We wound along Anderson Creek Canyon, emerged in a hollow near some dredges and a mongrel collection of shacks. Cookfires sputtered, monarch butterflies under cast-iron pots tended by women the color of ash. There were few children and no dogs. Any male old enough to handle pick, shovel, or pan was among the clusters of men stolidly attacking the earth, wading in the frigid water, toiling among the rocky shelves above the encampment.

Nobody returned my friendly nod. Nobody even really looked at me except for two men who observed the proceedings from a copse of scraggly cottonwoods, single-shot rifles slung at half-mast. My hackles wouldn't lie down until Hung led me through the camp to a building that appeared to be three or four shanties in combination. He ushered me through a thick curtain and into a dim, moist realm pungent with body musk and opium tang.

"Koenig, at last. Pull up a rock." Butler lay on a pile of bear pelts near a guttering fire pit. He was wrapped in a Navajo blanket, but clearly emaciated. His misshapen skull resembled a chunk of anthracite sufficiently dense to crook his neck. His dark flesh had withered tight as rawhide, and he appeared to be an eon older than his stentorian voice sounded. In short, he could've been a fossilized anthropoid at repose in Barnum's House of Curiosities.

Butler's attendant, a toothless crone with an evil squint, said, *"Mama die?"* She gently placed a long, slender pipe against his lips, waited for him to draw the load. She hooked another horrible glance my way and didn't offer to cook me a pill.

After a while Butler said, "You would've made a wonderful Templar."

"Except for the minor detail of suspecting Christianity is a pile of crap. Chopping down Saracens for fun and profit, that I could've done."

"You're a few centuries late. A modern-day crusader, then. An educated man, I presume?"

"Harvard, don't you know." I pronounced it Hah-vahd to maximize the irony.

"An *expensive* education; although, aren't they all. Still, a Pinkerton, tsk, tsk. Daddy was doubtless shamed beyond consolation."

"Papa Koenig was annoyed. One of the slickest New York lawyers you'll ever do battle with—came from a whole crabbed scroll of them. Said I was an ungrateful iconoclast before he disowned me. Hey, it's easier to shoot people than try to frame them, I've discovered."

"And now you've come to shoot poor Rueben Hicks."

"Rueben Hicks is a thief, a murderer, and a cannibal. Seems prudent to put him down if I get the chance."

"Technically a cannibal is one that feeds on its own species."

I said, "Rueben doesn't qualify as a member?"

"That depends on your definition of human, Mr. Koenig," Butler said, and smiled. The contortion had a ghoulish effect on his face. "Because it goes on two legs and wears a coat and tie? Because it knows how to say please and thank you?"

"Why do I get the feeling this conversation is headed south? People were talking about you in town. You're a folk legend at the whorehouse."

"A peasant hero, as it were?"

"More like disgraced nobility. I can't figure what you're doing here. Could've picked a more pleasant climate to go to seed."

"I came to Purdon ages ago. Sailed from London, where I had pursued a successful career in anthropology—flunked medical school, you see. Too squeamish. I dabbled in physics and astronomy, but primitive culture has always been my obsession. Its rituals, its primal energy."

"Plenty of primitive culture here."

"Quite."

"Mama die?" said the hag as she brandished the pipe.

Butler accepted the crone's ministrations. His milky eyes flared, and when he spoke, he spoke more deliberately. "I've been following your progress. You are capable, resourceful, tenacious. I fear Rueben will swallow you alive, but if anyone has a chance to put a stop to his wickedness it is you."

"Lead has a sobering effect on most folks." I said. "Strange to hear a debauched occultist like yourself fussing about wickedness. I take it you've got a personal stake in this manhunt. He must've hurt your feelings or something."

"Insomuch as I know he intends to use me as a blood sacrifice, I'm extremely interested."

"You ever thought of clearing out?"

"Impossible."

"Why impossible?"

"Gravity, Mr. Koenig." Butler took another hit. Eventually, he said in a dreamy tone, "I'm a neglectful host. Care to beat the gong?"

"Thanks, no."

"A reformed addict. How rare."

"I'll settle for being a drunk. What's your history with Hicks?"

"We were introduced in '78. I was in Philadelphia and had taken in the circus with some colleagues from the university. I fell in with a small group of the players after the show, Rueben being among this number. We landed in a tiny café, a decadent slice of gay Paris, and everybody was fabulously schnock-ered, to employ the argot. Rueben and I got to talking and we hit it off. I was amazed at the breadth and, I blush to admit, scandalous nature of his many adventures. He was remarkably cultured behind the provincial façade. I was intrigued. Smitten, too."

I said, "And here I thought Hicks was a ladies man."

"Rueben is an opportunist. We retired to my flat; all very much a night's work for me. Then…then after we'd consummated our mutual fascination, he said he wanted to show me something that would change my life. Something astounding."

"Do tell."

"We were eating mushrooms. A mysterious variety—Rueben stole them from P. T., and P. T. obtained them from this queer fellow who dealt in African imports. I hallucinated that Rueben caused a window to open in the bedroom wall, a portal into space. Boggling! Millions of stars blazed inches from my nose, a whole colossal bell-shaped galaxy of exploded gases and cosmic dust. The sight would've driven Copernicus insane. It was a trick, stage magic. Something he'd borrowed from his fellow performers. He asked me what I saw and I told him. His face…there was something wrong. Too rigid, too cold. For a moment, I thought he'd put on an extremely clever mask and I was terrified. And his mouth… His expression melted almost instantly, and he was just Rueben again. I knew better, though. And, unfortunately, my fascination intensified. Later, when he showed me the portal trick, this time sans hallucinogens, I realized he wasn't simply a circus performer. He claimed to be more than human, to have evolved into a superior iteration of the genus. A flawed analysis, but at least partially correct."

Hicks's rubbery grin bobbed to the surface of my mind. "He's crazed, I'll give you that."

"Rueben suffers from a unique breed of mycosis—you've perhaps seen the tumors on his arms and legs, and especially along his spinal column? It's consuming him as a fungus consumes a tree. Perversely, it's this very parasitic influence that imbues him with numerous dreadful abilities. Evolution via slow digestion."

"Dreadful abilities? If he'd showed me a hole in the wall that looked on the moon's surface I might've figured he was a fakir, or Jesus' little brother, or what have you. He didn't. He didn't fly out of Cedar Grove, either."

"Scoff as you will. Ignorance is all the blessing we apes can hope for."

"What became of your torrid love affair?"

"He and I grew close. He confided many terrible things to me, unspeakable deeds. Ultimately I determined to venture here and visit his childhood haunts, to discover the wellspring of his vitality, the source of his preternatural affinities. He warned me, albeit such caveats were mere inducements to an inquisitive soul. I was so easily corrupted." Butler's voice trailed off as he was lost in reflection.

Corruption begets corruption, copper. "Sounds very romantic," I said. "What were you after? The gold? Nah, the gold is panned out or property of the companies. Mating practices of the natives?"

"I coveted knowledge, Mr. Koenig. Rueben whispered of a way to unlock the secrets of brain and blood, to lay bare the truth behind several of mankind's squalid superstitions. To walk the earth as a god. His mind is far from scientific, and but remotely curious. One could nearly categorize him as a victim of circumstance in this drama. I, however, presumably equipped with superior intellect, would profit all the more than my barbarous concubine. My potential seemed enormous."

"Yes, and look at you now, Professor," I said. "Do these people understand what you are?"

"What do you think I am, Detective?"

"A Satan-worshipping dope fiend."

"Wrong. I'm a naturalist. Would that I could reinvent my innocent dread of God and Satan, of supernatural phenomena. As for these yellow folk, they don't care what I am. I pay well for my upkeep and modest pleasures."

"For a man who's uncovered great secrets of existence, your accommodations lack couth."

"Behold the reward of hubris. I could've done as Rueben has—descended completely into the womb of an abominable mystery and evolved as a new and perfect savage. Too cowardly—I tasted the ichor of divinity and quailed, fled to this hovel and my drugs. My memories. Wisdom devours the weak." He shuddered and spat a singsong phrase that brought the old woman scuttling to feed him another load of dope. After he'd recovered, he produced a leather-bound book from beneath his pillow. The *Dictionnaire Infernal*. "A gift from our mutual acquaintance. Please, take it. These 'forbidden' tomes are surpassingly ludicrous."

I inspected the book; de Plancy's signature swooped across the title page. "Did Rueben travel all this way to fetch you a present and off a few hapless miners as a bonus?"

"Rueben has come home because he must, it is an integral component of his metamorphosis. Surely you've detected his quickening purpose, the apparent degeneration of his faculties, which is scarcely a symptom of decay but rather a sign of fundamental alteration. Pupation. He has returned to this place to commune with his benefactor, to disgorge the red delights of his gruesome and sensuous escapades. Such is the pact between them. It is the pact all supplicants make. It was mine, before my defection."

My skin prickled at the matter-of-fact tone Butler affected. I said, "I don't get this, Professor. If you don't hold with demons and all that bunkum, what the hell are you worshipping?"

"Supplicating, dear boy. I didn't suggest we are alone in the cosmos. Certain monstrous examples of cryptogenetics serve the function of godhead well enough. That scholars invent fanciful titles and paint even more fanciful pictures does not diminish the essential reality of these organisms, only obscures it."

My suspicions about Butler's character were sharpening with the ebb and pulse of firelight. He lay coiled in his nest, a diamondback ready to strike. Not wanting an answer, I said, "Exactly what did you do to acquire this... knowledge?"

"I established communion with a primordial intelligence, a cyclopean plexus rooted below these hills and valleys. An unclassified mycoflora that might or might not be of terrestrial origin. There are rites to effect this dialogue. A variety of osmosis ancient as the sediment men first crawled from. Older! Most awful, I assure you."

"Christ, you've got holes in your brain from smoking way too much of the black O." I stood, covering my emotions with a grimace. "Next thing you'll tell me is Oberon came prancing from under his hill to sprinkle that magic fairy shit on you."

"You are the detective. Don't blame me if this little investigation uncovers things that discomfit your world view."

"Enough. Tell it to Charlie Darwin when you meet in hell. You want me to nail Hicks, stow the campfire tales and come across with his location."

"Rueben's visited infrequently since late spring. Most recently, three days ago. He promised to take me with him soon, to gaze once more upon the FatherMother. Obviously I don't wish to make that pilgrimage. I'd rather die a nice peaceful death—being lit on fire, boiled in oil, staked to an ant hill. That sort of thing."

"Is he aware of my presence in Purdon?"

"Of course. He expected you weeks ago. I do believe he mentioned some casual harm to your person, opportunity permitting. Rest assured it never occurred to him that I might betray his interests, that I would dare. Frankly, I doubt he considers you a real threat—not here in his demesne. Delusion is part and parcel with his condition."

"Where is he right now?"

"Out and about. Satiating his appetites. Perhaps wallowing in the Presence. His ambit is wide and unpredictable. He may pop in tomorrow. He may appear in six months. Time means less and less to him. Time is a ring, and in the House of Belphegor that ring contracts like a muscle."

"The house?"

Butler's lips twitched at the corners. He said, "A cell in a black honeycomb. Rueben's father stumbled upon it during his missionary days. He had no idea what it was. The chamber existed before the continents split and the ice came over the world. The people that built it, long dust. I can give directions, but I humbly suggest you wait here for your nemesis. Safer."

"No harm in looking," I said.

"Oh, no, Mr. Koenig. There's more harm than you could ever dream."

"Enlighten me anyhow."

Butler seemed to have expected nothing less. Joyful as a sadist, he drew me a map.

12.

The cave wasn't far from camp.

Long-suffering Hung Chan and his younger brother Ha agreed to accompany me to the general area after a harangue from Butler and the exchange of American currency.

We essayed a thirty-minute hike through scrub and streams, then up a steep knoll littered with brush and treacherous rocks. Invisible from a distance, a limestone cliff face split vertically, formed a narrow gash about the height of the average man. The Chan brothers informed me through violent gestures and Pidgin English they'd await my return at the nearby riverbank. They retreated, snarling to themselves in their foreign dialect.

I crouched behind some rocks and cooled my heels for a lengthy spell. Nothing and more nothing. When I couldn't justify delaying any longer, I approached cautiously, in case Hicks was lying in ambush, rifle sights trained on the rugged slope. Immediately I noticed bizarre symbols scratched into the occasional boulder. Seasonal erosion had obliterated all save the deepest marks, and these meant little to me, though it wasn't difficult to imagine they held some pagan significance. Also, whole skeletons of small animals—birds and squirrels—hung from low branches. Dozens of them, scattered like broken teeth across the hillside.

According to my watch and the dull slant of sun through the clouds, I had nearly two hours of light. I'd creep close, have a peek, and scurry back to the mining camp in time for supper. No way did I intend to navigate these backwoods after dark and risk breaking a leg, or worse. I was a city boy at heart.

I scrambled from boulder to boulder, pausing to see if anyone would emerge to take a pot shot. When I reached the summit I was sweating and my nerves twanged like violin strings.

The stench of spoiled meat, of curdled offal, emanated from the fissure; a slaughterhouse gone to the maggots. The vile odor stung my eyes, scourged deep into my throat. I knotted a balaclava from a handkerchief I'd appropriated from the Honeybee Ranch, covered my mouth and nose.

A baby? I cocked my ears and didn't breathe until the throb of my pulse filled the universe. No baby. The soft moan of wind sucked through a chimney of granite.

I waited for my vision to clear and passed through the opening, pistol drawn

13.

so beautiful.

I

14.

stare at a wedge of darkening sky between the pines.

My cheeks burn, scorched with salt. I've been lying here in the shallows of a pebbly stream. I clutch the solid weight of my pistol in a death grip. The Chan brothers loom, hardly inscrutable. They are pale as flour. Their lips move silently. Their hands are on me. They drag me.

I keep staring at the sky, enjoy the vibration of my tongue as I hum. Tralalala.

The brothers release my arms, slowly edge away like automata over the crushed twigs. Their eyes are holes. Their mouths. I'm crouched, unsteady. My gun. Click. Click. Empty. But my knife my Jim Bowie special is here somewhere is in my hand. Ssaa! The brothers Chan are phantoms, loping. Deer. Mirages. My knife. Quivers in a tree trunk.

Why am I so happy. Why must I cover myself in the leaves and dirt.

Rain patters upon my roof.

15.

Time is a ring. Time is a muscle. It contracts.

16.

colloidal iris

17.

the pillar of faces

18.

migrant spores

19.

maggots

20.

glows my ecstasy in a sea of suns

21.

galactic parallax

22.

I had been eating leaves. Or at least there were leaves crammed in my mouth. Sunlight dribbled through the gleaming branches. I vomited leaves. I found a trickle of water, snuffled no prouder than a hog.

Everything was small and bright. Steam seeped from my muddy clothes. My shirt was starched with ejaculate, matted to my belly as second skin. I knelt in the damp needles and studied my filthy hands. My hands were shiny as metal on a casket.

Butler chortled from a spider-cocoon in the green limbs, *"Now you're seasoned for his palette. Best run, Pinkerton. You've been in the sauce. Chewed up and shat out. And if you live, in twenty years you'll be another walking Mouth."* He faded into the woodwork.

I made a meticulous job of scrubbing the grime and blood from my hands. I washed my face in the ice water, hesitated at the sticky bur of my mustache and hair, finally dunked my head under. The shock brought comprehension crashing down around my ears.

I remembered crossing over a threshold.

Inside, the cave is larger than I'd supposed, and humid.

Water gurgling in rock. Musty roots the girth of sequoias.

Gargantuan statues embedded in wattles of amber.

The cave mouth a seam of brightness that rotates until it is a blurry hatch in the ceiling.

My boots losing contact with the ground, as if I were weightless.

Floating away from the light, toward a moist chasm, purple warmth.

Darkness blooms, vast and sweet.

Gibberish, after.

I walked back to Forty-Mile Camp, my thoughts pleasantly disjointed.

23.

Labor ground to a halt when I stumbled into their midst. None spoke. No one tried to stop me from hunching over a kettle and slopping fistfuls of boiled rice, gorging like a beast. Nor when I hefted a rusty spade and padded into Butler's hut to pay my respects. Not even when I emerged, winded, and tore through the crates of supplies and helped myself to several sticks of dynamite with all the trimmings.

I smiled hugely at them, couldn't think of anything to say.

They stood in a half moon, stoic as carvings. I wandered off into the hills.

24.

The explosion was gratifying.

Dust billowed, a hammerhead cloud that soon collapsed under its own ambition. I thought of big sticks and bigger nests full of angry hornets. I wasn't even afraid, really.

Some open, others close.

25.

After I pounded on the door for ten minutes, a girl named Evelyn came out and found me on the front porch of the whorehouse, slumped across the swing and muttering nonsense. Dawn was breaking and the stars were so pretty.

I asked for Violet. Evelyn said she'd lit a shuck from the Honeybee Ranch for parts unknown.

Octavia took in my frightful appearance and started snapping orders. She and a couple of the girls lugged me to a room and shoved me in a scalding bath. I didn't protest; somebody slapped a bottle of whiskey in my hand and lost the cork. Somebody else must've taken one look at the needle work on my arm and decided to snag some morphine from Doc Campion's bag of black magic. They shot me to the moon and reality melted into a slag of velvet and honey. I tumbled off the wagon and got crushed under its wheels.

"You going home one of these days?" Octavia squeezed water from a sponge over my shoulders. "Back to the Old States?" She smelled nice. Everything smelled of roses and lavender; nice.

I didn't know what day this was. Shadows clouded the teak panels. This place was firecracker hot back in the '50s. What a hoot it must've been while the West was yet wild. My lips were swollen. I was coming down hard, a piece of rock plunging from the sky. I said, "Uh-huh. You?" It occurred to me that I was fixating again, probably worse than when I originally acquired my dope habits. Every time my eyes dilated I was thrust into a Darwinian phantasm. A fugue state wherein the chain of humanity shuttered rapidly from the first incomprehensible amphibian creature to slop ashore, through myriad semi-erect sapiens formicating across chaotically shifting landscapes, unto the frantic masses in coats and dresses teeming about the stone and glass of Earth's megalopolises. I had vertigo.

"Any day now."

My ears still rang, might always.

Fading to a speck—the hilltop, decapitated in a thunderclap and a belch of dust. Boulders reduced to shattered bits, whizzing around me, a miracle I wasn't pulverized. Was that me, pitching like Samson before the Philistine army? More unreal with each drip of scented wax. My eyes were wet. I turned my head so Octavia wouldn't notice.

"Tommy Mullen came around today. You're still lookin' for Tommy. Right?"

"You see him?"

"Naw. Kavanaugh was talkin' to Dalton Beaumont, mentioned he saw Tommy on the street. Fella waved to him and went into an alley. Didn't come out again. Could be he's scared you'll get a bead on him."

"Could be."

Octavia said, "Glynna heard tell Langston Butler passed on. Died in his sleep. Guess the yellow boys held a ceremony. Reverend Fuller's talkin' 'bout ridin' to Forty-Mile, see that the professor gets himself a Christian burial." She became quiet, kneading my neck with steely fingers. Then, "I'm powerful sad. The professor was a decent man. You know he was the sawbones for three, four years? He did for the young 'uns as got themselves with child. Gentle as a father. Campion came along and the professor fell to the coolie mud. Shame."

My smile was lye-hot and humorless. "He didn't limit his moonlighting to abortions. Butler did for the babies too, didn't he? The ones that were born here at the Ranch."

Octavia didn't answer.

All those whore's babies tossed into a pitchy shaft, tiny wails smothered in the great chthonian depths. I laughed, hollow. "The accidents. Don't see many orphanages this far north."

Octavia said, "How do you mean to settle your tab, by the by?" She was getting colder by the second. She must've gone through my empty wallet.

"For services rendered? Good question, lady."

"You gave your *whole* poke to Violet?" Her disbelief was tinged with scorn. "That's plain loco, mister. Why?"

The room was fuzzy. "I don't suppose I'll be needing it, where I'm going. I did an impetuous deed, Octavia. Can't take back the bet once it's on the table." Where was I going? Into a box into the ground, if I was lucky. The alternative was just too unhappy. I listened for the tick-tock of transmogrifying cells that would indicate my descent into the realm of superhuman. Damnation; the bottle was dry. I dropped it into the sudsy water, watched it sink. Glowed there between my black and blue thighs.

"Musta been a heap of coin. You love her, or somethin'?"

I frowned. "Another excellent question. No, I reckon I don't love her. She's just too good for the likes of you, is all. Hate to see her spoil."

Octavia left without even a kiss good-bye.

26.

At least my clothes were washed and pressed and laid out properly.

I dressed with the ponderous calculation of a man on his way to a funeral. I cleaned my pistol, inspected the cylinder reflexively—it's easy to tell how many bullets are loaded by the weight of the weapon in your hand.

The whores had shaved me, and I cut a respectable figure except for the bruises and the sagging flesh under my eyes. My legs were unsteady. I went by the back stairs, unwilling to list through the parlor where the piano crashed and the shouts of evening debauchery swelled to a frenzied peak.

It was raining again; be snowing in another week or so. The mud-caked boardwalks stretched emptily before unlit shop windows. I shuffled, easily confused by the darkness and the rushing wind.

The hotel waited, tomb-dark and utterly desolate.

Like a man mounting the scaffold, I climbed the three flights of squeaking stairs to my room, turned the key in the lock after the fourth or fifth try, and knew what was what as I stepped through and long before anything began to happen.

The room stank like an abattoir. I lighted a lamp on the dresser, and its frail luminance caught the edge of spikes and loops on the bathroom door. This scrawl read, BELPHEGORBELPHEGORBELPHEGOR.

The mirror shuddered. A mass of shadows unfolded in the corner, became a tower. Hicks whispered from a place behind and above my left shoulder, "Hello again, Pinky."

"Hello yourself." I turned and fired and somewhere between the yellow flash and the new hole in the ceiling He snatched my wrist and the pistol went caroming across the floor. I dangled; my trigger finger was broken and my elbow dislocated, but I didn't feel a thing yet.

Hicks smiled almost kindly. He said, "I told you, Pinky. Close one hole, another opens." His face split apart at the seams, a terrible flower bending toward my light, my heat.

>←

The poem quoted above is cited as follows:

Baudelaire, Charles. "To A Madonna." *The Flowers of Evil* (sixth ed.), Trans. Anthony Hecht. Ed Marthiel and Jackson Mathews. New York: New Directions Publishing Corporation, 1989.

Red Goat Black Goat

Nadia Bulkin

IT HAD BEEN raining for five days. The Gunawan estate, riddled with wool and dung, was rank. Its position on a hill had saved the mountain villa from the floods wracking West Java, but the moon orchids were drowning, and the Mercedes was sinking in the mud. Twenty-some feral goats watched the driveway roll down the slope. Then they started to bleat, because a little human figure was slogging up the hill.

Ina Krisniati was covered in mud by the time she conquered the hill, but by then she was no longer feeling her aches. She had walked two miles, in rising waters and darkness. The small and the weak—frogs, stones, flowering weeds—had succumbed. And Kris had nearly given up too, halfway up the hill. She'd nearly decided to go home to Cililin and marry some fisherman on Saguling Lake. But her grandfather had fought in the war, partaken in the 1946 Sea of Fire—Kris came from strong stock. The goats followed her as she fought her way to the house. They watched with sad, beady eyes as she rinsed her hands in rain and wiped her flip-flops on the mat. When she rang the doorbell, they resumed bleating.

A woman came to the door. She was, to Kris's surprise, not a maid. She had bags under her eyes but she was dressed like a soap star. Behind her, the house was glowing with spun glass and gold. The warung-keeper in Bandung who told her about the job did say that the Gunawans were born lucky. The woman cleared her throat.

Kris mustered a smile and bent her head. "Assalamu'alaikum," she said.

It took the woman half a minute to answer in kind. "Wa'alaikum salam," she muttered. "Are you the new babysitter?"

Kris nodded.

"Ya Allah." Mrs. Gunawan rolled her eyes and stepped back from the door. "What a mess. Don't move." She threw towels at her until she stopped dripping. "You know you're late. And you'll have to wash those, of course."

"I'm sorry, ma'am. The bus I was on broke down. Then I took a wrong turn, back on Tunjukmanis…"

Mrs. Gunawan rolled her eyes. "Right. Well, you're here to watch the children, and they're already in bed. I expect you to watch them *constantly*. My husband took off, my son fell off a horse last week, and…" She took a deep breath and flexed her jeweled fingers. "You have experience with childcare, yes?"

"Four little brothers and sisters. It's been tough for my parents, my father was ill…"

Mrs. Gunawan gave her a long look. "Don't even think about sneaking a little extra. I'll make you regret it."

"Yes, ma'am."

"You didn't touch the goats, did you? The ones roaming around?"

They had seemed to want her to. They'd been nudging her, blocking her path, making needful little grunts. "No, ma'am."

"Good. Don't. Only the children and I can touch them. Oh!" She cocked her chin up and pointed. Whispers trickled from the second floor. Soon little footsteps came down the staircase, and little heads popped out of the shadows. "There they are. Number one and number two."

The children looked like a pair of big-eyed malu-malu. Two of those shy little primates had once climbed into a power switch center on Saguling Lake and fried themselves as well as the hydroelectric plant. Kris smiled at the children. They did not smile back.

Mrs. Gunawan made no introductions. "Take them to bed," she said, with a flip of her wrist.

The bedroom was so cold that Kris thought there had to be some kind of draft. She checked the windows in vain while the children sat side by side on the bed, eating chocolate goo out of plastic tubes. On the wall, over their heads, hung a protective charm made of wild goat hair.

"I guess it's just cold in here." Kris plastered on a smile and walked back to the children. The little girl was the older of the two. She looked like her mother, especially when she had her chin up so she could look down her nose. The little boy was cradling his arm, which was wrapped in a cast and a sling. "I'm Kris. I'm going to watch you from now on, okay?"

"I'm Putri," said the little girl. "This is Agus. And you're not going to be watching us, because we already have someone who does that." She poked her little brother in the shoulder. "Don't we."

He nodded vigorously, but only after a pause, and when he looked at his petrified arm he frowned.

"Really? And who's that?"

"The Goat-Nurse. She's taken care of us since we were born." She sniffed. "We've never had a babysitter."

"Well, that's fine if the Goat-Nurse wants to watch you too. But your mother wanted someone to come and make sure that you don't hurt yourself falling off horses anymore." She smiled at Agus, who made a quivering attempt to smile back.

"We can't trust people from outside the family," Putri said. "The Goat-Nurse says so."

Kris had wondered why such a rich family had no servants. "Well, you don't need to worry about me." She wiped the chocolate off their mouths, the little malu-malu. "I'm not going to hurt you."

In the daytime the children showed off the family's goat herd. These were not the feral goats that roamed the estate and the wild woods beyond—these were fat, gentle livestock, happy to spend their lives in a backyard enclosure before being sold off to butcheries. They passively chewed their grass while the children sat on their backs and braided their white wool. The goat keeper Tono spent most of his time lounging under trees and staring off at Mount Tangkuban Perahu.

"Don't they want more space?" Kris asked him.

Tono shook his head, cracking his knuckles. He'd been digging out the sunken Mercedes. "They're scared of the wild goats. The ones that eat up all the grass."

One such wild goat—thin but fearless, with a pair of odd gangly legs—was roaming in the bushes outside the idyll of the enclosure. It looked at Kris and there was something not-quite-right about its face.

"Those goats will charge you," said Tono. "But mine are a lot nicer. They know they have it good. You don't even need a stick to corral them."

He had given his herding stick to Putri to play with, and she lorded it over the animals like a kingpin. Now and then she'd bop them on the head for eating flowers or urinating, though it had no effect on their behavior. "I'm the Goat-Princess!" she declared, and her brother saluted her like soldiers saluted the general during parades, like the general saluted the flag.

Tono smiled at Kris, then bit down gently on his cigarette.

Putri refused to surrender the stick when it was time for afternoon prayer, so Tono let her keep it. Only when the Gunawans sat down to dinner did Mrs. Gunawan tell her the stick could not rest at the table. It fell on Kris to put it away.

The upstairs hall light had burned out. There was a window fifty feet away, but a rainstorm had rendered the moon useless. Kris crept down the hall, trying to remember how many doors away Putri's bedroom was. All the door knobs were cold. Oily. The walls felt coated with a wax that smelled of soil, and sweat, and corpses. When Kris tossed the herding stick onto the floor of Putri's room, it rolled back toward her in affection. The Goat-Nurse, she thought.

It had to be a ghost. Maybe she'd been a babysitter like Kris, some hundred years ago. Maybe she'd been Dutch. A prison nurse. Someone cruel. And maybe something horrible had happened to her, something that earned her such a nasty name. Maybe she lost her legs in an accident. Maybe they had to sew on a pair of goat legs as rudimentary prosthetics…

From the end of the hallway came a *clop clop*. Kris looked to her right into the dark. *Clop clop* again, but closer. Back at home she'd been able to pick a human shape out of a moonless night if she gave her eyes enough time. So far the hallway was a mess of undefined clumps, but they'd straighten out. They'd clear up.

"I'm not afraid of you," she said, but the days when she didn't fear the dark were gone.

Her eyes adjusted, and she saw something standing at the wall. It had a face, of a sort. A long neck. Below that was something like a body in a smock, and then—livestock legs. Bristled. Filthy. Complete with cloven goat hoofs. Then the entire shape shuddered and the facades of skin melted back like a drawn veil. Beneath it darkness came a-crawling.

Kris fell all over the tiles, unable to feel her legs. Some distant part of her reptilian brain realized that she had been shaking for the past five minutes. She tried to stand—no, her legs were leaden. No more *clop clop* now, just a rush of overboiled air. She glanced up once and saw a curled blackness filling the hallway, floor to ceiling, like smoke but thicker, heavier, almost woolen. Kris slapped her hands over her eyes.

Maybe you should lose your legs

Maybe I should have them

"Kris!" It was like being pulled from drowning. "What are you doing up there?"

Was there a safer world? The monstrous breathing had pulled back from her neck. She looked up through her fingers and the hallway was bare. Just curios lined with velvet. She shoved her numb feet beneath her body and staggered downstairs.

"I hope you weren't in my jewelry..."

The expression on Kris's face must have cut Mrs. Gunawan off.

"The hall light's burned out," Kris said, but she could not hear her own voice. Light bulbs were part of a surface world that was no longer relevant. Light bulbs and dinner plates and chandeliers. From some distant plateau, Mrs. Gunawan told her to tell Tono in the morning—but Mrs. Gunawan was a blur. So was the room. Only the children were in focus, with their bullet eyes and their heart-shaped mouths.

Dark things swirled on the periphery of the flashlight's ray. These things made a pretense of hiding, but it was purely symbolic, part of a great game they were all playing. Kris saw them and so did the children. Agus even traced their movements with his finger, as if they were watching a wayang performance.

"I don't think she likes you," Putri said, pulling her sheets up to her chin. "You should be careful."

"I thought all *she* did was take care of you."

"Yes, of *us,* and our goats. But she gets mad easy. Do you know where my daddy is?"

Kris shrugged. She assumed he was off cavorting in Bangkok or Bali. Possibly skulking in a Jakarta lounge popping shabu, but she doubted it.

"He had a fight with Mama about the Goat-Nurse. Then he walked into the forest. The Goat-Nurse says he's dead. She says he got eaten by a tiger."

Kris swallowed. She thought she heard a *clop clop.*

"She has *power,* Kris." With a sigh, Putri closed her eyes. "You *have* to be respectful."

Kris went next door. She didn't knock and would never knock on a door in this house again, not when the Goat-Nurse lurked in the walls. The little shape under the sheets jolted awake.

"I'm sorry," Kris whispered, quickly closing the door and kneeling by the bed. "I need to ask you something, okay? It's very important."

Agus chewed his cotton top-sheet.

"Did the Goat-Nurse break your arm?" Silence. "Gus...you need to tell me."

"I really did fall off the horse. He got all scared and went up on his back legs. I fell into the ditch. But the Goat-Nurse didn't catch me. Mama says she's supposed to make sure I never get hurt." After another pause: "Are horses scared of goats?"

The children's mother was smashing peanuts on the sofa when Kris rushed this information to her. Mrs. Gunawan raised her eyebrow. "Why do you think I brought you here?" she said flatly. "The damn Goat stopped looking after them. I don't know why, but...it is what it is."

Kris carefully perched on the edge of another chair. She didn't want to encroach, but Mrs. Gunawan was slouched over, looking breakable.

"The night he left, my husband told me the Goat took one of his brothers. Little brother, long time ago. And I told him—I thought this thing worked *for* your family—and he started..." she flailed her hands, "throwing plates."

"Ma'am...have you considered asking an imam to come?"

Mrs. Gunawan wiped her eyes and laughed. "She's not a jinn. God knows that would have made it easier. Imam get rid of toyol all the time, don't they?"

Yes, they did—Kris had seen it done, at a sideshow. A morose man brought the imam a glass jar, large enough to hold a baby, and said the toyol inside had gotten so out of hand—attacking small animals, biting people—that he couldn't use it to run errands anymore. The imam proceeded to pray over the jar, slap its lid, and scold the baby-jinn for bad behavior. Then he gave the jar back to the morose man and told him to bury it in the woods and let the spirit be at peace, for God's sake.

"You thought it was a toyol?"

"She made the crops grow! She gave us those fat goats in the shed! It was a *drought* the year they found her. Or she found them, I don't know." Mrs. Gunawan crushed a peanut shell. "My husband said the goats just came to the door one day. The wild ones, you know, the ones you shouldn't touch. They just came to the door, April 1962. Like God had sent them."

A few days later, Tono was caught taking money out of Mrs. Gunawan's purse. She drove him to the front stoop. First he made excuses—she owed him last month's payment, the money fell out and he was putting it back—and then he tried to return the five hundred thousand rupiah with a gap-toothed smile.

Mrs. Gunawan grabbed Tono by the wrist. He looked startled. "Keep it," she said. "And here. Something else to remember us by." She thrust a thick tuft of goat wool into his hand.

The wool was far too coarse to have been shorn from the sweet, docile goats in the enclosure. Tono made a horrified croak. He tried to drop the feral wool but it clung to him; he tried to rub it off like pollen but it spread. "Please!" he cried. "I'm *sorry!*"

She pointed, but it didn't matter anyway. Even if he huddled on the doorstep he'd still be marked for death. So Tono went off down the hill, sobbing. His threadbare shirt glowed white under the moon.

"You'll kill him," Kris said. "And you'll destroy Bandung."

Mrs. Gunawan slammed the door and bolted it. "But maybe she'll get a taste for other people." The blood-strained whites of her eyes were nearly unbearable to look at. She had been beautiful, once. "You don't want to die, right?"

Kris shook her head. The windows went dark and the electricity blinked as something large slipped over the roof, momentarily drowning the house in a deep digestive rumble. Mrs. Gunawan clenched her jaw so hard her chin shook. Kris cowered.

Then it passed. The walls settled as if exhaling. The water heater and refrigerator hummed, but all else was calm.

"Maybe you should leave," said Kris. "Before it comes back."

Mrs. Gunawan shook her head violently. *"She* is out *there. We* are safer *here."*

People had started screaming down below. Kris put her head in her hands. Trees broke and roofs collapsed, but they were only punctuations against the steady roar of the Goat in bloom.

"It's just like the Tasikmalaya earthquake," Mrs. Gunawan said melodically. "That's all. Just another earthquake, just another mudslide…just another volcano, ripping open…"

A gurgling cry arose from the staircase, where Agus stood with his hands clapped over his ears. His mother was catatonic, so Kris hurried to shush him.

"She's out killing," he whined. "I hate the noise she makes." As if the Goat heard him, a gut-wrenching aerial moan burst out from the city. It must have carried all the way to the crater of Tangkuban Perahu. The docile goats, crowded near the walls of the house for protection, were bleating plaintively.

They didn't see the Goat-Nurse for another two months. Those were not a happy two months, although they were bloodless. Bandung authorities had passed off the Goat's attack as a violent mid-season tropical storm. Twenty-one had died, but they'd been impaled on branches, crushed under roof beams. The only casualty who'd been consumed was Tono, whose head fell out of the sky and onto the front porch the day after.

The children were quiet; nervous. Kris counted the days and held her breath, waiting for a hoofstep or a grunt. And in her dreams she would lie in the goat shed, watching an endless herd of feral goats come trampling out of the stalls. Their wool would blanket her. They would nuzzle her and bare their teeth and smile.

"She isn't far," Putri said at breakfast. Kris couldn't tell if she was pleased.

That evening Mrs. Gunawan had a visitor: her father-in-law, accompanied by a mute, kowtowed son. He was wearing an old black button-down suit and centimeter-thick glasses. He took a deep sniff of the air and knew.

"Where is she? Where did she go?"

"Why don't you ask your son."

"If you chased her away, you ungrateful bitch…"

"Look, that monster—*she*—doesn't belong with us. She hurt my son, look what she did to his arm!"

The elder Mr. Gunawan leaned down and inspected Agus's cast with a jut of his jaw. He smelled heavily of menthol. He was missing several teeth, and Agus stared unabashed at the black spots eating away at his gums. The old man hissed at the evidence. "That's it? That's all? Do you have any idea what she *is?*"

"You promised me my kids wouldn't get hurt!"

"I promised that you'd have grandchildren." He knotted his lips in disdain. "Same promise that was made to me."

Yet the old man need not have worried. The Goat came back—on the eve of jum'at kliwon, no less, spirits' night. She descended onto the house and draped her many woolly arms over the windows, blocking out the moon. Then she seeped through the roof and drenched the walls with wool-grease and the dirt of twenty cities, the blood of six hundred. The house had always been hers.

Agus and Putri cuddled into the Goat's familiar warmth. Mrs. Gunawan woke up throwing the sheets back, gasping for air. Kris lay on her stomach like a snake, hoping the Goat would pass her by.

Mrs. Gunawan didn't get out of bed the next morning. They heard her coughing from the kitchen.

"Where's Mama?" Agus asked, while Kris tossed the fried rice.

"She's sick," said Kris. "We should go down to the market and buy her some jahe."

"I don't think we should go anywhere," said Putri, and that was that.

The house felt unbearably quiet—no Tono, no Mrs. Gunawan. Just a hovering stillness that left the children sleepy and Kris scrubbing oil off a coffee table. The spot wouldn't clean; the streaks kept morphing back into the shape of a goat head. She threw down her sponge. "Let's go outside."

"Why are you trying to separate us from her?" Putri asked, yawning.

"Because she is a danger to you!" She hissed this, because she was afraid.

"She would never hurt us, or leave us. Not like Mama and Daddy."

Kris groaned and helped Agus off the couch. "*We* are going to go for a walk. *You* may stay here with your Goat-Nurse, since you like her so much."

Putri looked disgruntled, almost hurt. In the backyard—they walked and walked, but could never step out from under a great gray cloud—Agus asked if his sister would be okay.

Kris snorted. "She'll be fine."

"Agus! Look at me!"

They looked over their shoulders. Putri had gone up to the second floor balcony and climbed the terracotta shingles until she was standing like a weather vane on the top beam of the roof.

"Ya Allah, Putri! Come down from there!"

"You watch! She'll save me!"

"No she *won't!*"

Putri grinned. Then she bent her knees and jumped, flapping her arms, giving over complete faith. As she dropped past the second-floor windows, smog emerged from the house and swarmed her little body. The enormous black cloud slowly drifted her down to a nest of grass. For a second the cloud seemed to have consumed her; then it dissipated, and left the unhurt child behind.

Putri was still smiling. "You see? She loves *me.*"

Agus hung back, looking at his own broken arm. Despite weeks of cast-life, the fracture just wouldn't heal. He began to gnaw at his shirt collar—and Kris was about to tell Putri to be nicer to her brother—when Putri reached her hand out toward him and said, "Never mind. Let's go see the goats."

Agus took Putri's hand after only a second of hesitation, and the two children walked solemnly through the grass to their inheritance.

Kris woke up sluggish. She had overslept, she could tell. How could it still be dark? She looked at her bedside clock, but it had jammed, apparently, at 5 a.m. The goats must have jammed too, because for once she didn't hear them mewling through the wall.

She had a flashlight, thank God. She fumbled her way into the main rooms of the house. All the clocks were stopped, and all the skies were dark. There was something too velvety about the night, like immense cosmic curtains had closed around the house.

Something was struggling upstairs. A muffled fight, but in a house so silent, Kris heard all. She found Mrs. Gunawan choking in her bed.

Kris rushed over out of occupational instinct—*what can I do for you, ma'am?*—but once she was leaning over the cursed bed she froze. Between the rows of perfect teeth, behind the bluish tongue, gobs of black wool were filling Mrs. Gunawan's throat. Kris clapped her hands to her own mouth as Mrs. Gunawan thrashed.

"I'll call the doctor," Kris muttered, but Mrs. Gunawan grabbed her wrist and made a wretched croaking sound, like she was trying to scream through the wool. Her eyes were peeled back so far that even the blood vessels writhed. Kris jerked back. In another second the seizures stopped and Mrs. Gunawan's eyes rolled backward. Wool poked through her lips. Kris said a little prayer, but there was no peace to be had.

There was a little sound behind her. It was the children, standing shock-still in the doorway. God only knew how long they'd been watching their mother die. They made eye contact with Kris, then bolted.

She chased the little white figures down the hallway. She called them— "Gus! Putri!"—but they had their backs to her. She'd had nightmares like this: running, chasing, and then the children would turn around with hissing kuntilanak faces. Kris caught up to them downstairs, and said a little prayer before grabbing their bony shoulders and spinning them around.

But no—they were children. Bitter and breaking, but still apple-cheeked. Kris threw her arms around them, spewing any and all bullshit that would calm them down, but Putri shoved her away.

"We don't need you! We don't need Mama!"

"I know you're sad." Hoofsteps were running rampant upstairs; doors were slamming. She heard a thump that had to be Mrs. Gunawan's body being dragged off the bed. "But you need to stay with me, okay, we need to go get help."

Agus started crying, and Putri's snarl escalated into a scream: "The Goat is our real mother! She is *everyone's* real mother!"

Kris bit her bottom lip so hard it drew blood. Then she grabbed hold of Putri's arm and dragged her out the back door. Agus came running after them, practically howling. They were still trapped behind the night-curtain. The yard was torn up, like someone tried to plow it, and Putri kept jamming her feet into little ruts in the soil. Kris kept yanking her forward.

"Come on! You think that thing is your mother, I want you to see what it does to its children!"

More screams. Kicking. Biting. But when they reached the goat enclosure, all resistance stopped. It was too quiet, and it smelled absolutely foul. Wet things squelched under their rubber flip-flops and oozed between their toes.

"Look at what it does!"

Kris turned the flashlight on, and immediately choked back vomit. There was a lot of red, a lot of bones. Stubby little horns and milky eyes lay scattered in a sea of lush wool.

Agus shrieked and buried his eyes in his hands. Putri said nothing, but as Kris leaned down to shake sense into her—she had loved these creatures, hadn't she? given them names?—tremors began to wrack the child. Putri was crying.

Kris teared up too, in relief. They were going to run. They were going to run down the hill toward Bandung and it would be all right. They'd go to a mosque or the mayor and the Goat-Nurse would fade into oblivion. She even had a fleeting thought of taking them home to Cililin. They'd be happier there. They could dive for snappers in Saguling Lake, wake up clear and unburdened for the first time in their lives. "Don't worry," she said, stroking their hair. Yes, they were going to survive. "Don't worry."

"Look! One of them's still alive!"

Near the shed, a little slip of flesh and bones rose on a pair of shaky stick-legs. It moved inch by inch, in trembling jerks. Under the flashlight's gaze, it looked fur-covered—it was certainly dripping blood. But those legs were the rods of a puppeteer; that was the shape of Arjuna pressed against the screen, not the god himself.

Kris told her no. She *screamed* it. She ran after Putri to strain and sideache, but the little girl was damn-near flying toward the shed. Kris pushed her leg muscles harder and they gave, as if they'd been sliced out. She skidded on the grass and landed chin-first in entrails.

The little slip had become elephantine. It was fundamentally shapeless, a lumbering mess of smoke and wool and a hideous desire to consume—and yet it wore a human face, strapped on like a dancer's mask. It was the grotesque, plasticized face of the feral goats, of the thing in the upstairs hall. Long and misshapen and *false*.

Kris scrambled to her feet. The Goat was at treetop-level now. She was swelling, breathing blood and matter. The human mask bent down toward Putri with its eternal tight-lipped smile, black wool pouring forth behind it. The child was whispering something—some plea with God? The Goat whip-snapped her into the air.

I love you I love you I love you most of all

"Kris, help me!"

"Reach for me, reach for me, reach for me!"

The faith had been ripped from her eyes. The Goat inhaled, exhaled, and swallowed her whole. Putri did not scream; her mind had already emptied out onto her babysitter, who pulled her own hair and clawed her own skin and unremittingly howled.

The Goat departed. She hovered briefly over Agus like a cloud—he peered up into her frothing underbelly as if hoping to see his parents and sister peeking out—but she had long deemed him unworthy of her love. She moved west.

Then came the feral goats, field-destroyers, farmers' bane, servants of an older god. They ate the blood-red remains of the docile herd with long tough teeth and slurping lips. They licked the goat shed clean. They gnawed off Kris's legs as she lay face-up in the grass with barely blinking eyes—and then they wandered into the forest, following the scent of the great and ever-wanting Goat.

Agus was left squatting in the grass with his broken arm, begging to be loved.

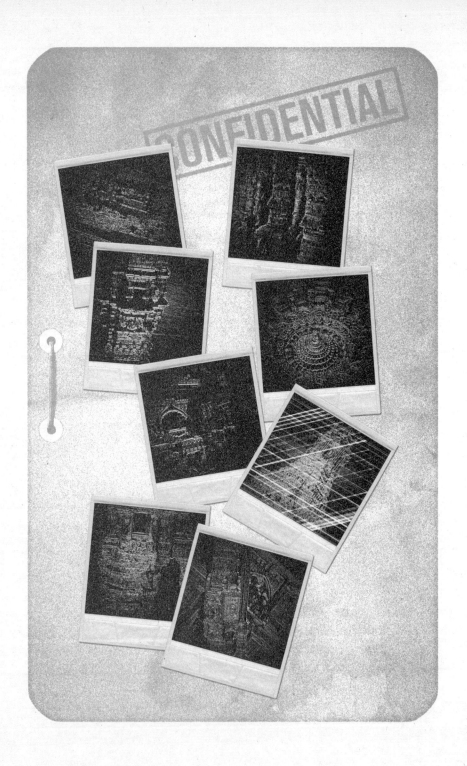

The Same Deep Waters as You

Brian Hodge

THEY WERE DOWN to the last leg of the trip, miles of iron-gray ocean skimming three hundred feet below the helicopter, and she was regretting ever having said yes. The rocky coastline of northern Washington slid out from beneath them and there they were, suspended over a sea as forbidding as the day itself. If they crashed, the water would claim them for its own long before anyone could find them.

Kerry had never warmed to the sea—now less than ever.

Had saying no even been an option? *The Department of Homeland Security would like to enlist your help as a consultant*, was what the pitch boiled down to, and the pair who'd come to her door yesterday looked genetically incapable of processing the word no. They couldn't tell her what. They couldn't tell her where. They could only tell her to dress warm. Better be ready for rain, too.

The sole scenario Kerry could think of was that someone wanted her insights into a more intuitive way to train dogs, maybe. Or something a little more out there, something to do with birds, dolphins, apes, horses…a plan that some questionable genius had devised to exploit some animal ability that they wanted to know how to tap. She'd been less compelled by the appeal to patriotism than simply wanting to make whatever they were doing go as well as possible for the animals.

But this? No one could ever have imagined this.

The island began to waver into view through the film of rain that streaked and jittered along the window, a triangular patch of uninviting rocks and evergreens and secrecy. They were down there.

Since before her parents were born, they'd always been down there.

It had begun before dawn: an uncomfortably silent car ride from her ranch to the airport in Missoula, a flight across Montana and Washington, touchdown at Sea-Tac, and the helicopter the rest of the way. Just before this final leg of the journey was the point they took her phone from her and searched her bag. Straight off the plane and fresh on the tarmac, bypassing the terminal entirely, Kerry was turned over to a man who introduced himself as Colonel Daniel Escovedo and said he was in charge of the facility they were going to.

"You'll be dealing exclusively with me from now on," he told her. His brown scalp was speckled with rain. If his hair were any shorter, you wouldn't have been able to say he had hair at all. "Are you having fun yet?"

"Not really, no." So far, this had been like agreeing to her own kidnapping.

They were strapped in and back in the air in minutes, just the two of them in the passenger cabin, knee-to-knee in facing seats.

"There's been a lot of haggling about how much to tell you," Escovedo said as she watched the ground fall away again. "Anyone who gets involved with this, in any capacity, they're working on a need-to-know basis. If it's not relevant to the job they're doing, then they just don't know. Or what they think they know isn't necessarily the truth, but it's enough to satisfy them."

Kerry studied him as he spoke. He was older than she first thought, maybe in his mid-fifties, with a decade and a half on her, but he had the lightly lined face of someone who didn't smile much. He would still be a terror in his seventies. You could just tell.

"What ultimately got decided for you is full disclosure. Which is to say, you'll know as much as I do. You're not going to know what you're looking for, or whether or not it's relevant, if you've got no context for it. But here's the first thing you need to wrap your head around: What you're going to see, most of the last fifteen presidents haven't been aware of."

She felt a plunge in her stomach as distinct as if their altitude had plummeted. "How is that possible? If he's the commander-in-chief, doesn't he...?"

Escovedo shook his head. "Need-to-know. There are security levels above the office of president. Politicians come and go. Career military and intelligence, we stick around."

"And I'm none of the above."

It was quickly getting frightening, this inner circle business. If she'd ever thought she would feel privileged, privy to something so hidden, now she knew better. There really were things you didn't want to know, because the privilege came with too much of a cost.

"Sometimes exceptions have to be made," he said, then didn't even blink at the next part. "And I really wish there was a nicer way to tell you this, but if you divulge any of what you see, you'll want to think very hard about that first. Do that, and it's going to ruin your life. First, nobody's going to believe you anyway. All it will do is make you a laughingstock. Before long, you'll lose your TV show. You'll lose credibility in what a lot of people see as a fringe field anyway. Beyond that...do I even need to go beyond that?"

Tabby—that was her first thought. Only thought, really. They would try to see that Tabitha was taken from her. The custody fight three years ago had been bruising enough, Mason doing his about-face on what he'd once found so beguiling about her, now trying to use it as a weapon, to make her seem unfit, unstable. *She talks to animals, your honor. She thinks they talk back.*

"I'm just the messenger," Colonel Escovedo said. "Okay?"

She wished she were better at conversations like this. Conversations in general. Oh, to not be intimidated by this. Oh, to look him in the eye and leave no doubt that he'd have to do better than that to scare her. To have just the right words to make him feel smaller, like the bully he was.

"I'm assuming you've heard of Guantanamo Bay in Cuba? What it's for?"

"Yes," she said in a hush. Okay, this was the ultimate threat. Say the wrong thing and she'd disappear from Montana, or Los Angeles, and reappear there, in the prison where there was no timetable for getting out. Just her and 160-odd suspected terrorists.

His eyes crinkled, almost a smile. "Try not to look so horrified. The threat part, that ended before I mentioned Gitmo."

Had it been that obvious? How nice she could amuse him this fine, rainy day.

"Where we're going is an older version of Guantanamo Bay," Escovedo went on. "It's the home of the most long-term enemy combatants ever held in U.S. custody."

"How long is long-term?"

"They've been detained since 1928."

She had to let that sink in. And was beyond guessing what she could bring to the table. Animals, that was her thing, it had always been her thing. Not

POWs, least of all those whose capture dated back to the decade after the First World War.

"Are you sure you have the right person?" she asked.

"Kerry Larimer. Star of *The Animal Whisperer*, a modest but consistent hit on the Discovery Channel, currently shooting its fourth season. Which you got after gaining a reputation as a behavioral specialist for rich people's exotic pets. You *look* like her."

"Okay, then." Surrender. They knew who they wanted. "How many prisoners?" From that long ago, it was a wonder there were any left at all.

"Sixty-three."

Everything about this kept slithering out of her grasp. "They'd be over a hundred years old by now. What possible danger could they pose? How could anyone justify—"

The colonel raised a hand. "It sounds appalling, I agree. But what you need to understand from this point forward is that, regardless of how or when they were born, it's doubtful that they're still human."

He pulled an iPad from his valise and handed it over, and here, finally, was the tipping point when the world forever changed. One photo, that was all it took. There were more—she must've flipped through a dozen—but really, the first one had been enough. Of course it wasn't human. It was a travesty of human. All the others were just evolutionary insult upon injury.

"What you see there is what you get," he said. "Have you ever heard of a town in Massachusetts called Innsmouth?"

Kerry shook her head. "I don't think so."

"No reason you should've. It's a little pisshole seaport whose best days were already behind it by the time of the Civil War. In the winter of 1927–28, there was a series of raids there, jointly conducted by the FBI and U.S. Army, with naval support. Officially—remember, this was during Prohibition—it was to shut down bootlegging operations bringing whiskey down the coast from Canada. The truth…" He took back the iPad from her nerveless fingers. "Nothing explains the truth better than seeing it with your own eyes."

"You can't talk to them. That's what this is about, isn't it?" she said. "You can't communicate with them, and you think I can."

Escovedo smiled, and until now, she didn't think he had it in him. "It must be true about you, then. You're psychic after all."

"Is it that they can't talk, or won't?"

"That's never been satisfactorily determined," he said. "The ones who still looked more or less human when they were taken prisoner, they could, and did. But they didn't stay that way. Human, I mean. That's the way this mutation works." He tapped the iPad. "What you saw there is the result of decades of change. Most of them were brought in like that already. The rest eventually got there. And the changes go more than skin deep. Their throats are different now. On the inside. Maybe this keeps them from speaking in a way that you and I would find intelligible, or maybe it doesn't but they're really consistent about pretending it does, because they're all on the same page. They do communicate with each other, that's a given. They've been recorded extensively doing that, and the sounds have been analyzed to exhaustion, and the consensus is that these sounds have their own syntax. The same way bird songs do. Just not as nice to listen to."

"If they've been under your roof all this time, they've spent almost a century away from whatever culture they had where they came from. All that would be gone now, wouldn't it? The world's changed so much since then they wouldn't even recognize it," she said. "You're not doing science. You're doing national security. What I don't understand is why it's so important to communicate with them after all this time."

"All those changes you're talking about, that stops at the seashore. Drop them in the ocean and they'd feel right at home." He zipped the iPad back into his valise. "Whatever they might've had to say in 1928, that doesn't matter. Or '48, or '88. It's what we need to know *now* that's created a sense of urgency."

Once the helicopter had set down on the island, Kerry hadn't even left the cabin before thinking she'd never been to a more miserable place in her life. Rocky and rain-lashed, miles off the mainland, it was buffeted by winds that snapped from one direction and then another, so that the pines that grew here didn't know which way to go, twisted until they seemed to lean and leer with ill intent.

"It's not always like this," Escovedo assured her. "Sometimes there's sleet, too."

It was the size of a large shopping plaza, a skewed triangular shape, with a helipad and boat dock on one point, and a scattering of outbuildings clustered along another, including what she assumed were offices and barracks for those unfortunate enough to have been assigned to duty here, everything laced together by a network of roads and pathways.

It was dominated, though, by a hulking brick monstrosity that looked exactly like what it was—a vintage relic of a prison—although it could pass for other things, too: an old factory or power plant, or, more likely, a wartime fortress, a leftover outpost from an era when the west coast feared the Japanese fleet. It had been built in 1942, Escovedo told her. No one would have questioned the need for it at the time, and since then, people were simply used to it, if they even knew it was there. Boaters might be curious, but the shoreline was studded at intervals with signs, and she imagined that whatever they said was enough to repel the inquisitive—that, and the triple rows of fencing crowned with loops of razor wire.

Inside her rain slicker, Kerry yanked the hood's drawstring tight and leaned into the needles of rain. October—it was only October. Imagine this place in January. Of course it didn't bother the colonel one bit. They were halfway along the path to the outbuildings when she turned to him and tugged the edge of her hood aside.

"I'm not psychic," she told him. "You called me that in the helicopter. That's not how I look at what I do."

"Noted," he said, noncommittal and unconcerned.

"I'm serious. If you're going to bring me out here, to this place, it's important to me that you understand what I do, and aren't snickering about it behind my back."

"You're here, aren't you? Obviously somebody high up the chain of command has faith in you."

That gave her pause to consider. This wouldn't have been a lark on their part. Bringing in a civilian on something most presidents hadn't known about would never have been done on a hunch—see if this works, and if it doesn't, no harm done. She would've been vetted, extensively, and she wondered how they'd done it. Coming up with pretenses to interview past clients, perhaps, or people who'd appeared on *The Animal Whisperer*, to ascertain that they really were the just-folks they were purported to be, and that it wasn't scripted; that she genuinely had done for them what she was supposed to.

"What about you, though? Have you seen the show?"

"I got forwarded the season one DVDs. I watched the first couple episodes." He grew more thoughtful, less official. "The polar bear at the Cleveland Zoo, that was interesting. That's 1500 pounds of apex predator you're dealing with. And you went in there without so much as a stick of wood between you and it.

Just because it was having OCD issues? That takes either a big pair of balls or a serious case of stupid. And I don't think you're stupid."

"That's a start, I guess," she said. "Is that particular episode why I'm here? You figured since I did that, I wouldn't spook easily with these prisoners of yours?"

"I imagine it was factored in." The gravel that lined the path crunched underfoot for several paces before he spoke again. "If you don't think of yourself as psychic, what is it, then? How *does* it work?"

"I don't really know." Kerry had always dreaded the question, because she'd never been good at answering it. "It's been there as far back as I can remember, and I've gotten better at it, but I think that's just through the doing. It's a sense as much as anything. But not like sight or smell or taste. I compare it to balance. Can you explain how your sense of balance works?"

He cut her a sideways glance, betraying nothing, but she saw he didn't have a clue. "Mine? You're on a need-to-know basis here, remember."

Very good. Very dry. Escovedo was probably more fun than he let on.

"Right," she said. "Everybody else's, then. Most people have no idea. It's so intrinsic they take it for granted. A few may know it has to do with the inner ear. And a few of them, that it's centered in the vestibular apparatus, those three tiny loops full of fluid. One for up, one for down, one for forward and backward. But you don't need to know any of that to walk like we are now and not fall over. Well…that's what the animal thing is like for me. It's there, but I don't know the mechanism behind it."

He mused this over for several paces. "So that's your way of dodging the question?"

Kerry grinned at the ground. "It usually works."

"It's a good smokescreen. Really, though."

"Really? It's…" She drew the word out, a soft hiss while gathering her thoughts. "A combination of things. It's like receiving emotions, feelings, sensory impressions, mental imagery, either still or with motion. Any or all. Sometimes it's not even that, it's just…pure knowing, is the best way I know to phrase it."

"Pure knowing?" He sounded skeptical.

"Have you been in combat?"

"Yes."

"Then even if you haven't experienced it yourself, I'd be surprised if you haven't seen it or heard about it in people you trust—a strong sense that you should be very careful in that building, or approaching that next rise. They can't point to anything concrete to explain why. They just know. And they're often right."

Escovedo nodded. "Put in that context, it makes sense."

"Plus, for what it's worth, they ran a functional MRI on me, just for fun. That's on the season two DVD bonuses. Apparently the language center of my brain is very highly developed. Ninety-eighth percentile, something like that. So maybe that has something to do with it."

"Interesting," Escovedo said, and nothing more, so she decided to quit while she was ahead.

The path curved and split before them, and though they weren't taking the left-hand branch to the prison, still, the closer they drew to it, darkened by rain and contemptuous of the wind, the greater the edifice seemed to loom over everything else on the island. It was like something grown from the sea, an iceberg of brick, with the worst of it hidden from view. When the wind blew just right, it carried with it a smell of fish, generations of them, as if left to spoil and never cleaned up.

Kerry stared past it, to the sea surging all the way to the horizon. This was an island only if you looked at it from out there. Simple, then: *Don't ever go out there.*

She'd never had a problem with swimming pools. You could see through those. Lakes, oceans, rivers...these were something entirely different. These were *dark* waters, full of secrets and unintended tombs. Shipwrecks, sunken airplanes, houses at the bottom of flooded valleys...they were sepulchers of dread, trapped in another world where they so plainly did not belong.

Not unlike the way she was feeling this very moment.

As she looked around Colonel Escovedo's office in the administrative building, it seemed almost as much a cell as anything they could have over at the prison. It was without windows, so the lighting was all artificial, fluorescent and unflattering. It aged him, and she didn't want to think what it had to be doing to her own appearance. In one corner, a dehumidifier chugged away, but the air still felt heavy and damp. Day in, day out, it must have been like working in a mine.

"Here's the situation. Why now," he said. "Their behavior over there, it's been pretty much unchanged ever since they were moved to this installation. With one exception. Late summer, 1997, for about a month. I wasn't here then, but according to the records, it was like…" He paused, groping for the right words. "A hive mind. Like they were a single organism. They spent most of their time aligned to a precise angle to the southwest. The commanding officer at the time mentioned in his reports that it was like they were waiting for something. Inhumanly patient, just waiting. Then, eventually, they stopped and everything went back to normal."

"Until now?" she said.

"Nine days ago. They're doing it again."

"Did anybody figure out what was special about that month?"

"We think so. It took years, though. Three years before some analyst made the connection, and even then, you know, it's still a lucky accident. Maybe you've heard how it is with these agencies, they don't talk to each other, don't share notes. You've got a key here, and a lock on the other side of the world, and nobody in the middle who knows enough to put the two together. It's better now than it used to be, but it took the 9/11 attacks to get them to even *think* about correlating intel better."

"So what happened that summer?"

"Just listen," he said, and spun in his chair to the hardware behind him.

She'd been wondering about that anyway. Considering how functional his office was, it seemed not merely excessive, but out of character, that Escovedo would have an array of what looked to be high-end audio-video components, all feeding into a pair of three-way speakers and a subwoofer. He dialed in a sound file on the LCD of one of the rack modules, then thumbed the play button.

At first it was soothing, a muted drone both airy and deep, a lonely noise that some movie's sound designer might have used to suggest the desolation of outer space. But no, this wasn't about space. It had to be the sea, this all led back to the sea. It was the sound of deep waters, the black depths where sunlight never reached.

Then came a new sound, deeper than deep, a slow eruption digging its way free of the drone, climbing in pitch, rising, rising, then plummeting back to leave her once more with the sound of the void. After moments of anticipation, it happened again, like a roar from an abyss, and prickled the fine hairs on the back of her neck—a primal response, but then, what was more primal than the ocean and the threats beneath its waves?

This was why she'd never liked the sea. This never knowing what was there, until it was upon you.

"Heard enough?" Escovedo asked, and seemed amused at her mute nod. *"That* happened. Their hive mind behavior coincided with that."

"What *was* it?"

"That's the big question. It was recorded several times during the summer of 1997, then never again. Since 1960, we've had the oceans bugged for sound, basically. We've got them full of microphones that we put there to listen for Soviet submarines, when we thought it was a possibility we'd be going to war with them. They're down hundreds of feet, along an ocean layer called the sound channel. For sound conductivity, it's the Goldilocks zone—it's just right. After the Cold War was over, these mic networks were decommissioned from military use and turned over for scientific research. Whales, seismic events, underwater volcanoes, that sort of thing. Most of it, it's instantly identifiable. The people whose job it is to listen to what the mics pick up, 99.99 percent of the time they know exactly what they've got because the sounds conform to signature patterns, and they're just so familiar.

"But every so often they get one they can't identify. It doesn't fit any known pattern. So they give it a cute name and it stays a mystery. This one, they called it the 'Bloop.' Makes it sound like a kid farting in the bathtub, doesn't it?"

She pointed at the speakers. "An awfully big kid and an awfully big tub."

"Now you're getting ahead of me. The Bloop's point of origin was calculated to be in the South Pacific…maybe not coincidentally, not far from Polynesia, which is generally conceded as the place of origin for what eventually came to be known in Massachusetts as 'the Innsmouth look.' Some outside influence was brought home from Polynesia in the 1800s during a series of trading expeditions by a sea captain named Obed Marsh."

"Are you talking about a disease, or a genetic abnormality?"

Escovedo slapped one hand onto a sheaf of bound papers lying on one side of his desk. "You can be the judge of that. I've got a summary here for you to look over, before you get started tomorrow. It'll give you more background on the town and its history. The whole thing's a knotted-up tangle of fact and rumor and local legend and god knows what all, but it's not my job to sort out what's what. I've got enough on my plate sticking with facts, and the fact is, I'm in charge of keeping sixty-three of these proto-human monstrosities hidden from the world, and I know they're cued into something anomalous, but I don't know what. The other fact is, the last time they acted like this was fifteen years ago, while those mics were picking up one of the loudest sounds ever recorded on the planet."

"How loud was it?"

"Every time that sound went off, it wasn't just a local event. It was picked up over a span of five thousand kilometers."

The thought made her head swim. Something with that much power behind it…there could be nothing good about it. Something that loud was the sound of death, of cataclysm and extinction events. It was the sound of an asteroid strike, of a volcano not just erupting, but vaporizing a land mass—Krakatoa, the island of Thera. She imagined standing here, past the northwestern edge of the continental U.S., and hearing something happen in New York. Okay, sound traveled better in water than in air, but still—*three thousand miles.*

"Despite that," Escovedo said, "the analysts say it most closely matches a profile of something alive."

"A whale?" There couldn't be anything bigger, not for million of years.

The colonel shook his head. "Keep going. Somebody who briefed me on this compared it to a blue whale plugged in and running through the amplifier stacks at every show Metallica has ever played, all at once. She also said that what they captured probably wasn't even the whole sound. That it's likely that a lot of frequencies and details got naturally filtered out along the way."

"Whatever it was…there have to be theories."

"Sure. Just nothing that fits with all the known pieces."

"Is the sound occurring again?"

"No. We don't know what they're cueing in on this time."

He pointed at the prison. Even though he couldn't see it, because there were no windows, and now she wondered if he didn't prefer it that way. Block it out with walls, and maybe for a few minutes at a time he could pretend he was somewhere else, assigned to some other duty.

"But *they* do," he said. "Those abominations over there know. We just need to find the key to getting them to tell us."

She was billeted in what Colonel Escovedo called the guest barracks, the only visitor in a building that could accommodate eight in privacy, sixteen if they doubled up. Visitors, Kerry figured, would be a rare occurrence here, and the place felt that way, little lived in and not much used. The rain had strengthened closer to evening and beat hard on the low roof, a lonely sound that built from room to vacant room.

When she heard the deep thump of the helicopter rotors pick up, then recede into the sky—having waited, apparently, until it was clear she would be staying—she felt unaccountably abandoned, stranded with no way off this outpost that lay beyond not just the rim of civilization, but beyond the frontiers of even her expanded sense of life, of humans and animals and what passed between them.

Every now and then she heard someone outside, crunching past on foot or on an all-terrain four-wheeler. If she looked, they were reduced to dark, indistinct smears wavering in the water that sluiced down the windows. She had the run of most of the island if she wanted, although that was mainly just a license to get soaked under the sky. The buildings were forbidden, other than her quarters and the admin office, and, of course, the prison, as long as she was being escorted. And, apart from the colonel, she was apparently expected to pretend to be the invisible woman. She and the duty personnel were off-limits to each other. She wasn't to speak to them, and they were under orders not to speak with her.

They didn't know the truth—it was the only explanation that made sense. They didn't know, because they didn't need to. They'd been fed a cover story. Maybe they believed they were guarding the maddened survivors of a disease, a genetic mutation, an industrial accident or something that had fallen from space and that did terrible things to DNA. Maybe they'd all been fed a different lie, so that if they got together to compare notes they wouldn't know which to believe.

For that matter, she wasn't sure she did either.

First things first, though: She set up a framed photo of Tabitha on a table out in the barracks' common room, shot over the summer when they'd gone horseback riding in the Sawtooth Range. Her daughter's sixth birthday. Rarely was a picture snapped in which Tabby wasn't beaming, giddy with life, but this was one of them, her little face rapt with focus. Still in the saddle, she was leaning forward, hugging the mare's neck, her braided hair a blonde stripe along the chestnut hide, and it looked for all the world as if the two of them were sharing a secret.

The photo would be her beacon, her lighthouse shining from home.

She fixed a mug of hot cocoa in the kitchenette, then settled into one of the chairs with the summary report that Escovedo had sent with her.

Except for its cold, matter-of-fact tone, it read like bizarre fiction. If she hadn't seen the photos, she wouldn't have believed it: a series of raids in an isolated Massachusetts seaport that swept up more than two hundred residents, most of whose appearances exhibited combinations of human, ichthyoid, and amphibian traits. The Innsmouth look had been well-known to the neighboring towns for at least two generations—"an unsavory haven of inbreeding and circus folk," according to a derisive comment culled from an Ipswich newspaper of the era—but even then, Innsmouth had been careful to put forward the best face it possibly could. Which meant, in most cases, residents still on the low side of middle-age…at least when it came to the families that had a few decades' worth of roots in the town, rather than its more recent newcomers.

With age came change so drastic that the affected people gradually lost all resemblance to who they'd been as children and young adults, eventually reaching the point that they let themselves be seen only by each other, taking care to hide from public view in a warren of dilapidated homes, warehouses, and limestone caverns that honeycombed the area.

One page of the report displayed a sequence of photos of what was ostensibly the same person, identified as Giles Shapleigh, eighteen years old when detained in 1928. He'd been a handsome kid in the first photo, and if he had nothing to smile about when it was taken, you could at least see the potential for a roguish, cockeyed grin. By his twenty-fifth year, he'd visibly aged, his hair receded and thinning, and after seven years of captivity he had the sullen look of a convict. By thirty, he was bald as a cue ball, and his skull had seemed to narrow. By thirty-five, his jowls had widened enough to render his neck almost nonexistent, giving him a bullet-headed appearance that she found all the more unnerving for his dead-eyed stare.

By the time he was sixty, with astronauts not long on the moon, there was nothing left to connect Giles Shapleigh with who or what he'd been, neither his identity nor his species. Still, though, his transformation wasn't yet complete.

He was merely catching up to his friends, neighbors, and relatives. By the time of those Prohibition-era raids, most of the others had been this way for years—decades, some of them. Although they aged, they didn't seem to weaken and, while they could be killed, if merely left to themselves, they most certainly didn't die.

They could languish, though. As those first years went on, with the Innsmouth prisoners scattered throughout a handful of remote quarantine facilities across New England, it became obvious that they didn't do well in the kind of environment reserved for normal prisoners: barred cells, bright lights, exercise yards…*dryness*. Some of them developed a skin condition that resembled powdery mildew, a white, dusty crust that spread across them in patches. There was a genuine fear that, whatever it was, it might jump from captives to captors, and prove more virulent in wholly human hosts, although this never happened.

Thus it was decided: They didn't need a standard prison so much as they needed their own zoo. That they got it was something she found strangely heartening. What was missing from the report, presumably because she had no need to know, was *why*.

While she didn't want to admit it, Kerry had no illusions—the expedient thing would've been to kill them off. No one would have known, and undoubtedly there would've been those who found it an easy order to carry out. It was wartime, and if war proved anything, it proved how simple it was to dehumanize people even when they looked just like you. This was 1942, and this was already happening on an industrial scale across Europe. These people from Innsmouth would have had few advocates. To merely look at them was to feel revulsion, to sense a challenge to everything you thought you knew about the world, about what could and couldn't be. Most people would look at them and think they deserved to die. They were an insult to existence, to cherished beliefs.

Yet they lived. They'd outlived the men who'd rounded them up, and their first jailers, and most of their jailers since. They'd outlived everyone who'd opted to keep them a secret down through the generations…yet for what?

Perhaps morality *had* factored into the decision to keep them alive, but she doubted morality had weighed heaviest. Maybe, paradoxically, it had been done out of fear. They may have rounded up over two hundred of Innsmouth's strangest, but many more had escaped—by most accounts, fleeing into the harbor, then the ocean beyond. To exterminate these captives because they were unnatural would be to throw away the greatest resource they might possess in case they ever faced these beings again, under worse circumstances.

Full disclosure, Escovedo had promised. She would know as much as he did. But when she finished the report along with the cocoa, she had no faith whatsoever that she was on par with the colonel, or that even he'd been told the half of it himself.

How much did a man need to know, really, to be a glorified prison warden?

Questions nagged, starting with the numbers. She slung on her coat and headed back out into the rain, even colder now, as it needled down from a dusk descending on the island like a dark gray blanket. She found the colonel still in his office, and supposed by now he was used to people dripping on his floor.

"What happened to rest of them?" she asked. "Your report says there were over two hundred to start with. And that this place was built to house up to three hundred. So I guess somebody thought more might turn up. But you're down to sixty-three. And they don't die of natural causes. So what happened to the others?"

"What does it matter? For your purposes, I mean. What you're here to do."

"Did you know that animals understand the idea of extermination? Wolves do. Dogs at the pound do. Cattle do, once they get to the slaughterhouse pens. They may not be able to articulate it, but they pick up on it. From miles away, sometimes, they can pick up on it." She felt a chilly drop of water slither down her forehead. "I don't know about fish or reptiles. But whatever humanity may still exist in these prisoners of yours, I wouldn't be surprised if it's left them just as sensitive to the concept of extermination, or worse."

He looked at her blankly, waiting for more. He didn't get it.

"For all I know, you're sending me in there as the latest interrogator who wants to find out the best way to commit genocide on the rest of their kind. *That's* why it matters. Is that how they're going to see me?"

Escovedo looked at her for a long time, his gaze fixated on her, not moving, just studying her increasing unease as she tried to divine what he was thinking. If he was angry, or disappointed, or considering sending her home before she'd even set foot in the prison. He stared so long she had no idea which it could be, until she realized that the stare *was* the point.

"They've got these eyes," he said. "They don't blink. They've got no white part to them anymore, so you don't know where they're looking, exactly. It's more like looking into a mirror than another eye. A mirror that makes you want to look away. So…how they'll *see* you?" he said, with a quick shake of his head and a hopeless snort of a laugh. "I have no idea *what* they see."

She wondered how long he'd been in this command. If he would ever get used to the presence of such an alien enemy. If any of them did, his predecessors, back to the beginning. That much she could see.

"Like I said, I stick with facts," he said. "I can tell you this much: When you've got a discovery like *them,* you have to expect that every so often another one or two of them are going to disappear into the system."

"The system," she said. "What does that mean?"

"You were right, we don't do science here. But they do in other places," he told her. "You can't be naïve enough to think research means spending the day watching them crawl around and writing down what they had for lunch."

Naïve? No. Kerry supposed she had suspected before she'd even slogged over here to ask. Just to make sure. You didn't have to be naïve to hope for better.

She carried the answer into dreams that night, where it became excruciatingly obvious that, while the Innsmouth prisoners may have lost the ability to speak in any known language, when properly motivated, they could still shriek.

Morning traded the rain for fog, lots of it, a chilly cloud that had settled over the island before dawn. There was no more sky and sea, no more distance, just whatever lay a few feet in front of her, and endless gray beyond. Without the gravel pathways, she was afraid she might've lost her bearings, maybe wander to the edge of the island. Tangle herself in razor wire, and hang there and die before anyone noticed.

She could feel it now, the channels open and her deepest intuition rising: This was the worst place she'd ever been, and she couldn't tell which side bore the greater blame.

With breakfast in her belly and coffee in hand, she met Escovedo at his office, so he could escort her to the corner of the island where the prison stood facing west, looking out over the sea. There would be no more land until Asia. Immense, made of brick so saturated with wet air that its walls looked slimed, the prison emerged from the mist like a sunken ship.

What would it be like, she wondered, to enter a place and not come out for seventy years? What would that do to one's mind? Were they even sane now? Or did they merely view this as a brief interruption in their lives? Unless they were murdered outright—a possibility—their lifespans were indefinite. Maybe they knew that time was their ally. Time would kill their captors, generation by generation, while they went on. Time would bring down every wall. All terrestrial life might go extinct, while they went on.

As long as they could make it those last few dozen yards to the sea.

"Have any of them ever escaped from here?" she asked.

"No."

"Don't you find that odd? I do. Hasn't most every prison had at least one escape over seventy years?"

"Not this one. It doesn't run like a regular prison. The inmates don't work. There's no kitchen, no laundry trucks, no freedom to tunnel. They don't get visitors. We just spend all day looking at each other." He paused in the arched, inset doorway, his finger on the call button that would summon the guards inside to open up. "If you want my unfiltered opinion, those of us who pulled this duty are the real prisoners."

Inside, it was all gates and checkpoints, the drab institutional hallways saturated with a lingering smell of fish. *Them,* she was smelling *them.* Like people who spent their workdays around death and decay, the soldiers here would carry it home in their pores. You had to pity them that. They would be smelling it after a year of showers, whether it was there or not.

Stairs, finally, a series of flights that seemed to follow the curvature of some central core. It deposited them near the top of the building, on an observation deck. Every vantage point around the retaining wall, particularly a trio of guard posts, overlooked an enormous pit, like an abandoned rock quarry. Flat terraces and rounded pillows of stone rose here and there out of a pool of murky seawater. Along the walls, rough stairways led up to three tiers of rooms, cells without bars.

This wasn't a prison where the inmates would need to be protected from each other. They were all on the same side down there, prisoners of an undeclared war.

Above the pit, the roof was louvered, so apparently, although closed now, it could be opened. They could see the sky. They would have air and rain. Sunshine, if that still meant anything to them.

The water, she'd learned from last night's briefing paper, was no stagnant pool. It was continually refreshed, with drains along the bottom and grated pipes midway up the walls that periodically spewed a gusher like a tidal surge. Decades of this had streaked the walls with darker stains, each like a ragged brush stroke straight down from the rusty grate to the foaming surface of their makeshift sea.

Fish even lived in it, and why not? The prisoners had to eat.

Not at the moment, though. They lined the rocks in groups, as many as would fit on any given surface, sitting, squatting, facing the unseen ocean in eerily perfect alignment to one another.

"What do you make of it?" he asked.

Kerry thought of fish she'd watched in commercial aquariums, in nature documentaries, fish swimming in their thousands, singularly directed, and then, in an instantaneous response to some stimulus, changing directions in perfect unison. "I would say they're schooling."

From where they'd entered the observation deck, she could see only their backs, and began to circle the retaining wall for a better view.

Their basic shapes looked human, but the details were all wrong. Their skin ranged from dusky gray to light green, with pale bellies—dappled sometimes, an effect like sunlight through water—and rubbery looking even from here, as though it would be slick as a wetsuit to the touch, at least the areas that hadn't gone hard and scaly. Some wore the remnants of clothing, although she doubted anything would hold up long in the water and rocks, while others chose to go entirely without. They were finned and they were spiny, no two quite the same, and their hands webbed between the fingers, their feet ridiculously outsized. Their smooth heads were uncommonly narrow, all of them, but still more human than not. Their faces, though, were ghastly. These were faces for another world, with thick-lipped mouths made to gulp water, and eyes to peer through the murky gloom of the deep. Their noses were all but gone, just vestigial nubs now, flattened and slitted. The females' breasts had been similarly subsumed, down to little more than hard bumps.

She clutched the top of the wall until her fingernails began to bend. Not even photographs could truly prepare you for seeing them in the flesh.

I wish I'd never known, she thought. *I can never be the same again.*

"You want to just pick one at random, see where it goes?" Escovedo asked.

"How do you see this working? We haven't talked about that," she said. "What, you pull one of them out and put us in a room together, each of us on either side of a table?"

"Do you have any better ideas?"

"It seems so artificial. The environment of an interrogation room, I mean. I need them open, if that makes sense. Their minds, open. A room like that, it's like you're doing everything you can to close them off from the start."

"Well, I'm not sending you in down there into the middle of all sixty-three of them, if that's what you're getting at. I have no idea how they'd react, and there's no way I could guarantee your safety."

She glanced at the guard posts, only now registering why they were so perfectly triangulated. Nothing was out of reach of their rifles.

"And you don't want to set up a situation where you'd have to open fire on the group, right?"

"It would be counterproductive."

"Then you pick one," she said. "You know them better than I do."

If the Innsmouth prisoners still had a sense of patriarchy, then Escovedo must have decided to start her at the top of their pecking order.

The one they brought her was named Barnabas Marsh, if he even had a use anymore for a name that none of his kind could speak. Maybe names only served the convenience of their captors now, although if any name still carried weight, it would be the name of Marsh. Barnabas was the grandson of Obed Marsh, the ship's captain who, as village legend held, had sailed to strange places above the sea and below it, and brought back both the DNA and partnerships that had altered the course of Innsmouth's history.

Barnabas had been old even when taken prisoner, and by human terms he was now beyond ancient. She tried not to think of him as monstrous, but no other word wanted to settle on him, on any of them. Marsh, though, she found all the more monstrous for the fact that she could see in him the puffed-up, barrel-chested bearing of a once-domineering man who'd never forgotten who and what he had been.

Behind the wattles of his expanded neck, gills rippled with indignation. The thick lips, wider than any human mouth she'd ever seen, stretched downward at each corner in a permanent, magisterial sneer.

He waddled when he walked, as if no longer made for the land, and when the two guards in suits of body armor deposited him in the room, he looked her up and down, then shuffled in as if resigned to tolerating her until this interruption was over. He stopped long enough to give the table and chairs in the center of the room a scornful glance, then continued to the corner, where he slid to the floor with a shoulder on each wall, the angle where they met giving room for his sharp-spined back.

She took the floor as well.

"I believe you can understand me. Every word," Kerry said. "You either can't or won't speak the way you did for the first decades of your life, but I can't think of any reason why you shouldn't still understand me. And that puts you way ahead of all the rest of God's creatures I've managed to communicate with."

He looked at her with his bulging dark eyes, and Escovedo had been right. It was a disconcertingly inhuman gaze, not even mammalian. It wasn't anthropomorphizing to say that mammals—dogs, cats, even a plethora of wilder beasts—had often looked at her with a kind of warmth. But *this*, these eyes…they were cold, with a remote scrutiny that she sensed regarded her as lesser in every way.

The room's air, cool to begin with, seemed to chill even more as her skin crawled with an urge to put distance between them. Could he sense that she feared him? Maybe he took this as a given. That he could be dangerous was obvious—the closer you looked, the more he seemed covered with sharp points, none more lethal than the tips of his stubby fingers. But she had to trust the prison staff to ensure her safety. While there was no guard in here to make the energy worse than it was already, they were being watched on a closed-circuit camera. If Marsh threatened her, the room would be flooded with a gas that would put them both out in seconds. She'd wake up with a headache, and Marsh would wake up back in the pit.

And nothing would be accomplished.

"I say God's creatures because I don't know how else to think of you," she said. "I know how *they* think of you. They think you're all aberrations. Unnatural. Not that I'm telling you anything you probably haven't already overheard from them every day for more than eighty years."

And did that catch his interest, even a little? If the subtle tilt of his head meant anything, maybe it did.

"But if you exist, entire families of you, colonies of you, then you can't be an aberration. You're within the realm of nature's possibilities."

Until this moment, she'd had no idea what she would say to him. With animals, she was accustomed to speaking without much concern for what exactly she said. It was more how she said it. Like very young children, animals cued in on tone, not language. They nearly always seemed to favor a higher-pitched voice. They responded to touch.

None of which was going to work here.

But Barnabas Marsh was a presence, and a powerful one, radiant with a sense of age. She kept speaking to him, seeking a way through the gulf between them, the same as she always did. No matter what the species, there always seemed to be a way, always something to which she could attune—an image, a sound, a taste, some heightened sense that overwhelmed her and, once she regained her equilibrium, let her use it as the key in the door that would open the way for more.

She spoke to him of the sea, the most obvious thing, because no matter what the differences between them, they had that much in common. It flowed in each of them, water and salt, and they'd both come from it; he was just closer to returning, was all. Soon she felt the pull of tides, the tug of currents, the cold wet draw of gravity luring down, down, down to greater depths, then the equipoise of pressure, and where once it might've crushed, now it comforted, a cold cocoon that was both a blanket and a world, tingling along her skin with news coming from a thousand leagues in every direction—

And with a start she realized that the sea hadn't been her idea at all.

She'd only followed where he led. Whether Marsh meant to or not.

Kerry looked him in his cold, inhuman eyes, not knowing quite what lay behind them, until she began to get a sense that the sea was *all* that lay behind them. The sea was all he thought of, all he wanted, all that mattered, a yearning so focused that she truly doubted she could slip past it to ferret out what was so special about *now*. What they all sensed happening *now*, just as they had fifteen years ago.

It was all one and the same, of course, bound inextricably together, but first they had to reclaim the sea.

And so it went the rest of the day, with one after another of this sad parade of prisoners, until she'd seen nearly twenty of them. Nothing that she would've dared call progress, just inklings of impressions, snippets of sensations, none of it coalescing into a meaningful whole, and all of it subsumed beneath a churning ache to return to the sea. It was their defense against her, and she doubted they even knew it.

Whatever was different about her, whatever had enabled her to whisper with creatures that she and the rest of the world found more appealing, it wasn't made to penetrate a human-born despair that had hardened over most of a century.

There was little light remaining in the day when she left the prison in defeat, and little enough to begin with. It was now a colorless world of approaching darkness. She walked a straight line, sense of direction lost in the clammy mist that clung to her as surely as the permeating smell of the prisoners. She knew she had to come to the island's edge eventually, and if she saw another human being before tomorrow, it would be too soon.

Escovedo found her anyway, and she had to assume he'd been following all along. Just letting her get some time and distance before, what, her debriefing? Kerry stood facing the water as it slopped against a shoreline of rocks the size of piled skulls, her hand clutching the inner fence. By now it seemed that the island was less a prison than a concentration camp.

"For what it's worth," the colonel said, "I didn't expect it to go well the first day."

"What makes you think a second day is going to go any better?"

"Rapport?" He lifted a Thermos, uncapped it, and it steamed in the air. "But rapport takes time."

"Time." She rattled the fence. "Will I even be leaving here?"

"I hope that's a joke." He poured into the Thermos cup without asking and gave it to her. "Here. The cold can sneak up on you out like this."

She sipped at the cup, coffee, not the best she'd ever had but far from the worst. It warmed her, though, and that was a plus. "Let me ask you something. Have they ever bred? Either here or wherever they were held before? Have *any* of them bred?"

"No. Why do you ask?"

"It's something I was picking up on from a few of them. The urge. You know it when you feel it. Across species, it's a great common denominator."

"I don't know what to tell you, other than that they haven't."

"Don't you find that odd?"

"I find the whole situation odd."

"What I mean is, even pandas in captivity manage to get pregnant once in a while."

"I've just never really thought about it."

"You regard them as prisoners, you *have* to, I get that. And the females don't look all that different from the males. But suppose they looked more like normal men and women. What would you expect if you had a prison with a mixed-gender population that had unrestricted access to each other?"

"I get your point, but..." He wasn't stonewalling, she could tell. He genuinely had never considered this. Because he'd never had to. "Wouldn't it be that they're too old?"

"I thought it was already established that once they get like this, age is no longer a factor. But even if it was, Giles Shapleigh wasn't too old when they first grabbed him. He was eighteen. Out of more than two hundred, he can't have been the only young one. You remember what the urge was like when you were eighteen?"

Escovedo grunted a laugh. "Every chance I get."

"Only he's never acted on it. None of them have."

"A fact that I can't say distresses me."

"It's just…" she said, then shut up. She had her answer. They'd never bred. Wanted to, maybe felt driven to, but hadn't. Perhaps captivity affected their fertility, or short-circuited the urge from becoming action.

Or maybe it was just an incredible act of discipline. They had to realize what would happen to their offspring. They would never be allowed to keep them, raise them. Their children would face a future of tests and vivisection. Even monstrosities would want better for their babies.

"I have an observation to make," Kerry said. "It's not going to go any better tomorrow, or the day after that. Not if you want me to keep doing it like today. It's like they have this shell around them." She tipped the coffee to her lips and eyed him over the rim, and he was impossible to read. "Should I go on?"

"I'm listening."

"You're right, rapport takes time. But it takes more than that. Your prisoners may have something beyond human senses, but they still have human intellects. More or less. It feels overlaid with something else, and it's not anything good, but fundamentally they haven't stopped being human, and they need to be dealt with that way. Not like they're entirely animals."

She stopped a moment to gauge him, and saw that she at least hadn't lost him. Although she'd not proposed anything yet.

"If they *looked* more human to you, don't you think the way you'd be trying to establish rapport would be to treat them more like human beings?" she said. "I read the news. I watch TV. I've heard the arguments about torture. For and against. I know what they are. The main thing I took away is that when you consult the people who've been good at getting reliable information from prisoners, they'll tell you they did it by being humane. Which includes letting the prisoner have something he wants, or loves. There was a captured German officer in World War Two who loved chess. He opened up after his interrogator started playing chess with him. That's all it took."

"I don't think these things are going to be interested in board games."

"No. But there's something every one of them wants," she said. "There's something they love more than anything else in the world."

And why does it have to be the same thing I dread?

When she told him how they might be able to use that to their advantage, she expected Escovedo to say no, out of the question. Instead, he thought it over for all of five seconds and said yes.

"I don't like it, but we need to fast-track this," he said. "We don't just eyeball their alignment in the pit, you know. We measure it with a laser. That's how we know how precisely oriented they are. And since last night they've shifted. Whatever they're cued in on has moved north."

The next morning, dawn came as dawn should, the sky clear and the fog blown away and the sun an actual presence over the horizon. After two days of being scarcely able to see fifty feet in front of her, it seemed as if she could see forever. There was something joyously liberating in it. After just two days.

So what was it going to feel like for Barnabas Marsh to experience the ocean for the first time in more than eighty years? The true sea, not the simulation of it siphoned off and pumped into the pit. Restrained by a makeshift leash, yes, three riflemen ready to shoot from the shore, that too, three more ready to shoot from the parapet of the prison...but it would still be the sea.

That it would be Marsh they would try this with was inevitable. It might not be safe and they might get only one chance at this. He was cunning, she had to assume, but he was the oldest by far, and a direct descendant of the man who'd brought this destiny to Innsmouth in the first place. He would have the deepest reservoir of knowledge.

And, maybe, the arrogance to want to share it, and gloat.

Kerry was waiting by the shallows when they brought him down, at one end of a long chain whose other end was padlocked to the frame of a four-wheel all-terrain cycle that puttered along behind him—he might have been able to throw men off balance in a tug-of-war, but not this.

Although he had plenty of slack, Marsh paused a few yards from the water's edge, stopping to stare out at the shimmering expanse of sea. The rest of them might have seen mistrust in his hesitation, or savoring the moment, but neither of these felt right. *Reacquainting,* she thought. *That's it.*

He trudged forward then, trailing chain, and as he neared the water, he cast a curious look at her, standing there in a slick blue wetsuit they'd outfitted her with, face-mask and snorkel in her hand. It gave him pause again, and in whatever bit of Marsh that was still human, she saw that he understood, realized who was responsible for this.

Gratitude, though, was not part of his nature. Once in the water, he vanished in moments, marked only by the clattering of his chain along the rocks.

She'd thought it wise to allow Marsh several minutes alone, just himself and the sea. They were midway through it when Escovedo joined her at the water's edge.

"You sure you're up for this?" he said. "It's obvious how much you don't like the idea, even if it was yours."

She glanced over at Marsh's chain, now still. "I don't like to see anything captive when it has the capacity to lament its conditions."

"That's not what I mean. If you think you've been keeping it under wraps that you've got a problem with water, you haven't. I could spot it two days ago, soon as we left the mainland behind."

She grinned down at her flippers, sheepish. Busted. "Don't worry. I'll deal."

"But you still know how to snorkel…?"

"How else are you going to get over a phobia?" She laughed, needing to, and it helped. "It went great in the heated indoor pool."

She fitted the mask over her face and popped in the snorkel's mouthpiece, and went in after Marsh. Calves, knees…every step forward was an effort, so she thought of Tabby. *The sooner I get results, the quicker I'll get home.* Thighs, waist…then she was in Marsh's world, unnerved by the fear that she would find him waiting for her, tooth and claw, ready to rip through her in a final act of defiance.

But he was nowhere near her. She floated facedown, kicking lightly and visually tracking the chain down the slope of the shoreline, until she saw it disappear over a drop-off into a well that was several feet deeper. *There he is.* She hovered in place, staring down at Marsh as he luxuriated in the water. Ecstatic—there was no other word for him. Twisting, turning, undulating, the chain only a minor impediment, he would shoot up near the surface, then turn and plunge back to the bottom, rolling in the murk he stirred up, doing it again, again, again. His joyous abandon was like a child's.

He saw her and stilled, floating midway between surface and sand, a sight from a nightmare, worse than a shark because even in this world he was so utterly alien.

And it was never going to get any less unnerving. She sucked in a deep breath through the snorkel, then plunged downward, keeping a bit of distance between them as she swam to the bottom.

Two minutes and then some—that was how long she could hold her breath.

Kerry homed in on a loose rock that looked heavy enough to counter her buoyancy, then checked the dive compass strapped to her wrist like an oversized watch. She wrestled the wave-smoothed stone into her lap and sat cross-legged on the bottom, matching as precisely as she could the latest of the southwesterly alignments that had so captivated Marsh and the other sixty-two of them. Sitting on the seabed with the Pacific alive around her, muffled in her ears and receding into a blue-green haze, as she half expected something even worse than Marsh to come swimming straight at her out of the void.

Somewhere above and behind her, he was watching.

She stayed down until her lungs began to ache, then pushed free of the stone and rose to the surface, where she purged the snorkel with a gust of spent air, then flipped to return to the seabed. Closer this time, mere feet between her and Marsh as she settled again, no longer needing the compass—she found her bearing naturally, and time began to slow, and so did her heartbeat in spite of the fear, then the fear was gone, washed away in the currents that tugged at her like temptations.

Up again, down again, and it felt as if she were staying below longer each time, her capacity for breath expanding to fill the need, until she was all but on the outside of herself looking in, marveling at this creature she'd become, amphibious, neither of the land nor the water, yet belonging to both. She lived in a bubble of breath in an infinite now, lungs satiated, awareness creeping forward along this trajectory she was aligned with, as if it were a cable that spanned the seas, and if she could only follow it, she would learn the secrets it withheld from all but the initiated—

And he was there, Barnabas Marsh a looming presence drifting alongside her. If there was anything to read in his cold face, his unplumbed eyes, it was curiosity. She had become something he'd never seen before, something between his enemies and his people, and changing by the moment.

She peered at him, nothing between them now but the thin plastic window of her mask and a few nourishing inches of water.

What is it that's out there? she asked. *Tell me. I want to know. I want to understand.*

It was true—she did. She would wonder even if she hadn't been asked to. She would wonder every day for the rest of her life. Her existence would be marred by not knowing.

Tell me what it is that lies beyond…

She saw it then, a thought like a whisper become an echo, as it began to build on itself, the occlusions between worlds parting in swirls of ink and oceans. And there was so *much* of it, this was something that couldn't be—who could build such a thing, and who would dream of finding it *here,* at depths that might crush a submarine—then she realized that all she was seeing was one wall, one mighty wall, built of blocks the size of boxcars, a feat that couldn't be equaled even on land. She knew without seeing the whole that it spanned miles, that if this tiny prison island could sink into it, it would be lost forever, an insignificant patch of pebbles and mud to what lived there—

And she was wholly herself again, with a desperate need to breathe.

Kerry wrestled the rock off her lap for the last time, kicking for a surface as far away as the sun. As she shot past Barnabas Marsh she was gripped by a terror that he would seize her ankle to pull her back down.

But she knew she could fight that, so what he did was worse somehow, nothing she knew that he *could* do, and maybe none of these unsuspecting men on the island did either. It was what sound could be if sound were needles, a piercing skirl that ripped through her like an electric shock and clapped her ears as sharply as a pressure wave. She spun in the water, not knowing up from down, and when she stabilized and saw Marsh nearby, she realized he wasn't even directing this at her. She was just a bystander who got in the way. Instead, he was facing out to sea, the greater sea, unleashing this sound into the abyss.

She floundered to the surface and broke through, graceless and gasping, and heard Colonel Escovedo shout a command, and in the next instant heard the roar of an engine as the four-wheeler went racing up the rock-strewn slope of the island's western edge. The chain snapped taut, and moments later Marsh burst from the shallows in a spray of surf and foam, dragged twisting up onto the beach. Someone fired a shot, and someone else another, and of course no one heard her calling from nearly a hundred feet out, treading water now, and they were all shooting, so none of them heard her cry out that they had the wrong idea. But bullets first, questions later, she supposed.

His blood was still red. She had to admit, she'd wondered.

It took the rest of the morning before she was ready to be debriefed, and Escovedo let her have it, didn't press for too much, too soon. She needed to be warm again, needed to get past the shock of seeing Barnabas Marsh shot to pieces on the beach. Repellent though he was, she'd still linked with him in her way, whispered back and forth, and he'd been alive one minute, among the oldest living beings on the earth, then dead the next.

She ached from the sound he'd made, as if every muscle and organ inside her had been snapped like a rubber band. Her head throbbed with the assault on her ears.

In the colonel's office, finally, behind closed doors, Kerry told him of the colossal ruins somewhere far beneath the sea.

"Does any of that even make sense?" she asked. "It doesn't to me. It felt real enough at the time, but now…it has to have been a dream of his. Or maybe Marsh was insane. How could anyone have even known if he was?"

Behind his desk, Escovedo didn't move for the longest time, leaning on his elbows and frowning at his interlaced hands. Had he heard her at all? Finally he unlocked one of the drawers and withdrew a folder; shook out some photos, then put one back and slid the rest across to her. Eight in all.

"What you saw," he said. "Did it look anything like this?"

She put them in rows, four over four, like puzzle pieces, seeing how they might fit together. And she needed them all at once, to bludgeon herself into accepting the reality of it: stretches of walls, suggestions of towers, some standing, some collapsed, all fitted together from blocks of greenish stone that could have been shaped by both hammers and razors. Everything was restricted to what spotlights could reach, limned by a cobalt haze that faded into inky blackness. Here, too, were windows and gateways and wide, irregular terraces that might have been stairs, only for nothing that walked on human feet. There was no sense of scale, nothing to measure it by, but she'd sensed it once today already, and it had the feeling of enormity and measureless age.

It was the stuff of nightmares, out of place and out of time, waiting in the cold, wet dark.

"They've been enhanced because of the low-light conditions and the distance," Escovedo said. "It's like the shots of the *Titanic*. The only light down that far is what you can send on a submersible. Except the Navy's lost every single one they've sent down there. They just go offline. These pictures… they're from the one that lasted the longest."

She looked up again. The folder they'd come from was gone. "You held one back. I can't see it?"

He shook his head. "Need to know."

"It shows something that different from the others?"

Nothing. He was as much a block of stone as the walls.

"Something living?" She remembered his description of the sound heard across three thousand miles of ocean: *The analysts say it most closely matches a profile of something alive.* "Is that it?"

"I won't tell you you're right." He appeared to be choosing his words with care. "But if that's what you'd picked up on out there with Marsh, then maybe we'd have a chance to talk about photo number nine."

She wanted to know. Needed to know as badly as she'd needed to breathe this morning, waking up to herself too far under the surface of the sea.

"What about the rest of them? We can keep trying."

He shook his head no. "We've come to the end of this experiment. I've already arranged for your transportation back home tomorrow."

Just like that. It felt as if she were being fired. She hadn't even delivered. She'd not told them anything they didn't already know about. She'd only confirmed it. What had made that unearthly noise, what the Innsmouth prisoners were waiting for—that's what they were really after.

"We're only just getting started. You can't rush something like this. There are sixty-two more of them over there, one of them is sure to—"

He cut her off with a slash of his hand. "Sixty-two of them who are in an uproar now. They didn't see what happened to Marsh, but they've got the general idea."

"Then maybe you shouldn't have been so quick to order his execution."

"That was for you. I thought we were protecting you." He held up his hands then, appeasement, time-out. "I appreciate your willingness to continue. I do. But even if they were still in what passes for a good mood with them, we've still reached an impasse here. You can't get through to them on our turf, and I can't risk sending you back out with another of them onto theirs. It doesn't matter that Marsh didn't actually attack you. I can't risk another of them doing what he did to make me think he had."

"I don't follow you." It had been uncomfortable, yes, and she had no desire to experience it again, but it was hardly fatal.

"I've been doing a lot of thinking about what that sound he made meant," Escovedo said. "What I keep coming back to is that he was sending a distress call."

She wished she could've left the island sooner. That the moment the colonel told her they were finished, he'd already had the helicopter waiting. However late they got her home again, surely by now she would be in her own bed, holding her daughter close because she needed her even more than Tabby needed her.

Awake part of the time and a toss-up the rest, asleep but dreaming she was still trying to get there. Caught between midnight and dawn, the weather turning for the worse again, the crack and boom of thunder like artillery, with bullets of rain strafing the roof.

She had to be sleeping some of the time, though, and dreaming of something other than insomnia. She knew perfectly well she was in a bed, but there were times in the night when it felt as if she were still below, deeper than she'd gone this morning, in the cold of the depths far beyond the reach of the sun, drifting beside leviathan walls lit by a phosphorescence whose source she couldn't pin down. The walls themselves were tricky to navigate, like being on the outside of a maze, yet still lost within it, finding herself turning strange corners that seemed to jut outward, only to find that they turned in. She was going to drown down here, swamped by a sudden thrashing panic over her air tank going empty, only to realize…

She'd never strapped on one to begin with.

She belonged here, in this place that was everything that made her recoil.

Marsh, she thought, once she could tell ceiling from sea. Although he was dead, Marsh was still with her, in an overlapping echo of whispers. Dead, but still dreaming.

When she woke for good, though, it was as abruptly as could be, jolted by the sound of a siren so loud it promised nothing less than a cataclysm. It rose and fell like the howling of a feral god. She supposed soldiers knew how to react, but she wasn't one of them. Every instinct told her to hug the mattress and melt beneath the covers and hope it all went away.

But that was a strategy for people prone to dying in their beds.

She was dressed and out the door in two minutes, and though she had to squint against the cold sting of the rain, she looked immediately to the prison. Everything on the island, alive or motorized, seemed to be moving in that direction, and for a moment she wondered if she should too—safety in numbers, and what if something was *driving* them that way, from the east end?

But the searchlights along the parapet told a different story, three beams stabbing out over the open water, shafts of brilliant white shimmering with rain and sweeping to and fro against the black of night. *A distress call,* Escovedo had said—had it been answered? Was the island under attack, an invasion by Innsmouth's cousins who'd come swarming onto the beach? No, that didn't seem right either. The spotlights were not aimed down, but out. Straight out.

She stood rooted to the spot, pelted by rain, lashed by wind, frozen with dread that something terrible was on its way. The island had never felt so small. Even the prison looked tiny now, a vulnerable citadel standing alone against the three co-conspirators of ocean, night, and sky.

Ahead of the roving spotlights, the rain was a curtain separating the island from the sea, then it parted, silently at first, the prow of a ship spearing into view, emerging from the blackness as though born from it. No lights, no one visible on board, not even any engine noise that she could hear—just a dead ship propelled by the night or something in it. The sound came next, a tortured grinding of steel across rock so loud it made the siren seem weak and thin. The ship's prow heaved higher as it was driven up onto the island, the rest of it coming into view, the body of the shark behind the cone of its snout.

And she'd thought the thunder was loud. When the freighter plowed into the prison the ground shuddered beneath her, the building cracking apart as though riven by an axe, one of the spotlights tumbling down along with an avalanche of bricks and masonry before winking out for good. She watched men struggle, watched men fall, and at last the ship's momentum was spent. For a breathless moment it was perfectly still. Then, with another grinding protest of metal on stone, the ship began to list, like twisting a knife after sticking it in. The entire right side of the prison buckled and collapsed outward, and with it went the siren and another of the searchlights. The last of the lights reeled upward, aimed back at the building's own roofline.

Only now could she hear men shouting, only now could she hear the gunfire.

Only now could she hear men scream.

And still the ground seemed to shudder beneath her feet.

It seemed as if that should've been the end of it, accident and aftermath, but soon more of the prison began to fall, as if deliberately wrenched apart. She saw another cascade of bricks tumble to the left, light now flickering and spilling from within the prison on both sides.

Something rose into view from the other side, thick as the trunk of the tallest oak that had ever grown, but flexible, glistening in the searing light. It wrapped around another section of wall and pulled it down as easily as peeling wood from rotten wood. She thought it some kind of serpent at first, until, through the wreckage of the building, she saw the suggestion of more, coiling and uncoiling, and a body—or head—behind those.

And still the ground seemed to shudder beneath her feet.

It was nothing seismic—she understood that now. She recalled being in the majestic company of elephants once, and how the ground sometimes quivered in their vicinity as they called to one another from miles away, booming out frequencies so deep they were below the threshold of human hearing, a rumble that only their own kind could decipher.

This was the beast's voice.

And if they heard it in New York, in Barrow, Alaska, and in the Sea of Cortez, she would not have been surprised.

It filled her, reverberating through rock and earth, up past her shoes, juddering the soles of her feet, radiating through her bones and every fiber of muscle, every cell of fat, until her vision scrambled and she feared every organ would liquefy. At last it rose into the range of her feeble ears, a groan that a glacier might make. As the sound climbed higher she clapped both hands over her ears, and if she could have turtled her head into her body she would've done that too, as its voice became a roar became a bellow became a blaring onslaught like the trumpets of Judgment Day, a fanfare to split the sky for the coming of God.

Instead, *this* was what had arrived, this vast and monstrous entity, some inhuman travesty's idea of a deity. She saw it now for what it was to these loathsome creatures from Innsmouth—the god they prayed to, the Mecca that they faced—but then something whispered inside, and she wondered if she was wrong. As immense and terrifying as this thing was, what if it presaged more, and was only preparing the way, the John the Baptist for something even worse.

Shaking, she sunk to her knees, hoping only that she might pass beneath its notice as the last sixty-two prisoners from Innsmouth climbed up and over the top of the prison's ruins, and reclaimed their place in the sea.

To be honest, she had to admit to herself that the very idea of Innsmouth, and what had happened here in generations past, fascinated her as much as it appalled her.

Grow up and grow older in a world of interstate highways, cable TV, satellite surveillance, the Internet, and cameras in your pocket, and it was easy to forget how remote a place could once be, even on the continental U.S., and not all that long ago, all things considered. It was easy to forget how you might live a lifetime having no idea what was going on in a community just ten miles away, because you never had any need to go there, or much desire, either, since you'd always heard they were an unfriendly lot who didn't welcome strangers, and preferred to keep to themselves.

Innsmouth was no longer as isolated as it once was, but it still had the feeling of remoteness, of being adrift in time, a place where businesses struggled to take root, then quietly died back into vacant storefronts. It seemed to dwell under a shadow that would forever keep outsiders from finding a reason to go there, or stay long if they had.

Unlike herself. She'd been here close to a month, since two days after Christmas, and still didn't know when she would leave.

She got the sense that, for many of the town's residents, making strangers feel unwelcome was a tradition they felt honor-bound to uphold. Their greetings were taciturn, if extended at all, and they watched as if she were a shoplifter, even when crossing the street, or strolling the riverwalk along the Manuxet in the middle of the day. But her money was good, and there was no shortage of houses to rent—although her criteria were stricter than most—and a divorced mother with a six-year-old daughter could surely pose no threat.

None of them seemed to recognize her from television, although would they let on if they did? She recognized none of them, either, nothing in anyone's face or feet that hinted at the old, reviled Innsmouth look. They no longer seemed to have anything to hide here, but maybe the instinct that they did went so far back that they knew no other way.

Although what to make of that one storefront on Eliot Street, in what passed for the heart of the town? The stenciled lettering—charmingly antiquated and quaint—on the plate glass window identified the place as THE INNSMOUTH SOCIETY FOR PRESERVATION AND RESTORATION.

It seemed never to be open.

Yet it never seemed neglected.

Invariably, whenever she peered through the window Kerry would see that someone had been there since the last time she'd looked, but it always felt as if she'd missed them by five minutes or so. She would strain for a better look at the framed photos on the walls, tintypes and sepia tones, glimpses of bygone days that seemed to be someone's idea of something worth bringing back.

Or perhaps their idea of a homecoming.

It was January in New England, and most days so cold it redefined the word bitter, but she didn't miss a single one, climbing seven flights of stairs to take up her vigil for as long as she could endure it. The house was an old Victorian on Lafayette Street, four proud stories tall, peaked and gabled to within an inch of its moldering life. The only thing she cared about was that its roof had an iron-railed widow's walk with an unobstructed view of the decrepit harbor and the breakwater and, another mile out to sea, the humpbacked spine of rock called Devil Reef.

As was the custom during the height of the Age of Sail, the widow's walk had been built around the house's main chimney. Build a roaring fire down below, and the radiant bricks would keep her warm enough for a couple of hours at a time, even when the sky spit snow at her, while she brought the binoculars to her eyes every so often to check if there was anything new to see out there.

"I'm bored." This from Tabitha, nearly every day. *Booorrrrred,* the way she said it. "There's nothing to do here."

"I know, sweetie," Kerry would answer. "Just a little longer."

"When are they coming?" Tabby would ask.

"Soon," she would answer. "Pretty soon."

But in truth, she couldn't say. Their journey was a long one. Would they risk traversing the locks and dams of the Panama Canal? Or would they take the safer route, around Argentina's Cape Horn, where they would exchange Pacific for Atlantic, south for north, then head home, at long last home.

She knew only that they were on their way, more certain of this than any sane person had a right to be. The assurance was there whenever the world grew still and silent, more than a thought…a whisper that had never left, as if not all of Barnabas Marsh had died, the greater part of him subsumed into the hive mind of the rest of his kind. To taunt? To punish? To gloat? In the weeks after their island prison fell, there was no place she could go where its taint couldn't follow. Not Montana, not Los Angeles, not New Orleans, for the episode of *The Animal Whisperer* they'd tried to film before putting it on hiatus.

She swam with them in sleep. She awoke retching with the taste of coldest blood in her mouth. Her belly skimmed through mud and silt in quiet moments; her shoulders and flanks brushed through shivery forests of weeds; her fingers tricked her into thinking that her daughter's precious cheek felt cool and slimy. The dark of night could bring on the sense of a dizzying plunge to the blackest depths of ocean trenches.

Where else was left for her to go but here, to Innsmouth, the place that time seemed to be trying hard to forget.

And the more days she kept watch from the widow's walk, the longer at a time she could do it, even while the fire below dwindled to embers, and so the more it seemed that her blood must've been going cold in her veins.

"I don't like it here," Tabby would say. "You never used to yell in your sleep until we came here."

How could she even answer that? No one could live like this for long.

"Why can't I go stay with Daddy?" Tabby would ask. *Daddeeeee*, the way she said it.

It really would've been complete then, wouldn't it? The humiliation, the surrender. The admission: *I can't handle it anymore, I just want it to stop, I want them to make it stop*. It still mattered, that her daughter's father had once fallen in love with her when he thought he'd been charmed by some half-wild creature who talked to animals, and then once he had her, tried to drive them from her life because he realized he hated to share. He would never possess all of her.

You got as much as I could give, she would tell him, as if he too could hear her whisper. *And now they won't let go of the rest*.

"Tell me another story about them," Tabby would beg, and so she would, a new chapter of the saga growing between them about kingdoms under the sea where people lived forever, and rode fish and giant seahorses, and how they had defenders as tall as the sky who came boiling up from the waters to send their enemies running.

Tabby seemed to like it.

When she asked if there were pictures, Kerry knew better, and didn't show her the ones she had, didn't even acknowledge their existence. The ones taken from Colonel Escovedo's office while the rains drenched the wreckage, after she'd helped the few survivors that she could, the others dead or past noticing what she might take from the office of their commanding officer, whom nobody could locate anyway.

The first eight photos Tabby would've found boring. As for the ninth, Kerry wasn't sure she could explain to a six-year-old what exactly it showed, or even to herself. Wasn't sure she could make a solid case for what was the mouth and what was the eye, much less explain why such a thing was allowed to exist.

One of them, at least, should sleep well while they were here.

Came the day, at last, in early February, when her binoculars revealed more than the tranquil pool of the harbor, the snow and ice crusted atop the breakwater, the sullen chop of the winter-blown sea. Against the slate-colored water, they were small, moving splotches the color of algae. They flipped like seals, rolled like otters. They crawled onto the ragged dark stone of Devil Reef, where they seemed to survey the kingdom they'd once known, all that had changed about it and all that hadn't.

And then they did worse.

Even if something was natural, she realized, you could still call it a perversity.

Was it preference? Was it celebration? Or was it blind obedience to an instinct they didn't even have the capacity to question? Not that it mattered. Here they were, finally, little different from salmon now, come back to their headwaters to breed, indulging an urge eighty-some-years strong.

It was only a six-block walk to the harbor, and she had the two of them there in fifteen minutes. This side of Water Street, the wharves and warehouses were deserted, desolate, frosted with frozen spray and groaning with every gust of wind that came snapping in over the water.

She wrenched open the wide wooden door to one of the smaller buildings, the same as she'd been doing every other day or so, the entire time they'd been here, first to find an abandoned rowboat, and then to make sure it was still there. She dragged it down to the water's edge, plowing a furrow in a crust of old snow, and once it was in the shallows, swung Tabby into it, then hopped in after. She slipped the oars into the rusty oarlocks, and they were off.

"Mama...?" Tabitha said after they'd pushed past the breakwater and cleared the mouth of the harbor for open sea. "Are you crying?"

In rougher waters now, the boat heaved beneath them. Snow swirled in from the depths overhead and clung to her cheeks, eyelashes, hair, and refused to melt. She was that cold. She was *always* that cold.

"Maybe a little," Kerry said.

"How come?"

"It's just the wind. It stings my eyes."

She pulled at the oars, aiming for the black line of the reef. Even if no one else might've, even if she could no longer see them, as they hid within the waves, she heard them sing a song of jubilation, a song of wrath and hunger. Their voices were the sound of a thousand waking nightmares.

To pass the time, she told Tabby a story, grafting it to all the other tales she'd told about kingdoms under the sea where people lived forever, and rode whales and danced with dolphins, and how they may not have been very pleasant to look at, but that's what made them love the beautiful little girl from above the waves, and welcome her as their princess.

Tabby seemed to like it.

Ahead, at the reef, they began to rise from the water and clamber up the rock again, spiny and scaled, finned and fearless. Others began to swim out to meet the boat. Of course they recognized her, and she them. She'd sat with nearly a third of them, trying trying trying to break through from the wrong side of the shore.

While they must have schemed like fiends to drag her deep into theirs.

I bring you this gift, she would tell them, if only she could make herself heard over their jeering in her head. *Now could you please just set me free?*

A Quarter to Three

Kim Newman

SOMETIMES THE NIGHTS get to you, right? When there's no-one pushing coins into it, the juke plays Peggy Lee over and over again. "Fever." The finger-click backing track gets into your skull. Like a heartbeat, you've got it in there for the rest of your life. And in the off-season, which when you're talking about the 'Mouth is—let's face it—all year round, sometimes you go from midnight 'til dawn with no takers at all. Who can blame them: we serve paint stripper au lait and reinforced concrete crullers. When I first took the graveyard shift at Cap'n Cod's 24 Hour Diner, I actually liked the idea of being paid (just) to stay up all night with no hassles. Maybe, I'd get to finish *Moby-Dick* before Professor Whipple could flunk me. Anyway, that's not the way it worked out.

Two o'clock and not a human face in sight. And in late November, the beachfront picture window rattles in the slightest breeze. The waves shattered noisily on the damn useless shingles. The 'Mouth isn't a tourist spot, it's a town-sized morgue that smells of fish. All I'd got for company was a giant cardboard cut-out of the Cap'n, giving a scaly salute and a salty smile. He hasn't got much of a face left, because he used to stand outside and get a good sloshing whenever the surf was up. I don't know who he was in the first place—the current owner is a pop-eyed lardo called Murray Something who pays in smelly cash—but now he's just a cut-out ghost. I'd talk to him, only I'd be worried that some night he'd talk right back.

It's a theme diner, just like all the others up and down the coast. Nets on the ceiling, framed dead fish on the walls, formica on the tables, and more sand on the floor than along the seashore. And it's got a gurgling coffee machine that spits out the foulest brew you've ever tasted, and an array of food under glass that you'd swear doesn't change from one month to the next. I was stuck in a groove again, like Peggy if I forget to nudge the juke in the middle of that verse about Pocahontas. It's that damn chapter "The Whiteness of the Whale." I always trip over it, and it's supposed to be the heart of the book.

I didn't notice her until the music changed. Debbie Reynolds, singing "It Must Have Been Moonglow." Jesus. She must have come in during one of my twenty-minute "blinks." She was sitting up against the wall, by the juke, examining the counter. Young, maybe pretty, a few strands of blonde hair creeping out from under her scarf, and wearing a coat not designed for a pregnant woman. It had a belt that she probably couldn't fasten. I'm in Eng. Lit. at MU, not pre-med, but I judged that she was just about ready to drop the kid. Maybe quins.

"Can I help you, ma'am?" I asked. Murray likes me to call the mugs "sir" and "ma'am" not "buddy" and "doll" or "asshole" and "drudge." It's the only instruction he ever dished out.

She looked at me—big hazel eyes with too much red in them—but didn't say anything. She looked tired, which isn't surprising since it was the middle of the night and she was about to give birth to the Incredible Bulk.

"Coffee?" I suggested. "If you're looking for a way to end it all, you could do worse. Cheaper than strychnine. Maybe you want ice cream and pickles?"

"That's crap," she said, and I realised that she really was young. If she weren't pregnant, I'd have accused her of being up after her bedtime. Sixteen or seventeen, I guessed. Cheerleader-pretty, but with a few lines in there to show she had more to worry about than who's dating Buddy-Bob Fullback these days or how she'll get through the Home Ec. quiz next Friday. "About cravings, that's crap. You don't want to eat weird stuff. Me, I don't want to eat at all, ever again. But you gotta, or you disintegrate. It's like having a tapeworm. You eat as much as you can, but you still go hungry. The fo-etus gets all the goodies."

Fo-etus. That was how she pronounced it. I kind of liked the sound of it.

"Well, what does your fo-etus fancy this morning?"

"A cheeseburger."

"This is a fish place, ma'am. No burgers. I can melt some cheese on a fishcake and give it to you in a bap."

"Sounds like shit. I'll have one, for the mutant…"

Julie London was on now, "Cry Me a River." "Cryyyyy me a river, cuh-ry me a river, I cried a reever over you." That has one of the best rhymes in the English language in it; "plebean" with "through with me an'…now you say you're lonely…"

I slapped the frozen cake on the hotplate and dug out some not-too-senile cheese. We don't stock the kind that's better if it's got mould on it.

"Have you got liquor?"

"Have you got ID?"

"Shit, how come you can get knocked up five years before you can have a drink in this state?"

The ice in the cake popped and hissed. Julie sounded broken-hearted in the background. It must be a tough life.

"I don't make the rules."

"I won't get drunk. The fo-etus will."

"He's underage too, ma'am."

"It's an it. They did tests."

"Pardon?"

"Ginger ale…"

"Fine."

"…and put a shot of something in it."

I gave in and dug out the scotch. Not much call for it. The highlander on the label had faded, a yellowing dribble down his face turning him leprous. I splashed the bottom of a glass, then added a full measure of soft drink. She had it down quickly and ordered another. I saw to it and flipped the cake over. I wish I could say it smelled appetising.

"I'm not married," she said. "I had to leave school. There goes my shot at college. Probably my only chance to get out of the 'Mouth. Oh well, that's another life on the rocks. You must get a lot of that."

"Not really. I don't get much of anyone in here. I think the Cap'n will be dropping the 24 Hour service next year. All his old customers drowned or something. It's entropy. Everything's winding down. You have to expect it."

I melted the cheese and handed her her cheesefish bap. She didn't seem interested in it. I noticed she had a pile of quarters stacked in a little tower on the bar. She was feeding the juke regularly.

"This is my song," she said. Rosemary Clooney, "You Took Advantage of Me." "The bastard certainly did."

She was a talker, I'd spotted that early. After midnight, you only get talkers and brooders. I didn't really have to say anything, but there'd be pauses if I didn't fill in the gaps.

"Your boyfriend?"

"Yeah. Fuckin' amphibian. He's supposed to be here. I'm meeting him."

"What'll happen?"

"Who knows. Some folks ain't human."

She pushed her plate around and prodded the bap. I had to agree with her. I wouldn't have eaten it, either. Murray never asked me if I could cook.

"Look, the lights…" She meant the sea lights. It's a localised phenomenon in the 'Mouth. A greenish glow just out beyond the shallows. Everyone freaks first time they see it. "He'll be here soon. Another ginger ale plus."

I gave her one. She took it slower. Captain Ahab looked insanely up from the broken-spined paperback on the counter, obsessed with his white whale. Crazy bastard. I'd love to see him on a talk show with one of those Greenpeace activists.

There was someone coming up from the beach. She shifted on her stool, uncomfortably keeping her pregnancy away from the rim of the counter. She didn't seem interested one way or the other. "It's him."

"He'll be wet."

"Yeah. That he will."

"It don't matter. I don't do the mopping up. That's the kid who gets the daytime haul."

It was Sinatra now. The main man. "It's a quarter to three…"

"No-one in the place except you and me," I said, over the Chairman of the Board. Her smile was cracked, lopsided, greenish. She had plaque.

The door was pushed inward, and in he waddled. As you might expect, he didn't look like much. It took him a long time to get across the diner, and he wasn't breathing easily. He moved a bit like Charles Laughton as Quasimodo, dragging wetly. It was easy to see what she had seen in him; it left a thin damp trail between his scuffed footprints. By the time he got to the counter, she had finished her drink.

He got up onto a stool with difficulty, his wet, leather-linked fingers scrabbling for a grip on the edge of the bar. The skin over his cheeks and neck puffed in and out as he tried to smile at her.

"…could tell you a lot," sung Frankie, "but you've got to be true to your code…"

She put her glass down, and looked me in the eye, smiling. "Make it one for my baby, and one more for the toad."

The Dappled Thing
William Browning Spencer

WHEN *Her Glory of Empire* rolled out of the jungle and stopped at the edge of the black river, two dozen green and yellow parrots exploded from the trees. Sir Bertram Rudge, unsealing the topside hatch, emerged in time to see the birds blow across the river like gaudy silks, but the sight stirred no aesthetic shivers within his stout frame. He and his team were heading into the wild heart of the jungle, and he had no time for beauty's wiles. This savage land had swallowed Wallister's party, which included Lord Addison's grand-daughter, Lavinia, a girl of twelve when Rudge had last seen her and now, by all accounts, a willful and beautiful young woman who had shocked high society and sundered a dozen foppish hearts when she left London to cross the Atlantic on the *Cloud King*, a chartered zeppelin, in the company of Henry Wallister, famous explorer, member of the Royal Geographical Society, and, according to Lord Addison, a thorough scoundrel.

"Lavinia's a good girl," Lord Addison had declared. "Spirited, not utterly without brains, but a fool for a rogue like Wallister." His Lordship, face red, eyes maddened by the hearth's fire, fixed Rudge with a wild stare. "Bring her back to me, Bertie. By force, if you must."

With the opening of the hatch, a railing of gleaming steel pipes rose up from the silvery surface of the great sphere and snapped into place with a hydraulic exhalation. Rudge gripped the railing and leaned out to study the river below. Here was a test he didn't relish.

"Hot down there!"

Rudge turned at the voice and saw that Tommy Strand, the expedition's naturalist, had come up from below and was wiping his face with a cloth. A hank of his blond hair fell forward and, in profile, he looked like an addled cockatoo. The day was dying, and a large bird swooped low over the river. This inspired Strand, who spread his arms wide, something a cockatoo might do in preparation for flight, but this flight, alas, was merely verbal. He recited:

"I wandered lonely as a clown
Whose heart of red is filled with rue,
When all at once I saw an owl,
A bird of nighttime, nocturnal,
Up in the sky and all a-hooting,
A lovely balm for my heart's soothing."

Why, Rudge wondered, were supposedly educated young men so often inclined to declaim in meter? Rudge recognized the quoted poet, the insufferable Wadsworth, one of the fashionable Lake Poets (although where, one might ask, were the corresponding numbers of River Poets, Pond Poets, Bog Poets?).

Strand continued to bellow out Wadsworth, and Rudge unfurled the rope ladder he'd brought from below, secured it to two of the steel posts, tested his knots with a yank, and methodically descended the ladder. He was huffing a bit by the time his boots met the mud, but still—and the thought pleased him—steady on his legs, hale and hearty (by God!) in a world where so many of his old comrades were content to drowse in armchairs, poor old sweats muttering about some bloody wog, some worthless *apke wasti*.

On the ground, where a fishy smell contended with the green odor of rotting vegetation, Rudge walked to the very edge of the water and looked down. He saw no piranhas, no fer-de-lance, no giant anaconda, no cunning crocodile. The only animate life he observed was the vile cloud of black flies and mosquitoes that rose up from the mud to greet him. He tried to ignore them, as he had done in a younger life in another jungle, but the years of his retirement had drained some of his stoicism. He swatted and cursed the mindless buggers, then turned to regard the rescue vehicle.

Her Glory of Empire was a vast silver sphere, easily big enough to contain several row houses, and it burned in the twilight, pink and gold, with an authority that reduced the surrounding elements (the clutter of greenery, the outlandish verdancy of the jungle) to a shadowy backdrop. The machine was presently feeding, a strange business that Rudge found endlessly fascinating. Great mechanical tentacles, armored like the carapace of a millipede, stretched to the tree tops, clutched branches, and broke them with its segmented strength or severed them with small spinning blades. The thin, tapered end of a tentacle would wrap itself around a leafy bundle and carry it to an open hatch that glowed with ruddy light. The furnace within could devour any sort of vegetation by subjecting the green and unpromising material to a series of processing containers—rather like the multiple stomachs of a cow—before turning the altered material into a blazing motive force.

Her Glory of Empire was the fevered brainchild of the eccentric and fabulously wealthy Hugh Edmonds, whom Rudge had met only once, briefly, when Lord Addison had driven Rudge to Edmonds's estate. There they had found the estate's master in avid conversation with one of his gardeners.

Since Edmonds was a notorious recluse, Rudge's friends would ask what the man was like, and, in the privacy of his club, Rudge would respond by saying that the man was well-spoken, erudite, somewhat small and frail with an unusually large penis, a description that gave some people pause. One had to understand that Hugh Edmonds was a devout Christian who believed that hiding one's nakedness was "giving in to the serpent." He never wore clothes while at home.

Edmonds was a self-taught scientist, a not uncommon condition among English madmen of independent means, and had been the architect of this immense traveling rotundity, discovering new principles for the science that informed it, and offering detailed instructions for its manufacture.

The machine had not been designed expressly to rescue Lord Addison's granddaughter, but Providence had nicely timed its completion to correspond with that task, and this was its maiden voyage.

Rudge watched as the furnace hatch closed. The several tentacles retreated into the body of the sphere, and iris-like portals closed behind them. Rudge turned his back on the vehicle and regarded the sunset. *I'm too old for this,* he thought.

When Rudge climbed back down into the bowels of the vehicle, he found Mallory already strapped into the pilot's chair, checking the various gauges and wrestling his arms into the appendage lacings. A red-faced, whiskered man,

Mallory was always slightly damp and became quickly soaked with perspiration when exerting himself. He wore—and apparently slept in—a dirty linen outfit that looked to be of some unknown military lineage, with mud-spattered puttees wrapping his calves and even his forearms, as though he had planned to mummify himself but had been distracted by other, more pressing matters.

It was hot in the enclosed space, and only two of the duct fans were running. Rudge could hear the furnace rumble and the hiss of pipes as valves obeyed the engineer's commands.

This circular floor space, with its bolted chairs and equipment, comfortably accommodated its five travelers. Had the expedition contained twice that number, it would have been crowded indeed. Returning with Wallister's group might prove difficult, Rudge thought—if, of course, Wallister and his party were still alive. Rudge was not a pessimist, but he'd lived long enough to know that hope had to be kept on a short leash.

Six weeks ago a column of smoke had drawn the attention of the denizens of a nearby mission, and after a day's trek into the forest, the mission's priest and his companions had come upon a clearing and the fire-ravaged remains of a zeppelin. Since the skeletal frame was still intact, the priest concluded that the conflagration was not the result of a crash. No charred corpses were discovered amid the airship's remains. Various scorched artifacts revealed its identity as that of the luxury cruiser *Cloud King*. All of the passengers were missing, their whereabouts a source of much conjecture. Perhaps Wallister's group had found refuge with one of the tribes to the north of the Negro, although the priest thought it more likely they had been captured or killed by hostile, deep-forest denizens he referred to as the Yami. "Crazy peoples," the priest had said. "Eat you up. Of your head, they make a jar."

Rudge had heard stories of the Yami or a similar tribe inhabiting the same region. These natives of the deep rain forest filed their teeth to points, fought constantly with neighboring tribes and with members of their own tribe, and taught their children violence—a young boy who beat his sister was praised. They ate the dead.

"All right, then," Mallory said, his voice returning Rudge to the moment. "Here we go."

The machine began to rumble and shiver as Rudge took his seat and strapped himself in. From his position behind the engineer, Rudge could see the panel of instruments and the glass portal that offered a view of weeds and mud and the river beyond.

The outer shell, the hull, began to move and the rat-scrambling sound of the steel brushes that generated a weak Faraday Effect as they spun between the inner and outer shells set Rudge's teeth on edge. Now the view portal flickered, no longer a direct view of the landscape beyond but an ever-changing image retrieved by mirrors from ports that opened and closed as the behemoth rolled forward.

The floor swayed some, like the deck of a ship in open sea, but it was marvelously steady considering that portions—and sometimes the entirety—of the outer hull was moving, a gleaming, rolling monstrosity that thundered down the muddy bank and into the rushing black water. Directly, water spit and hissed from the two open fan ducts, and Jon Bans, the fifth member of the crew, slapped the portals closed with a curse, his tall, seaman's frame contorted over the walking cage that allowed him to move easily across the floor. Rudge felt his lungs contract in the visceral certainty that the meager bubble of air that now sustained them beneath the river would be breached by black torrents.

The weak radiance created by the Faraday Effect made blocky shadows of the men within. The view portal was useless now, and they would have to depend on the compass and the questing touch of mechanical tentacles to guide them to the other side.

"I'm sending some air tubes up," Mallory said. He pulled several levers and a hollow clattering announced the rise of the tubes. He studied the dials, then nodded. "That should do her." He turned his head and shouted to Jon Bans. "Open four, five and six above and the furnace feeds."

The fans spit briefly and then the cool air above the river blew through the cabin, and Rudge felt the tightness go out of his chest.

Now they moved without the rolling hull, dragged forward by grapples and propelled by bundles of uneven, jointed pipes that sprouted from the base of the vehicle to produce a slow, lumbering motion, a falling forward, then catching, then falling again that translated to the ship's floor as a lazy, rocking-horse gallop.

In the blackness, time congealed. Rudge became convinced that they were making no progress at all, that they were stuck in mud, rocking back and forth, like some poor idiot who has lost his way in the night and seeks to console himself by hugging his knees and aping a pendulum or the clapper in a bell.

Something exploded, echoing in his skull. Booming, scratching, rending sounds sent Rudge's heart racing as he imagined some monstrous water beast attempting to rip open this hard-shelled egg and lap up the life within.

"It's all right!" Mallory shouted. "It's a submerged tree."

Stolid Mallory, sweat beading on his forehead, moved his arms as though fondling a ghost, and external tentacles obeyed his pantomime. The vessel clambered against the current, and the sunken branches grasped for them with a scorned lover's desperation. Rudge tried to picture it: a drowned tree wrestling with a mechanical squid whose belly was full of people (soft flesh over breakable bones) and all in black murk, an invisible battle raging, meaningless and unimaginable to some beast or savage gazing at the river's roiling surface.

So Sir Bertram Rudge contemplated the unutterable strangeness of his situation, and this acknowledgment of his insignificance and vulnerability calmed him, as it always did at such times.

They lunged and grappled, fought to escape, were hopelessly mired, and then, in an instant, as though the struggle had been a game, a tug-of-war with a giant who had abruptly lost interest and abandoned his end of the rope, they were free and rising into shallower water, and aground again.

There was little light in the sky by then, but they traveled on, not wishing to camp too close to the river. That night, all but Mallory pitched their tents outside the vehicle and slept swaddled in mosquito netting, weapons by their sides. They might have been safer within *Her Glory of Empire*'s armored orb, where no wild beasts could find them, but, for the moment, their hearts were done with dank, enclosed enterprises, and they preferred to take their chances on the ground.

Snug in his tent, Rudge reached out to douse the kerosene lamp and a small round object bounced twice as though dropped from the ceiling. Rudge jerked his hand back, wary of spiders and other stinging, biting vermin. Leaning forward, he saw a tiny pale frog. He moved his hand slowly over it—with no thought except to test his reflexes—and snatched it. He slowly uncurled his fingers and looked at the pop-eyed creature. It was walnut-sized, its skin transparent so that you could see the organs within. Turning the creature toward the light, Rudge could see its tiny beating heart, the twist of its intestines (like a water-drowned worm), and its fragile green bones. Rudge leaned forward, stretched his arm out and under the tent flap, and opened his hand. The creature leapt away, and Rudge pulled his empty hand back inside the tent and lay down again. *You are far from green England's cozy hearth,* he thought.

It was the dry season, a relative term, and Rudge cursed a so-called *dry* season that could grow mold on a man's skin and generated a pale mist in which monsters seemed to lurk.

Their progress through this world was loud and violent. *Her Glory of Empire* was not designed for stealth. It moved by thrashing and sawing its way through the jungle, pulling trees down or climbing them like an ungainly spider until they bent beneath its weight. Sometimes monkeys would scream from the trees, following the vehicle for days, hooting with outrage or, perhaps, a kind of carnival glee, delighting in destruction, as Rudge had seen men do in the frenzy of war.

He was fascinated with *Her Glory of Empire,* but there was something about the machine that he distrusted. It was, Rudge thought, against Nature, by which he did not mean that it was some kind of Devil's work, but that, being fashioned by immutable physical laws, and, consequently, itself a creature of Nature, its destruction of the natural world seemed a perversity, a subverting of those laws God had stamped on His Creation. Rudge could not have explained this to anyone, and if, somehow, he *had* managed to voice his reservations, no one would have taken him seriously. They would have been amused, would have seen him as some foolish old codger at odds with inevitable change.

Well, he was old and set in his ways. Maybe that was all there was to it.

On the eleventh day of travel beyond the site of the burned zeppelin, they had a bit of good luck. They came upon a small village of round huts, a village they might have passed if the cacophony of their passage hadn't attracted the natives, who were friendly and showed some acquaintance with civilization, even to the point of wearing clothing and emulating Jesus by pushing thorns into the palms of their hands. Rudge's manservant, Jacobs, had a gift with languages, or, more precisely, communication itself. A small, swarthy man, Jacobs possessed a gray explosive mustache that suggested belligerence, but he was, in fact, as calm as a cat, and capable of getting the meaning from any human being with vocal chords.

After talking at length to the village elder, Jacobs was able to relate the good news. Wallister's party had passed this way heading north. "He says he warned them about the Yami, but they seemed unperturbed on that score," Jacobs said.

He added, "The old fella says he thought they might have been earth or water spirits because they didn't know things that even a child knows."

Rudge asked what that would be.

"He said they didn't know that they could die."

The next day, they ate lunch in a small clearing with a bright stream running through it. The stream was bordered by thin pale-green trees and lush black-green ferns. When Rudge went off to relieve his bladder by the edge of the forest, tiny blue butterflies fluttered around the stream of his urine and settled on the wet grass as though he were spilling a rare elixir.

When he returned, Rudge found Tommy Strand sitting by the brook. Strand started declaiming immediately, as though Rudge's presence required it. It was another poem:

"Glory be to God for dappled things,
For skies of couple-color as a brinded cow,
For rose-moles all in stipple upon trout that swim;
Fresh-firecoal chestnut-falls, finches' wings;
Landscape plotted and pieced, fold, fallow and plough..."

It went on like that for a while. Rudge thought the verse was apt enough: a jungle was definitely dappled, light tumbling through the leaves, water, always moving, the light within it alive, mottled and animate. But it was a stretch to compare the sky to a cow. Poets often did that: started out well enough but then let go of the reins, let language get the best of them in their zeal.

Strand said the poem was by a fellow named Manly Hopkins. Rudge didn't think of poets as being all that manly, except for that Kipling fellow who had some grit in his lines and knew how to tell a story.

Another nine days of travel were consumed in slow progress northward. The jungle was crisscrossed with a hundred nameless tributaries, none deep enough to require harrowing underwater descents but the sum of them creating a daunting maze that made *Her Glory of Empire*'s steady compass-guided route seem arbitrary and futile. Morale was suffering, and the spongy, sodden ground—dry season, indeed!—required that Rudge and his men spend their nights within the vehicle. In this forced, uncomfortable proximity, it was no surprise that Jon Bans and Tommy Strand got in a scuffle, nor was it any surprise that the older, hard-muscled sailor won. The manifestations of Strand's defeat were minor (a bloody nose, a black eye, a swollen lip) but Rudge couldn't let the fight pass unremarked. He tried to sort out the altercation's cause.

Apparently Strand had objected to the way Bans had referred to a woman, calling her, among other things, a "doxy." Bans, in his defense, said that the woman he was referring to was his own wife. He loved his wife but felt that he was better acquainted with her than some young dandy stuffed full of fairy dust whose sole knowledge of women came from reading love poetry (which, everyone knew, was designed to seduce women not to portray them accurately) and who had no business, in any event, instructing a man on the proper way to describe his own wife.

When the two cooled off, Rudge sat them down and addressed them solemnly. "I will not tolerate fighting," he said. "We are on a rescue mission, and personal differences must be put aside." He added, wistfully, "There was a time when I could have had the both of you shot." There: he was getting nostalgic again, an old man's affliction.

As more days passed, the sun began to send long shafts of light down through the trees, yellow light like celestial grain pouring from some angelic silo, and Rudge felt that God was surely in His Heaven and looking out for those denizens of His most cherished island, dear emerald England.

God does not, however, wish anyone to lie too easy in his hammock, complacency being a sin that can easily escalate into pride. The next day, around noon, just after he'd finished his lunch and was folding his tarp, Rudge looked up to see a man, naked except for a black patch above his groin, poised between two trees not ten yards away and staring at Rudge over the sharp stone point of an arrow.

Civilization had dulled Rudge's survival instinct, and, instead of taking immediate evasive action, he shouted, "I say!" and might have added something equally inane like "That won't do!" The arrow snatched the folded tarp from his hands and pinned it to a tree.

The old warrior within him was roused by the attack. Rudge knew better than to turn and flee and take an arrow in the back. He charged the man and slapped soundly into him before the savage had another arrow notched. Down they both went. Rudge was roaring now: "Bloody bastard!"

The savage was not a big man, but he was strong and feral-fast and hissed like a snake and his body was slick with sweat or animal oils, and Rudge couldn't pin him. Rudge had knocked the man down, and they both rolled on the ground, thrashing amid the wet leaves and mud, and doing this for an inordinately long time, exchanging blows, making pig noises and grunts of menace, and then the savage was on top of him, his knees slamming into Rudge's chest and Rudge couldn't catch his breath, and he saw that the hand raised above him held a sharp killing-stone, and Rudge raised his forearm to block the blow.

The man leaned back slightly. Rudge could see the swollen scars that marked the man's cheeks and the way his eyes suddenly widened, and Rudge felt his own lungs gasp for air as the weight of his attacker seemed to lift.

The savage uttered a sharp cry, bird-like and quick, and he floated away, rising up into the trees, squeezed magically small by perspective, twisting and kicking and howling now, and Rudge saw the thick, gleaming coil that encircled the man's chest and fell away like a burnished silver vine, and he swung his head to follow the arc of the silver cord, his eye still sorting details while the logic of what he saw lagged behind. The great sun-struck curve of the shining mirrored orb showed his own reflection, and he saw where the tentacle protruded from the vessel, and his eye traced it back again and up to where the man squirmed high and small in the canopy of trees.

In an instant, Rudge understood what had happened. Mallory had witnessed the attack from within the vessel and had acted quickly, sending a segmented tentacle stretching to the edge of the clearing to snatch Rudge's assailant and haul him skyward.

As Rudge sorted this out, he was surprised by a hand on his shoulder. It was Jacobs. "Are you all right, Sir Bertram?"

"Yes," Rudge said, getting to his feet and brushing muck from his thighs. "Bit out of breath, but—"

He was interrupted by the body that came crashing and tumbling down from the trees to land on its back with a wet smack on the forest floor. Mallory had either released the man or the man had wriggled out of the tentacle's grasp without reflecting on the consequences of that maneuver.

The man's eyes were open as was his mouth. He was dead and wore a dumbfounded expression, as though the other side was not at all what he expected.

"Sir!" Jacobs said, and Rudge looked up to see more naked men, armed with spears and bows and arrows, moving out of the trees and into the sunlight.

"Over here," another voice shouted, and Rudge looked over his shoulder and saw Jon Bans and Tommy Strand. Jon Bans was aiming an ancient Enfield Musketoon at one of the natives, but Rudge felt that the odds of Bans killing anyone other than himself were slim. Rudge had examined the moldering gun weeks ago and pronounced it worthless. Tommy Strand was holding Rudge's own Lee-Metford, a fine bolt-action rifle that Rudge trusted with his life. He did not, however, trust the abilities of the feckless naturalist who was presently holding it. Rudge wondered how many savages Mallory could wring the life out of with his mechanical tentacles.

But the savages seemed uninterested in Rudge or any of his comrades. They surrounded the dead man and began talking and grunting and slapping each other on the back. One of the men threw his feet up in the air, threw his arms wide, and sprawled on his back to the accompaniment of loud hoots and grunts which Rudge identified as expressions of mirth.

"These boys have a hell of a sense of humor, don't they?" The man who had just walked out of the forest and uttered this remark was dressed as though for tennis, or, perhaps, croquet. He was smoking a cheroot with an insouciant air, and a black-rimmed monocle was screwed into his left eye.

"Wallister!" Rudge blurted. He'd never met the man, but his likeness was famously familiar.

"I am," the man said. "I don't know who you are, but I bet you are looking for Lavinia. There's always someone chasing after her."

The Yami village was less than a mile away, and Rudge and his men accompanied Wallister on foot. Mallory followed behind in *Her Glory*, maintaining a distance of several hundred yards so that the falling trees and flying branches that were an inevitable byproduct of the vehicle's progress wouldn't maim anyone. The natives walked ahead of Rudge and Wallister.

"Didn't know that fellow was going to try to shoot an arrow through you," Wallister said, as they pressed on through the jungle. "I wouldn't have stood still for that if I'd seen it coming. Sorry though. I should have been paying more attention." He shot a glance at Rudge. "Although you know how to look out for yourself. I can see that. That was quite a trick with that machine of yours. Never seen anything like that."

They were silent for a while, and then Wallister said, "Lord Addison sent you, didn't he?" and Rudge nodded and said that Lavinia's grandfather had been concerned for her welfare, and that Rudge had volunteered to find her and report on her safety. He'd become, of course, much more worried when he and his men came upon the burned out shell of the zeppelin.

Wallister was surprised to learn that the zeppelin had burned—"wasn't burning when we set off," he said—but he didn't seem particularly upset. He had a cavalier manner that suited his heavy-lidded eyes and too-full lips, and the slightly vexed expression of a man often misunderstood by his inferiors. He moved through the jungle with a twisting of hips and shoulders that suggested a man wending his way through a party crowd with the bar as his destination. Rudge better understood Lord Addison's antipathy for Wallister and, consequently, felt less ambivalent about getting Lavinia back to England and her grandfather by whatever means necessary.

Their arrival at the village was heralded by a dozen or so small children, who ran down the path to meet them, silent, swift, pale creatures, weaving and darting and ogling the new intruders and then running on down the path to where *Her Glory of Empire* was shaking the jungle and throwing up debris. They would flee it, then stop, turn, and run toward it, stand wiggling and flapping their arms and uttering rude noises, then flee again.

When Rudge and his companions arrived at the village, they found every man, woman, and child who had not set out to greet them, the lot standing in a fleshy mass of expectancy, and, as Rudge entered the clearing, the crowd parted to reveal a hut from which a young woman emerged, a strikingly beautiful girl with raven hair that fell loosely from under a pith helmet decorated with pink and purple orchids. She seemed dazed by the sunlight; she brought a hand to her throat, and her eyes widened, blue eyes that pierced old Rudge's memory and brought her name to his lips, reflexively. Could this vision be the precocious twelve-year-old he had known so long ago?

But before her name could pass his lips, a voice shouted in his ear: "Vinia!" And he saw Lavinia's eyes grow yet wider, impossibly large, and she began to run toward him, and he felt something like pain—perhaps acute embarrassment at an old man's fancy—when he realized she was not running toward him but toward the man who had just raced by Rudge to close the distance in mere seconds, take Lavinia in his arms and spin her in the air while she laughed with that merriment that only the young have access to.

Tommy Strand and Lavinia Addison hugged and kissed, sobbed and laughed, aware perhaps of their audience—as the young so often are—and portraying two besotted lovers with a skill well beyond that of the most accomplished thespians.

⊰⊱

It was the evening of the next day. The sun was still in the sky, but, in less than an hour, it would slide precipitously into the water. Rudge stood at the end of a ramshackle pier, which, he suspected, had not fallen into disrepair but been born in that state. A sizeable lake spread out in front of him, its mirrored surface full of the cloudy sky, not a dimple on its surface (curious, that). There was no sign of life at all, and a strange, dank odor filled the air. Nonetheless, Rudge was delighted to have evaded, if only briefly, the chatter of the Yami, their idiotic bluster and pomp. Primitive peoples did not inspire Rudge, who saw in them the worst aspects of human nature, reminding him that superstition, ignorance, violence, and cruelty were inherent human traits, first impulses, and that civilization was a cheap coat of paint over a rotten edifice.

He was not, he decided, angered by Tommy Strand's subterfuge. The young man was not a naturalist, a fact which should have been apparent from the beginning; he was, in truth, the feckless son of Arthur Strand, a powerful industrialist who had prevailed upon Lord Addison to take his son on board for this rescue mission. Neither Arthur Strand nor Lord Addison had any idea that young Tommy and Lavinia were enamored of each other—or had been until an unfortunate misunderstanding had led to a heated argument which had prompted Lavinia, obeying an impulse not uncommon in young people, to put an entire ocean between herself and her unhappy suitor.

She had quickly come to regret this. Wallister proved an unpleasant man, a "brute," (although he had not, according to Lavinia, indulged in any sexual impropriety beyond a certain sly familiarity and presumption). The jungle had failed to improve her disposition, and the insufferable Yami were the last straw, a noisy, foul-smelling lot who wore no clothes except—how stupid was this?—a small black patch to cover the navel, a kind of spiritual precaution, since demons tended to enter a person via this umbilical entrance. You were just asking for trouble if you didn't hide your navel under a mollusk shell or bit of sloth hide.

In any event, the lovers were reunited, and it looked like a happy—

The sky seemed to die and fall upon him. A cold fist squeezed his heart. He fell to his knees. Suddenly it was as though his body were fashioned from clay; surely this numbness heralded his death, and yet this mortal fear was nothing compared to an overwhelming sense of desolation. If he had been told that everyone he knew and cared for had died, hideously, that might have engendered such despair; a palpable evil, a malevolent spirit, had settled in his mind with the authority of truth, bringing with it a suffocating terror, a need to run, to flee, but robbing him of volition.

Somehow he managed to stagger to his feet and gaze down into the water from which this malign psychic force seemed to emanate. The water was clear, and he saw the lake's bottom, which rippled with shadows, black blotches that shifted and danced, as though cast by broad leaves shivering in a strong wind. He had thought the lake deeper, even here at the end of the pier, and this shift in perception created a kind of panicky vertigo. What did it matter how deep—? Then he understood. He was not looking at the lake's bottom; he was gazing down upon the back of some unknowable beast. It was gliding under the water, a vast, translucent creature, shapeless, or shifting in shape, a kind of ovoid whale-sized jellyfish. The mottled, black shapes within it pulsated and moved, and these black undulating inkblots were not organs beating to some animal pulse—how Rudge knew this he could not say; but know it he did— they were mouths opening and closing to reveal a terrible hunger, more ancient and ravenous than any jungle beast or mythical monster.

Rudge did not know if he walked or ran or crawled back down the pier and over the ground and back to the hut. He had some memory of falling upon his blankets and being seized by a deep and unrelenting lethargy, which a scientist of the mind might have identified as a strategy of the subconscious designed to defend the self from a horror it found untenable.

In the morning, when Jacobs brought him his tea, Rudge came awake, groggy but in full possession of the previous night's horror.

The old man could speak English, having spent four years in a mission before deciding that one god was not enough for a jungle life, and now, having heard Rudge out, he nodded.

"This in-the-lake thing big. Very big, very bad. It not live here. It from some other. It splash into this world and very angry, and it kill-kill everything and eat up everything. Mostly, it stay in the night, wait for the night when the sun is shy. We Yami, we try to kill it. It eat up Yami. Ha ha!" The old shaman laughed and slapped his thigh. "We stick him with spear. We stick him with arrow. He eat up spear and arrow and Yami!" The old man glowered, as though suddenly struck with the seriousness of this Yami-eating business.

"It make slave of some Yami. It catch Yami and make him fetch food and trick other Yami to lake, but it take Yami soul to make of him slave, and we see that. We say, 'That man, he have no soul,' and we kill him."

The Yami were not fools. They had discovered several things about the beast. It could not travel on land, and its substance, its flesh, was, consequently, trapped within the lake. It needed to eat, to feed, and it had done that until there was nothing left for it to eat. No birds, no fish, no frogs, no turtles, nothing. It would die in its dead lake.

"We kill it with nothing," he said, his smile revealing half a dozen ragged black teeth.

Rudge was about to ask something about the Yami slaves when a series of high-pitched screams made him leap to his feet and run outside.

The screams were coming from the lake, and as soon as Rudge rounded a gnarled clump of trees, he understood what was happening. So much for the shaman's assertion that the creature shunned the daylight. It was, no doubt, growing desperate.

Wallister and Lavinia were both kneeling on the end of the pier, clutching the weather-battered logs and desiccated vines that comprised it. The pier had been ripped from the shore and was moving out into the lake, riding the back of the beast, a raft surrounded by white turbulence and leaving a wild, frothing wake.

Rudge saw Tommy Strand running toward the lake. He stood on the edge, preparing to dive in and swim valiantly after his beloved, but a shout stopped him, and Rudge turned too, and spied Mallory, standing atop *Her Glory of Empire* and urging Strand to hurry.

Mallory disappeared before Strand reached the vehicle, and a silver tentacle reached out and lifted the young man up to the hatch. Rudge marveled at Mallory's skill. He was an artist with old Edmonds's invention.

Her Glory rolled into the lake and water rollicked all over the banks and then, amid several flying tentacles and the ball-ended air tubes, it disappeared beneath the surface. The steady progress of the bobbing tubes was all that marked its journey. Those air tubes gained on the floundering pier, and suddenly a tentacle reached out of the water and encircled Lavinia's waist. The girl screamed, no doubt thinking the beast had her, and continued to scream until, suddenly, she fell from the tentacle's clasp. The tentacle sank beneath the waves, and so did Lavinia. On the bank, Rudge shouted, appalled, crazy in his helplessness. Then Lavinia's head and shoulders broke the surface, and Tommy Strand could be seen behind her. Lavinia's eyes were closed, but Tommy had his arm around her and was in no danger of losing her. With strong, purposeful strokes he drew her to the shore.

Rudge turned back to where the pier now lay motionless in the middle of the lake. Wallister was nowhere to be seen, and *Her Glory of Empire* had failed to resurface.

Time passed. The crowd of naked men, women, and children, silent at first and keeping a cautious distance from the shore, began to talk excitedly and gesture among themselves.

Rudge spied Tommy and Lavinia on the shore to his right. Tommy had an arm around her shoulders and she was sitting up, coughing. Rudge was about to set off in their direction when a great funnel of water erupted and *Her Glory of Empire* rose up, all twelve of its tentacles thrashing, shimmering in the blazing sun, seeming to dance upon the water. It was up and on the shore in an instant, and then it was among the Yami who screamed and fled in all directions. The machine snatched them up, each tentacle moving of its own accord, independent of all others. Mallory's skill was nothing like this. Men, women, and children were tossed in the air, slammed against tree trunks, torn to bits by tentacles that sliced them with gleaming blades. An old warrior's head bounced at Rudge's feet. He jumped back as it rolled past, blood splattering his boots.

And then this great machine stood tall on six tentacles, in defiance of all engineering principles, and Rudge saw the slumped form of Wallister, sodden and surely lifeless, bound by several coils of a single tentacle, and the machine, moving with an unholy ease that suggested a decisive intelligence, darted into the jungle, parting trees and brush in a welter of sound and fury—and was gone. In less than five minutes, its progress could no longer be marked by the noise that accompanied it, although Rudge could still discern the cloud of dust and twigs and leaves that rose above it.

As he walked to meet Tommy and Lavinia, Rudge saw, on the lake's bank, a litter of pipes and seals and broken gauges, the mechanical guts of *Her Glory*, instruments of no interest to the creature that now wore the vehicle like a suit of armor.

All's well that ends well. That's what Rudge told himself on his return to England. And certainly Lord Addison was pleased to have his granddaughter safely home.

But what is the end? When, six weeks after his disappearance, Wallister walked out of the jungle, miraculously whole, was that the end? When the great explorer abandoned his travels and devoted his fortune to industry, was that the end? When a factory in Sheffield began producing great hollow steel orbs that dwarfed the men who made them, and when the public learned that these were the prototypes of a new and glorious engine based on Hugh Edmonds's invention, what was one to make of that?

People said that Wallister had changed, was serious, almost solemn, and the flamboyance that had delighted the public and annoyed his fellows was gone for good. Was there anyone in England who could discern the absence of a soul?

Rudge would have liked to know if these manufactured steel casings awaited cunning furnaces and engines and navigational devices. Or did they await creatures in need of external skeletons? If these empty spheres were waiting upon the latter, then that, Rudge thought, might well be the end.

Inelastic Collisions

Elizabeth Bear

TOO EASY BY half, but a girl had to eat.

Tamara genuflected before the glistening white sphere, a black one peeking over its top. She bent over the felted slate table like a sacrifice—a metaphor more ironic than prophetic—letting her shirt hike up her nubby spine. The balls were round, outside her domain, but that was a detail too insignificant to affect Tamara's understanding of the geometry involved.

All that mattered were the vectors.

BORED, Gretchen murmured, as the cue stick slipped curveless through Tamara's fingers. BORED BORED BORED BORED BORED.

The cue stick struck the cue ball. The cue ball jolted forward, skipping into the eight ball and stopping precisely as its momentum was transferred. An inelastic collision. *Thump. Click.* The eight ball glided into the corner pocket, and Tamara lifted her head away from the table, shaking razor-cut hair from her neck. She showed her teeth. To her sister, not to the human she'd beaten.

Gretchen leaned her elbows on the pool table, pale bones stretching her skin gorgeously. Tendons popped as she flexed her fingers. The shape she wore was dough-pale, sticky and soft, but hunger made it leaner. Not enough leaner.

"You lose," Gretchen said to Tamara's prey.

The male put a gold ring on the edge of the table, still slick inside with fat from his greasy human skin. Gretchen slipped a fingernail through the loop and scraped it up, handling it by the edges. She was dirty herself, of course, dirty in a dirty human body. It didn't make human grease any nicer to touch.

Gretchen tucked the ring into her pocket. She nagged. **HUNGRY.**

Tamara, reaching for the chalk, stopped—and sighed, though she could not get used to the noises made by the meat—and let the blunt end of her cue stick bump the floor. "Play again?" the human asked. "I'd like a chance to win that back." He pointed with his chin at Gretchen's pocket.

He was dark-haired, his meat firm and muscular under the greasy toffee-colored skin. Disgusting, and looking at him didn't help Tamara forget that she too was trapped in an oleaginous human carcass, with a greasy human tongue and greasy human bones and a greasy human name.

But a girl had to eat.

"Actually"—she said, and showed her teeth to the human, willing him to snarl back. No. *Smile* back—"how do you feel about dinner?"

Gretchen was furious. Tamara felt it as from twitching tail-tip to shivering pricked ears. Her human cage had neither, but *she* still remembered what it was to be a Hound. Gretchen's flesh-clotted legs scissored to crisp ninety degree angles. Her razor-cut hair snapped in separate tendrils behind her.

YOU'RE ANGRY, Tamara said, finally, desperately. It was wrong to have to ask why, wrong to have to *ask* anything. Between sisters, between terrible angels, there should be consensus.

Gretchen did not answer.

The May night was balmy. Tamara wrapped her fingers around her shoulders and pressed them against the ridge of bone she could feel through cloying meat. She set her heels.

Gretchen stalked ten steps further and halted as sharply as if someone had popped her leash. An inelastic collision. Her heeled shoes skittered on parking lot gravel.

Tamara waited.

YOU KNEW I WAS HUNGRY, Gretchen said. **YOU LET HIM GET AWAY.**

I DIDN'T!

But Gretchen turned toward her, luminous green-brown eyes unblinking above the angles of her cheekbones, and Tamara looked down. Wrong, *wrong*, that she could not hear what her sister was thinking. **I DIDN'T**, she insisted.

YOU SHOWED YOUR TEETH.

I SMILED AT HIM.

SISTER, Gretchen said sadly, **THEY CAN TELL THE DIFFERENCE.**

They sold the ring at a pawnshop and took the money to another bar. While Gretchen thumbed quarters into the pool table, Tamara worried. Worry was a new thing, like distance from her sister. Exile on this round spinning world in its round spinning orbit was changing them; Tamara had learned to count its revolutions and orbits, as the humans did, and call them *time* now that she could no longer sense the real time, the Master's time, inexorable consumption and entropy.

She had been its warden, once. The warden of the real time, immaculate and perfect, as unlike the messy, improvisational sidereal time of the meat puppets as a diamond crystal was unlike a blown glass bauble. But she and her sister had failed to bring to justice a sorcerer who had upset the true time, and unless they could regain the Master's favor, they would not rejoin their sisters in Heaven.

All the painful curves of this world: the filthy, rotting, organic bodies that stayed fleshy and slack no matter how thin the sisters starved them; the knotted curves of roots and veins and flower petals were slow poison.

Tamara had lost her home. Exile was costing her her sister, as well.

She hunched on the barstool—her gin and tonic cradled in her right hand, gnawing the rind of the lime—and watched Gretchen rack the balls. The second bar was a smoky little place with canned music and not much of a crowd. Some male humans sat at the bar nursing beers or boilermakers, and a female whose male companion wasn't drinking fiddled with a plate of hot wings and a cosmopolitan in a booth on the wall. Gretchen rattled the rack one last time and lifted it with her fingertips. A human female's hands would have trembled slightly. Gretchen's stayed steady as if carved.

She turned away to hang the rack up, and when she looked back, she bared her teeth.

She didn't care what Gretchen said; Tamara *couldn't* tell the difference. She shredded the rind of the lime between her teeth and washed its bitterness down with the different bitterness of the gin and tonic. When she got up to go to Gretchen, she left her glass on the bar so somebody might offer to buy her another one.

It was hard, playing badly. Hard to miss once in a while. Hard to look like she was really trying, poking a sharp triangle of tongue between taut lips, narrowed eyes wrinkling the bridge of her nose. Gretchen, walking past, patted her on the haunches.

Tamara sucked her tongue back into her mouth, smiled against the cue stick, and broke.

She had to let Gretchen win two games before they attracted any interest. The squeak of rubber on the wood floor caught her ear, but she didn't raise her head until the human cleared his throat. She straightened and turned, already alerted by her sister's posture that something unusual was happening.

The male paused before her sat in a wheelchair, his hands folded across his lap. He was ugly even by human standards, bald and bristly and scalded-looking, with heavy jowls and watery eyes that squinted through thick thumbprint glasses. He pointed to the rack of cues over Gretchen's shoulder and said, "There's only one table. Mind if I play the winner?"

His voice was everything his body wasn't. So rich and comforting, full of shadowy resonances like the echoes off of hard close planes. Tamara recognized him: he was the male who had been with the dark-haired female eating the chicken wings. Tamara glanced toward the door, but his companion seemed to have left. He smelled of salt water and beer, not grease and rotten meat the way most humans did. "I'm Pinky Gilman," he said, as if Tamara had answered, and extended his hand.

CRIPPLED, Gretchen murmured. WEAK. Tamara made sure to keep her teeth covered when she smiled. PREY, she answered, and felt Gretchen laugh, tongue lolling, though her human cage remained impassive. "Tamara," Tamara said. She reached out gingerly squeezed thick human fingers. "Gretchen is my sister."

"I see the resemblance," he said. "Am I interrupting?"

"No." Gretchen turned to reach another stick down. "I was going to take a break."

Tamara disentangled her fingers from the meat-puppet's, and stepped back. Her tongue adhered to the roof of her weird blunt-toothed mouth. "Can you?…"

"Well enough," he said, and accepted the cue stick Gretchen extended across the table at arm's length.

Gretchen patted Tamara on the arm as she went by. "Do either of you want a beer?"

Tamara was learning so many new emotions in her cage, and so many nuances on the old ones. Worry, discontent, and now another: surprise.

Because she didn't have to try not to beat Pinky Gilman too easily. Rather, he was making her work.

The first game, she let him break, and never chalked her stick. In fact, Tamara handled Pinky's cue more than her own, because he passed it to her to hold while he manipulated the wheelchair.

He sank three balls on the break, chose solids, and proceeded to clear the table with efficiency and a series of small flourishes, mostly demonstrated when he spun his wheelchair into position. By the time he reached the eight ball, though, he looked up at her and winked.

Gretchen had just returned with the beer. She pushed her hair behind her shoulder with the back of her fingers and handed Tamara a drink. I DON'T BELIEVE IT.

CAN MEAT PUPPETS *do* THAT?

SHOOT POOL?

win AT POOL. Gretchen leaned her shoulder on Tamara's so her bones bruised her sister's cage's flesh. Tamara sighed, comforted.

APPARENTLY, she answered, SOME CAN.

The male, leaning forward in his wheelchair to peer the length of the cue stick, did not glance at them. His eyes narrowed behind the glasses and the stick flicked through his fingers like a tongue. It struck the scuffed white ball, and the white ball spun forward, rebounding from the wall and striking the black at an angle. *Click. Hiss. Clunk.*

Eight ball in the corner pocket.

Pinky laid his stick across the table, spun the wheels of his chair back six inches, and turned to Tamara, holding up his hand. "Shark," she said, and put the beer into it instead of accepting the greasy clasp.

Pinky smiled at her and swallowed deeply as Gretchen passed her a second bottle. She was thirsty. She was always thirsty. "Go again?"

Beer was bitter in her mouth, cold and foaming where it crossed her tongue. She swallowed and rubbed her cage's tongue against its palate for the lingering texture, then gulped once more. The cold hurt the teeth of her cage. "Gretchen," she said, stepping backwards, "you play."

Gretchen beat him, but just only, and only because she broke. He laughed like a drain as she sunk the smooth, black eight ball, and raised his cue stick in his hands, holding it overhead as if it were a bar he meant to chin himself upon.

He had blunt nails, thick enough that Tamara could see the file marks across them, and the tendons of his forearms ridged when he lifted them. "So," he said, "how would you feel about playing for forfeits?"

Gretchen smiled, and Tamara could see the difference. "What do you have in mind?"

The human lowered his cue stick and shrugged. "If I win, you come back to my place and let me feed you dinner." Tamara started, and he held up his hand. "Never fear; I don't have improper designs. And there are two of you, and only one of me, after all."

Tamara looked at Gretchen. Gretchen looked at Tamara, her luminous eyes huge, the pupils contracted to pinpricks. "Not to mention the wheelchair," Tamara said.

"Not to mention the wheelchair," he agreed. "And if you win, you can make *me* dinner." He let his cue stick fall forward so that it rested on the edge of the table.

Tamara smiled at him.

Tamara lingered in the bathroom, scraping her fingertips across pungent white soap to fill the gaps so her nails would stay clean. Through the wallboard, she could hear the clink of dishes and the rumble of the human's voice, the occasional answering chirp of Gretchen's. She turned the water on with the heel of her hands and cupped it to her mouth in brimming palmfuls. It tasted faintly of Dial and made her blunt human teeth ache, her throat stretch and hurt when she gulped.

The smell of the alcohol the human was pouring reached her from the kitchen. She swallowed more tap water, filling the hollow spaces inside her, squinching her eyes against the following, welcome pain.

She straightened and turned off the tap, then checked her nails to see if the white crescents of soap had gotten loose. They gave her hands the appearance of a careful manicure. She stuffed them into her pockets as she walked down the hall.

As Tamara came down the hall, she saw Gretchen bent over the breakfast bar in the kitchen, a strip of pale skin revealed between her shirt and the band of her jeans. The male stumped about the kitchen on elbow crutches, which he had produced when Gretchen and Tamara helped him into his car. The wheelchair was because he couldn't shoot pool with something in his hands, he said.

Tamara had been all for eating him in the parking lot, but Gretchen had thought it better to wait. For privacy, and leisure, in which to enjoy their first good meal in days.

Tamara cleared her throat. And Gretchen jumped a little—guiltily? Tamara flinched in silent sympathy. *We cannot live like this. We just cannot.*

It was an effort to think *we,* and that almost moved her to tears. It was an effort, too, to remember divinity. To remember certainty. To remember what it had been like to be clean.

HUNGRY, she said, and felt Gretchen stretch inside her skin. Gretchen grinned and ran her tongue over her teeth, and together they moved forward. Soon there would be blood and sinew, bone and flesh—and if not an end to thirst and hunger, sweet surcease, for as long as the dining lasted.

The air was cool and full of rich smells. Tamara's feet were springy on the floor. One more step forward. One more.

Over the spit of bacon, without turning, the male said, "I'd reconsider that if I were you."

Gretchen checked, and Tamara hesitated a half-step later. She hissed between her teeth as the male lifted bacon from the grease with tongs, set it on a paper napkin, and turned off the heat under the pan. Only then did he turn, leaning heavily on his elbow crutches.

TAMARA? Gretchen said, and Tamara's breath almost sliced her; the name struck her like a cue ball. Sisters did not need names. Not between sisters. Names were a human-thing, part of the lie.

She bit blood from her cheek as Gretchen said, again. TAMARA?!

The human male said, "He won't take you back, you know. You can starve yourself to the bone, starve yourself until you're blades, starve yourselves until your human hearts stop—and he will never forgive you. Time does not offer second chances. History does not give do-overs. It doesn't matter how hard you try to be entropy's angels again. The only kind of angel you can ever be from now on is fallen."

That whine. That was *her.* Or was it Gretchen?

The male—not a human male, no, she'd been fooled by his disguise, but she knew from his words that he must be an angel too, of some one of the dark Gods or another—continued. "Or you can learn to live in the world."

She should have stepped forward, rent him with her nails, shredded with her teeth. But she could taste it already, the grease of his flesh, the fat and the soil. She drove her nails into her own palms again. Gretchen crouched beside her. "You're not the Master's. You are not a Hound."

"No," the male said, leaning on his crutches so they squeaked on the linoleum. "I was born to the Father of Frogs. But I belong to myself now. Like you."

"You failed. You *fell.*"

"I climbed, my angels."

And that explained why he smelled of sea air and not sour maggoty meat. Unlike Tamara, who could feel her own flesh rotting on the bones when she breathed too deep.

Filthy. Greasy. Everything was dirt. Tamara sobbed and licked blood from her nails, tasting the soap, stronger than ever. Some of it was her own blood. She wished that some of it was the watery blood of this smiling monster.

"I *won't* be dirty. I won't be hungry," Gretchen said, her hands bridged on the tile, one knee dropped. Her voice rose. "I won't be dirty forever. I *won't.*"

The male's face was soft. Compassionate. Sickening. He tilted his head. "You'll be dirty," he said, pitiless as the Master, "or you'll be dead. Being hungry is being human. Can they bear more than you?"

Gretchen recoiled. Tamara thrust her thumb into her mouth, sucked the clean moon crescent of soap onto her tongue. She swallowed, hard, and again, and again, sucking each finger clean, feeling the soap reach her stomach, acid and alcohol hissing around it.

The male would *not* stop talking. She didn't think he'd stop if she jammed her fingers in her ears. "And that's the human condition. None of us can get clean. The world is sticky."

"And we don't have to like it."

"But you can't be an angel any more. So you're going to have to learn to talk to each other."

YOU CAN'T KNOW THAT

Tamara didn't know if she'd said it, or Gretchen. Gretchen, from the lift of her shoulders, the upward glance, did not know either. The sound was dim, broken.

"I know," Pinky said, and held out one ugly hand, with its filed thick nails and its bulging knuckles. The webs that stretched between the fingers were vestigial, greenish, vascular along the underside of the membrane. He spread them wide. "I used to be a terrible angel too."

The soap, the words, the dirt, the blood. Something was coming back up. Something. Tamara went to her knees beside Gretchen, smacked down on the slate floor (so smooth, so hard, so planar). She retched. A thin stream of frothy bile trickled between her gritted teeth. She heard Gretchen whine.

And then someone was there, holding her, stroking her hair, pushing the flat feathered strands out of her eyes, his sleek aluminum props splayed out on either side. "Shh," said the monster, the fallen angel, the inhuman man. "Shhh," he said, and held her head as she bent down again and vomited soap and liquor on what had been a scrubbed floor, her belly clenched around cramping agony. "We don't eat soap," he said, and petted her until she stopped choking. "We don't eat soap. Silly angel."

She lifted her head, when she could, when the yellow slaver no longer dripped down her jowls. Pinky Gilman leaned over her, his wattled throat soft, tender, so close to her aching jaws. She lifted her head and saw her sister staring back at her.

A held breath. A quick shake of the head. Sharp silence, so hard that it might have ricocheted.

And Tamara, looking at Gretchen, heard the answer not because she *knew* it, but because she would once have known.

Remnants

Fred Chappell

I.

ECHO WAS THRASHING and muttering in her sleep and would soon have cried out if Vern had not crawled over in the dark to her pallet and addressed her ear, making only a whisper-noise and no words. "Psss, psss, psss."

"Psss psss psss," she answered, imitating his exact sibilance, as she always did.

"Hush now," he murmured. "Don't cry out."

These five words she repeated also, her inflection reproducing his. She had not wakened.

"What is it?" he said, speaking ever so softly. "Is it a shiny? Is it a waggly? Is it a too-bright?"

All this she mimicked.

"No," he said. "Say what."

"No. Say what." Then, in a while: "Dirt. Broke dirt."

"Broken dirt," her brother said. He was trying to lengthen the loop of her phrases so that more information would filter into its sequence of repetition. He was four years older than she; he was going on sixteen now, but he had learned to be almost tirelessly patient. He looked to see if Moms had been wakened by the girl's unrest, but she seemed to sleep soundly, lying in the leaf pile with her face turned away and covered with scraps of cloth and burlap and canvas. She shivered a little; it was impossible to sleep warmly in their cave behind the waterfall, and they were reduced to rags for blankets.

"Broke dirt," Echo said.

"Why broke-dirt? What for broke-dirt? Where is broke-dirt?"

"Psss psss psss. Hush now. Don't cry out. What is it? Is it a shiny…" She had started from the beginning again, her voice copying his in every breath, but not becoming louder, so probably what disturbed her sleep was not an Old One sweeping a thought-probe through the landscape in random search, as they so often did. The black mixed collie, Queenie, lay watching the brother and the sister, and she was peaceful, with her head on her paws and not bristling. Nor was she growling in that dangerous but almost inaudible manner that meant she understood that Echo had detected something perilous nearby.

Vern decided he could go back to sleep. Whatever Echo had encountered could wait till morning. She was a little easier to communicate with when she was awake, but communication required an immense store of calmness.

Which I have not got, he thought, as he lay down in his place and re-covered himself over with rags and leaves. I have just about run out of calm, the way I have run out of ideas about where to find food.

He thought about that, staring into the darkness above. The stream whose bed roofed the cave in which they lived offered fish, the small speckled trout native to these mountains. In summer there were berries and rabbits and other small game, but that season was dwindling and the trees were dropping their leaves so quickly they seemed to be racing to denude themselves. The family had not managed to put much by for the winter. The Old Ones and their shog-goth slaves had been active in this area all through the summer, so Vern and Moms had foraged less often than they desired. Also, Moms and Vern did not like to leave Echo alone in the cave, even with Queenie there to disguise her mind and to protect her.

This was the main reason they shared food with Queenie. The dog thought in the same way that Echo did. She thought in pictures and not in words; she thought in terms of smell and sound as much as in visuals, and this was true too of Echo. The Old Ones who swept a casual thought probe through would probably identify Echo as a dog or an opossum or raccoon. If Vern and Moms kept their feelings at a low level and were as careful as possible not to think in large generalizations like "weather," "time," "yesterday," "the future," and so forth, the pictures in the heads of Queenie and Echo would pretty well mask the ways of thought of Vern and Moms.

Of course, if the Olders—as Vern called them—set out to make a thorough and deliberate search, there would be no way to hide. And no way to defend themselves. They would be captured, examined inside and out, and when that bloody, shrieking inventory was complete, they would be discarded, unless the Olders found something in one of their minds to isolate and store in their cyborganic memory banks.

But this latter possibility was extremely unlikely. In their family, only their father, Donald Peaslee, had known anything that could have been of use to the Olders. They took it from him, whatever it was, along with his sanity first and then with his life.

Vern would not think about that. If he thought about the way his father, or what was left of him, had looked the last time he saw him, his emotions would rise like a scarlet banner run up a flagpole and then maybe an Older would notice and come hunting. Or maybe the Older would send a throng of their stupid and disgusting shoggoths to search them out. The cosmetic ministrations those creatures wreaked on humans prettified them no more than did the interrogations of the Olders.

But something had nudged Echo's sleeping mind with its strange faculties and it was needful to know what that might have been.

When morning came, he would make an attempt, if she had not forgotten… Well, no, Echo was incapable of forgetting anything. Everything that had ever happened to her, everything she had seen and felt and heard and smelled and tasted was all there in her mind. But it was hard to draw it out because she had no categories. You had to find a specific detail and then add that to another and then another and another until some sort of picture was suggested.

He sighed and turned to sleep and just as he was letting go, he fancied that something touched his own mind too, with just the whisper of a whisper. Then he decided he was only imagining; he lacked Echo's quick, delicate talent.

Vern wanted to question his sister the first moment the three of them were awake, but there was no chance of that. For Echo, everything had to fall into place in a customary routine. First, Vern had to go outside and "scout," as Moms put it—meaning that he had to find a tree and take a leak, fill a can with stream water, and look for dangers or for nothing until Moms had cleaned up Echo and brushed her hair as best she could and made her feel Echo-ish. This was one of the few times she enjoyed being touched by others, except for petting and hugging Queenie and guiding Vern's hand during the drawing sessions.

So out he went into a gray, chilly dawn with its sky streaked here and there with scores of dropping meteorites. This time he really did look about for signs of danger because of Echo's restlessness and his own vague feeling that something was waiting to happen. He toured the small, handy game traps he had set, but they were empty this morning. He had been seeing raccoon sign by a little streamlet that fed into the waterfall stream and was pretty sure he could capture it some soon morning before dawn. That would be glad news for the family, meat and pelt together. He did not bother to look into the fish trap set at the farther end of the waterfall pool; he had seen yesterday evening that a large brook trout was captured in the willow-withe cage and he would let it stay there to keep fresh. They already had stocked two smoked trout in the cave, one for now and one for the other meal of the day.

He let himself recall, for the most fleeting of moments, the great, lush blackberries he had gathered some forty-odd days ago, so juicy-sweet they had made Echo tremble as she crammed them into her mouth by handfuls while Moms watched her with teary eyes.

Then he turned the thought away. It might make his emotions rise to a detectable level. The Olders…

Time now to go back. Inside, he saw Echo all freshened up to the best of her mother's ability. She was hugging Queenie and singing her wake-up song: "All night all night all night…"

He found his length of steel—a flattened lever two feet long—and went to the ember hole, lifted off the slate covering, and dug out one of the cylinders of foil. The other he left for supper. He covered the hole over again and brought the trout to where Moms and Echo sat waiting.

Moms looked more tired than yesterday, he thought, but Echo was as happy as ever she could be. She liked the taste of the trout smoked in foil but more than that she liked the anticipation of eating it. She drummed her hands on her crossed legs, smiling and murmuring softly her song, "All night all night."

"Thank you, Vern," Moms said when he handed her the packet. "Did you sleep well?"

"Echo was hearing something," he said. "She was almost awake."

"I know." Moms took the one metal knife they possessed from her belt and divided the fish. Her belt held up the britches she had stitched together with nylon fishing leader from an old, mostly rotten tent they had found in the woods. They needed to find some more fabric soon or roam around naked.

Echo would not like that; she must have her many-colored robe, cloth scraps of every kind held together with pins and wire bits and paper clips and whatnot. She would squall if she had to go naked.

"There is something she wants to tell us about," Vern said.

"The Old Ones?"

"I don't know. Should we try to find out?"

"Maybe we should. I heard once long ago that they make parts of forests like this one into preserves and stock them with all sorts of animals that might harm us. To this particular environment, they might import grizzly bears and gray wolves and panthers. Wolves and panthers used to inhabit here."

"I know," Vern said. But he didn't know and he wouldn't inquire. *I heard once long ago*—this was Moms' phrase to indicate something her husband had told her. Best never to say his name, for sorrow would rise in them and such a feeling—or any strong feeling—was so alien to the Olders that they could detect it at fairly long range.

His father had known many things: history and science and music and numbers and stars. He had known too much about the stars. He had known too much about everything. See what grief his learning had brought them… Vern turned aside these thoughts.

But Moms had remembered some of the history her husband knew. He had told her of the caves in this part of the mountains where remnants of the Cherokee nation hid out when the soldiers came to drive them away, and to rape and kill and burn. Those who did not hide in the caves were herded on the Trail of Tears, to suffer and die on the brutal march westward. Vern had found signs and leavings in their own cave. A rose-colored flint knife was his special treasure.

Queenie had trotted out of the cave when they began eating the fish. She would scout the area, ranging farther than Vern had done, and then return for her own meal. It had taken a long time to reconcile her to this routine, but they needed a sentry in this hour. When Echo ate, she could concentrate on nothing else until the breakfast ritual was complete. When Queenie returned, Vern would feed the dog the smoked opossum buried in the ember hole. Now he passed to his mother and sister the can of water brought from the stream. Each drank, then both washed their hands and faces, Echo mimicking Moms' actions closely.

Tasks awaited Vern. He needed to fashion new traps from whatever pliable materials he could find. He already had a good-sized stock; the woods were full of discarded things, trash that was treasure for the family. He also needed to pile wood to dry for burning and to fashion into rude tools to dig and scrape with. But he was concerned about what Echo might have discovered. This was a good time to try to talk to her; she was calm and good-natured after feeding.

He sat on the earth floor beside her and began slowly. "Echo?"

She shook her head and would not look at him. Sometimes she was shy about contact; sometimes she seemed only to be teasingly coy, but of course she was incapable of such an attitude.

"Echo?" He kept repeating her name until she did look at him, her bright gray eyes staring into his face, her gaze now locked to his.

"Broke dirt. Do you remember? Broke dirt. Dirt broken. Do you remember?"

Yes, she remembered. She never forgot anything. But getting her to speak of one specific subject in the past was difficult because she knew no past. Everything was immediate.

"Broke dirt," he said again and, for a wonder, she repeated the phrase— three times in a row.

"What for, broke dirt?"

She repeated this phrase too for a while and then interrupted the loop. "Go. Go broke dirt."

"Where is it?"

This question would make no sense to her and he regretted asking it. Sometimes when words made no sense, she would fall into a spooky silence and sit unspeaking, unmoving, for hours.

He had found out, though, that something had spoken in her mind, or to it, saying that the three of them must travel to Broken Dirt, wherever and whatever that was. He waited and then said, "Draw?"

She nodded, solemn-faced.

"Let's go to the drawing sand," he said and when she nodded again, he crawled over to a space toward the cave mouth where the light was brighter. Moms took Echo's hand and they joined him and Moms sat beside Echo, to be near and reassure her.

This space was a circle about four feet in diameter. Vern had cleared away the pebbles and smoothed the floor and brought fine sand from the bottom of the stream and poured it and spread it out. This was where they wrote and drew and Moms taught Vern mathematics and geometry and a little geography. Here too Echo and Vern drew the pictures that came into Echo's mind. Echo had many words in her head, but she could not order them into concepts;

she could not abstract. Her world was made up of separate, individual things that could be, and sometimes had to be, placed in rote positions. She had no categories to put things into. Queenie did not belong to the family of dogs; she belonged to the family of Queenie and there were no other members. For all the masses of words heaped in her capacious, seemingly unlimited memory, Echo could not know what a *word* was.

It made everything extremely difficult, for she was their best detector of the Olders. She could hear sounds as acutely as Queenie, perhaps, and she could see even better, for the dog was less receptive to color. As for odors, there Queenie had it all over the girl. Queenie was particularly sensitive to the Old Ones' smell and if it became too strong she was uncontrollable, yelping and howling and snapping. She might bite even Vern in her terror.

"Let's draw how dirt is broken," Vern said. "Show me how." He took up the curved stick lying by the sand circle and held it in his right hand. It was a slightly arced, two-foot length of a sapling maple branch he had trimmed and sharpened.

It took some time before Echo would touch him, but at last she laid her small, porcelain-like hand on the back of his wrist and with slight but not ten-tative movements began to guide. The marks she directed Vern to make were incomprehensible, but he had learned to wait for the process to conclude. First a mark here by her knee, then one over there so that he had to lean to make it and then one to the left almost out of the circle... Vern could not draw things in that way himself and he was always surprised when the marks joined together to form an image.

This time the picture would be of Broken Dirt, whatever that might be, but when Echo took her hand from his wrist and snuggled her face into Moms' shoulder, he thought that she must not have finished the picture and had given up. He had been struck by this fear before, that Echo was only making random scratches. She never closed her eyes to concentrate. It was as if she saw an image already in the sand and was merely tracing it out. So he leaned close and studied.

It was not a picture of an animal or a person or of one of the Olders. Echo could not have drawn one of the latter without crying out in terror and retreat-ing into herself for a long time. It was no machine that Vern could puzzle out; the lines were too far apart. Maybe it was some building or monument the Olders had constructed, or that they were constructing now. They were always busy, always remaking the world around them into something it should not be, something that made Vern queasy when he saw it. Echo's picture was of nothing that plied through the sky like the monstrous flying machines that whispered back and forth in the upper air on unguessable errands.

Maybe it was something in the stream. There was a wavy line between two sets of straight-line segments that were joined. There were squiggly circles and lines disposed about the line-segments. He peered more closely at the wavy line between the segment sets; it was broken in two places with small empty spaces.

Echo was watching him look, her face expressionless. When he pointed at one of the broken places and asked, "Is it a waggly?" she buried her face in Moms' shoulder. Then she looked out again to watch him examine it.

So, whatever, the hiatus indicated, it was not something that flapped or waved or fluttered in the breeze. Those irregular movements fascinated Echo; they were to her the salient parts of any landscape.

"Is it a too-bright?"

Echo rocked back and forth, excited, but she did not smile.

A too-bright would be something that flashed or glittered or glimmered. There were two of them, so it probably wouldn't be something that emitted a steady shine as an artificial light would probably do. What things in nature flashed or flickered intermittently?

Well, it was a stream, of course, or a river. When the three of them went to bathe in the stream in the warm summer, the thing that captured Echo's attention most firmly was the way the sunlight reflected off the wavelets. She was transfixed, watching these changing lights as fixedly as if she were trying to decipher a code.

So then, if the wavy line were a stream, the surrounding segments would represent the banks. The squiggly circles and other lines would represent bushes and grasses.

Except that Echo could not "represent" with abstract symbols. She always guided Vern's hand to draw, as closely as the sand-medium would allow, the exact lineaments of the thing to be seen. So his interpretation must be wrong and these disjointed marks composed a realistic picture of something he could not recognize.

Or—

Or maybe it was a true-to-life drawing of the picture that was in her mind. Maybe it had come to her just as it was laid out here in the sand, a schematic diagram of a place. In that case, it must have been sent to her as a message—and not from the Olders or any of their slaves. Their aura about it would ravage his sister. She would crouch with her face to the cave wall, clutching her knees and wailing.

He looked at her, safe in Moms' arms, watching him. She was not frightened. The message had come from something or someone else other than they knew, an entity that had searched to find a receptive mind and had encountered Echo. This was not the first of her extrasensory episodes. Such experiences had been re-marked as fairly widespread among autistics, even before the advent of the Olders had heightened, in greater and less degree, according to individuals, those powers among humans. Some person, or group of persons, was trying to make contact, either with Echo alone or with the whole family by means of Echo.

He examined the drawing again. Was he looking at a map? Did these scattered lines represent a specific place? He could not ask. "Place" would mean nothing to Echo. If she arrived at the location suggested by her drawing, she almost certainly would not be able to recognize it. It would be too detailed and, to her, would bear no resemblance to the lines in the sand.

Well then, supposing that this telepathic being, whatever it might be, really had transmitted a map to Echo's mind, and, supposing that Vern had interpret-ed the hiatuses in the wavy line correctly, how would the sender have known to include a representation of a "too-bright" in the scheme? The telepath would have to know her mind thoroughly, understanding the way Echo experienced things and reacted to them. But that would not be possible without her knowl-edge and if she had felt someone rummaging through her mind-pictures, her fear and trembling would alert her mother and brother.

If, however, the telepath understood the *kind* of mind it had touched, it would not need intimate knowledge of its contact. If she or he or it recognized autism and had had previous commerce with autistic personalities, it would know how to contact them and how to communicate information without distressing that person. Echo had been disturbed; she had murmured in her sleep, reacting to the encounter, but she had not been distressed. The telepath was not immediately threatening… But the further intentions might not be benevolent.

Now, supposing that his first two notions were not groundless, the situation would be that some being had made purposeful contact with the family, or at least with Echo, and had transmitted a map, though one with limited geo-graphical information. Perhaps it had transmitted only as much as it estimated that Echo could receive and pass on.

Why had it done so? Did it desire that the family travel to the mapped place?

He passed his hand above the sand drawing and looked at Echo, into her unwavering stare, and asked, "Go here?"

For a long time she did not respond and when she did, it was only to sing one of her songs. "All night all night all night…"

"Queenie, play with Echo," Vern said, and the big black dog rose and came to his sister and nuzzled her elbow and suffered herself to be petted. This was one way to break Echo's verbal cycles, but it did not always work.

She had retreated from his question, Vern realized, because *here* meant to her not the place the diagram represented but the sand itself. Echo did not want to go sit in the circle and destroy her drawing; she was always proud when she had guided Vern to draw a picture that was in her head.

She would never be able to say, "Yes, let us travel to the place we have drawn the map of. Something wants us to be there and it is important." Those wishful sentences Vern furnished for himself in his anxiety to comprehend, and this fancy was a signal of his frustrated impatience.

There might be other explanations for the contact. Vern knew that others had retreated to these caves to escape the onslaught of the Olders. In their small university town, most people had been killed with dreadful weapons or left to the mercies of the slave-organisms called shoggoths that had no notion of what mercy might be, and so killed lingeringly, as if taking enjoyment from the spectacle and music of the final agonies. A number of persons had been taken away to the colossal laboratory structures the Olders had reared and there they were divested of the knowledge the dire creatures judged might be useful to their purposes—whatever those might be.

Among those who had managed to flee and hide in the caves that had once sheltered the abused Cherokee people, there might be another autistic with some of the extrasensory powers that Echo possessed.

The question would still remain, however. Why should such a person transmit a map? Whoever sent it had sent an invitation. Or a summons.

They were as well prepared as they could be to leave the cave and journey. Moms and Vern had made a list and gathered the accessories necessary for travel. "Someday," she had said, "the Old Ones will come into our territory. They are always expanding their reach, tearing down our world and rebuilding it to suit them, remaking it in their own image. So we must gather supplies and put them away in the cave and be prepared. *I heard once long ago* that it is best always to Be Prepared."

So they had scavenged for twine and for whatever other binding materials they could find, for cloth of any kind that might warm, shelter, and hide them, and for any handy pieces of metal that could be beaten into useful shape or sharpened to an edge. There was no way to preserve foodstuffs, so Vern had laid several fish traps in the stream below the waterfall. An early autumn rain had washed away two of them, but there were three left, though only one now contained a trout.

We have enough to travel a short way if we must, he thought. He thought too about how people used to discard all sorts of good things, now useful for the family. That time was a world ago and the kind of time it had existed within could never return.

But if they were to travel, answering that summons, where would they go?

He looked at the drawing again. The line segments crowded near the wavy line upon its left-hand side, but on the other side they were set farther away. So if the wavy line was indeed a stream that sparkled intermittently, the right bank was farther from its center. Or maybe that was just the angle of vision. If the right bank only appeared to be farther, it would mean that the stream was deep in a ravine and the map showed it from the right-hand side. The stream they lived beneath ran to the south and as it rolled down the mountainside, it had cut, over the millennia, deep declivities. Vern thought that if they decided to answer the summons, they should follow the stream, descending the mountain until they found a place that fit the map.

He sighed. It was all very chancy, but this was the best interpretation he could come up with. He would talk it over with Moms in the evening. Now he would go to his daily chores, gathering food and fuel where he could and collecting any shard or scrap or leaf or root that might help to keep them alive. Then this evening they would hold council and decide.

This was the best part of the day for them, although Echo, if she were overtired in the evening, would be fretful for a tedious time before settling to nestle in Moms' lap. Vern and Moms were by this hour good-tired, the cessation of the long, active day pleasant after their labors were accomplished. This was the hour they talked, making plans and sometimes recalling the good things they had stored in memory.

During this time they would also debate courses of action and this evening Vern had asked Moms whether it would be wise to try to find the place Echo had depicted.

"You say it is an invitation or a summons from someone or some people we cannot know," Moms said.

"That's how I make it out."

"She is not in a state. She is not frightened by this…message."

They watched Echo. She had gone back to the circle and was playing with the sand, pouring the grains into one hand and then into the other and letting them spill through her fingers. Over and over she did this, over and over, while crooning a wordless song.

"That is one reason I think I should try to find it."

"You?" Moms asked. "That cannot be. It would have to be the three of us together."

"I could go find it and, if I can figure out what is going on and see whether it's safe, then I could take us there."

"But if you did not come back, Echo and I would perish."

"If we all go, we all might die."

"That would be better." Her eyes moistened and she turned her head away. Vern heard her taking deep breaths to calm her emotions.

"It would be hard traveling with three. Faster for me to go and come back and go again."

"But you can't be sure you have found the right place unless Echo is with you. She will know the place when she arrives there."

"She might not."

"Whoever is sending the message now will tell her when she has arrived."

"What if it is some plan of the Olders to draw humans out?"

"You have already rejected that idea or you would not even consider going. And if there was any slight hint of the Old Ones about it, Echo would smell them out. She is more sensitive to them than we are."

"Could they not find a way to disguise their presence?"

"I don't think so. I can't pretend to understand their psychology; I don't know that such a concept can even apply to them. But when I try to translate their 'attitude,' if I can call it that, to our terms, I would describe it as *contemptuous* in regard to humans. They probably hold us in less esteem than those amoebean slaves they created, those shoggoths. They think themselves invincible on our planet and maybe within the whole cosmos, as I heard once long ago. They would not think of hiding or disguising their presences. They do not confer upon us the dignity of being considered their opponents. We are, at most, mere nuisances."

"Yes." Vern let the image of the star-headed monstrosity slip into his mind and then imagined its disappearance before it could bring up his emotional temperature. But their handiwork, all those immense towers and cyclopean, steeply sloped pyramids with ridged ramps, all that bewildering hyper-geometry of almost unvisualizable angles—these images and many others he allowed to register in his mind. They would not attract the attention of a probe, for they were only pictures of things that existed and any animal might be gazing upon them. "Yes," he said, "we are only minor pests to them. But we know that they have enemies much more powerful than we are. They have battled Cthulhu and triumphed and were defeated and then triumphed again. This is something I heard once long ago. It may be that this call—this invitation or summons—is intended to entrap an enemy more dangerous than humans."

"But in that case the call would be cast in terms utterly alien to us. I do not think Echo could even react to it."

Again Vern looked at his sister. The world outside had darkened as the hour deepened and the sound of the curtaining waterfall seemed to grow louder. Echo, with her silvery long hair and porcelain-pale skin almost glowed ghostlike in the dim cave. She had stopped pouring sand and was gathering it into little mounds spaced out evenly from one another. After mounding a fifth small pile, she stopped and sat up cross-legged with her hands in her lap, looking toward the cave mouth.

"Well, what do you think we should do?" Vern asked.

"It is time to go to sleep. Maybe you'd like to scout around outside a little. Maybe when Echo goes to sleep tonight, she will receive another message and maybe it will be clearer than this map diagram she drew."

Moms' suggestion was what Vern had expected. He supposed that prudence was probably their best policy, but he was apprehensive. Someone or something knew of their existence. They went on with their hardscrabble daily lives as if the Olders did not know about them, keeping as closely as possible to narrowly settled routines, to behavior that did not arouse their feelings or require unusual degrees of mental activity. Quietude was their only camouflage. If they had to journey, the stress of traveling with Echo might rouse attention, but if pursuers were closing in, there would be no choice but to travel.

It was dark here; the detestable five-pointed orange moon was not in the sky—and he was grateful for that. Skirting around the waterfall by a familiar but barely traceable pathway over the rocks, Vern walked a little way down the stream edge. Then he stopped and breathed in the night air that was growing ever colder with the season. He shivered. The scraps of canvas and plastic and cloth Moms had spliced into a motley robelike garment was draughty, to say the least. He hugged his chest.

And then he thought he heard a sound different from the customary night noises. A thin, high yelping far, far away. Perhaps the Olders had introduced an animal new to this forest, some strain of wolf, or an animal of their own engineering.

Then he heard it no more and decided that his imagination was overly exercised and he turned and headed back to the cave where Echo and Moms would be ready for sleep by now.

Despite his apprehensions, Vern was sleepy. Although his day had been physically a little less active than usual, anxiety had depleted his mental energy. He lay for a few minutes, listening. He could tell that Moms was not asleep; she was surely thinking through their discussion. Echo was asleep in her own way, though sometimes Vern wondered if she ever actually slept, the way that he and Moms and Queenie did—as Queenie was doing now, her large head laid on her large paws.

Almost as soon as he closed his eyes, he began to dream. His viewing floated like an invisible balloon, bodiless, and traversed one of the Olders' cities, if that was what they were to be called. He envisioned entering underground through a huge doorless opening. If he were making this journey in his body, his every nerve would be pulsing with fear as he passed tremendous pentagonal pools of unknown, black liquids and drifted through rooms filled with curious and inexplicable utensils of myriad sorts. Then there were colossal caverns filled with intricate machines whose purposes he could not guess. They were all motionless until he came to one larger than the rest. It was so large that the top of it must have extended through the cavern roof into the outside world. It seemed to buckle inward and outward continuously, the matte gray planes of its panels opening and closing simultaneously, as if it were a strange doorway allowing both entrance and exit in the same vertiginous movement. This machine uttered a high-pitched piping sound and it seemed to Vern that the noise was like the sound of the faraway yelping or baying he had thought he heard outside by the stream.

Then he woke.

Queenie was awake too, making her dangerous, nearly inaudible growl. And Echo was awake and Moms was sitting up straight, her eyes wide and glistening in the dark. The three of them listened to that piping; it was still far away, still small among the sounds of the waterfall and of the forest at night, but it was dreadfully intelligible:

"Tekeli-li Tekeli-li."

2.

"Ship?"

"Yes, Captain."

"Are all things well?"

"Very well. The mission is proceeding according to procedure."

"That is good," I said and truly I felt a happy relief in my organism. "Am I sober enough to take command?"

"You are not entirely cleansed of deepsleep narcosis," Ship said, "but you are rational and your body is highly operable, though it needs exercise, as do the bodies of the other crew members."

"Please find if they are well and sober," I said. "Doctor, Navigator, Seeker—how do they fare?"

"They fare well… No. Disregard. Fare well is a phrase suitable for departures. The crew fare good. They are beginning to awake."

"I will address them when all is sober."

"The correct would be, When all are sober," said Ship.

"Are you certain?"

"Eighty-four point oh-two certain."

"Our mission dialect is difficult," I said.

"The English is," Ship said. "There are other planetary languages more difficult; there are others less so. Part of the problem is that we have taken our knowledge of these languages from what remained of the libraries of relic spaceships. The electronic was primitive and much has been lost to age-deterioration and other damage."

"But we must persevere," I replied, "for if our mission performance is well, we must be ready to converse."

"All the crew have been instructed during normal sleep periods and also during deepsleep, but that is not the same as speaking. We all must practice."

"I will write my account in English," I said. "That will be strong practice."

"We salute your pluck," Ship said, speaking for the Alliance, I presumed.

While Ship was waking the rest of the crew, I undertook the prescribed medicines and waters and endured the exercises. During the stretches and lunges, I reviewed the tasks that awaited. The Starheads had taken over the planet third from the sun to use as a base for offensive strikes and architectural experiment. As usual, they had almost eradicated the dominant intelligent species and there remained only scattered Remnants that were like my siblings and myself. Our own home had been destroyed and the four members left of my family had been rescued by a small party of scientists who were members of the Radiance Alliance, the ancient foes of the Starheads. The Alliance are a highly advanced race (in our local mission world they were called the Great Ones) and they have thought it desirable to try to preserve all the different species of life that they could rescue. The Starheads (locally known as the Old Ones) regard every other species of intelligent beings but themselves as enemies, active or potential. For this reason, they kill all. But if any can be saved from slaughter, the Great Ones strive to that end and send out disguised spying machines where the Starheads are active to find if some few survivors escaped their attentions. Traces of Remnants had been detected here and Ship and crew had been dispatched.

So here we were. Our task was to find and rescue as many fugitives from the Old Ones as possible.

It was no easy job and to accomplish it, we had only the four of us and Ship. We were not in direct contact with the Alliance for fear that the Starheads might trace signals back to our base and thereupon wreak destruction.

I desisted from my exercises and greeted my shipmates as they left their cubes and entered the control room one by one.

First there came my younger brother whom Ship had designated navigator and now we used this English instead of his actual name. It is best to call him Navigator in this narrative in case information might be gleaned from his own name. Though he is younger than I, he is more muscled and usually bests me in the pan-agon arena where we exercise martially. Still, I have been designated Captain and he must receive my orders, which he does mostly patiently and sometimes not. His duty is to cooperate with Ship to keep knowledgeable of our spatial locations, of the happenstances in our space environment, and to locate and trace the movements upon the planetary surface of any Remnants we might contact.

My sister, who is only slightly younger than myself, Ship names Doctor because it is her duty to tend the health of us three others. She monitors not only illness but also signs of emotional disturbance and of sudden, untoward changes in our mental states. She must keep watch that the thought-probes of Starheads do not disrupt our minds or displace them completely to make us to be crawlers and droolers, bereft of rationality, trying to do away with ourselves and with one another. She is always glancing at graph-screens and listening to corporal rhythms that Ship relays to her about our bodies.

My youngest sister we call Seeker, a name not so pretty by far as her own true name. I should not write so here perhaps, but she is my favorite person in the cosmos and also she is the favorite of all the crew. Whereas Navigator and Doctor are largish of corpus and darkly haired and complected, Seeker is as white as a gleaming mineral and her skin seems to glow, almost. Her eyes are green but become violet-like of color when she makes mind contact with others. Her hair is silver silk. All female telepaths belong to this physical type, Ship says, or at least the hominids do, though I believe none others universally can be so pretty as Seeker.

Her duty is the most demanding, for she must make mind contact with a Remnant group and persuade it to come to a place within the planet where we can guide them and let them know we are not perilous and mean them no injury and that we are all trying to escape and hide from the Old Ones now and maybe in time to come grow strong and do them grievous hurt so that the cosmos will not be only Starheads and their slaves and nothing else that thinks and feels.

Here now they stood before me, the three, still a little wrinkled in spirit from deepsleep and slightly confused. But they answered cheeringly when I spoke to each and congratulated on wakefulness. "Do we all know what is to come?" I asked.

They said Yes.

Then Ship directed us to the small mess hall and we partook solid food instead of venous alongside some happy water and were much refreshed.

Then we returned to control and set up our routines.

Millions and millions of light years we had traveled, Ship had informed Navigator. Our vessel, disguised as a comparatively leisurely meteor had skated across the orbit of the fourth planet and soon would pass the single moon of the third planet.

Navigator suggested that we call this third planet Terra, a word from an ancient and long-deceased speech known as Latin. "We cannot very well call it Earth," he said. "All home planets are Earths. Confusion must ensue."

"Terra is sound," I said. "Soon we shall be in its farther gravitation and perhaps Seeker can begin to search for whispers or traces of hominid Remnant mentation."

"I shall begin when our approach is closer," she said. "It would require powerful amplification of telepathic signal to scan the surface from here. Amplification of such magnitude the Starheads would notice."

"Now that we are in the Terran sun-system, let us call them Old Ones," I said. "We do not wish to confuse the Remnant group when we make contact."

"Very well, Captain," she said. She wore a pretty smile when she said that. I thought how it was or seemed unright that she, the smallest and most delicate of the crew, must perform the most difficult duties and engage the greatest risks. After all the millions of light years we had traversed through underspace, Seeker must calibrate her last tasks in terms of English yards, feet, inches and fractions of inches. It is a little like, I thought, leaping from an immensely tall tower and coming to rest lightly upon a grain of sand. While she was doing so, distractions would be taking place violently.

If any of us others could have done it for her, we would so, but we lacked the telepathic talents that are hers. We each possessed rudimentary telepathic ability, as Ship says that almost every intelligence must own, and Ship is able to link us tenuously with Seeker when necessary, but each faint contact is not voluptuously profitable. None could take Seeker's place, but we would be aiding in all possible ways, and eagerly too.

I read through the long list of protocols and drills that Ship inscribed on my screens and during the next eight waking periods, I went through them with the crew until it would no longer help to do so.

Thereafter we rested and played games among us, though Seeker and Ship kept alert.

Then on the next watch, Seeker reported that she detected mental activity nothing like that of the Old Ones. It was a small group hiding away, she said, three or four of them. Of three she was certain, but the fourth was unclear.

One of the three was a telepath, sending strange, nearly random signaling, though of course not directed at Seeker. "This telepath is un-normal of mind," she said. She wrinkled her brow as she bent to her screens and scopes and auditories. Her console and all its instruments were nervily active, blinking and trilling, and her hands fluttered over them like white ribbons wafting in strong air convection.

"Is the Terran telepath deranged?" I asked.

"I do not know," Seeker said, and Doctor said, "Not exactly deranged." She was busy at her instruments also. Her console was collecting medical information from Seeker's instruments and filtering for Doctor.

"What then?" I asked

She hesitated then said, "I believe the Terran term is *autistic.*"

"Autistic?" I said.

She paused again, listening, and then repeated what Ship told her screen: *"Autistic* defines a mental condition or disposition lacking ability to generalize and to form conclusions aiding useful or even necessary actions. It is marked by a profound, imprisoning subjectivity. Many autistic individuals possess rudimentary telepathic capacities; some of them are well advanced in the talent."

"Profound, imprisoning subjectivity sounds like derangement," I said. "Is this autist able to travel distances?"

She studied for a while and then replied. "I think so, yes. But it will be difficult for her."

"The telepath is female?"

"Yes, a she."

"Being autistic, does she know she is telepathic?" I asked Seeker.

She studied. "We are too far. I cannot read. She may be mind-linked to a slave organism."

"That does not bode good," I said.

"We need to be nearer." Her face wrinkled as she concentrated and I recalled her description of the difficulties of receiving such mental fields or auras and the messaging therein. "It is like trying to feel a photon with a fingertip," she said. We marveled at that notion, Doctor and I. Navigator only shook his head impatiently. I think that he is sometimes a little envious of Seeker's abilities. It is good he keeps good temper, for if we quarreled and made spats, our concentration would suffer harm.

In the ruins of the old spaceship libraries there were many descriptions of Terra's moon. The scientific accounts put its orbital revolution at 27⅓ days at a distance of 384,403 kilometers from the planet. Its bright albedo was remarked and attributed to its surface of glassy crystalline soil. There was a great amount of similar minutiae, important to Terrans because a moon base was in process of construction when the Old Ones came again. This satellite inspired poets to write of it incessantly, often in terms not faithful to astronomical fact. They frequently spoke of it in terms of silver, as "striding the night in silver shoon" or "gifting its silver smile to the still waters."

If there were any poets upon the planet still composing, they spoke no more of a "silver orb." The Old Ones had sculpted the satellite into a five-pointed construction, angry red-orange in color, mottled with pyramidal protrusions disposed in groups of five, a geometry vaguely suggesting the shapes of the crania of the Old Ones. The rubble from this immense project was still falling upon Terra in shower after shower of meteors and meteorites. This was one reason Ship was cloaked in the guise of a meteor. So many of such bodies were striking Terran atmosphere, it had been thought that we might be undistinguished amid the number of them.

On such frail hopes and forlorn details our enterprise depended.

I could not always keep my apprehensions at bay. The four of us, with no useful experience to rely on, dropping through its sun-system to an obscure planet, no more than a speck on the outer shoals of this galaxy, our vessel disguised and ridged and pocked as if by collisions, a mote thousands of times smaller than the watery world toward which we drifted… What madness had come upon the Great Ones to entrust us with so important a mission?

Then it came to me that our ignorance and inexperience were the factors that had determined the choice. We were a more expendable crew than most of the other search teams. Those who had survived encounters and rescued Remnant groups would be sent to more prominent fronts to undertake larger and more urgent missions. Our little family was dispatched to an odd little corner of the conflict. If the Old Ones exterminated us, the loss would be relatively unimportant—unless we let slip, through carelessness or under stress, information that might help tease out the locations of important Alliance posts.

Dreadful but necessary measures had been installed to prevent that from happening.

We kept gazing at the ugly orange moon-sculpture as it filled twelve of our visiscreens. I thought that it seemed to pulse its coloration, the orange brightening and darkening at irregular intervals, but set the impression aside as an illusion born of tensed nerves.

"Navigator," I said, "how fare we?"

He glanced at his instruments and sighed. "Well enough, I think, though there are some slight anomalies I cannot account for. Distances seem to change irrespective of our velocity."

"Seeker?"

"I think the Starheads—I mean, the Old Ones—may be distressing the local space-weave," she said. "They are probably constructing some of those colossal engines we were taught about. The energies exchanged are so enormous they may twist space-time here."

Navigator said this might account for his observations.

Then Seeker asked us to fall quiet. "I may be feeling something," she said. "Silence will help me to concentrate. I am picking up fearful emotions. At least, I think perhaps."

"The crew will silence," I said.

Seeker had spoken before of the fear the fugitives on Terra must be enduring and I understood that these would be stark and continuous, but I wondered how they would feel if they knew the extent of the Old Ones' desecrations. Worlds on worlds, across all the cosmos, were crumbled to rubble or blown away to radioactive cloud, millions of nations, tribes, and civilizations were mangled to bloody ruin, the grandest achievements of art, science, religion, and philosophy had gone dark like lights turned off on a space cruiser.

The Terrans had known something of the Old Ones before this time. They had learned, but they had forgotten—almost purposefully, it seemed. In one of the relic spaceship libraries was a long document concerning something called Miskatonic Expedition 1935. This exploration project had discovered in land-mass Australia "certain traces" the Old Ones had left "in rocks even then laid down a thousand million years…laid down before the true life of [Terra] had existed at all." The Terrans, according to this history, knew about the struggles of the Old Ones against the "spawn" of Cthulhu and the abominable Mi-Go and about some of the interstellar subjugations and massacres. These things they knew, but when the ancient evils rose again from the sea or "seeped down" from the stars, they were not prepared.

Their lack of realization had been pointedly described by their best historian of Cthulhu and the Old Ones and Great Ones. He spoke candidly of their failure, imputing it to "the inability of the human mind to correlate all its contents." He drew a dark, disheartening view of his species: "We live on a placid island of ignorance in a black sea of infinity, and it was not meant that we should voyage far."

They had not voyaged far, but black infinity had come upon them, and few were left and those scattered few must endure miserable, terror-filled days and nights. These Terrans probably would not be counted among the greatest of races in the cosmos; they were not the widest thinkers or most accomplished builders or the most generous of spirit. Yet they had achieved things fine in their way, however modest. Their erasure would be a waste, pathetic if not tragic. They had struggled against the Old Ones, this planet full of nations. Now we four individuals must struggle against the same implacable force.

I ordered myself not to allow this mood of thought to dominate my spirit.

After the next sleep period, Seeker told us that she had located geographically the Terran telepath and her group. It was a family of four, including the mysterious ancillary member whose thoughts Seeker could partially read but only sometimes. "She too is a female, this other one, and, like the telepath, she has extremely limited language skills, so that it is difficult to understand her thought patterns. She mostly thinks without words and possesses sensory organs different from those of her companions. She may belong to a different species."

"Yet you say she is not enslaved," I said.

"It is an arrangement we do not have ourselves," she said.

"Does she see herself as part of the group?"

"Yes. But I need more information."

"We will now orbit-out three locator flyers," I said. "They will triangulate the source-point of the telepathic signals, just as we rehearsed."

Ship gave a slight lurch, having dispatched the flyers as I was speaking. Each flyer contained amplifiers to reinforce the signals from Terra. They transmitted simultaneously pictures of the planetscape to the ship screens and to Seeker's mind. If all performed according to scheme, we would have pictures of the close environs of the Remnant family in eight hours or fewer.

But it was a tiring interlude for Seeker. I watched her at work, her neck and shoulders tense in concentration. I could see the muscles strain as she bent to her console. Her lightweight, white robe emphasized her taut slenderness and she frowned and smiled alternately, as the signal strengthened or faded. I could almost read Seeker's mind as she seined through the blasts of data she intook, making innumerable decisions almost instantaneously.

Doctor too was concentrating. Her mechanisms were now principally focused upon Seeker, monitoring her physical conditions to the finest detail. If something touched Seeker's mind, the event would show on Doctor's screens and she would decide whether Ship must go dark, maybe forever.

Navigator was occupied with directing the flyers, maneuvering them within the Terran atmosphere in accordance with the directionals of the Remnants' telepath.

All this went on for long and long.

"The signals are stronger now," Seeker said. Her voice was a musical whisper that floated above the steady mechanical humming of the control room. "I have a closely approximate placement. They are in a wilderness terrain. The locator flyers send pictures of the area. Can Navigator direct a beacon landing near?"

He considered for a time. "Yes," he said, and described briefly the landscape at large, with particular emphasis upon a river in its midst and a high bluff that hung above its lower stretches. "But we must be secret and exquisite of touch. The plateau there is close upon a place where the Old Ones are laboring. I cannot make out exactly what they are constructing, but their presence will be strong there and the beacon cannot be placed any farther downstream. Even so, that plateau is the best choice."

"Have the flyers recorded pictures Seeker can send?"

"Yes," he said.

"Seeker?" I asked.

"Have forbearance," she said. "Contact is complex."

"The Old Ones are close upon them," I said. "There is a concern of time."

"Have forbearance."

Then in another while she said she was contacting and the rest of us could not help directing much attention, though we did not neglect our urgent duties. How could we not watch our most precious sister when she must undergo the rigors of contact with an alien species? The mind-frames of otherworlders are so different from ours that sometimes they can tatter the rationality of both telepathic parties. The Great Ones had described Terrans as being much like ourselves, but complete likeness was not possible and the margin of unlikeness, the forceful tension of sheer otherness, would cause a fearful strain on the mind-spirit of Seeker and perhaps a worse consequence. She once said it was like plunging down and down into a boiling sea within which unknown creatures drifted and darted, their shapes and size ungraspable until after long acquaintance. If the Terran telepath was indeed deranged, there was a possibility that her condition would infect Seeker's mind.

I believed I could not do the thing my sister was doing, even if I possessed her abilities. One must be strong of selfhood and sometimes that is insufficient. According to Alliance records, a number of telepaths have been contacted by Starhead minds. Those pale individuals lived out the rest of their days in the state that the English call catatonia, though the term falls short. In catatonia the mind is inoperable, but with Old Ones' telepathic damage, the mind no longer exists. Some other, indescribable mode of unconsciousness supplants it.

"I am receiving more strongly," Seeker said. "Is it nighttime where the signal emits? I think she may be sleeping. Some send stronger when they sleep, in particular if they are un-normal. Sleeping, they are less distracted."

"It is nighttime at the emission point," Navigator said.

"What does she signal?" I asked.

"She sends large smells of an animal friendly to her. It is not a slave organism, as we feared. It is a parasite or symbiote in complex and close relationship. I do not comprehend. Her name for it is a queenie. I think that must mean companion or helpmeet."

"May it be telepathic, this animal? Is it of normal mind?"

Seeker said nothing for long and then made a hand gesture of disappointment. "I cannot know," she said. "But the autist is calmly receptive while sleeping. As soon as we find a beacon place, I can tell her where."

"This Remnant group is safe from the Old Ones for the moment?"

Now she became more and more intent, enmeshed with Ship so closely in the mind-contact it was as if she were wearing the network of amplifiers and transceivers as a robe wrapped around her thinking. "Somewhere there is something perilous," she said. Her expression was darkening. "I cannot say what as of yet."

"Perhaps—" I began to say.

"Seeker, withdraw!" Doctor said.

Her face grew even more white and her eyelids fluttered. She thrashed her hands against her upper arms.

"Seeker, withdraw now!" Doctor said.

Her voice was high and thin and shrill when she said the words the autist on Terra must have been hearing. *"Tekeli-li."*

"Seeker!" cried Doctor and cried we all as well.

3.

Vern was fairly pleased with the progress they had made today. His rough estimate was that he had brought Moms and Echo about a kilometer and a half along the streamside before evening came into the woods and visibility was hindered and the first faint pipings—*Tekeli-li*—were heard from the west. Now it was time to find shelter, the best hiding place they could discover.

They were following the stream as it ran south down the mountainside. The decline was steep enough that it kept a fairly straight course, though it curled around the bases of some of the prominent peaks and widened out in some of the more level hollers. He had reasoned that if the picture Echo had guided him to draw were indeed a ravine with a stream at the bottom, that water would almost necessarily be the same under which their cave was located and, if that were the case, it would be to the south where the force of its falling would have carved deeply between the hills.

That was a big *if* and Vern trusted his reasoning less than Moms did. She had more faith in him than he had in himself. Or perhaps she only pretended to, bolstering his confidence.

In any case, they must find a place to eat and sleep and to try to hide. Tonight was not as cold as last night and they would be warmer if they went into the woods a little way from the cold stream. He wanted to get some distance from the sound of the water too, so that they might better hear anything moving through the forest.

That thin shrilling, the nerve-wracking piping of the shoggoths, had not come closer and Vern estimated that the group of them must be at least two kilometers away. The dreadful sound carried far, especially at night in these otherwise silent mountains. But the sound was close enough to cause Echo fearful distress.

He did not know if she had ever seen one of the creatures. Probably she had not, for the sound of their shrilling would recall their image and that would send her into paroxysms. He had seen them only once, two of them, as they fell upon a deer and did not devour so much as absorb it. Shapeless or nearly shapeless they were, composed of a viscous jelly which looked like an agglutination of bubbles, and these would be about fifteen feet in diameter when spherical. Yet they had a constantly shifting shape and volume, throwing out temporary developments—arms, pseudopods, tentacles—and forming, deforming and reforming organs of sight and speech. *Tekeli-li* was the word, as nearly as Vern could approximate the sound with human phonemes, that they spoke to one another almost continuously, though the slight variations in pitch and timbre he was able to perceive suggests that this one utterance was capable of a plenitude of meanings. That word had been recorded by the old historians of the nineteenth and twentieth centuries.

He had been stalking the same deer himself, a young doe that had not learned caution, and had been so horrified when the monsters burst out of the foliage upon their prey, that he swooned away for a few moments. That was a piece of good luck. If he had cried out, they would have made an end of him.

They would have ended the lives of Moms and Echo too—and of Queenie, for there was an intense detestation of those creatures for dogs and of dogs for them. Shoggoths, as the humans supposed, communicated telepathically with the Old Ones their masters and the presence of Vern in that glade where the doe was ingested, or rather, digested, would have been made known. Then the Old Ones would come to search this part of the forest and they would unfailingly find Echo, though they might not comprehend the origin of her kind of mind-pictures.

Echo had tired of walking and clambering over the rocks and Vern and Moms had taken turns carrying her for the past hour or so. She was in Moms' arms now and, as the four of them came to the edge of a large streamside boulder, Vern signaled for Moms and Echo to stay behind, while he searched for a suitable place to last out the night.

They had arrived at a fairly level place on the mountainside. The stream widened out here and was less voluble over its stones. If he could find a spot forty or so yards from its edge, they ought to be able to hear forest sounds clearly and to distinguish those that signaled danger. A cave would be ideal, but this place could offer nothing like that.

There was a dense laurel thicket bordering a ferny glade and when he skirted it, he found a small opening. Echo would be frightened to crawl into this little tunnel in the foliage, but she would not be terror-stricken. He explored it for about fifteen yards and then could go no farther, the tightly meshed branches and twigs forming a prickly wall. Cozy, Vern thought. He realized that it had sheltered an animal not long ago, perhaps a fawn or maybe one of the black bears common in these hills. It would be a good place. Maybe they could even chance a tiny fire.

But when he brought the family inside this den, he decided against the fire. The smoke might not easily be visible at night, but they would have to crowd closely to the flame and Echo would be so transfixed by the sight of it that she might not be able to communicate. Flashing water, trembling fronds, twinkling lights—these sent her into a trancelike state, so fixedly that she could concentrate on nothing else.

So Vern and Moms tried their best to approximate the evening routine they had clung to when they lived in the cave. He crawled out of the brambly little tunnel to "scout," while Moms primped Echo and combed her hair. Then Vern returned with a tin flask of water and Moms opened the canvas bag with the decal that read University Bookstore and brought out jerky for Vern and herself and smoked fish for Echo. Sometimes Echo's teeth were painful and she would refuse to chew the dried deer meat.

After this meal, Vern and Moms arranged leaf piles for bedding. The fallen laurel leaves were thick here but made unsatisfactory mattresses, cold and slick and noisy. Uneasy sleep was guaranteed.

Now Moms took Echo in her arms and held her closely. This was their quiet time and Vern wanted to use it to question Echo, but he could not think how to ask what they needed to know.

"What voices do you hear inside?"

She shook her head, not meeting his eyes, and Vern looked to Moms for aid.

Moms said, "I know that we need to know what to look for, the source of the call or summons to her, but I don't know how to ask, either."

"If it is a person or a group of people, we must see them before they see us," Vern said. "If we don't like the look of them, we won't make ourselves known."

"But if we approach closely, they will sense we are there. It may be that they already know we are traveling toward their signal."

"Shiny," Echo murmured. Then she turned the word into a little song. "Shiny, shy-nee, shiny, shy-nee." She was carefully not looking at Vern or Moms.

"Shiny?" Vern asked. "What is shiny, Echo?"

For a long time she only repeated the word, but at last added another. "Wall. Shiny, shy-nee wall. Shine wall."

"Go there?" Vern asked. "Are we to go to a shiny wall?"

She nodded and looked at him and smiled. The picture in her mind of this shiny wall made her happy.

"Is it a too-bright?" Moms asked. "Does it hurt Echo's eyes?"

Slowly she wagged her head No. "Wall of shy-nee," she said.

"It must be a place," Vern said. "Maybe a building."

"Yes," Moms said. "A structure of some kind. Are there any buildings positioned by a ravine that would not be built by the Old Ones?"

"I don't know," Vern said. "I had thought that all the human things in this area had been destroyed. Maybe it is not a building but a machine. If it looks like a wall to Echo, it could be a big machine."

"Only the Old Ones have large machines now."

"They would not be sending a call to Echo. If they knew where she was, we would already be killed."

"Let us suppose that it is some sort of machine made by someone other than the Old Ones. If they wanted us to come to their machine, why didn't they place it or send it close to where we were?"

"I don't know," Vern said. Then in a moment: "Maybe because if things don't work out, if something goes wrong, we could still get back to our cave and be safe there, since the Olders don't know about it. If this shiny wall was discovered by them, they would search close by and find our cave."

"Perhaps," Moms said. "Anyway, we have decided that we should answer the summons. Does the singing of the shoggoths seem to be getting closer to us? It may be that we need to find this shiny wall soon."

"As soon as we can," Vern said. "Let us try to get some rest."

He had not said "sleep" and he suspected that Moms' night was as unrestful as his own. *Tekeli-li* had sounded continuously and the shrillness came from different quarters. It seemed to be advancing upon them, but perhaps that was an illusion brought on by anxiety. Queenie did not behave as if shoggoths were closing in and Vern trusted her senses.

The morning routine matched that of the evening, except that Vern actually did scout, trying to make sure the area was free of traces of the Olders and to acquire an idea of the topography they were to travel through. He found a tall poplar with one branch low enough to give access to the upper branches and climbed easily. The months of outdoor survival had given him a wiry, purposeful musculature and a sureness of foot, hand, and eye. He was not even breathing heavily when he made it to the nearly leafless top and stood on a sturdy limb.

From here he could see the stream as it wound out of the holler, disappeared around a bend, and reappeared below, all whitewater and jumbled rock. Above the stream at that point reared a cliff, its level top a treeless, grassy sward. He decided it would be more informative to leave the streamside and climb along the ridges to that cliff. Even if it did not border the ravine shown in Echo's map, it would offer a prospect of the southern reaches, so that if they did return to streamside, he would have some notion of where they were located in the forest.

Following the ridges would be no easy task, he thought, and indeed it was not. Echo found the trail-less climb hard going; she wanted to stop often and fix her attention on ragged leaves waving in the breeze upon ragged oak limbs. Then Moms would carry her for a while, shifting her from one arm to the other. And then Vern would carry, giving to Moms the book bag containing their provisions.

Still, they went forward, halting often to rest but then pushing on. Echo was not easy to manage, with so many new sights tugging at her faculties, but Vern and Moms got accustomed to her rhythms and Queenie showed canny trail-sense, finding openings and pathways that Vern would have overlooked.

A little after midday they came to a clearing full of goldenrod and orchard grass and Joe Pye weed and there, unexpectedly close, loomed the cliff face. There was a ridge leading close to the top on the western side and Vern thought that if they followed it at the rate of speed they had been making, they would gain the plateau before nightfall.

They did make pretty good time, but Vern had been deceived by the land-folds. The ridgeline led not to the cliff plateau but wandered off farther westward and there was no way to attain the top except by scrambling down to the very bottom and climbing the perilous-looking path that zigzagged up the face. Echo would not like those heights; the cliff looked to be about 250 feet high. She might struggle violently against being taken up, but their choices were nonexistent.

The climb was, however, steeper and more toilsome than he had counted on and, though Echo did not writhe and struggle, she refused to walk and proved a heavy burden. The day began to darken toward a chilly twilight and they had gotten only about halfway up. When they halted for a rest, Vern debated with himself whether to continue climbing or to go back down and find a night place.

Then when the ancient trail doubled back upward, there opened a hole in the cliff-wall, a cave that had not been visible from below because a projecting ledge hid it from the sightline. He motioned for Moms and Echo to stay in the trail and he and Queenie went toward the opening. Queenie sniffed all around the cave mouth, but she did not seem disturbed and Vern let her enter before him. The natural thing to fear in this spot was a rattlesnake den. Some of the caves in these mountains were filled with hundreds of serpents, coiled side by side among rocks and stretched out upon ledges. But Queenie went in without barking. She came out in a few minutes and gave Vern a quizzical gaze and he followed as she reentered.

This cave was handmade, like the path that had been carved into the cliff face. The Cherokee must have maintained this place to evade the soldiers that herded their nation so murderously westward. There were many hiding places like this, cellar-like holes dug out in the woods, large cubbyholes chopped into thorny blackberry thickets. In one of the latter Vern had found a flint hatchet. Other sites yielded shards of pots.

In here, though, he found no trace of the Cherokee and the one utensil was a pewter pitcher which lay in the deep dust. Disposed around it in disorder were eight skeletons. Three of these were of children and the others, to judge by size and structure, belonged to adults of varying ages. Clothing had rotted away, but remains of shoes and boots clung to the pedal bones of the adults. Two skeletons lay with some of the upper-body bones entangled, as if that couple had died in an embrace.

It was likely that they had died so. Vern imagined that here had come a family or an enclave of refugees from one of the scattered settlements; they would have been of like faith and resolve. They had killed themselves, Vern thought, and before him in the dust lay the pewter pitcher in which they has passed round the poison. This group of intimates had found it nobler and easier to die by their own hands than to be done in coolly, methodically, and agonizingly by the Old Ones—or in disgusting, viscous horror as victims of the shoggoths.

Here was a sorrowful sight and Vern spent a long minute in dark thought. There was a recess in the back of the cave, small but with adequate room to pile these bones in, and he did so, lifting them as carefully—and as tenderly—as he knew how. He deposited them in one place, all piled together, and mounded as much dust over them as he was able to gather. It was a sad task, but not the worst he had had to perform.

He felt that he ought to say some proper words over these rueful remains, but all that came to mind was the one familiar phrase and he mumbled it as he stood above the bones and poured over them a last scraping of dust.

"Rest in peace."

Well, they had made up their minds to do that and now they rested. The task for Vern was to try to make sure they did not disturb Echo's rest. If the toothy grins and hollow eye sockets frightened her, she might shriek for minutes, then moan for hours, rocking back and forth in Moms' arms. She would not be able to communicate information about the shiny wall or anything else. He removed all the other traces he could find of the sad departed. He would warn Moms to keep Echo away from the back of the cave.

For the evening meal, they had only a little water left in the flask, barely enough to wash down their nine mouthfuls of food. It was insufficient to slake Echo's thirst and she complained, whining and twisting her torso so that her make-shift dress was in danger of falling apart. Moms finally quieted her by crooning an improvised lullaby. Queenie got only a single strip of dried meat and no water. She was growing weak.

Vern and Moms were thirsty too—and hungry. Whatever the plateau might offer tomorrow, water and food must be found. How far could it be to the shiny wall of Echo's vision? They could last only a few more hours without some replenishment. When their scanty food scraps ran out, they would share the fate of the last occupants of this cave, but in a more lingering fashion.

Unless they jumped.

Vern wondered about that misfortunate group. What had been the final straw, the situation that convinced them to effect their own ends? Might it have been the shrilling of the shoggoths, *Tekeli-li,* from the streamside below? His imagination failed in the attempt to picture those amorphous, globular ag-glutinations climbing the cliff side. Perhaps those people had heard the sound from above, from the cliff top that Vern and Moms and Echo and Queenie were trying to reach. That area looked treeless from below and those pursued would be exposed.

Best for Vern to reconnoiter the place just at daybreak. He did not know whether he could summon the strength to climb the steep trail, observe the scene, and then return and lead the others there. He would have to decide about that in the morning; maybe sleep would refresh him sufficiently.

Echo was still resting in Moms' arms. Her eyes were closed and she seemed to be listening, though Moms had left off her lullaby. Vern crept over to them and murmured "shiny wall, shiny wall," though he expected that Echo was too tired and sleepy to be able to converse.

She did respond, though, repeating Vern's phrase in his own intonation. "Shiny wall." Then she stopped and a lovely, quiet smile came to her face. To Vern, this was as surprising and delightful as a rainbow. Echo rarely smiled— almost never.

Then, before he could speak further, she fell asleep and Moms laid her down, just as she was, on the floor of the cave and stretched out to sleep beside her. Queenie slept, always with her head on her outstretched paws, and only Vern was awake.

And then he was not.

The skeletons came crawling toward them, of course, clacking their bones in this weary darkness in which their nasty, eternal grins glowed and flickered. Vern knew that he was dreaming and was not frightened. He tried to dismiss the dream so that he could sleep more soundly, but it persisted, its loathsome images and sounds ever more vivid until he woke with a start and looked instantly to see if Moms and Echo were safe.

They had not moved from where they had dropped, but their breathing was excited and irregular, and he knew that they too were dreaming, though probably not of skeletons. The three of them had gathered enough nightmare material to furnish out bad dreams for the remainders of their lives.

He lay still for a long time. Just before sunrise a wind sprang up and the mouth of the cave resounded with strange humming. Vern listened hard but could hear no whistling of shoggoths in the wind. If only this cave were near water, he thought, it would be ideal to live in.

Best not to dwell on fancies...

When the light was bright enough to make out details—the paws of Queenie protruding from beneath her nose, the porcelain-pale hands of Echo on her tatterdemalion dress—he sat up and began to move about.

It was not easy to do. His muscles were sore and his knees ached. It would be miraculous if he could get them to the top. Moms would be even more exhausted than he, so he would have to carry Echo the larger part of the way.

Yet let them rest now, he thought, as long as they are able. He rose and went out onto the cliff-side path. In the early light the stream below seemed far away and he saw how it ran southward into the shadow of another cliff on the other side and it came to him that if they reached the top and went south upon the plateau, they would find a place that matched the map that Echo had drawn.

Maybe it is not hopeless, after all, he thought.

But when he reentered the cave and saw Moms ministering to Echo, massaging his sister's swollen feet and crooning soothing encouragement, he felt anew the weight of the responsibilities he had taken on and doubt crept over his spirit. Moms and Echo looked at him expectantly and he made himself smile as he began to arrange their scanty breakfast.

And so, in a short few minutes, they were out of their shelter and struggling up the path that grew steeper with every step. Vern realized that they would have to stop often to rest and that the duty of mollifying Echo's fear would grow more onerous, but there could be no turning back now.

The weather was in their favor, with a mild blue sky and little wind, even at this height, and they made better going than he had reckoned they would. At the last sharp turn before the top, Vern told Moms to stop for a rest and mind Echo while he went up to see what lay before them on the plateau.

The path they had been climbing was steeply graded, but the last eight feet or so had been cut into steps. These gave Vern an opportunity to peek over the edge, exposing only his head, so that his view of the prospect was at ground level. The area before him extended about fifty yards on three sides; the turf was short grass, composing what was traditionally called a "bald" in these mountains. At its south end was a long border of wildflowers—ironweed, jewelweed, bee balm, and the like—and these water-loving blooms held the promise of a spring. Beyond the flowers was a stand of low firs which cut off the long vista of the south.

There were no signs of shoggoths or other animals or of the Old Ones. A preternaturally peaceful silence reigned over this grassy bald.

Vern returned to the switchback in the path where Moms and Echo and Queenie waited, Moms was crooning earnestly to Echo, and Queenie snuggled against the pale girl, as if she, like Moms, were trying to stop Echo from looking down toward the stream.

Vern did not know why he whispered the report of his discoveries to his mother and sister. Maybe the information was too happy to speak of in normal tones. Moms whispered too: "Oh, I do hope there is water."

"We will let Queenie go up first," Vern said. "If there is water, she will find it."

So it was Queenie who led the way to the gentle greensward, bounding up the weather-rounded steps and springing joyfully over the edge. By the time Vern brought Echo and Moms into the sky-tented field, the dog was already halfway to the border of flowers. She had smelled water.

Moms crawled onto the level surface, to sit cross-legged, and received Echo as Vern handed her up. Then Vern squirmed over too and the three of them sat for a few moments, to rest muscles and joints and to gaze back toward the way they had come, down the twinkling stream and over the tumbled, bushy hills, and through the shady glades and hollers to the foot of the treacherous but hospitable cliff. They shared a feeling of achievement. Whatever happened next, they had come this far safely, answering the summons. They had overcome great odds, greater than they had realized during their hard march.

Then Vern stood and turned toward the south and gazed upon a different world. Behind him was a landscape of forest, mountains, and green-blue valleys. Before him, beyond the flowers and the little firs, beyond the edge of this brief plateau, lay a vast panorama of immense, sky-spearing, cyclopean structures. So tall were these angular monuments, oblongs and cubes and spiry pyramids, that clouds obscured some of their tops. Their angles were all wrong, so that Vern experienced a fleeting vertigo.

Wrongness—that was the first salience that attacked his senses and his instincts. He could not estimate how far away these structures stood, piled one past the other in an infinitely regressing series, because they seemed to be erected in a different *kind* of space than that which obtained here on the plateau. They seemed also to inhabit a different kind of time, so that if you traveled toward them—that is, if you *could* travel toward them—you would leave behind the now you were in and stand in a different now, a kind of time to which your body, mind, and spirit were direly unsuited.

This knowledge flooded into his mind and gut all at once, as if from a suddenly unveiled black star.

He did not cry out; he did not swoon. But the sight of this monstrous, incomprehensible landscape, mindscape, was so alien that he fell to his knees. Then he fell forward on his hands, retching and heaving for breath and grasping the grass in his fingers as if these handfuls of turf were his only desperate hand-hold upon the planet.

I will not look up, he thought. I will not look at these things.

He heard from behind a muffled moaning and knew that Moms and Echo were gazing upon this nightmare prospect. It was Moms who had uttered that soul-stricken, heartsick moan. She was standing upright, hugging herself with both arms, and silver tears streamed gleaming upon her cheeks. There was an expression of desolate comprehension in her eyes. She must have known better than Vern could know what these gigantic shapes that crushed the southern horizon implied and that what was implied had to be the thing she most loathed and feared, except for the striking-down of her children.

"In their own image!" she cried.

Vern understood. The Olders were remaking the world, the whole planet, in accordance with their icy intellectual designs. They were not building machines and monuments upon the planetary surface; they were reconfiguring the molecular structures of the world, from core to crust, from pole to pole. Earth was in process of losing its identity. No longer would it be an Earth; it would be an alien object, an implement or instrument, a tool whose purposes might be unimaginable.

Moms stood transfixed with horror, but Echo was not shrieking in terror, as Vern had supposed that she would be. She too was transfixed, but her expression was one of wonderment. Those unthinkably huge planes and angles and cleavages that folded inward and projected outward simultaneously in momentously slow formings and reformings exercised upon the autistic mind the same hypnotic fascination that a flickering light or a wind-trembled branch or a lightly dancing snowfall would produce. The fascination might be different by enormous degree, but it would not be different in kind from that which other and more familiar phenomena brought upon Vern's sister.

When he saw that Echo did not lose herself in terror, that she was not beating her face with her fists as she did when fear was too terrible in her, Vern came to himself a little. Even with the calming image of Echo before him, it took an effort almost beyond his powers for him to collect his senses and something of his reasoning power.

He walked slowly to where Moms was standing and knelt and took the canteen from the book bag she had dropped in the grass. He grasped it in both hands and, keeping his gaze firmly turned toward the ground, never raising his eyes to the mind-wrenching panorama, trudged into the little marshy area outlined by the ranks of wildflowers.

In a minute or so, he came to a thin, oily streamlet that oozed among clumps of marsh-grassed turf. He bent and filled the flask and tasted the water. Musky and muddy, it was not toxic. He drank a little more before carrying the flask back to the females. Queenie bounded out of the herbage and trotted along beside him. No more than Echo was she disturbed by the sight of the world in ruin.

He fed Echo a grateful swallow at a time and she looked at him with her bright gray eyes brimming with gratitude. Moms seemed to find it difficult to drink; she rinsed her mouth and took the humus-tasting liquid in small sips. Then she dropped to the grass and stretched her legs out before her.

She spoke to the air and the grass when she said, "We cannot live in a world like this." She shook her head. "At least, I cannot." She looked up at her son, into his weather-lined face with its sparse blond beard. "I feel I am on the verge of losing my sanity. I was afraid we would have no future. Maybe we can have one, but I do not want it. And now I think we have no past either."

"Last night we shared our shelter with some people that felt like you do," Vern said.

"What do you mean? I don't know what you mean. Don't talk in riddles." Her voice rose almost to a shout. "Say something that means something."

He shrugged. "Maybe nothing means anything."

He made himself look again, staring with renewed horror at the immensities of those grotesque cubes and cylinders, cube-clusters, and five-angled projections. His mind could not divide this phantasmagoric panorama into parts, but it seemed to him that gigantic bridges arched over seemingly limitless abysses and that those bridges did not attach to the surfaces they touched but penetrated into the stone with the continuous motionless movement that a great cataract of water presents to vision. The simultaneous opening and closing of the five-angled edges gave the impression that the matter of which those pinnacles were constructed was both material and immaterial. More dimensions than four were in play; that vertiginous rampart that struck its bulk over a half kilometer of empty space extended into time as well as into space. It was what it was—and yet it was in process of becoming what it already was, and becoming something other and beyond that also.

And it was all of a color that was no color at all.

Moms spoke more quietly than Vern had heard her speak before. "I cannot bear it," she said. "No one can."

Vern said, "Echo does not give up."

He pointed to his sister. Echo was clapping her hands and swaying in an excited dance, her face full of joy. "Shy-nee shiny shiny shiny shy-nee," she sang. She left off dancing and broke into a clumsy run. The air was bright there at the cliff-edge and Echo ran to enter into it, to plunge into empty space.

4.

Tekeli-li.

This transliterated approximation was the closest Terran English could approach to the piercing command-trilling the Old Ones' shoggoths made as they traveled, each telling its whereabouts to its sibling organisms. It had been anciently recorded in the unfinished narrative left by Arthur Gordon Pym and further attested by later writers and adventurers and it always carried with it a nauseating feeling of dread.

Seeker held her face in her hands and drew deep, harsh breaths. She had not withdrawn from the Terran's mind and the sound of that trilling had shaken her.

"How close are the shoggoths to the Remnant?" I asked.

She was silent a space, gathering her thoughts. Then she said she could not tell. "That sound is vivid in her mind because of her great fear, but I cannot judge distance."

"Navigator?" I asked.

He studied his panel for some time. "Not so near as to be deadly, I think," he said. "It is very difficult to judge distances."

"We have found where this Remnant is," I said. "We also have pictures from the locators. Where shall we set down the beacon?"

"Not so close as to attract the Old Ones to them nor so far that the autist cannot travel to it."

"We must put the beacon down soon," Seeker said, "so that it can set the Gate in place. I will have to go down to planet surface."

Three of us said No at once.

"The danger is too huge," I said. "If the Old Ones are close, your mind could be erased. A shoggoth could sense what you are. If you are lost to us, the Remnant is lost and so are we."

She looked at us steadily, each in turn. "If I do not exhibit myself in my own person, just as I have pictured me to the autist Echo and her queenie, they will not come through the Gate and we cannot bear them away. Then truly all will be lost."

"How have you pictured you?" I asked.

"Looking as I do, but with all pleasantness and all welcoming and offering safety to the family. I have tried to picture myself happily to the queenie, but I do not know if she knows and interprets in the same manner as the others. She has strong smell-sense; I would like to transmit odors to her but cannot."

"Are you certain it is needed for you to descend?"

"Yes," Seeker said.

"There is no other way?"

She indicated No.

"Then let us rehearse the protocols and do all speedily," I said, and once more and assiduously we bent to our tasks.

There was one procedure we could not rehearse.

If the Old Ones mind-touched Seeker, they would recognize our mission and why and how. Then they would try to trace us back and locate the Great Ones' operational point for this mission. The disaster that followed would endanger and probably result in the slaughter of many races on many planets and the Old Ones would then take care that no Remnants were left. They would scour clean every planet and sun-system.

To prevent, I would kill Seeker. That is, I would order Ship to kill her before her mind could reveal its contents or before the Old Ones could assimilate. If the instruments detected that I did not emit the order quickly enough, Ship would enact its final program and detonate itself and all of us to atomic gas. There would be nothing left for the Old Ones to trace—but they would have been warned, and there would be consequences of that.

But Seeker declared that she must descend in her own person and not by image transmission to planet surface. She knew the minds we others could not know. And she would not imperil the mission needlessly. So I reviewed the steps and all seemed to be in order and we had to do everything quickly and with no mistakes.

There was a complication. Navigator had found a desirable site; the locators furnished detailed pictures of a green plateau above a river and the unactivated beacon was on its way, disguised, like Ship, as debris. It hurtled toward Terra, along with a flock of moon-chunks, and once it was surfaced, Ship would activate it for a brief time so that Seeker's mind-signals could be amplified to the female telepath and directions would be vivid to her, though not a picture of the site, which Seeker explained would mean nothing or too much. Then the beacon would be deactivated, so as not to attract attention. When the time came, *the exact moment,* it would power up again and set the Gate in place and keep it open—again for the briefest of periods. In that short space, Seeker would appear to the autist and her queenie and welcome them through.

But Navigator was finding precise measurement difficult. We had thought that the distortion of the local space-weave was accidental, a product of the great interdimensional engineering the Old Ones were undertaking. As an ancillary quality, the distortion would remain constant and the anomalies could be taken into account. The distortion was increasing, Navigator told us, and he now thought it was not accidental. The Old Ones were transforming local space-time.

"They are not satisfied to remake the objects of the cosmos," he said. "They are changing the makeup of the vessel that contains the cosmos. It begins with Terra and will spread, wave upon wave, throughout the whole universe. We will be unable to ascertain when or where anything is."

"How can they change the nature of space without destroying themselves?" Doctor asked.

"I do not know," Navigator said.

"Perhaps underspace will not be affected," I said. "And this transformation— if it is really taking place—will require a very long time to complete. We must rescue this Remnant promptly and return to the Great Ones. They will understand how to halt the process."

"Perhaps," Navigator said. His voice was doubtful. "I will try to work out a mathematics for the rate of distortion and we will follow our plan whether it is useful or not."

"That is best," I said because I could think of nothing else to say.

And then it was time for Seeker to go down. The beacon was in place and had already proved its worth. The Terran telepath had received Seeker's pictures most clearly and Navigator reported that the family was marching toward the plateau. He suggested that we configure the beacon transceivers in a different way and thus access some of the energy the Old Ones were using to distort space-time. We could do so undetected, so much of that energy was surplusage and not closely tabulated.

"It would require too long," I said. "Those shoggoths are too near, are they not?"

He watched his screens and scopes for a little and then agreed.

Seeker went into the Gate-entrance chamber. She had freshened her robe and made her long hair brighter. Doctor and I kept our gazes upon each other, for though our sister strode into the exchange chamber steadily and with all purpose, we knew that she must have been enduring most horrible fears. She was descending into the territory of the Old Ones and she absorbed the terror of them ferociously, being in contact with the Remnant that survived just outside the verge of their icy intelligences and had witnessed what things they had done.

We tested the communications and Seeker said she could well hear me.

"Good," I said, "because you must mark the instant for Navigator and for Ship. It has to be precisely exact."

"I know." She spoke bravely, but there was a quiver in her voice, only little, but it betrayed her slightly, and I looked at Doctor and she was concerned but also smiled bravely to let me know Seeker would not lose consciousness.

We waited and waited but not, I now think, as long as it seemed we waited.

Seeker stood straight with her shoulders held back and her eyes glowing now with more color than ever I had seen in them. She brought her hands away from her sides and rested them slightly on the Gate posts.

Then she said, *"Now,"* and I will not forget the sound of that word ever.

Ship heard and activated the beacon and the welcoming Shiny Wall-Gate was in place, so we thought.

5.

Vern was certain that he could never get to her in time. He sprinted as hard as he could, but though Echo was severely uncoordinated and could often not walk in a straight line, she had a long head start. She was singing and babbling her Shiny Wall song and maybe that slowed her. Yet when he caught her, only inches from the fall that would crush her, and wrestled her to the turf, he had to use all his strength to hold her down. She struggled and cried and slapped at him. She was scarlet-faced and weeping but still singing, when she could find breath, "Shy-nee, shiny, shiny…" Moms began wailing too, uttering a cry so full of grief and horror, that it chilled Vern even in the heat of his exertions.

And now in the midst of these commotions, Queenie came bounding past. Vern hardly had time to turn his head and follow her flight as she raced by him and the caroling Echo and launched herself, as if arcing into a lake to fetch a stick, over the cliff edge into the abyss.

Finally he was able to turn Echo on her back. He knelt on her, pinning her shoulders with his knees. She looked up at him with an expression of puzzled sorrow. "Shy-nee," she said.

Then it was visible to Vern. It stood, or hovered, exactly upon the cliff edge, a rectangle of blue-white shimmer, mottled and interlaced with glowing threads that pulsed silver and violet and orange-red. It looked as if it ought to emit sound—a small sonic clap upon its appearance, or the snap and sizzle of electronic static—but it was eerily silent. Vern could feel that no heat emanated from this object that Echo called a wall.

He took his weight off his sister and stood her up and clasped her tightly. She was not pushing him away now or attempting to run. She was transfixed, hypnotized by the shiftings and sparklings of the threaded workings upon or within the seemingly flat surface. She even nestled a little in his embrace as she often did with Moms.

Moms came behind Vern and put her arms around her shoulder, so that the three of them stood holding tight in mutual embrace. Vern wanted to speak to Moms but could not.

The girl who stepped out of Echo's Shiny Wall resembled Vern's sister in many ways. She was thin and her skin was pale as porcelain and her hair was bright blond, although it was not raddled and stringy like Echo's but done up in feathery swirls that appeared to float about her head. She was wearing a white robe that cupped the sunlight into little pools of color, subtle yellows and blues.

Then she spoke in a clear, treble voice, her syllables like chimes. "You will be pleased to come away. The shoggoths are near. There is small time before the gate must shut."

Echo laughed delightedly. Vern could say nothing and it was Moms who asked, in a quavering but determined tone, "Who are you?"

"I am Seeker. Echo knows who I am. You can see how she is not fearing. You must come. *Now.* They are almost upon us."

Vern heard. They must have been advancing upon them from the north ridge. *Tekeli-li Tekeli-li.* Those beasts that looked like decomposing flesh could not come up the cliff-side path. They must have come along the other side of the bald.

Moms said, "We don't know how. We are exhausted and frightened and you are strange to us."

"You must trust me," the girl said. "Your queenie is already aboard."

"Queenie?"

"Please."

The shrilling was very near. *Tekeli-li.*

"We have no choice, Moms," Vern said.

Her voice was vacant. "Maybe you were right, Vern, to say that nothing means anything anymore. I don't want to see this world the way it is now. How could anything be worse than what is here? So I will go first."

She walked to stand by the girl in the white robe. The girl motioned her forward and Moms did not turn to look at Echo and Vern but stepped into the sheet of silver fire that opened over the abyss.

"Now—so as to avoid those Old One things," the girl said.

Tekeli-li…

Almost upon the greensward, almost within sight.

Echo was still frozen in fascination, so Vern scooped her up and carried her into the wall-sheet of energy and the girl in the colorful white robe followed, backing in and looking with horrified loathing at what was out there and then all that scene went away.

It was cold and sharp. It was like stepping through the waterfall that had protected their cave, except that it was not wet.

On the other side of the Shy-nee Wall was sleep.

6.

Ship had changed the combination of gases so that our vessel atmosphere conformed more closely to the Terran. For us crew members, the heavier air was not unpleasant, but it was a little more difficult to breathe. We wanted our Remnant guests to be as comfortable as possible, for all must seem highly strange to them. We were in space, where the Old Ones ranged abroad. That would be threatening, we thought maybe.

As soon as the necessities were done with, we all went to our deepsleep berths and Ship filtered in the proper narcotics and we plunged into underspace. This happened in the shortest of times. We did not know if we had been seen or, had we been, if we were traceable. We did not know if underspace was changed—or "wrecked," as Navigator called it.

Ship was to awaken us after four periods. At that point, we would be one hundred watches' flight from the Alliance Remnant Reclamation Consigning Base, a station located where a sun system formerly had revolved. The Old Ones had annihilated every planet and moon there and the dim little central star now hung alone. There were no outposts near this deserted space and it was a lonely place wherein to stand waiting and planning.

After the crew had been awakened, Echo and the queenie were brought to full consciousness and their needs attended to. They required more bodily attention than the young man and his mother. Seeker spent a long time period communicating with the animal—"dog," it was classified—and the autistic female; they could all speak to each other in a rudimentary mental speech, and Echo, once she was assured that her mother and brother were alive and well, was happy. She no longer echoed, repeating the phrases and words and sounds of others. Now, with Seeker, she had her own voice.

Then Vern was wakened and he reported immediately that he felt wonderfully well. This was not surprising. Ship had massaged and exercised him and rid him of unhealthy microorganisms and prepared healthy, Terran-like food, which he ate with lavish enjoyment.

He asked a great many questions—as we had expected he would ask.

"You look so cool and white," he said. "You seem delicate."

"We were rescued from our home planet by the Radiance Alliance almost two of your years ago. We have been enclosed in the station and aboard ship since then. So we have not...planetary...physiques. But now, after we are restored to strength, we will be going to a world like the one you left, like ours that the Old Ones murdered. We will develop our physical nature on the new planet."

"I like the clothes you gave me," he said. "I never wore a robe before. It is comfortable and very pink. It is very pink."

"I am glad you adore it," I said.

"There are lots of things I do not understand," he said. "I thought Echo would fall off the cliff and die. I thought Queenie had already fallen."

I explained that the scene was arranged to deceive the foe. "Echo is an autistic and sees *everything* the way it really is. You and I see what we expect to see, but autistics do not see predicted patterns. The Old Ones see only patterns, all things arranged schematically. If they saw the grass blades depressed by the edge of the gate, they would attribute that to the wind bending them over. But it was the gate pressing down, though it was not yet visible. Echo saw what it really was and went through the gate to Seeker."

"But the gate *was* visible," Vern said. "It was silver, with other colors. I saw it."

"Ship made it visual for you and your mother. Otherwise, you might not have entered."

He was silent for a while. Then he said, "Thank you for rescuing us. Thank you for saving our lives."

"It is our mission. In the world we are going to there are other Terra-like Remnants hidden away. They were rescued too. The Alliance is trying to preserve as many species as possible. The greater number of them does not look like us." I could not help smiling. "Some of them look very different."

"Have you and the crew rescued many Remnants?"

"Only your family," I said. "We were all apprehensive because we had no experience. We are immature."

"What do you mean, immature?" Vern asked.

"In terms of Terran cycles, I am fifteen years old, Doctor is fourteen, Navigator is twelve, and Seeker is ten. We are orphans. We are Remnants, as you are. Our home was obliterated and we were rescued, though our escape was not so narrow as yours."

Vern thought, then wagged his head. "Why would your Great Race send out children for such a mission? It seems not very brilliant."

"But if we were adults and thought in complicated patterns, the way older beings do, the Old Ones could detect us more easily. They are not so closely attuned to the thought-patterns of children or of animals—or of autistic beings."

"This is hard to take in," Vern said.

"Is it not better for you here than it was on Terra?"

"Yes. May we wake Moms now?"

"She had to stay asleep longer. Her mind is more torn because the world she lived in so long is unrecognizable to her now. She will take longer to recover."

"I had a sister younger than Echo," Vern said. "Her name was Marta. The Old Ones destroyed her when they murdered my father. We could never say her name because we would cry and become too upset. That was not safe."

Ship sounded some noises to signal that Moms had awakened.

Moms was sitting in a grand, plush chair shaped like a quarter moon beside her deepsleep rectangle. Queenie sat beside her in regal attitude. They looked as if they were granting audience. Moms' robe was of a softer-looking material than Vern's and Echo's and it was a dark, peaceful blue. It lapped over Queenie's paws. When she saw Vern and Echo and all the crew come to greet her, she began to laugh and cry. Her face formed different expressions and Vern saw how confused she was.

But she was happy.

"Oh children," she said. "How fine you look! And you are all dressed up! Is there going to be a party?"

"I don't know," Vern said.

So Ship announced that a celebration was scheduled in two hours in the large conference bay. Everyone is invited, Ship said. Please attend. I am proud to know you.

"And we are all cosmically proud of Seeker," I said. "She has done what all others could not."

"I am awfully grateful," Vern told her. "Is Seeker your real name?"

"In your English sounds, it would be something like Inanna," I said.

He tried to pronounce it.

"Seeker," I said, "say your name to Vern."

"In a moment," she said. She brushed the air with her hand. Her forehead was wrinkled and we knew she was mind-feeling something probably distant, but we could not know what.

Love Is Forbidden, We Croak and Howl

Caitlín R. Kiernan

ERE'S THE SCENE: One hour past twilight on the night of a full Hay Moon—so an evening in June—an hour and spare change, and the last bend of the Castle Neck River vomits out the estuaries and salt marshes and sand bars that is, by turns, known as Essex Bay and Innsmouth Harbor. Lovecraft called the river the Manuxet, but that was never its true name. That was only some portmanteau spun from Algonquian—*man,* island fused with *uxet,* "at the river's widest part." Not inaccurate, as the Castle Neck here abandons any pretense at *being* a river, and is, instead, only the sluggish maze of shallow streams, sloughs, impassable tracts of swamps, dunes, and thickly wooded islands prefacing Essex Bay (id est, Innsmouth Harbor). On this night in June of 1920 the Hay Moon has only just cleared the horizon and shines low and red across the Atlantic beyond Ipswich Bay. To men and women alien to the decaying seaport of Innsmouth, that moon might bring a shiver. It might cause one to look away, because it could be the single eye of any god gazing out across a world to which it means to do mischief. The peculiar inhabitants of the seaport, however, revel on these nights. They strip and swim through the cold water out to the low granite spine of Devil Reef, and, by the moonlight, there they do cavort with the sorts of beings their slow metamorphoses will one day make of them. This has been the way of things since Captain Obed Marsh returned from the South Seas prior to the year of someone else's lord, 1846 (possibly as far ago as the early 1820s), sailing back on the *Sumatra Queen* with new prosperity for an ailing town and the gift of transcendence and ever-lasting life for all. Returning to preach the gospel of Father Dagon and Mother Hydra.

But this is neither a geography nor a history lesson. This is something else.

Some would say this is a love story. Alright, let's settle for that, if only for the sake of convenience. Some would go so far as to make an analogy with Shakespeare's *Romeo and Juliet*, though that may be interjecting an unnecessary and, too, inappropriate degree of sentimentality into what is to come.

Once upon a time, there was a ghoul who fell in love with a daughter of the port of Innsmouth. To say the least, her parents would hardly have looked upon this as an acceptable state of affairs. She, destined one day to descend through abyssal depths to the splendor of many spired Y'ha-nthlei in the depths well beyond the shallows of Jeffreys Ledge. She might have the fortune to marry well, perhaps, even, taking for herself a husband from among the amphibious Deep Ones who inhabit the city, or, at the very least, a fine and only once-human devotee of the Esoteric Order. She would be adorned in nothing more than the fantastic, partly golden alloy diadems and bracelets and anklets, the lavalieres of uncut rubies, emeralds, sapphires, and diamonds. What caring parent would *not* be alarmed that their only daughter might foolishly forsake so precious an inheritance, and all for an infatuation with so lowborn and vile creature as a ghoul?

The girl's name is (or was, if you dislike tense shifts) Elberith Gilman, and on the night in question she is a few months past her sixteenth birthday. Likely, she has long since been betrothed and is only awaiting the completion of her transition.

The ghoul has no name that could ever be spoken in any tongue of man. With a small tribe of his kind, he passes the days in the moldering tunnels beneath the Old Hill Burying Ground, those passages roofed with long-emptied, shattered caskets and the roots of elderly oaks and hemlocks. Unlike Elberith, the ghoul has not much more to look forward to but a few fresh corpses here and there, the gnawing of dry bones devoid of the least scrap of marrow, and the grumbling company of his own vicious kin. Possibly, if great luck should someday shine down upon him, the ghoul may one day descend into the underworld of the Dreamlands, and dwell on peaks of Thok, above the Vales of Pnath (carpeted with a billion skeletons), where the most celebrated ghouls never lack for the fleshiest of rotted corpses.

On a night almost a full year before *this* night, the ghoul first emerged from the tunnels—something his race rarely does—and crept almost seven miles across field and wood and fen down to Innsmouth town. For he is an uncommon sort of ghoul, given to curiosities, fascinations, and obsessions not entirely healthy for subterranean creatures who wisely shun the cruel light of the sun. And he'd heard rumors of the seaport, and of its peculiar citizens, and of the pact they'd made with those immortal beings who are neither frogs nor fish, but bear a striking (some would say discomfiting, even nauseating) resemblance to both at once. He much desired to look upon such things for himself. It seemed unlikely he would be missed, so occupied are most with their own grisly and individual affairs. Surely, he could escape the eyes of man and be back before dawn. So it was he climbed the forty-seven steps up and up and up to the mausoleum whose bronze door led out into the forbidden World Above.

On that night, when the moon was still several nights from full, Elberith went with her mother and father and three sisters (it was the greatest tragedy in her father's life that he had no sons) to the nightly services in the Hall of Dagon at New Church Green, the same building that had once held the port's Masonic temple. With her family and her fellow inhabitants of Obed Marsh's fair community, she raised her coarse voice in the rattling, gurgling hymns to the Father and the Mother and to Great Cthulhu. She much enjoyed singing the hymns, and, as it happens, was said to possess one of the finest voices in all Innsmouth. Following the services, she walked along the wharves with her family and that of Mister Zebidiah Waite, savoring the muddy reek of an especially and unexpectedly low tide. It was almost midnight by the time the Gilmans at last returned to their listing and somewhat dilapidated home on Lafayette Street.

Never before had the ghoul imagined such wonders—almost beyond comprehension to one who has lived his life in the darkness below a bone yard—as the cobbled streets, the gas- and candlelight through windows, the fieldstone and redbrick chimneys, steeples, the widow's walks and cupolas of Georgian architecture, the handful of rusting automobiles parked here and there. The ghoul could not see, of course, all the signs of disuse and neglect that shrouded the avenues and alleys of Innsmouth, having no point of reference. Even the boarded windows and doorways seemed the product of amazing skill. The parallel lines of abandoned railways and telegraph poles that had long since lost their wiring to one or another nor'easter or hurricane were evidence of a carefully calculated brilliance he had never suspected could exist. The ghouls knew the World Below, and they knew very little else. Indeed, he had been taught it was anathema to *seek* anything more, as such an act would surely be an offense to the gods who guarded and watched over carrion feeders.

It was only happenstance that he chose to squat beneath the bedroom window of Elberith Gilman. Most of Lafayette Street was dark and deserted (which, so far as the ghoul knew, was a normal condition for any town), so it was, naturally, the yellow-orange glow of the windows of her house that drew his attention. Perhaps, then it was *not* happenstance, but quite the opposite. It may have been the inevitability that so often attends curiosity. Darkness and shadows were familiar to the ghoul; lighted windows, however, these were a novelty. In a patch of weeds and beneath the limbs of an elderberry tree, he squatted and listened intently to the noises—all quite routine, though he had no way of knowing this—of Elberith readying herself for bed. He pressed his ear to the weathered grey clapboard, savoring every sound. But it wasn't until he heard the creak of mattress springs, not until the light from the room was extinguished, that the ghoul summoned the courage to rise on his hooved and shaggy, fetlocked hindlimbs and gaze in through the windowpane.

It so happened that Elberith had not yet even closed her eyes, much less drifted away and down to her usual and sweet, welcomed dreams of the bioluminescent terraces and silt courtyards of Y'ha-nthlei, or of that nameless sunken city in the Middle Sea of the Dreamlands which lies in the strait between Dyath-Leen and the city of Oriab. When the ghoul began softly tapping and scraping on the glass, at first she took it for nothing more than a breeze causing the branches of the elderberry tree to brush against the house. But then the tap-tap-tapping grew more insistent, and she sensed in it both a purpose and a pattern that never could be attributed to wind and tree limbs. So she rose and went to the window. She was met by the scarlet eyes of the ghoul's peering in at her and its wet nose pressed to the pane.

At first she was taken aback by such a monstrous sight and very nearly called for her father, whom she still trusted to keep her safe from all the malevolent bogeys and goblins that go bump in the night.

Seeing the beauty of her, another thing completely alien to the ghoul, he quite unintentionally—or, at least, without forethought—coughed out a short bark and a few words of wonder. Of course, Elberith didn't speak the language of ghouls, and this was only the guttural din that might be heard from any animal. But she didn't recoil, and she didn't scream. She stared back, and the ghoul tapped several more times on the glass.

"If you meant to do me harm," she asked aloud, "would you not simply shatter the glass and crawl in across the sill?"

As the ghoul didn't know the language of humans, not even that of humans evolving into that which may no longer be considered human, the question meant no more to him than his utterances had meant to her.

Linguists would call this unfortunate situation a "language barrier."

"You would do that, wouldn't you?" asked Elberith Gilman. "You would, and by now I would have been slaughtered and near to half devoured."

Catching the absence of fear in the girl's voice, the ghoul raised its eyebrows and twisted its short muzzle into the grimace that passes as a smile among ghouls. Elberith did wince the tiniest bit at the sight of his rows of crooked yellowed teeth, the canines robust as those of any wolf or black bear. She bravely pressed her open palm and outstretched fingers against the windowpane, and certainly the ghoul took this as a sign of welcome. In response he did the same, though his hand was not a hundredth as fair as hers and his talons clicked loudly upon the glass even when he didn't intend them to do so.

"You mean me no harm," she said, "and if I raise the sash you won't eat me," she said, having silently arrived at this unlikely conclusion. "You want to be friends, I do believe. It may be that, whatever manner of a beast you are, you want nothing more than to dispel a loneliness that has long troubled your heart."

Elberith had always been a bold girl, and one given to questionable deductions.

She unlocked the window, lifted it, and then stared face to face with the ghoul who'd walked all the way from Ipswich. Uncertain of what he ought do next, he took a step back, lest he make some move that would startle the girl. All the men and women and children he'd ever glimpsed had been dead and consigned to their narrow houses (though others he knew had peered out at gravediggers, mourners, and ministers), but none had been anywhere near as beautiful as *this* human girl. Her forehead sloped slightly backwards, and she had hardly any chin at all. Her lips were uncommonly thick (if the corpses upon which he'd stolen and fed were any indication), her skin vaguely irides-cent in the moonlight, and there were the faintest folds on each side of her throat. Her green eyes bulged more than he would have expected. Her long yellow hair was pulled back in a braid, and when she'd opened the window the ghoul had noted a sort of webbing between her long fingers.

"Well, there," she said, "I've gone and done it. So, if you mean to eat me, do be quick about it, please."

The ghoul did his best to decipher her words, but it was hopeless. Instead, he decided upon another action that he did hope would be taken as friendly. He held out one hand to her, that which he'd used to tap and scratch at the girl's window. His long arm reached into the room, and for almost a full minute, she regarded the proffered hand with what Elberith considered the necessary dose of caution and suspicion. The skin was calloused, with tufts of coarse hair sprouting here and there in no discernable pattern. The claws could easily have gutted a shark, should the opportunity arise, and several plainly unwholesome species of fungus grew upon the ghoul's flesh. But then, arriving at one of her questionable verdicts, she took the ghoul's hand. It was altogether warmer than she'd expected it would be.

The ghoul, unaccountably pleased by the gesture, folded up her hand in his. And that's how it went on the first night. For a time, they stood there, holding hands and staring at one another with ever increasing fondness. Until, somewhere in the seaport, a clock chimed the hour, so startling the ghoul that he released her and scampered away from the window and the elderberry trees, back down empty lanes and once more into the marshes. He did make it back to the bronze door of the mausoleum well before dawn. As for Elberith, she stood staring at her hand and the smudgy, moldy stain the ghoul had left on her jaundiced skin until at last she grew sleepy, closed the window, locked it against less amiable visitors, and crawled back into bed. This night, she did not dream of submarine palaces or of her grandparents and aunts and uncles and cousins who'd long since gone down to the sea without ships, rising to the surface only on appointed nights to cavort upon the jagged strata of Devil Reef. Rather, she dreamt of the ghoul, of his face and the touch of his hand upon her own.

The Sect of the Idiot

Thomas Ligotti

> The primal chaos, Lord of All...the blind idiot god—Azathoth.
> —*Necronomicon*

THE EXTRAORDINARY IS a province of the solitary soul. Lost the very moment the crowd comes into view, it remains within the great hollows of dreams, an infinitely secluded place that prepares itself for your arrival, and for mine. Extraordinary joy, extraordinary pain—the fearful poles of a world that both menaces and surpasses this one. It is a miraculous hell towards which one unknowingly wanders. And its gate, in my case, was an old town whose allegiance to the unreal inspired my soul with a holy madness long before my body had come to dwell in that incomparable place.

Soon after arriving in the town—whose identity, along with my own, it is best not to bring to light—I was settled in a high room overlooking the ideal of my dreams through diamond panes. How many times had I already lingered in mind before these windows and roamed in reverie the streets I now gazed upon below.

I discovered an infinite stillness on foggy mornings, miracles of silence on indolent afternoons, and the strangely flickering tableau of neverending nights. A sense of serene enclosure was conveyed by every aspect of the old town. There were balconies, railed porches, and jutting upper stories of shops and houses that created intermittent arcades over sidewalks. Colossal roofs overhung entire streets and transformed them into the corridors of a single structure containing an uncanny multitude of rooms. And these fantastic crowns were echoed below by lesser roofs that drooped above windows like half-closed eyelids and turned each narrow doorway into a magician's cabinet harboring deceptive depths of shadow.

It is difficult to explain, then, how the old town also conveyed an impression of endlessness, of proliferating unseen dimensions, at the same time that it served as the very image of a claustrophobe's nightmare. Even the nights above the great roofs of the town seemed merely the uppermost level of an earthbound estate, at most an old attic in which the stars were useless heirlooms and the moon a dusty trunk of dreams. And this paradox was precisely the source of the town's enchantment. I imagined the heavens themselves as part of an essentially interior decor. By day: heaps of clouds like dust balls floated across the empty rooms of the sky. By night: a fluorescent map of the cosmos was painted upon a great black ceiling. How I ached to live forever in this province of medieval autumns and mute winters, serving out my sentence of life among all the visible and invisible wonders I had only dreamed about from so far away.

But no existence, however visionary, is without its trials and traps.

After only a few days in the old town, I had been made acutely sensitive by the solitude of the place and by the solitary manner of my life. Late one afternoon I was relaxing in a chair beside those kaleidoscopic windows when there was a knock at the door. It was only the faintest of knocks, but so unanticipated was this elementary event, and so developed was my sensitivity, that it seemed like some unwonted upheaval of atmospheric forces, a kind of cataclysm of empty space, an earthquake in the invisible. Hesitantly I walked across the room and stood before the door, which was only a simple brown slab without molding around its frame. I opened it.

"Oh," said the little man waiting in the hallway outside. He had neatly groomed silver hair and strikingly clear eyes. "This is embarrassing. I must have been given the wrong address. The handwriting on this note is such chaos." He looked at the crumpled piece of paper in his hand. "Ha! Never mind, I'll go back and check."

However, the man did not immediately leave the scene of his embarrassment; instead, he pushed himself upwards on the points of his tiny shoes and stared over my shoulder into my room. His entire body, compact as it was in stature, seemed to be in a state of concentrated excitement. Finally he said, "Beautiful view from your room," and he smiled a very tight little smile.

"Yes, it is," I replied, glancing back into the room and not really knowing what to think. When I turned around the man was gone.

For a few startled moments I did not move. Then I stepped into the hallway and gazed up and down its dim length. It was not very wide, nor did it extend a great distance before turning a windowless corner. All the doors to the other rooms were closed, and not the slightest noise emerged from any of them. At last I heard what sounded like footsteps descending flights of stairs on the floors below, faintly echoing through the silence, speaking the quiet language of old rooming houses. I felt relieved and returned to my room.

The rest of the day was uneventful, though somewhat colored by a whole spectrum of imaginings. And that night I experienced a very strange dream, the culmination, it seemed, of both my lifetime of dreaming and of my dreamlike sojourn in the old town. Certainly my view of the town was thereafter dramatically transformed. And yet, despite the nature of the dream, this change was not immediately for the worse.

In the dream I occupied a small dark room, a high room whose windows looked out on a maze of streets which unraveled beneath an abyss of stars. But though the stars were spread across a great reaching blackness, the streets below were bathed in a stale gray dimness which suggested neither night nor day nor any natural phase between them. Gazing out the window, I was sure that cryptic proceedings were taking place in sequestered corners of this scene, vague observances that were at odds with accepted reality. I also felt there was special cause for me to fret over certain things that were happening in one of the other high rooms of the town, a particular room whose location was nevertheless outside my cognizance. Something told me that what was taking place there was specifically devised to affect my existence in a profound manner. At the same time I did not feel myself to be of any consequence in this or any other universe. I was nothing more than an unseen speck lost in the convolutions of strange schemes. And it was this very remoteness from the designs of my dream universe, this feeling of fantastic homelessness amid an alien order of being, that was the source of anxieties I had never before experienced. I was no more than an irrelevant parcel of living tissue caught in a place I should not be, threatened with being snared in some great dredging net of doom, an incidental shred of flesh pulled out of its element of light and into an icy blackness. In the dream nothing supported my existence, which I felt at any moment might be horribly altered or simply ended. In the most far-reaching import of the phrase, my life was of *no matter*.

But still I could not keep my attention from straying into that other room, sensing what elaborate plots were evolving there and what they might mean for my existence. I thought I could see indistinct figures occupying that spacious chamber, a place furnished with only a few chairs of odd design and commanding a dizzying view of the starry blackness. The great round moon of the dream created sufficient illumination for the night's purposes, painting the walls of the mysterious room a deep aquatic blue; the stars, unneeded and ornamental, presided as lesser lamps over this gathering and its nocturnal offices.

As I observed this scene—though not "bodily" present, as is the way with dreams—it became my conviction that certain rooms offered a marvelous solitude for such functions or festivities. Their atmosphere, that intangible quality which exists apart from its composing elements of shape and shade, was of a dreamy cast, a state in which time and space had become deranged. A few moments in these rooms might count as centuries or millennia, and their tiniest niche might encompass a universe. Simultaneously, this atmosphere seemed no different from that of the old rooms, the high and lonely rooms, I had known in waking life, even if *this* room appeared to border on the voids of astronomy and its windows opened onto the infinite outside. Then I began speculating that if the room itself was not one of a unique species, perhaps it was the occupants that had introduced its singular element.

Though each of them was completely draped in a massive cloak, the places in which the material of these garments pushed out and folded inwards as it descended to the floor, along with the unnatural contrivance of the chairs whereupon these creatures were situated, betrayed a peculiarity of formation that held me in a state of both paralyzed terror and spellbound curiosity. What were these beings that their robes should adumbrate such unaccountable configurations? With their tall, angular chairs arranged in a circle, they appeared to be leaning in every direction, like unsettled monoliths. It was as if they were assuming postures that were mysteriously symbolic, locking themselves in patterns hostile to mundane analysis. Above all it was their heads, or at least their topmost segments, that were skewed most radically as they inclined toward one another, nodding in ways heretical to terrestrial anatomy. And it was from this part of their structures that there came forth a soft buzzing noise which seemed to serve them as speech.

But the dream offered another detail which possibly related to the mode of communication among these whispering figures who sat in stagnant moonlight. For projecting out of the bulky sleeves dangling at each figure's side were delicate appendages that appeared to be withered, wilted claws bearing numerous talons that tapered off into drooping tentacles. And all of these stringy digits seemed to be working together with lively and unceasing agitation.

At first sight of these gruesome gestures I felt myself about to awaken, to carry back into the world a sense of terrible enlightenment without sure meaning or possibility of expression in any language except the whispered vows of this eerie sect. But I remained longer in this dream, far longer than was natural. I witnessed further the fidgeting of those shriveled claws, a hyperactive gesticulating which seemed to communicate an intolerable knowledge, some ultimate disclosure concerning the order of things. Such movements suggested an array of repulsive analogies: the spinning legs of spiders, the greedy rubbing of a fly's spindly feelers, the darting tongues of snakes. But my cumulative sensation in the dream was only partially involved with what I would call the *triumph of the grotesque*. This sensation—in keeping with the style of certain dreams—was complicated and exact, allowing no ambiguities or confusions to comfort the dreamer. And what was imparted to my witnessing mind was the vision of a world in a trance—a hypnotized parade of beings sleepwalking to the odious manipulations of their whispering masters, those hooded freaks *who were themselves among the hypnotized*. For there was a power superseding theirs, a power which they served and from which they merely emanated, something which was beyond the universal hypnosis by virtue of its very mindlessness, its awesome idiocy. These cloaked masters, in turn, partook in some measure of godhood, passively presiding as enlightened zombies over the multitudes of the entranced, that frenetic domain of the human.

And it was at this place in my dream that I came to believe that there obtained a terrible intimacy between myself and those whispering effigies of chaos whose existence I dreaded for its very remoteness from mine. Had these beings, for some grim purpose comprehensible only to themselves, allowed me to intrude upon their infernal wisdom? Or was my access to such putrid arcana merely the outcome of some fluke in the universe of atoms, a chance intersection among the demonic elements of which all creation is composed? But the truth was notwithstanding in the face of these insanities; whether by calculation or accident, I was the victim of the unknown. And I succumbed to an ecstatic horror at this insight.

On waking, it seemed that I had carried back with me a tiny, jewel-like particle of this horrific ecstasy, and, by some alchemy of association, this darkly crystalline substance infused its magic into my image of the old town.

⊰⊱

Though I formerly believed myself to be the consummate knower of the town's secrets, the following day was one of unforeseen discovery. The streets that I looked upon that motionless morning were filled with new secrets and seemed to lead me to the very essence of the extraordinary. A previously unknown element appeared to have emerged in the composition of the town, one that must have been hidden within its most obscure quarters. I mean to say that while these quaint, archaic facades still put on all the appearance of a dreamlike repose, there presently existed, in my sight, evil stirrings beneath this surface. The town had more wonders than I knew, a cache of unwonted offerings stored out of sight. Yet somehow this formula of deception, of corruption in disguise, served to intensify the town's most attractive aspects: a wealth of unsuspected sensations was now provoked by a few slanting rooftops, a low doorway, or a narrow backstreet. And the mist spreading evenly through the town early that morning was luminous with dreams.

The whole day I wandered in a fevered exaltation throughout the old town, seeing it as if for the first time. I scarcely stopped a moment to rest, and I am sure I did not pause to eat. By late afternoon I might also have been suffering from a strain on my nerves, for I had spent many hours nurturing a rare state of mind in which the purest euphoria was invaded and enriched by currents of fear. Each time I rounded a streetcorner or turned my head to catch some beckoning sight, dark tremors were inspired by the hybrid spectacle I witnessed—splendid scenes broken with malign shadows, the lurid and the lovely forever lost in each other's embrace. And when I passed under the arch of an old street and gazed up at the towering structure before me, I was nearly overwhelmed.

My recognition of the place was immediate, though I had never viewed it from my present perspective. Suddenly it seemed I was no longer outside in the street and staring upwards, but was looking down from the room just beneath that peaked roof. It was the highest room on the street, and no window from any of the other houses could see into it. The building itself, like some of those surrounding it, seemed to be empty, perhaps abandoned. I assessed several ways by which I could force entry, but none of these methods was needed: the front door, contrary to my initial observation, was slightly ajar.

The place was indeed abandoned, stripped of wall-hangings and fixtures, its desolate, tunnel-like hallways visible only in the sickly light that shone through unwashed, curtainless windows. Identical windows also appeared on the landing of each section of the staircase that climbed up through the central part of the edifice like a crooked spine. I stood in a near cataleptic awe of the world I had wandered into, this decayed paradise. It was a venue of strange atmospherics of infinite melancholy and unease, the everlasting residue of some cosmic misfortune. I ascended the stairs of the building with a solemn, mechanical intentness, stopping only when I had reached the top and found the door to a certain room.

And even at the time, I asked myself: Could I have entered this room with such unhesitant resolve if I truly expected to find something extraordinary within it? Was it ever my intention to confront the madness of the universe, or at least my own? I had to confess that though I had accepted the benefits of my dreams and fancies, I did not profoundly believe in them. At the deepest level I was their doubter, a thorough skeptic who had indulged a too-free imagination, and perhaps a self-made lunatic.

To all appearances the room was unoccupied. I noted this fact without the disappointment born of real expectancy, but also with a strange relief. Then, as my eyes adjusted to the artificial twilight of the room, I saw the circle of chairs.

They were as strange as I had dreamed, more closely resembling devices of torture than any type of practical or decorative object. Their tall backs were slightly bowed and covered with a coarse hide unlike anything I had ever beheld; their arms were like blades and each had four semicircular grooves cut into them that were spaced evenly across their length; and below were six jointed legs jutting outwards, a feature which transformed each piece into some crablike thing with the apparent ability to scuttle across the floor. If, for a stunned moment, I felt the idiotic desire to install myself in one of these bizarre thrones, this impulse was extinguished upon my observing that the seat of each chair, which at first appeared to be composed of a smooth and solid cube of black glass, was in fact only an open cubicle filled with a murky liquid which quivered strangely when I passed my hand over its surface. As I did this I could feel my entire arm tingle in a way which sent me stumbling backward to the door of that horrible room and which made me loathe every atom of flesh gripping the bones of that limb.

I turned around to exit but was stopped by a figure standing in the doorway. Though I had previously met the man, he now seemed to be someone quite different, someone openly sinister rather than merely enigmatic. When he had disturbed me the day before, I could not have suspected his alliances. His manner had been idiosyncratic but very polite, and he had offered no reason to question his sanity. Now he appeared to be no more that a malignant puppet of madness. From the twisted stance he assumed in the doorway to the vicious and imbecilic expression that possessed the features of his face, he was a thing of strange degeneracy. Before I could back away from him, he took my trembling hand. "Thank you for coming to visit," he said in a voice that was a parody of his former politeness. He pulled me close to him; his eyelids lowered and his mouth widely grinned, as if he were enjoying a pleasant breeze on a warm day.

Then he said to me: "They want you with them on their return. They want their chosen ones."

Nothing can describe what I felt on hearing these words which could only have meaning in a nightmare. Their implications were a quintessence of hellish delirium, and at that instant all the world's wonder suddenly turned to dread. I tried to free myself from the madman's grasp, shouting at him to let go of my hand. "*Your* hand?" he shouted back at me. Then he began to repeat the phrase over and over, laughing as if some sardonic joke had reached a conclusion within the depths of his lunacy. In his foul merriment he weakened, and I escaped. As I rapidly descended the many stairs of the old building, his laughter pursued me as hollow reverberations that echoed far beyond the shadowy spaces of that place.

And that freakish, echoing laughter remained with me as I wandered dazed in darkness, trying to flee my own thoughts and sensations. Gradually the terrible sounds that filled my brain subsided, but they were soon replaced by a new terror—the whispering of strangers whom I passed on the streets of the old town. And no matter how low they spoke or how quickly they silenced one another with embarrassed throat-clearings or reproving looks, their words reached my ears in fragments that I was able to reconstruct because of their frequent repetition. The most common terms were *deformity* and *disfigurement*. If I had not been so distraught I might have approached these persons with a semblance of civility, cleared my own throat, and said, "I beg your pardon, but I could not help overhearing.... And what exactly did you mean, if I may ask, when you said...." But I discovered for myself what those words meant—*how terrible, poor man*—when I returned to my room and stood before the mirror on the wall, holding my head in balance with a supporting hand on either side.

For only one of those hands was mine.

The other belonged to them.

Life is a nightmare that leaves its mark upon you in order to prove that it is, in fact, real. And to suffer a solitary madness seems the joy of paradise when compared to the extraordinary condition in which one's own madness merely emulates that of the world. I have been lured away by dreams; all is nonsense now.

Let me write, while I still am able, that the transformation has not limited itself. I now find it difficult to continue this manuscript with either hand. These twitching tentacles are not suited for writing in a human manner, and I am losing the will to push my pen across this page. While I have put myself at a great distance from the old town, its influence is undiminished. In these matters there is a terrifying freedom from the recognized laws of space and time. New laws of entity have come to their work as I look helplessly on.

In the interest of others, I have taken precautions to conceal my identity and the precise location of a horror which cannot be helped. Yet I have also taken pains to reveal, as if with malicious intent, the existence and nature of those same horrors. Be that as it may, neither my motives nor my actions matter in the least. They are both well known to the things that whisper in the highest room of an old town. They know what I write and why I am writing it. Perhaps they are even guiding my pen by means of a hand that is an extension of their own. And if I ever wished to see what lay beneath those dark robes, I will soon be able to satisfy this curiosity with only a glance in my mirror.

I must return to the old town, for now my home can be nowhere else. But my manner of passage to that place cannot be the same, and when I enter again that world of dreams it will be by way of a threshold which no human being has ever crossed…nor ever shall.

Jar of Salts

Gemma Files

FOR H. P. LOVECRAFT'S BIRTHDAY

I found it here, under the floorboards,
labelled in a spidery hand: O nameless name,
old ancestor, return. I swear, if I am asked,
to speak these words, pray to no known god,
burn herbs, pour out the contents,
mix well with blood (my own will do), and wait.
The stopper, a plug of wax, is flecked
with grains of dusty incense—
a charnel odor at the back of the tongue,
unexpellable, susurrant, sere.

Who knows who hid it here? Who laid
these clues, a widdershins path, for me
to follow? Who sends me dreams of deep
and rocky fathoms, drowned bells tolling?
I only know I was not made like others,
my jawbones traced with the fluting
of unopened gills. How, reading these labels,
I feel my eyes already burn, begin to bulge.
The smell of salt is everywhere, sick-fragrant,

like decay—muck and silt, old entrails, slime.
All the varying grossness of some fruiting trench
that rings this world, Leviathan-vast,
where sunken Ys's gates gape still, waiting.

This much I feared, even before I opened it:
Those of my blood live long, then fall
forward, into water. The open hole
at the dead sea's bottom. So what matter
whose name I call now, in the gathering dark?
Our echo thrums forever, cleaving stone to bone.

Black as the Pit, from Pole to Pole

Howard Waldrop & Steven Utley

I

N AN EARLY American spring, the following circular was sent to learned men, scholars, explorers, and members of the Congress. It was later reprinted by various newspapers and magazines, both in the United States and abroad.

St. Louis, Missouri Territory, North America
April 10, 1818
I declare that the Earth is hollow; habitable within; containing a number of solid concentric spheres; one within the other, and that it is open at the pole twelve or sixteen degrees. I pledge my life in support of this truth, and am ready to explore the hollow if the world will support and aid me in the undertaking. John Cleves Symmes of Ohio, Late Captain of Infantry.

N.B. I have ready for the press a treatise on the principles of Matter, wherein I show proofs on the above proposition, account for various phenomena, and disclose Dr. Darwin's "Golden Secret."

My terms are the patronage of this and the new world; I dedicate to my wife and her ten children.

I select Dr. S. L. Mitchel, Sir H. Davy, and Baron Alexander Von Humboldt as my protectors. I ask 100 brave companions, well-equipped, to start from Siberia, in the fall season, with reindeer and sledges, on the ice of the frozen sea; I engage we find a warm and rich land, stocked with thrifty vegetables and animals, if not men, on reaching one degree northward of latitude 82; we will return in the succeeding spring. J. C. S.

From the Introduction to *Frankenstein; or, The Modern Prometheus*, revised edition, 1831, by Mary Wollstonecraft Shelley:

Many and long were the conversations between Lord Byron and Shelley, to which I was a devout but nearly silent listener. During one of these, various philosophical doctrines were discussed, and among others the nature of the principle of life, and whether there was any possibility of its ever being discovered and communicated. They talked of the experiments of Dr. Darwin (I speak not of what the Doctor really did, or said that he did, but, as more to my purpose, of what was then spoken of as having been done by him) who preserved a piece of vermicelli in a glass case, 'til by some extraordinary means it began to move with a voluntary motion. Not thus, after all, would life be given. Perhaps a corpse would be reanimated; galvanism had given token of such things; perhaps the component parts of a creature might be manufactured, brought together and imbued with vital warmth....

It ends here.

The creature's legs buckled. His knees crunched through the crust as he went down. The death's-head face turned toward the sky. The wind swept across the ice cap, gathering up and flinging cold dust into his eyes.

The giant, the monster, the golem, closed his fine-veined eyelids and fell sideways. He could go no farther. He was numb and exhausted. He pressed his face down into the snow, and his thin, black lips began to shape the words of an unvoiced prayer:

It ends here, Victor Frankenstein. I am too weary to go on. Too weary even to cremate myself. Wherever you are now, whether passed into Heaven, Hell, or that nothingness from which you summoned me, look upon me with pity and compassion now. I had no choice. It ends here. At the top of the world, where no one shall ever come to remark on the passing of this nameless, forsaken wretch. It ends here, and the world is rid of me. Once again, Victor, I beseech you. Forgive me for my wicked machinations. Even as I forgave you yours.

He waited for death, his ears throbbing with the ever-slowing beat of his hand-seled heart. Spots of blackness began to erupt in his head and spread, overtaking and overwhelming the astonishingly vivid assortment of memories which flickered through his mind. *Such a pretty little boy. I will not eat you, do not scream. Be quiet, please. I mean you no harm. Please. I want to be your friend. Hush now. Hush. Hush. I didn't know that he would break so easily. There is open sea not far from where I sprawl in the snow, awaiting death. The sea is the mother of all life. Save mine. The young man's name was Felix, and he drove me away. I could have crushed his skull with a single casual swat with the back of my hand. And I let him drive me away. Such a pretty little boy. Such a pretty little boy. Why was I not made pretty? Tell me now, Frankenstein. It is important that I know. Do I have a soul? Felix. Felix. I will be with you on your wedding night. I will be with you. Do I have a soul, Victor Frankenstein?*

He suddenly pushed himself up on his elbows and shook ice from his eyelids. He could see the sea before him, but it was too bright to gaze upon. It seemed to burn like molten gold, and it was as though the very maw of Hell were opening to receive him.

He collapsed, burying his face in the snow, and lay there whimpering, no strength left now, no sensation in his legs and hands. *Do I have a soul?* he demanded a final time, just as he felt himself sliding, sliding, about to take the plunge into oblivion. There was time enough for a second question. *If so, where will it go?* And then there was no time at all.

He had not felt so disoriented since the night of his first awakening. He sat up painfully and glared around in confusion. Then tears streamed from his eyes and froze upon his cheeks, and he shrieked with rage and frustration.

"Fiend! Monster! *Damn you!*"

He struggled to his feet and tottered wildly, flailing the air with his mismatched fists. And he kept screaming.

"*This* is the full horror of your great achievement! Death won't have me, Frankenstein! Hell spews me forth! *You made me better than you thought!*"

His thickly wrapped legs, aching with the slow return of circulation, began to pump stiffly, driving him across the ice. He kicked up clouds of cold snow dust. Then glass-sliver pain filled his lungs, and his mad run slowed to a walk. Fury spun and eddied in his guts, hotter by far than the fire in his chest, but it was fury commingled with sorrow. He sat down abruptly, put his face into his hands, and sobbed.

Death had rejected him again.

At the instant of his birth on a long-ago, almost forgotten midnight, he had drawn his first puzzled breath, and Death had bowed to Life for the first time, had permitted a mere man to pry its fingers from the abandoned bones and flesh of the kirkyard and the charnel house. Death had never reclaimed that which had been taken from it. Time and again, Death had chosen not to terminate his comfortless existence.

I was never ill, Frankenstein. I survived fire and exposure. I sustained injuries which would have killed or at least incapacitated even the hardiest of human beings. Even you could not kill me, you who gave me life. That should make you proud. You shot me at point-blank range after I killed your beautiful Elizabeth. You couldn't kill me, though. Perhaps nothing can kill me.

His sobbing subsided. He sat in the snow and dully rolled the bitter thought over and over in his mind. Perhaps nothing can kill me. Perhaps *nothing* can kill me. When Victor Frankenstein had shot him, the ball struck him low in the left side of the back and emerged a couple of inches above and to the right of the incongruous navel. The impact had knocked him from the sill of the château window through which he had been making an escape. Doubled up on the ground beneath the window, he had heard Frankenstein's howl of anguish over the murdered Elizabeth. Then, clutching his abdomen, he had lurched away into the night.

The bleeding had ceased within minutes. The wounds were closed by the following morning and, at the end of a week's time, were no more than moon-shaped, moon-colored scars. He had wondered about his regenerative powers but briefly, however, for his enraged creator was breathing down his neck in hot, vengeful pursuit. There had been no time for idle speculation during the trek across Europe, across Siberia, into the wind-swept Arctic.

He pushed his tongue out and licked his frostbitten lips. Words started to rumble up from the deep chest, then lost all life of their own, and emerged dull-sounding and flat. "You cheated me, Victor Frankenstein. In every way, you cheated me."

He paused, listening. The wind moaned like the breath of some immense frost-god wrapped in unpleasant dreams. Muffled thunder rolled across the ice from the direction of the now-leaden sea.

"I owe you nothing, Victor. *Nothing.*"

He got to his feet again and began moving toward the edge of the ice. Plucking bits of ice from his face and hair, his mind bubbling and frothing, he was suddenly stopped in his tracks by a particularly vicious gust of wind. His eyes filled with salt water. The cold cut through his parka, flesh, and bone, and he cried out in pure animal misery. He sucked on his frozen fingers and tried to stamp warmth back into his limbs. In the sky, its bottom half under the horizon, the heatless, useless sun mocked him. He snarled at it, shook his fist at it, turned his back on it.

And could not believe what he saw before him.

Hanging between the northern edge of the world and the zenith was a second, smaller sun.

II

In the year 1818, *Frankenstein; or, The Modern Prometheus* was published. Mary Shelley was twenty-one years old.

John Cleves Symmes, late of the Ohio Infantry, published his treatise about the hollow earth. He was a war hero and a Missouri storekeeper. He was thirty-eight years old.

Herman Melville would not be born for another year.

Jeremiah N. Reynolds was attending Ohio University but would soon become a doctor and a scientist. He would also fall under the spell of Symmes.

Edgar Allan Poe, nine years old, was living with his foster parents.

Percy Shelley, Lord Byron, and Dr. Polidori sailed as often as possible in the sloop *Ariel* on Lake Como.

In New Bedford, Massachusetts, young Arthur Gordon Pym sailed around the harbor in his sloop, also christened *Ariel.* His one burning desire was to go to sea.

In the South Seas, Mocha Dick, the great white whale, was an age no man could know or guess. Mocha Dick was not aware of aging, nor of the passing of time. It knew only of the sounding deeps and, infrequently, of the men who stuck harpoons into it until it turned on them and broke apart their vessels.

Victor Frankenstein's patchwork man was similarly unaware of the passing of time. The creature did not know how long he had slept in the ice at the top of the world, nor was he able to mark time within Earth.

It became subtly warmer as the mysterious second sun rose in time with the ice cap's apparent northerly drift. The creature kept telling himself that what he saw was impossible, that there could be no second sun, that it was merely an illusion, a reflected image of the sun he had always known, a clever optical trick of some sort. But he was too miserable to ponder the phenomenon for very long at a time.

He subsisted on the dried meat which he had carried with him from Siberia in the pouch of his parka. He had little strength for exercise, and the circulation of his vital fluids often slowed to the point where he was only semiconscious. His eyes began playing other tricks on him. The horizon started to rise before him, to warp around him outrageously, curving upward and away in every direction, as though he had been carried over the lip of an enormous bowl and was slowly, lazily sliding toward its bottom. He could account for none of it.

He was dozing, frozen, in the shelter of an ice block when a shudder passed through the mass beneath him. He blinked, vaguely aware of something being wrong, and then he was snapped fully awake by the sight and *sound* of a gigantic blossom of spray at the edge of the sea. The thunder of crumbling ice brought him up on hands and knees. He stared, fascinated, as the eruption of water hung in the air for a long moment before falling, very slowly, very massively, back into the sea.

Then panic replaced fascination. He realized what was happening.

The ice was breaking up. He spun, the motion consuming years, took two steps and sank, howling, into snow suddenly turned to quicksand. He fell and scrambled up in time to see an ice ridge explode into powder. The shelf on which he stood pitched crazily as it started to slide down the parent mass's new face. The scraping walls of the fissure shook the air with the sound of a million tormented, screaming things. Dwarfed to insignificance by the forces at play around him, the giant was hurled flat. The breath left his lungs painfully.

He pushed himself up on elbows and sucked the cold, cutting air back into his tormented chest. The world beyond his clenched fists seemed to sag, then dropped out of sight. A moment later, clouds of freezing seawater geysered from the abyss as the shelf settled and rolled, stabilizing itself.

The creature turned and crawled away from the chasm. He kept moving until he was at the approximate center of the new iceberg. He squatted there, alternately shaking and going numb with terror.

He had seen the abyss open inches from him.

He had looked down the throat of the death he had wanted.

He had felt no temptation.

He cursed life for its tenacity. He cursed, again, the man whose explorations into the secrets of life had made it impossible for him to simply lie down, sleep, and let the Arctic cold take him.

He could not help but brood over his immunity to death. What would have happened, he wondered, had he been precipitated into the fissure when the shelf broke off? Surely he would have been smeared to thin porridge between the sliding, scraping masses. But—

There was another rumble behind him. He turned his head and saw a large section of the berg drop out of sight, into the sea.

It doesn't matter, he reflected as he dug into his parka for a piece of meat. The ice is going to melt, and I will be hurled into the sea. I wonder if I can drown.

He did not relish the prospect of finding out.

His virtually somnambulistic existence resumed. He ate his dried meat, melted snow in his mouth to slake his thirst, and fully regained consciousness only when the berg shook him awake with the crash and roar of its disintegration. The sun he had known all of his life, the one which he could not think of as other than the *real* sun, at last disappeared behind him, while the strange second sun now seemed fixed unwaveringly at zenith. The horizon was still rising, rolling up the sky until it appeared behind occasional cloud masses and, sometimes, above them. It was as though the world were trying to double over on itself and enfold him.

He amused himself with that image between naps. Nothing was strange to him anymore, not the stationary sun, not the horizonless vista. He was alive, trapped on a melting iceberg. He was in Hell.

It was only when he began to make out the outlines of a coast in the sky that he experienced a renewed sense of wonder. In the time which followed, a time of unending noon, of less sleep and more terror as the berg's mass diminished, the sight of that concave, stood-on-edge land filled him with awe and a flickering sort of hope which even hunger, physical misery, and fear could not dispel.

He was alive, but merely being alive was not enough. It had never been enough.

He was alive, and here, sweeping down out of the sky, rolling itself out toward him in open invitation was…what?

He stood at the center of his iceberg and looked at his hands. He thought of the scars on his body, the proofs of his synthesis, and he thought:

What *was* my purpose, Victor Frankenstein? Did you have some kind of destiny planned for me when you gave me life? Had you not rejected me at the moment of my birth, had you accepted responsibility for my being in the world, would there have been some sort of fulfillment, some use, for me in the world of men?

The berg shivered underfoot for a second, and he cried out, went to his knees, hugged a block of ice desperately. The dark landmass swam in the air. When the tremor had subsided, he laughed shakily and got to his feet. His head spun, grew light, filled with stars and explosions. He reached for the ice block in an effort to steady himself but fell anyway and lay in the snow, thinking.

Thinking, This is no natural land before me, Frankenstein, and perhaps there are no men here.

Thinking, I could be free of men here, free of everything.

Thinking, This is going to be *my* land, Frankenstein.

Thinking, This is no natural land, and I am no natural man.

Thinking.

The berg had begun crunching its way through drifting sheets of pack ice when the creature spotted something else which stood out against the brilliant whiteness of the frozen sea. He watched the thing for a long time, noting that it did not move, before he was able to discern the sticklike fingers of broken masts and the tracery of rigging. It looked like some forgotten, bedraggled toy, tossed aside by a bored child.

The ship was very old. Its sides had been crushed in at the waterline, and the ice-sheathed debris of its rigging and lesser masts sat upon the hulk like a stand of dead, gray trees. A tattered flag hung from the stern, frozen solid, looking to be fashioned from thick glass.

When his iceberg had finally slowed to an imperceptible crawl in the midst of the pack, the creature cautiously made his way down to the sheet and walked to the ship. When he had come close enough, he called out in his ragged voice. There was no answer. He had not expected one.

Below decks, he found unused stores and armaments, along with three iron-hard corpses. There were flint, frozen biscuits, and salt pork, kegs of frozen water and liquor. There was a wealth of cold-climate clothing and lockers packed with brittle charts and strange instruments.

He took what he could carry. From the several armaments lockers, he selected a long, double-edged dagger, a heavy cutlass and scabbard, a blunderbuss, and a brace of pistols to supplement the one he had carried throughout his Siberian trek. There had been two pistols originally—he had stolen the set before leaving Europe and had used them on a number of occasions to get what he needed in the way of supplies from terrified Siberian peasants. One of the pistols had been missing after his departure from the whaling vessel. He supposed that it had fallen from his belt when he leaped from the ship to the ice.

There was enough powder in several discarded barrels to fill a small keg. He found shot in a metal box and filled the pouch of his parka.

He did not bother himself with thoughts about the dead men or their vanished comrades. Whoever they had been, they left in a hurry, and they had left him their goods. He was still cold, tired, and hungry, but the warm clothing was now his, and he could rest in the shelter of the derelict. He had hardtack and meat and the means to make fire. And he had weapons.

He returned to the deck for a moment and contemplated the upward-curving landscape ahead.

In this world, perhaps, there are no men.

He waved the cutlass, wearily jubilant, and, for the first time in his life, he began to feel truly free.

III

John Cleves Symmes published a novel in 1820, under the name Adam Seaborn. Its title was *Symzonia: A Voyage of Discovery* and it made extensive use of Symmes's theories about the hollow world and the polar openings. In the novel, Captain Seaborn and his crew journeyed to the inner world, where they discovered many strange plants and animals and encountered a Utopian race. The explorers eventually emerged from the interior and returned to known waters. They became rich traders, exchanging Symzonian goods for cacao and copra.

In 1826, James McBride wrote a book entitled *Symmes' Theory of Concentric Spheres.* Meanwhile, Congress was trying to raise money to finance an expedition to the North Pole, largely to find out whether or not there were indeed openings at the northern verge.

Symmes traveled about the United States, lecturing on his theory and raising funds from private donors in order to finance his proposed expedition to the north. The Russian government offered to outfit an expedition to the Pole if Symmes would meet the party at St. Petersburg, but the American did not have the fare for the oceanic crossing. He continued to range throughout the Midwest and New England, lecturing and raising money. His disciple, Jeremiah N. Reynolds, accompanied him during the last years of his life.

During his winter lecture tour of 1828, Symmes fell ill and returned to Hamilton, Ohio, where he died on May 29, 1829.

The ice pack eventually yielded to snow-covered tundra, spotted here and there with patches of moss and lichens. In a matter of a long while, he entered a land marked by ragged growths of tough grass and stunted, wind-twisted trees. There was small game here, mainly rodents of a kind he did not recognize. They appeared to have no fear of him. Killing them was easy.

Larger game animals began to show themselves as he put still more distance between the ice-bound sea and himself. He supplemented his diet of biscuits, salt pork, and rodents with venison. He walked unafraid until he saw a distant pack of wolves chase down something which looked like an elk. But wolves and elk alike looked far too large, even from where he observed them, to be the ones he had known in Europe.

After that, he kept his firearms cleaned, loaded, and primed at all times, and he carried his cutlass like a cane. When he slept, he slept ringed by fires. For all of his apprehensions, he had only one near-fatal encounter.

He had crested a hillock, on the trail of giant elk, when he saw several dozen enormous beasts grazing some distance away. The animals looked somewhat like pictures of elephants he had seen, but he recalled that elephants were not covered with shaggy reddish-brown hair, that their tusks were straighter and shorter than the impressively curved tusks of these woolly beasts.

The creature pondered the unlikelihood of his blunderbuss bringing down one of the beasts and decided to skirt the herd in the direction of a thicket.

He was almost in the shadow of the ugly trees when he heard a bellow and a crash. A massive, shaggy thing as large as a coach charged him, mowing down several small trees as it burst from the thicket. Frankenstein's man dropped his blunderbuss and cutlass and hurled himself to one side as his attacker thundered past, long head down, long horn out. The beast did not turn. It galloped straight past and disappeared over the hillock. In the thicket, something coughed.

Retrieving his weapons, the creature decided to skirt the thicket.

>∈<

Below the ice and snow, beyond the pine forests that were the domain of strange and yet familiar mammals, beyond glaciers and a ring of mountains were the swampy lowlands. The bottom of the bowl-shaped continent turned out to be a realm of mist and semigloom, of frequent warm rains and lush growth. Cinder cones and hot springs dotted the landscape.

It was a realm of giants, too, of beasts grander and of more appalling aspect than any which the creature had previously thought possible.

He saw swamp-dwelling monsters six times larger than the largest of the odd woolly elephants. Their broad black backs broke the surface of fetid pools like smooth islets, and their serpentine necks rose and fell rhythmically as they nosed through the bottom muck, scooping up masses of soft plants, then came up to let gravity drag the mouthfuls down those incredibly long throats.

He saw a hump-backed quadruped festooned with alternating rows of triangular plates of bone along its spine. Wicked-looking spikes were clustered near the tip of the thing's muscular tail. It munched ferns and placidly regarded him as he circled it, awed, curious, and properly respectful.

He saw small flying animals which, despite their wedge-shaped heads, reminded him irresistibly of bats. There were awkward birds with tooth-filled beaks here, insects as big as rats, horse-sized lizards with ribbed sails sprouting along their spines, dog-sized salamanders with glistening polychromatic skins and three eyes. He could not set his boot down without crushing some form of life underfoot. Parasites infested him, and it was only by bathing frequently in the hot springs that he could relieve himself of his unwanted guests. Clouds of large dragonflies and other, less readily named winged things exploded from the undergrowth constantly as he slogged across the marshy continental basin, driven by the compulsion to explore and establish the boundaries of *his* world. There was life everywhere in the lowlands.

And there was the striding horror that attacked him, a hissing, snapping reptile with a cavernous maw and sharklike teeth as long as his fingers. It was the lord of the realm. When it espied the wandering patchwork man, it roared out its authority and charged, uprooting saplings and small tree ferns with its huge hind feet.

The creature stood his ground and pointed the blunderbuss. Flint struck steel, the pan flared, and, with a boom and an echo which stilled the jungle for miles, the charge caught the predator full in its lowered face.

The reptile reared and shrieked as the viscid wreckage of its eyes dribbled from its jowls and dewlap. Lowering its head again, it charged blindly and blundered past its intended victim, into the forest, where it was soon lost from sight, if not from hearing.

The creature quickly but carefully reloaded the blunderbuss and resumed his trek. A short while later, one of the blinded monster's lesser cousins, a man-sized biped with needlelike teeth and skeletal fingers, attacked. The blunderbuss blew it to pieces.

He got away from the twitching fragments as quickly as he could and watched from a distance as at least half a dozen medium-large bipeds and sail-backed lizards converged unerringly upon the spot. He turned his back on the ensuing free-for-all and, cradling the blunderbuss in his arms, looked longingly at the ice-topped mountains encircling the basin.

He had found the cold highlands infinitely more to his liking. He could not comprehend mountain-big reptiles who did nothing but eat. He was tired of being bitten and stung by insects, sick to death of mud and mist and the stench of decaying vegetation. He was, he frankly admitted to himself, not at all willing to cope with the basin's large predators on a moment-to-moment basis. The beasts of the highlands had been odd but recognizable, like parodies of the forms of that other world, the world of men.

He chuckled mirthlessly, and when he spoke, his voice sounded alien, out of place, amid the unceasing cacophony of the basin denizens' grunting, bellowing, shrilling, croaking, screeching, chittering.

What he said was, "We are all parodies here!"

It was extremely easy to become lost in the lowlands. The mists rose and fell in accordance with a logic all their own. He walked, keeping the peaks before him whenever he could see them, trusting in his sense of direction when he could not. Encounters with predatory reptiles came to seem commonplace. His blunderbuss was capable of eviscerating the lesser flesh-eating bipeds, and the cutlass was good for lopping off heads and limbs. He could outrun the darting but quickly winded sail-backed lizards. He made very wide detours around the prowling titans.

And he got lost.

He began to notice many holes in the ground as he blundered through the land of mist. He supposed that these might lead back to the world of men, but he did not care to find out. He knew where he wanted to be. He would be more than glad to let the basin's carnivorous lords have their murky realm, just as he was happy to leave men to their own world.

He finally came to a cave-pocked escarpment. Two great rivers emptied noisily into hollows at the base of the towering formation. The basalt mass rose into the mists, higher than he could see. It was isolated from his yearned-for mountains. There was no point in attempting to scale it.

He ranged back and forth across the base of the escarpment for some time, from one river to the other. He ate the eggs of the flying reptiles who made their nests on the cliff face. He slept in the caves. He sulked.

At last, he began to explore the caves which honeycombed the escarpment.

IV

Jeremiah N. Reynolds stood at the aft rail of the *Annawan* as she slid from the harbor into the vast Atlantic, windy already in October, and cold. But the *Annawan* was bound for much colder waters: those of the Antarctic.

To starboard was the *Annawan*'s sister, the *Seraph*. Together, they would cross the Atlantic along its length and sail into the summer waters of the breaking ice pack. Reynolds hoped to find Symmes's southern polar opening. He was not to have much luck.

The *Annawan* and *Seraph* expedition got as far as 62° South—far south indeed, but Antarctica had already been penetrated as deeply as 63°45' by Palmer in 1820. A landing party was sent out toward the Pole, or, as Reynolds hoped, toward the southern verge. Symmes had thought that the concavities toward the interior world would be located at or just above latitude 82°. Reynolds and his party had come so close, but bad weather forced them to wait, and then supplies ran low. The party was rescued just in time. The expedition headed northward before the Antarctic winter could close on them.

It was while Reynolds was with his ill-fated landing party that John Cleves Symmes died in Ohio, but Reynolds was not to learn this for nearly a year. Off the coast of Chile, the *Seraph*'s crew mutinied, put Reynolds and the officers ashore, and took off for a life of piracy.

Jeremiah N. Reynolds devoted the next three or four years to various South Seas expeditions, to whaling, to botanical and zoological studies in the Pacific. He continued to defend Symmes's theories and traveled about the United States to gain support, as Symmes had done before him, for a gigantic assault upon the interior world.

The creature went down.

He lost his way a second time and could only wander aimlessly through the caves, and he went down.

Into another world.

Into the world containing the great open sea, fed by the two great rivers that drained into hollows beneath the great escarpment. This second interior world was illuminated by electrical discharges and filled with constant thunder. There was a fringe of land populated by a few small animals and sparse, blighted plants.

The creature could not find his way back up to the basin. He had no choice but to pass through the world of the great open sea, into a third interior world.

There was a fourth world, a fifth, a sixth, and probably more which were not in line with his burrowing course. He moved constantly, eating what he could find, amazed and appalled by the extremes represented by the various worlds. He caught himself dreaming of the sun and moon, of days and nights. But, if he ever felt the old stirrings of loneliness now, he did not admit as much to himself. Good or bad, he told himself, these worlds were his to claim if he chose to do so. He did not need companionship.

Even so, even so, he left his mark for others to see.

There was an ape in one of the interior worlds. It was the largest ape that had ever lived in or on the Earth, and, though it was an outsider to all of the ape tribes in its cavernous habitat, it ruled over them like some human monarch. It came and went freely from band to band. What it wanted, it took. This ranged from simple backrubs to sexual favors. While it was at one of the females in a given band, the erstwhile dominant males would go off to bite mushroom stalks or shake trees or do some other displacement activity. Had they interfered the great ape would have killed them.

Frankenstein's creature tripped over the ape as the latter slept in a tangle of dead plant stalks.

The patchwork man lost the third finger on his left hand.

The great ape lost its life, its hide, and some of its meat. A pack of lesser pongids came across the carcass after the victor had departed. They gave the place a wide berth thereafter, for they reasoned among themselves—dimly, of course—that no animal had done this. No animal could have skinned the great ape that way. Something new and more terrible stalked the world now, something too dangerous, too wild, for them to understand.

They heard from other tribes that the thing which had taken the skin carried it over its shoulders. The thing looked much like a hairless ape. It made the lightning-flames with its hands and placed meat in the fire before eating it.

They would nervously look behind themselves for generations to come, fearing the new thing infinitely more than they had ever feared the great ape whose skin it had taken.

V

The Franklin expedition set out for the North Pole in the summer of 1844. Sir John Franklin took with him two ships, the *Erebus* and the *Terror*. These were powerful, three-masted vessels with steam screws. They were made to conquer the Arctic.

The Franklin expedition was lost with all 129 members. The Arctic was the scene of a search for survivors for more than forty years afterward. During the course of these rescue missions, more of the north was mapped than had previously been dreamed possible.

In the 1860s, an American lived for several years among the Esquimaux to the north and west of Hudson Bay. He continually troubled them with questions, perhaps in the hope of learning something of the last days of the Franklin expedition.

He finally came to a village in which the storyteller, an old woman, told him of a number of white men who had pulled a boat across the ice. The American plied the storyteller with questions and soon realized that she was not talking about survivors of the Franklin expedition of fifteen years before. She was recounting the story of some survivors of one of Frobisher's voyages, three hundred years before, in search of the Northwest Passage.

The creature fought his way through other lands, and somewhere he passed by the middle of the Earth and never knew it.

The next world he conquered, for human beings lived there.

VI

Some Navaho, all of the Hopi, and the Pueblo Indians of the American Southwest each have a legend about the Under-Earth People, their gods.

The legends all begin:

It was dark under the Earth, and the people who lived there wanted to come up. So they came up through the holes in the ground, and they found this new world with the sun in the sky. They went back down and returned with their uncles and their cousins. Then, when they all got here, they made us.

In the center of the villages are *kivas*, underground structures in which religious ceremonies are held. In the center of the floor of each kiva is a well, going far down out of sight. It is from the wells that the first men are said to have come to the outside world.

The memory of the Hopi may be better than that of the Esquimaux. The Hopi remember further back than Frobisher. If you ask them, they will tell of Esteban, the black slave of Cabeza de Vaca. They will tell of the corn circle they made when Coronado came, and of the fight in the clouds of the highest pueblo, and how many had to jump to their deaths when the village was set afire by the Spaniards.

But, mostly, the Hopi remember Esteban, the second outsider whom they ever saw. Esteban was tall and black. He had thick lips, and he loved to eat chili peppers, they will tell you.

That was 1538.

And in the center of each pueblo is a kiva, where the first men came from inside the Earth.

He saw them first as they paddled animal-hide boats through the quietness of a calm lake where he drank. They were indistinct blobs of men, difficult to see in the perpetual twilight of this new interior world. But they were men.

The creature withdrew into the shadows beneath the grayish soft-barked trees and watched thoughtfully as the men paddled past and vanished into the gloom.

Men. Men *here*. In *his* world. *How?* He weighed the blunderbuss in his hands. Could mere men have fought their way this far into the Earth? Even with ships in which to cross the Arctic sea, even with firearms and warm clothing and the strength of numbers, could poor, weak human beings do what he had done? How could there be men here? How? Were they native to this subterranean world? He shrugged in his ape-hide cloak, and a frown creased his broad forehead.

I know what to expect of men. I will leave this place and go....

Where? Back to the cavern of the apes? Back to the land of heat and molten rock? Back to the great open sea?

No, he thought, then said the word aloud. "No." The inner world belongs to me. All of it. I won't share it with men. He made a careful check of his firearms, shouldered the blunderbuss and set out to find these human beings.

He tried to remain alert and wary as he walked, for there were dangers other than men in this world. Once, from a safe distance, he had seen a vaguely bearlike beast tearing at a carcass. Another time, he had watched as an obviously large flying reptile, larger by far than the delicate horrors he had observed in the basin, glided past, a black silhouette against the swirling gray murk overhead. Yet another time, he had happened upon the spoor of a four-footed animal whose claw-tipped paws left impressions six inches wide. Only a fool would not have been cautious here. But, still, his mind wandered.

I could attack these men, he told himself. I have weapons, and I have my great strength. And I cannot die by ordinary means. I would have the element of surprise in my favor, too. I could charge into their camp and wipe them out easily. And then, once again, I would be free to come and go as I please. If I do not kill them now, when the odds favor me, they'll find out about me eventually, and then I'll have to fight them anyway. They will not tolerate my existence once they know.

But... He stopped, perplexed by a sudden thought. But what if these men are different from those I knew before? Idiotic notion! Don't delude yourself. You know what men are like. They hate you on sight. You don't belong with men. You aren't a man, and you have no place among men. But what if...?

He had eaten several times and slept twice when he finally located a squalid village built on the shore of a deep inlet. From a vantage point among the trees, the creature could see that the village consisted of perhaps two dozen lodges, crudely fashioned of poles and hides. He saw women smoking fish on racks and chewing animal skins to soften them while the men repaired their ungainly boats at the water's edge. Naked children ran among the lodges, chasing dogs and small piglike animals.

The men, he noted, were armed mainly with spears, though a very few also had what appeared to be iron swords of primitive design at their sides. He smiled grimly, envisioning the psychological impact his blunderbuss's discharge might have upon such poorly armed opponents.

He was thinking about tactics when a long, low craft hove into view at the mouth of the inlet and sped toward the beach. The men on the shore shouted and waved. The women put aside their skins, and the children raced a yelping horde of dogs to the water's edge. As soon as the canoe had been beached, its passengers—about ten men—were mobbed. The sounds were jubilant. The sounds were of welcome. In his place of hiding, Frankenstein's man unexpectedly found himself sick at heart.

Now, whispered a part of himself. Creep down now, and begin killing them while their attention is diverted.

He regarded the blunderbuss in his hands. At close range, it could probably kill two or three people at once, and possibly maim others. He felt the pistols digging into his skin where his belt held them against his abdomen. He closed his eyes and saw heads and bellies splitting open as he strode through the village, swinging the cutlass in devastating arcs. He saw all of the villagers dead and mutilated on the ground before him. The palms of his hands started to itch. Kill them off.

A celebration was getting underway in the village. Eyes still closed, the creature listened to the thin, shrill laughter, to the bursts of song. Something twisted a knife in his heart, and he knew that he was helpless to do anything to these people.

He wanted to go down into the village. He wanted to be with these people. He wanted to be of them. He had not known that he was so painfully lonely. I still want people, he bleakly admitted to himself. Frankenstein made me a fool. I am a monster who wants friends. I want to have a place among men. It isn't right that I should be so alone.

Cold reason attempted to assert itself. *These people will kill you if they have the chance. They don't need you. They don't want you. Your own creator turned his back on you. Frankenstein put his curse on you. Frankenstein made you what you are, and that is all you can be. A monster. An abomination in the eyes of men. A—*

Frankenstein is dead.

His work lives on.

Frankenstein has no power over me now. I control my own life.

He was on his feet, walking into the village, and, within himself, there were still screams. *Will you throw your life away so easily? Will you—*

I want people. I want friends. I want what other men have.

Bearlike in his shaggy cloak of ape skin, he entered the village.

If Victor Frankenstein had made him a monster, the blunderbuss made him a god.

The men who had arrived in the long boat were obviously home from a fairly successful raiding trip. A quantity of goods had been heaped at the approximate center of the village. Nearby was a smaller pile of grislier trophies: severed heads, hands, feet, and genitals. The villagers had started drinking from earthen vessels, and many of them were already inebriated.

But one of the children spotted the creature as he stepped out of the shadows. A cry of alarm went up. The women and youngsters scattered. The men lurched forward with spears and swords at the ready.

The creature had stopped dead in his tracks as soon as the commotion began. Now he swung the blunderbuss up and around. He blew a patch of sod as big around as his head from the ground in front of the warriors, then watched, immensely gratified, as the spears and swords slipped, one and two at a time, from trembling hands.

"We are going to be friends," he said. And laughed with wicked delight. "Oh, Victor, were you but here!"

The creature had just had an inspired thought.

Before eighteen months had passed in the outer world, the creature was the leader of the largest war party ever seen in the interior. His firearms, coupled with his demonic appearance, guaranteed him godhood, for the barbarians who lived on the shores of the great lake were a deeply superstitious lot. They dared not incur his wrath. Their petty animosities were forgotten, or at least ignored, as he conquered village after village, impressing the inhabitants into his service.

With three hundred warriors at his back, he finally left the lake and followed a lazily winding river until he came to the first of the city-states. It was called Karac in the harsh tongue of the inner-world, and it was almost magnificent after the rude villages of the lake dwellers. Karac sent an army of five hundred men to deal with the savages howling around the walls. The creature routed Karac's army, slept, and marched into the city.

Ipks fell next, then Kaerten, Sandten, Makar, until only Brasandokar, largest of the city-states, held against him by the might of its naval forces.

Against that city the creature took with him not only his mob of warriors but also the armies of his conquered city-states, ripe for revenge. They had been under the domination of Brasandokar for a long time, and they wanted its blood. Under the creature, they got it. Two thousand men attacked in the dim twilight, from the land, from the great river. They swarmed over the gates and walls, they swept the docks and quays. Flames lit the air as the raiders ran through the stone-paved streets. They plundered, and Frankenstein's man ravaged with them.

He stopped them only when he saw the woman.

Her name was Megan, and she was the second daughter of the War Leader of Brasandokar. The creature looked up from his pillaging and saw her in the window of a low tower toward which the invaders were sweeping. He stopped the rapine and went to the tower and escorted her down. He could not say why he did this. He knew that not even the woman whom his accursed creator had begun to fashion for him had moved him so much. Megan had stood in the tower window, her head turned to the side, listening to the battle raging below. Brave? Foolish?

It took him a moment after he found her in the tower to realize that she was blind. He placed her small, pale hand upon his arm and silently led her down the stairs. Together, they entered the courtyard, and his panting, blood-spattered men parted to let him pass, and all that he could think was, I have found my destiny.

Glow-lamps fashioned from luminous weed hung everywhere. The city-state of Brasandokar seemed laid out for a masked ball, but there were still embers to be found in fire-gutted buildings, and the streets were still full of the stench of drying blood. Widows sat in doorways and sang songs of mourning. The sounds of their grief were punctuated by shouts and hammerings.

In the tower where he had first seen her, the creature sat across from Megan. She toyed restlessly with his gift, a black jewel taken from the coffers of Sandten.

I have never before seen such a beautiful woman, he thought. And then that dark and seething part of himself which had once urged the extermination of the villagers hissed, *Fool, fool...* He shook his head angrily. No. Not this time. Not a fool. Not a monster. A man. An emperor. A god.

A god in love for the first time in his life.

"Sir," said the Lady Megan, setting the jewel aside.

"Yes?"

"I ask you not to go on with this suit."

There was a mocking laugh inside his head. He shuddered and ground his teeth together. "Do I offend you?" he asked, and his voice sounded thick and strange.

"You are a conqueror, sir, and Brasandokar is yours to do with as you please. Your power is unlimited. A word from you, and your armies—"

"I am finished with this city, Lady Megan. I am finished with my armies.

Brasandokar will show no sign of having been invaded within a matter of…"
He trailed off helplessly. There were no weeks in a timeless world.

She nodded slightly. "I hear people working outside. But I hear wives
crying for their husbands, too. My father is still abed with his wounds, and my
brother-in-law is still dead. You are still a conqueror. I cannot consider your
suit. Take me as is your right, but—"

"*No.*"

Lady Megan turned her blind eyes in the direction of his voice. "You may
be thought a weak king otherwise, sir."

He rose to his full height and began pacing back and forth across the room.
Not much of an emperor after all, he thought bitterly. Certainly not much of a god.

"Why do you not take me?" Lady Megan asked quietly.

Because. Because. "Because I am in love with you. I don't want to take you
against your will. Because I am very ugly."

Because I am a monster. Life without soul. A golem. A travesty. Thing. It.
Creature. He stopped pacing and stood by the window from which she had
listened to the sack of Brasandokar. At his orders, his followers labored alongside the citizens to repair the damage inflicted upon the city. His empire would
bear few scars.

Ashes in my mouth. Shall I leave now? Take away their god, and these
people will soon go back to their squabbles and raids. And where can a god
go now? Yes. Downriver. To the great flat river beyond Brasandokar. Into new
worlds. Into old hells.

He started when he felt her hands upon his back. He turned and looked
down at her, and she reached up as far as she could to run her fingers across his
face and neck.

"Yes," Lady Megan said. "You are very ugly. All scars and seams." She
touched his hands. "You are mismatched. Mismatched also is your heart. You
have the heart of a child in the body of a beast."

"Shall I leave you, Lady Megan?"

She backed away and went unerringly to her seat. "I do not love you."

"I know."

"But, perhaps, I could come to love you."

VII

Edgar Allan Poe's first published story, "MS Found in a Bottle," was about

Symmes's Hole, although Poe did not know it at the time. It wasn't until 1836, while editing Arthur Gordon Pym's manuscript, that Poe came across one of Jeremiah N. Reynolds's speeches to the U.S. House of Representatives, urging them to outfit an expedition to the South Seas. In the same issue which carried the opening installment of Pym's memoirs, Poe had an article defending both Reynolds and the theories of the late Captain Symmes.

A year after the publication of *The Narrative of Arthur Gordon Pym*, Reynolds published his book on whaling in the South Pacific, memoirs of his days as expedition scientist aboard the *Annawan*. In this book, he gave the first complete accounts of the savage white whale, Mocha Dick, who terrorized whaling fleets for half a century.

Poe and Reynolds never met.

They were married in Brasandokar. The creature had to wear his wedding signet on his little finger, since his ring finger had been bitten off by the great ape. After the ceremony, he took his Lady Megan to the tallest tower in the city and gently turned her face up so that her dead eyes peered into the murk.

"There should be stars there," he told her, "and the moon. Lights in the air. A gift to you, were I able to make it so."

"It sounds as if it would be wonderful to see."

If only I could make it so.

Sex was difficult for them, owing to the way he had been made. They managed nonetheless, and Lady Megan bore him a stillborn son. She was heartbroken, but he did not blame her. He cursed himself, his creator, the whole uncaring universe, and his own words to Victor Frankenstein came back to haunt him: "I shall be with you on your wedding night."

Frankenstein would always be with him, though he was long since dead.

In what would have been, in the outer world, the third year of their love, Kaerten revolted. Within Brasandokar, there was dissent: his generals wanted him to launch an all-out attack and raze Kaerten to the ground.

He stood in his tower and spoke to them.

"You would be as I once was. You would kill and go on killing. Otherwise, all this land would have been empty with my rage. Do you understand? I would not have stopped until everyone was dead. Then my men and I would have turned on each other. I have come to know a stillness in my soul. It came when I stopped killing. We can do the same as a people."

Still they pressed for war. The armies were restless. An example needed to be made of Kaerten, lest the other cities regard his inaction as a mark of weakness. Already, conspiracies were being hatched in Karac, in Ipks, in Makar. Brasandokar itself was not without troublemakers.

"If you want so badly to kill," he finally snarled, "come to me. I'll give you all the killing you can stomach!"

Then he stomped away to his chambers.

Lady Megan took his giant hand in both of hers and kissed it. "They will learn," she said soothingly. "You'll show them. But, for now, they can't stand that you've taught yourself not to kill."

He remained pessimistic.

"War! War! War!"

He felt Megan shiver alongside him. He drew her closer and hugged her gently, protectively. Her head rested upon his shoulder, and her hand lay upon his pale, scarred chest.

In the courtyard below, the army continued to chant. "War! War! War! War!"

He had left his bed at one point to look down upon them. Many of his original followers were in the crowd. He had shaken his fist at them.

"I'm afraid now," Megan confessed. "I remember listening at my window in my father's house when you took the city. I was frightened then, but I was curious, too. I didn't quite know what to expect, even when you came in and escorted me down. Now I'm afraid, really afraid. These men were your friends."

"Hush. Try to sleep. I've sent word to my officers. I'll make them disperse the soldiers. Or, if worse comes to worst, I'll call on the units that are still loyal to me."

He kissed her forehead and lay back, trying to shut out the chant. Let the army level Kaerten. Let the empire shudder at my wrath. But leave me in peace.

The chant abruptly broke off into a bedlam of yells punctuated by the clang of swords. The creature rolled away from the Lady Megan and sprang to the window in time to see his personal guards go down before the mob. Shrieks and curses began to filter up from the floors below.

Lady Megan sat up in bed and said, quietly, "It's happened, hasn't it?"

He made no reply as he pulled on his breeches and cloak, then went to an ornately carved wooden cabinet.

"What are you going to do?" she asked when she heard the rattle of his cutlass in its scabbard. There was a rising note of terror in her voice now.

"They still fear the firearms," he growled as he began loading the pistols. There was just enough powder and shot to arm each of the weapons, including the blunderbuss. He tossed the keg and the tin box aside, thrust the pistols and a dagger into his belt, and cradled the blunderbuss in the crook of his arm. The sounds of battle were closer. Too close.

"Stay here until I return. Bolt—"

The door bulged inward as something heavy was slammed against it on the other side. Lady Megan screamed. The creature held the muzzle of the blunderbuss a foot away from the door and fired. Within the confines of his bedchamber, the roar of the discharge hurt his eardrums, but it failed to completely drown out cries of agony.

A spear poked through one of the several holes he had blown in the door. He grabbed it away and thrust the barrel of a pistol through the hole. A second spear snaked through another hole and jabbed him in the wrist. A third stabbed him shallowly in the left side. He roared with fury and emptied his pistols into the attackers. When he had run out of firearms, he stepped back, stooped, and picked up the spear he had previously snatched.

Then the door came off its hinges and fell into the room, followed by the heavy iron bench which had battered it down. The creature impaled the first man through the door. A sword nicked him across the forearm as he whipped the cutlass out of its scabbard, catching the swordsman in the sternum. Assassins spilled into the room, stumbling over the bench and the corpses, losing hands and arms and the tops of skulls, falling and creating greater obstacles for those behind. A blade drove through his side, snapping ribs. A spear slid under his sword arm, into his belly. Another sword went into his thigh. He howled. And swung the cutlass, grunting as something crunched beneath the blade. There was no end to them. They kept coming, more than he could count, faster than he could kill them. He swung the cutlass and missed, and someone stabbed him in the groin. He swung and missed again, and someone caught him on the cheek with the flat of a blade. He swung and missed and dropped the cutlass, and something hot and sharp pierced him high in the chest, and he went down. They had killed him for the time being.

Flanked by his bodyguards, he lumbered through the streets of one of his cities. The Lady Megan, second daughter of the War Leader of Brasandokar, rode at his side in a litter borne by four strong men who panted and grumbled as they tried to match his long stride. From time to time, he would glance at the woman and smile fleetingly. She did not love him, but she had told him that she might come to love him. That was enough for now, he kept telling himself.

His people, on the other hand, would probably never learn to love him. He had their respect and their obedience. But they could not love what they feared. Their children ran away at the sight of him, and the hubbub of the marketplace diminished noticeably as he passed through. Nevertheless, he enjoyed touring the city afoot, and he was happy that Lady Megan had agreed to accompany him. He paused occasionally to describe things to her. The luster of jewels from Sandten. The patterns in cloth woven in Ipks. The iridescent scales of strange fish hauled up from the river's bottom. He took her by the quays and told her of an incredible motley of vessels, skin-hulled canoes, sail-less galleys, freight barges, flatboats, and rafts.

And one rose on the docks to confront him, and that one was Victor Frankenstein, a pale corpse with opaque eyes, frostbitten cheeks, and ice beaded on the fur of his parka.

I am waiting for you to join me, Frankenstein said. His voice was the same one which had lurked in the creature's head, calling him fool, urging him to commit monstrous deeds.

I see you at last, the creature replied.

Frankenstein looked past him to Lady Megan. You will lose everything, he told the creature, not taking his eyes from the beautiful blind woman. Even as I lost everything. We two are joined at the soul, monster, and our destinies run parallel to each other.

You're dead, Frankenstein, and I am free. Go back to the grave.

Not alone, demon. Not alone. Frankenstein laughed shrilly and, without taking a step, reached forward, his arm elongating nightmarishly, his hand darting past the creature's head toward Lady Megan's face.

Yes! Alone! He tore Victor Frankenstein to pieces on the spot, then led Lady Megan back to her tower.

The top of Megan's head came to his breastbone. She had long, fine hair of a light, almost silvery hue. Her flesh was pale, the color of subtly tinted porcelain.

She had small, pointed breasts, a firm, delicately rounded belly, and slim hips. She was not much more than a girl when he married her, but she knew about sexual techniques—there was no premium set on virginity in Brasandokar— and she did not mock him for his virtually total ignorance of such matters. She was the first woman he had ever seen naked.

And after their first clumsy copulation, Victor Frankenstein materialized at the foot of the bed to regard him scornfully. Megan seemed oblivious to the apparition.

Even in this respect you are a travesty, said Frankenstein, pointing at the creature's flaccid penis. You remove the beauty from all human functions.

The sin is with my maker.

The sin is that you have broken the promise you made at my deathbed. You live on, monster.

I have little choice in the matter. The creature rolled from the bed to drive the ghost away, but his knee buckled as soon as he put his weight on it, and he went sprawling on the floor. Pain exploded in his head, his torso, his limbs. He lay upon his face and gasped for breath. The earth closed in and smothered him.

It took him forever to claw his way up to the surface. The closer he got, the worse the pain became. The taste of blood was in his mouth. He moaned, raised his head, and dully looked around at the carnage. Nothing made any sense. A splintered door, knocked from its hinges. An iron bench. A litter of weapons. Blood everywhere. He dropped his head back into his hands and puzzled together the things he had seen.

Megan. Lady Megan. Where was the Lady Megan?

Horror began to gnaw within him. He dragged himself forward across the floor until he reached the corner of the bed, pushed himself up on hands and knees. Looked. Looked. Looked. Looked.

Until the sight of the bloody meat on the bed doubled him up on the floor. Until he saw only a huge swimming red ocean before him. Until he heard himself scream in animal pain and loss.

They heard him in the streets below, heard a sound like all of the demons in whom they half-believed set loose at once, and some of them unsheathed swords and made as though to return to the tower in which they had slain the conqueror, his woman, his few supporters. They stopped when they saw him at his window.

"I'll show you war!" he howled, and a metal bench crashed into their midst. Cries and moans filled the courtyard. He disappeared from the window. Moments later, a heavy cabinet sailed through the window and shattered on the pavement. It was followed by chairs, a wardrobe, the bodies of warriors.

Then he came down with his cutlass in his hand, and they broke and ran in the face of his fury, casting away their weapons, trampling those who fell. He flew at their backs, his wounds forgotten. He drove them before him, killing all whom he could reach.

He raged the breadth of Brasandokar. He demolished booths and slaughtered penned animals in the marketplace. He overturned braziers and kicked over tables laden with goods. He smashed open casks of liquor and heaved a disemboweled soldier into a public well. He grabbed a torch and set fires everywhere, and the city's burning began to light the cavern sky for miles around. He dragged people from their homes and butchered them in the gutters.

At last, he staggered to the docks, dazed, exhausted, in shock. Lowering himself onto a raft, he cut it loose and entered the current. Behind him, Brasandokar blazed, and he was tiredly certain that he had destroyed it for all time. He shook his fist at the flames.

"No scars on the face of my empire!" he shouted, but there was no feeling of triumph in his heart. Megan was still dead. Megan was dead.

Screaming, crying, he fell to the bottom of the raft. It drifted toward the great flat river where men did not go.

The creature awoke just before the river entered a low, dark cavern.

How long he had drifted to this, he did not know, nor could he tell how long and how far he traveled through the cave. The river flowed smoothly. The raft sometimes nudged an invisible bank, sometimes floated aft-foremost along the water. The walls of the cavern sometimes glowed with the balefire of mushroom clusters, sometimes with a wonder of animals shining on the ceiling like moving stalactites.

More often than not, though, there was the darkness, impenetrable before and behind.

From one hell to another I go, he thought, dipping up a handful of water from the river. The water was cooler now, but were not underground streams always cool? Had he not lived in caves before, hunted by men, despised by all natural things, and had not the underground waters been cool then? He could hardly remember but decided that the matter was unimportant anyway.

What is important is that this river leads somewhere, away from the lands of men, where I can be free of their greeds, their fears. I am warm in my cloak. My wounds heal. I still have my cutlass. I am still free. He curled up on the raft and tried to ignore the first pangs of hunger. The top of Lady Megan's head comes to my breastbone. She has long, fine hair of a light, almost silvery hue. Her flesh is...

He eventually noticed the river's current slowing and its bed becoming wider and shallower. He peered into the gloom and, from the corner of his eye, saw the movement of light. He turned his head. The light vanished. The waters lay black around him.

The light reappeared in front of the raft. He stared into the water. There were small movements below: a series of dots undulated, darted away, returned. He put his hand into the water. The dots flashed away into the depths. He kept his hand in the water.

Presently, the dots snaked into sight again. He lunged, felt contact, and squeezed. Something struggled in his hand. He hauled his long arm up and over and smashed its heavy burden against the deck. The thing tried to flop away. He slammed it against the deck a second time, and it lay still. Its glow faded swiftly.

He looked around and saw more of the dots moving in the water. There was a noisy splash behind the raft. The light winked out.

Soon the raft entered another lighted place. The light was from bracket mushrooms halfway up the walls of the cavern. The creature poled close to the bank and, as he passed, snapped off a piece of fungus. Some of its luminescence came off on his hand.

He poled back to the middle of the river, then knelt to examine the thing he had dragged from the water. It was a salamander, perhaps three feet long. Along its dorsal side was the row of phosphorescent dots that had given it over to death. The skull was flat and arrowhead-like.

He ate it happily. With his hunger quelled, he took more notice of his surroundings. The walls of the cavern were gradually curving away to the sides. The bracket mushrooms grew more thickly as he drifted farther, and the waters frequently parted where fish broke the surface. The river grew shallower, though there were places where his pole could not touch bottom. He let the weakening current carry him past these places. He wondered what might dwell at the bottoms of those deep places.

He was poling the raft forward at one point when he heard the sloshing of a large thing ahead. The water stretched flat and unbroken before him. Nothing moved below the surface. Something had frightened away the salamanders and fish. There was another splashing noise. He raised the pole like a harpoon and waited, but nothing happened. Gradually, the dotted lines reappeared in the water.

In a little while, the sides of the river slid out of sight. There was almost no current. Overhead were faint smudgy patches of light, arcing out forever before and to either side of him. Here, he thought, was the end of the great river. A vast subterranean lake. Perhaps it drained into other worlds. Perhaps it opened up to the exterior. He shrugged, willing to accept anything, and lay down on the deck to rest.

He was awakened by soft, dry rain pelting his face. He opened his eyes and, for the first time in many years, thought he saw the stars. But underground? And rain? In a cave?

The creature sat up and shook his head to clear it. This was a rain such as men had never seen. Tiny luminous things bounced off the deck of the raft. Fish swirled and turned in the water and flopped onto the deck in attempts to get the things.

He reached into his hair and drew out a pupal case, then looked up again, blinking against the cascade. From the dimly lit ceiling was falling a faintly glowing snow, and tiny winged shapes fluttered beneath the ceiling.

The creature rolled the pupal case in his hand. The worms were hatching, and the fish were going crazy with gluttony. He scooped up and killed the larger fish that flopped onto the raft, brushed piles of insect cases into the water and left the rain of pupal cases as unexpectedly as he had entered it. As he started to eat one of his fish, he heard splashes of panic behind him as something large wallowed through the feeding schools. He could see nothing.

But, later, he was sure that he saw hazy white shapes swim past at a distance.

VIII

The dark-haired little man was dying, in delirium.

Two ward heelers had gotten him drunk that election day in Baltimore, Maryland, and taken him from place to place and had him vote under assumed names. It was common practice to gather up drunks and derelicts to swell the election rolls.

Neither of the two men knew who it was that they dragged, moaning and stumbling, between them. The man was Edgar Allan Poe, but Poe so far gone into the abyss that even the few friends he had would not have recognized him. Opium and alcohol had done their work on a mind already broken by a life of tragic accidents.

They left Poe in a doorway when the polls closed. He was found there by a policeman and taken to a small hospital. He burned with fever, he tossed in his bed, he mumbled. The hospital staff could not keep him quiet.

Early the next morning, Edgar Allan Poe stiffened and sat up in bed.

"Reynolds!" he said. "Reynolds!"

And lay back and died.

Have you no name, sir? the Lady Megan asked.

I have been called Demon, the creature replied. And worse, he added to himself. My soldiers call me the Bear, or the Ape, or the Shatterer.

But a *name,* she persisted, a real name. I cannot call you Bear or Ape.

Victor Frankenstein did not christen me.

Who was Vitter Frang—? She shook her head, unable to utter the odd syllables. Who was he? She? A friend, a god?

He told her. She looked horrified, then disappeared.

He lay on the raft and felt tears on his face. He had been crying in his sleep.

He heard their raucous cries long before he saw them. The high, worm-lit cavern ceiling sloped down before him, brightening ahead. The sounds grew louder as he drifted toward the sloping roof, and he glimpsed indistinct white shapes in the water from time to time.

He stripped the rope from one end of the pole and sharpened it with his dagger. It would make a crude but lethal spear.

White shapes awaited his coming. They screamed at him and began piling into the water on either side of his raft. They were as tall as men, with large beaks, webbed feet, and the merest vestiges of wings.

Behind them was a circle of brighter light. He bellowed his challenge at the things splashing around him and poled forward. They were too heavy to climb onto the raft, but they managed to slow his advance by massing in his path. He stabbed at them with the pole until he felt the raft crunch against the bottom. Then he leaped into the calf-deep water and sloshed toward the circle of light, swinging the pole like a club, beating a path through a cawing mass of white feathers and beaks. The light was a cool white circle ahead: the mouth of a tunnel. Eggs cracked under his feet, young birds squirmed and died as he passed.

One of the giant birds rose to block his path. A shock ran up his arm as he broke the improvised spear over its skull. Leaping over the carcass, he dashed toward the light, into the tunnel. Into a world of nightmare-polished stone of deepest ebony.

A wave of white horrors pursued him. He ran through corridors chiseled out of the rock by something far older than human beings. He glimpsed carvings on the walls and sculptures which no human hand had made, but he did not slow his feet until he had emerged into the light of a large central opening. Tunnels yawned to right and left. Above the opening was a grayish sheet of ice. It arched to form a dome. The floor of the chamber was littered with the rubble which must once have formed the roof.

The creature heard the vengeful white birds screeching at his back and plunged into one of the tunnels to find himself at the foot of a spiral ramp. It was cold there, and it had the smell of dust and antiquity. It had the smell of tumble-down churches he had seen, of dark mold and dead leaves on the forest floor. He shivered in spite of himself as he began to ascend.

He came out in a hall of glass cases and strode, wondering, past incomprehensible displays and strange machinery. Here were strangely curved hand tools, levers, and wheels in riotous profusion, brassy colors, iron, gold, silver. In one case was a curve-bladed cutting tool like a halberd-pike. The creature banged on the glass with the stump of his pole, to no effect. He put his arms around the case and toppled it, and one pane broke with a peculiarly metallic crash.

It was followed by a dim, echoing sound. A gong was being struck somewhere.

The creature pulled the pike-ax from its mountings and examined it. It was made entirely of metal. It was curiously balanced. It had never been designed to be hefted by a being with hands. He was pleased with it, nonetheless, and when the first of the white birds burst into the hall and charged him, he sheared its head off with a casual swing. The gong continued to clang, and the sound was everywhere now. He ran. The decapitated bird thrashed on the floor. Its angry, squawking brethren flowed into the room.

It was in a second ascending tunnel that he first saw the beings that the clangor had summoned. Shapes out of nightmare; sight beyond reason. They were paralleling his course through the tunnel. There were few of them at first, but each time he came to a lighted connecting tunnel, there were more, blocking the paths so that he could not turn aside. Their voice piped and echoed through the halls and tunnels, and he saw tentacles, cilia, myriad dim eyes as he ran.

He turned a corner, and three of the things stood in his way, their pikes raised, their bodies hunched as low as barrel-thick cones could be lowered.

His halberd chopped into the nearest of the things just below its bunched eyestalks and cilia. The top of the cone described a green-bleeding arc and ricocheted off the wall, and the trunk toppled forward, the pike slipping from tentacles. Five sets of leathery wings, like the thin arms of a starfish, began to beat and buzz spasmodically.

The creature did not pause with that ax-stroke but stepped closer and caught the second cone with his backswing. The blade stuck in the trunk. It swung its pike at his head.

He dived to the floor as the halberd whistled past, grabbed the base, and heaved. The thing went backward into the third cone. Both fell into a struggling heap. He threw himself upon them, seized bunches of eyestalks in his hands, and ripped them free. The cones' high, distressed pipings ceased when he opened the trunks with a pike. It was like splitting melons.

Then he was on his way once more, his feet slippery with green ichor. More pipings sounded ahead, commingled with the raucous voices of the great white birds.

Twice he turned aside when the cones blocked his way. The third time, he realized that they were desperate to keep him out of the interconnecting tunnels. Were they guarding something? Their ruler? Their children?

He was on another group before they knew it. Piping screams of warning came too late to save the first two guards in his path. He was through them before they recovered. The pipings behind him rose in pitch and volume as he raced through the tunnel. He saw movement ahead: there was a room at the end, and two cones were slashing the air with their pikes, warning him away. Behind them, a third cone seized a wheel with its tentacles and turned it. A panel began to slide from the ceiling and close off the room.

He yelled and leaped. The cones dropped their pikes and fled. He watched them go, then looked around at the chamber. At the far side of the room was a huge metal door, studded with bolts, deadplates, and slides leading…where? Into darker recesses? Hell? A weapons room, a nursery? The machinery in the room gave him no clue.

The creature abruptly noted a thick, sickening smell which overlay the place's scent of antiquity. The odor seemed to be coming through cracks in that gigantic door. He stepped nearer and heard a sloshing, rolling sound, as if a putrefying carcass of vast size were being dragged. He raised his halberd.

Two cones appeared to one side. They saw him approaching the door and started to hoot and honk, their tentacles and cilia beating, their wings buzzing, their eyestalks writhing, as though imploring him to stay away from the portal. Whatever lay beyond the door, they obviously did not want him to see it. He sought only escape. Perhaps it lay there.

One of the cones threw a flask at him but missed. There was a pop and an explosion as the vial hit the wall, and fire spread an orange tongue across the floor.

For an instant, the creature felt panic, then saw that the fire separated him from the two cones but not a panel of levers and dials set in the wall next to the door. He seized levers and threw his weight upon them. Nothing happened. He tried other levers. Nothing. The helpless cones wailed with terror.

And the room began to shake.

The door through which he had come reopened. Past the snakes of flame, he saw masses of the cones pour in from the tunnel. One threw a small hatchet at him. It smashed dials near his hand. Far, far below, tremors rocked some gigantic machinery. The huge door groaned, the groan rising to a shriek of protesting metal, and, slowly, ponderously, opened. It swung away on huge rollers and hinges, and a smell of death and rotting things filled the room.

The creature, huddled to one side, poised to leap through the flames, through the door to safety, stared in horror as something oozed from the opening. It flowed out forever, skirting the flames behind which he stood, moving faster and faster until it reached the hindmost of the cones now trying to escape through side tunnels. There was a greasy sucking sound, and a cone disappeared into the mass. Other cones screamed. Some fluttered their wings, rose from the floor, circled, banged into the walls like blinded canaries. They fell, and sticky edges of the gelatinous horror covered them.

There was an explosion somewhere below, and the floor sagged, cracked, yawned open. The oozing thing rippled and twisted, then slid into the fissure.

As it fell from sight, another mass emerged through the door, skirted both fire and fissure, and squeezed its bulk into one of the tunnels. Screams and whistles ended in mid-note. A third horror came through, then a fourth, a fifth. The earth trembled, and a seam ran from the hole in the floor to the wall and upward. Dust sifted down from the ceiling.

The creature, driven back by the fire, saw the crack open. It reached the roof of the chamber and stopped, a forty-five-degree slash up the wall. He bounded forward, squeezed himself into the rent, and started making his way up, away from the flames, away from the shapeless nightmares from behind the great portal. The pike hampered him, but he refused to abandon it.

He climbed through the ceiling and found himself in another circular chamber. The place shook and rocked, a bedlam of moving things, shrieks and groans in the air and in the earth. Smoke billowed up from below. Piping cones swept past him and paid him no attention. He ran with them, into tunnels that led upward. Always upward. He passed machinery noisily tearing itself to pieces. He passed the flightless white birds and did not bother to wonder whether they had invaded the tunnels en masse to find him or were merely some sort of livestock maintained by the cones.

Once, he saw a cone run past the mouth of a side tunnel. Pseudopodia shot out of the tunnel, snared it, and pulled it back out of sight. Once, the earth heaved and smashed him to the floor.

Upward. Always upward.

Upward, into the sunlight.

The creature followed some of the birds through a rent into a light-filled tunnel whose ceiling had fallen in. Clouds of ash fell all around. In the distance, a volcano sputtered and spat. There was a sound of continuous thunder in the air, and of masses of ice breaking up, of water turning to steam, of the earth sundering.

He screamed as the white, hot ash touched him. The birds squawked as if on fire beneath the deadly rain. The snow steamed. He hurled himself down and rolled in the snow, trying to escape, and as he rolled, he heard a roar that drowned out everything else. His ears turned his eyes in the direction of the roar. He gasped.

A crack had opened in the world. It ran straight and true across the ice cap, and down the crack came a wall of water. Roiling and seething, the waters swept past with the speed of a tornado.

He thought of the spewing volcano and of the unbridled energy which would be released when the cold water met the magma. He picked himself up, the halberd still clasped in his fist, and slogged away. The ash swirled about his head, blinding him, and covered him from head to foot.

There was a sound like the universe breaking. A giant hand struck him from behind and threw him headlong into the steaming snows. Broken white birds tumbled past. He was rolled and carried by the sound. Steam, slivers of ice, and hot ash blew past in a gale. New furies of cinders fell on him.

He picked himself up and ran. For the sea, for water, for relief from the falling hellish rain which scoured his skin. It lay ahead, a troubled line of gray against the white tongues of the land. The crack through which the cataract ran pointed like the finger of God to escape from the ash. He ran, covered with hot dust. He ran, and, overhead, birds appeared, disturbed from some ethereal rookery or nest, giving voice to harsh echoing cries as they made their way through the burning air. He ran, and the flightless birds from the caverns below fled with him. He ran, and the ghost of Victor Frankenstein uncoiled in his head, a serpent rising to sink its fangs into him.

Welcome to the Pit, Frankenstein said. And laughed. And the white ash continued to fall.

IX

Herman Melville published *Moby-Dick; or, The Whale* in 1851, to generally scathing notices. Less than four thousand copies of the novel were sold during the next four and one-half decades; it was not until 1921 that the book began to receive plaudits, and by 1921, Melville had been dead for thirty years.

The cataract worked terror on the land through which it tore. The white banks gave way and caved in. Behind was a mountain-sized wall of steam, at the heart of which could be seen the reddish glow of the volcano's maw.

Looking like a snowman built by crazy children, the creature came at last to the coast. Two miles to his left was the mouth of the crack. Most of the waddling white birds had struck out for the torrent at once, drawn by the lure of cold water. There was no doubt in his mind that the current had swept them back toward the depths below.

It must close, he thought, watching as hillocks of ice bobbed and shattered in the cataract. It must close, or the sea will fill the interior of the Earth. He imagined the dark waters rushing through the tunnels of the underground city, engorging the great river, backing up to flood Brasandokar, Sandten, to the cavern of the great apes, to the cavern of magma. Another explosion, another cataclysm. The world bursting open like a ripe fruit. Good riddance to it all.

He turned and began to run around the headland, away from the roaring river. After a time, its roar diminished noticeably. He sat down on the ice, exhausted, and stared out to sea, oblivious even to the cinders which continued to fall. He could go no farther.

Welcome to the Pit, Frankenstein said again.

Go away, he thought wearily, burning with the torment of the white ash.

This is where it ends, said Frankenstein. Feel the heat of the ash, demon. Listen to the thunder of water rushing to meet magma. Hell, demon. Hell. You are home.

The creature peered into the darkness gathering over the sea. On the waters was a canoe. It was being carried toward the cataract.

He clambered to his feet, picked up the halberd, and stumbled to the edge of the sea. Two figures could be seen in the canoe, one seated in the prow, the other aft. As the canoe drew nearer, he saw that the men looked haggard, listless, and did nothing to try to alter their course. The one in the prow seemed more active, turning his face to stare at the creature on the shore.

The canoe crunched nose-first against the shore, spun in the current, rocking and heaving as it cartwheeled through the choppy waters.

The creature swung the pike-ax high over his head, out over the water, and snagged a gunwale. The ice beneath his feet threatened to crumble as he strained backward, drawing the unwieldly vessel with him, fighting the craft's weight and momentum and the pull of the current. He growled inarticulately, feeling pain in his shoulder sockets, the corded muscles of his back and legs. Wounds in his thighs opened and seeped blood.

But the long canoe came out of the water, onto the shelf.

The man at the bow was too stunned to resist. He could only stare, wide-eyed. Then the creature grabbed him and hurled him onto the ice. The man landed heavily and did not move.

The man in the stern called out feebly, his voice barely more than a croak, as the creature dragged the canoe farther inland. Ice dust lifted as the shelf shuddered and cracked, letting chunks of itself swirl away toward the cataract.

When he had gained safety, the creature wrenched the halberd from the gunwale. The man in the stern waved an oar, weakly menacing. The pike clove him from pate to clavicle.

There was a dead black man in the bottom of the canoe. He pulled out both corpses, lay the halberd in the boat, and started dragging it across the ice cap, away from the cataract, away from the ash and heat. Victor Frankenstein appeared at his side, keeping pace.

You can still kill after all, Frankenstein noted with satisfaction.

Yes. I can still kill.

Where now, demon? Hell is not to your liking?

There isn't room here for both of us, Victor.

Birds passed overhead on their way out to sea. *Tekeli-li*, they screamed. *Tekeli-li*.

X

Late in June 1863, Professor Otto Lidenbrock, of the University of Hamburg, arrived with his nephew Axel and a guide on the rim of the Icelandic volcano Sneffel. They descended into the crater, determined to reach the interior of the Earth by way of a chimney on the crater floor.

A Frenchman edited Axel Lidenbrock's subsequent account of the expedition, and it appeared in *Hetzell's Young Peoples Magazine for Education and Recreation* in 1864.

In New England, seventeen-year-old Abner Perry read geology and paleontology texts and tinkered together curious little inventions in the attic of his father's house.

He sculled the canoe for a long time. Even this far out, he could not rest, for the current still nibbled gently at the boat. If he rested, he might lose ground. Somehow, he had to keep paddling until he outran the pull of the waterfall to the center of the Earth.

The ragged curtain of fire and ash in the air had begun to settle. The air seemed full of dust. The sun hung on the horizon like a sinking ship. It was dim and the color of blood.

He turned his gaze toward the prow and saw what he at first took to be a similarly blood-red island. A calved ice cake, perhaps, like the one which had borne him into the Earth—how many years before?

Then the island sank from sight, to reemerge a hundred yards off the port gunwale. Twin corkscrews of foam rose and fell. The creature watched in awe.

The whale went under with hardly a ripple, as smoothly as a surgeon's blade slides under the skin. For a few seconds, the sea was flat, like glass, with only a few dimples as ash sifted onto it.

The whale broke the sea into a million liquid mirrors as it breached. It was huge, huge, and it stood in the air like a trout fighting to free itself of a hook. Its eyes were tiny in comparison with its bulk, and it took in the world to each side: on this, the calm sea; on that, one of the hated boats. But the boat did not pursue. A single creature stood in it.

The whale was white, white as land ice, marbled with patches like sooted snow. Its redness came from the setting sun. To the monster, the patchwork being in the boat, it was the biggest thing in the universe. It stood apart from heaven and Earth. In its side were innumerable harpoons and lances, tangled lines, all covered with barnacles, unlike the whale's smooth white skin. It hung in the air like a heavy cloud, then slowly, so slowly, went back into the ocean.

The creature's heart leaped with it, and he danced in the stern of the boat.

"Free!" he yelled as the whale breached a second time, farther away. "Free! Free! Free!"

He watched, smiling, until the great whale was lost to sight. It seemed to him that God had passed through this part of the world and found it good.

A long twilight began as the sun slipped behind the horizon. The creature sculled with the sweeps, ignoring the Antarctic cold which was finally displacing the heat of the recent cataclysm. He was bound northward for the lands of men.

The stars came out slowly. Above, the twin smudges of the Magellanic Clouds shone dimly. They had lighted the way for sailors for three hundred years. They would light his.

He rowed happily, willing, for the moment, to accept whatever lay ahead. And Victor Frankenstein sat in the prow, frowning. And could say nothing.

Waiting at the Crossroads Motel

Steve Rasnic Tem

WALKER NEVER THOUGHT of himself as any kind of genius, but he knew that at least his body was never wrong. If his body told him not to eat something, he didn't. If his body told him not to go into a place, he stayed outside. If his body wanted to be somewhere, Walker let his body take him there. He figured he got his body from his father, who he never knew, but he knew his father had been someone remarkable, because his body knew remarkable things.

"Blood will tell," his mother used to say, in pretty much every situation when an important decision had to be made. He eventually understood this referred to the knowledge he had inherited from his father, held in his blood, and which informed his body which seemed to know so much. Walker's blood never said anything too loudly—it whispered its secrets so softly he couldn't always hear. But he could feel it pull in this or that direction, and that had been the compass that had brought them here.

The motel was small, all one story, just a row of doors and square windows along the inner side of an L-shaped building, with a dusty parking lot and no pool. Walker heard there used to be a pool, but they'd had a hard time keeping the water sanitary, so they'd filled it in with sand. A few cacti and thorny bushes now grew in that faded bit of rectangular space, but none too well.

The maid—a withered-looking woman well into her seventies—tried confiding in Walker from day one. "There's something wrong with this dirt, and the water ain't never been quite right. You buy bottled water for your family while you're here—especially them kids." But Walker made them all drink right out of the rusty taps, because that was the drink his own blood was thirsting for.

If anything Walker felt more at home at the Crossroads than he had anywhere in years. He'd drink the water and he'd breathe the dry desert air, taking it deep into his lungs until he found that trace of distant but unmistakable corruption he always knew to be there. He'd walk around outside barefoot at night, feeling the chill in the ground that went deeper than anyone else could know. He'd walk around outside barefoot during the middle of the day letting the grit burn into his soles until his eyes stung with unfamiliar tears.

Angie had started out asking nearly every day how long they'd be staying at the Crossroads, until he'd had enough and given her a little slap. He didn't really want to (he also didn't want *not* to), but it seemed necessary, and Walker always did what his body told him was necessary.

That was the thing about Walker—he could take people, or he could leave them. And he felt no different about Angie. His body told him when it was time to have sex with her, and his body told him to hide her pills so he could father some kids by her, but Walker himself never much cared either way.

"The four of us, we'll just stay here in the Crossroads until I hear about a new job. I have my applications in, and I've been hearing good things back." She never even asked how he could have possibly heard good things, waiting there in the middle of nowhere. He never called anyone. But she'd never asked him any questions about it. Angie was as dumb as a cow.

Somehow he'd convinced her that the Crossroads Motel was the perfect place for them to be right now. From the Crossroads they could travel into New Mexico, Arizona, Utah, or turn around and head back towards Denver. They could even go back home to Wyoming if they had a particularly desperate need to visit that state ever again. In order to do any of those things, though, they'd have to get a new car—theirs had barely made it to the Crossroads before falling apart. "But we have a world of choices." That's what he told her. Of course he'd lied. She was an ignorant cow but the dumbest thing she ever did was fall in love with him.

Their fourth day there he'd made an interesting discovery. He'd always whittled, not because he liked it particularly, he just always did. He'd grabbed a piece of soft wood and gone out to that rectangular patch where the cacti grew and the swimming pool used to be—he called that area the "invisible swimming pool" sometimes, or just "the pool"—and sat down cross-legged in the sand, the sun bearing down on him like a hot piece of heavy iron press-ing on his head, and started to carve. He was halfway through the piece—a banana-shaped head with depthless hollows for eyes and a ragged wound of mouth—when suddenly the hand holding the knife ran it off the wood and into the fatty part of his hand—slow and deliberate and unmindful of the consequences.

He permitted the blood to drip, then to pour heavily into the sand before stopping it with a torn-off piece of shirt-tail. Then it thickened, blackened, spread into four flows in different directions. Then each of those flows hardened and contracted, rose from the sand into four legs attempting to carry the now rounded body of it away. It had begun to grow a head with shining eyes when the entire mass collapsed into a still shapelessness.

Not strong enough, he thought. *But that will change.*

Walker spent most of the next few days sitting in an old lawn chair he'd set up behind the motel. The cushion was faded and riddled with holes—rusty stuffing poked through like the organs of a drowned and bloated corpse. The whole thing smelled like sea and rot—odd because it was so dry here, miles from anything larger than a car wash puddle—but it was an aroma he'd always found comforting. It was like the most ancient smell of the world, what the lizards must have smelled when they first crawled out of the ocean.

He had the chair set up so he could gaze out across the desert that spread out behind the motel, away from the highway that fed out through the southwest corner of Colorado and into the rest of the West. That desert was as flat and featureless and as seamlessly light or as seamlessly dark as the ocean, depending on the time of day and the position of the sun and the moon. So much depended on those relative positions, and the things that waited beyond, much more than most human beings were destined to know.

Out on the distant edges of that desert, out at the farthest borders the sharp-est human eye could see, lay shadowed dunes and hard rock exposures, ancient cinder cones and mesas, flat top islands in the sky. He had never been to such a place, but it had been a location fixed in his dreams for most of his life.

Every day Walker sat there in the chair, the eaves of the motel roof providing some minimal protection from glare, a notepad in his lap, a blue cooler full of beer at his feet, and watched those barely distinguishable distant features, waiting for something to change or appear, or even just for some slight alteration in his own understanding. "I'm working out our future plans and finances," was what he told Angie, and of course she'd believed him. If she'd only taken a peek at that notepad she would have seen the doodles depicting people and animals being consumed by creatures whose only purpose was to consume, or the long letters to beings unknown using words few human tongues could say. But no doubt she would not have understood what she was seeing, in any case. If he had a sense of humor he might say, "It's a letter from my father." But since he had never seen the utility of humor he did not.

Angie had never asked him why they had to travel so far just to wait for the results of some job applications, especially when there were no jobs at Crossroads or anywhere within a hundred miles of that place. He hadn't even bothered to concoct a story because he'd been so sure she wouldn't ask. This woman was making him lazy.

Once or twice he'd told her directly how stupid she was. She'd looked as if she might break apart. Part of him wanted to feel sorry for what he'd said. Part of him wanted to know what the feeling was like, to feel like your face was going to break. But he didn't have the capacity in him. He supposed some people were born victims. And some people were born like him. *Predator* was a good word for people like him, he supposed. There were a great many predators on this planet.

Their two kids had been climbing the walls. Not literally, of course, but that's the way Angie had expressed it. The only place they had to play was the motel parking lot. As far as he was concerned they should let them loose out there—the children could learn a few lessons about taking care of themselves. If they saw a car coming, let them learn to get out of the way. But Angie wouldn't allow it. He was their father, of course—they had his wise blood in their bodies. He could have insisted. But sometimes you let the mother have the final say where the care of the children is concerned.

Walker's own mother let him wander loose from the time he was six years old—that had been her way. It didn't mean she had no caring in her for him. Actually, he had no idea how she felt. She could have felt anything, or nothing. That was simply the way she was.

He'd never met his father, but he felt as if he knew him—certainly he could feel him. She'd lain with a hundred men or more, so it could have been anyone, or anything he supposed. But Walker felt he'd know his father if he saw him, however he manifested himself. It never bothered him. And if he did see this creature, his father, he wasn't even sure he'd say hello. But he might have questions. He might want a sample of his blood. He might want to see what happened if he poured his father's blood onto the grounds of the Crossroads.

The boy—they'd named him Jack—threw something at the girl. Gillian, or Ginger, depending on the day. Walker had never quite found a name he'd really liked for her, or even remembered from one day to the next. Walker didn't know what the boy tried to hit her with—he never saw anything. He didn't watch them very closely. And there was no sense in asking them—they were both little liars. That was okay with him—in his experience most human beings didn't respond well to the truth in the best of cases. These children were probably better off lying.

But Angie wouldn't stop. "They're going to grow up to be monsters! Both of them! Jack slaps her. Gillian kicks him. This crap goes on all day! Do you even care how they might turn out?"

"Of course I care," he'd lied. Because it would have been inconvenient if Angie had fully understood his basic attitude toward their children. He couldn't have her attempting to take the children and leave before things had completed. "I'll talk to them." The relief in her face almost made him smile.

The children looked up at him, sullenly, defiantly. This was good, he thought. Most children were naturally afraid of him. "Jack, what did you throw at her?" he asked.

"It was a rock," Gillian or Ginger said. Walker slapped her hard across the face, her little head rocking like a string puppet's.

"I asked Jack," he explained.

She didn't cry, just stared at him, a bubble of blood hanging from one nostril.

"It was a rock," Jack said quietly. Walker examined his son's face. Something dark and distant appeared to be swimming in his light green eyes. Angie's eyes were also that color, but Walker had never seen anything swimming there.

"Would it have made you feel badly if you had really hurt her?"

Jack stared up at him dully. Then the boy turned to his sister and they looked at each other. Then they both looked back up at Walker.

"I don't know," Jack replied.

"If you continue to behave this way where other people can see you, eventually you may be detained and imprisoned. It's your decision, but that is something to think about. Right now, you are upsetting your mother. You do not want to do that. You upset her and she becomes troublesome for me. You do not want that, do you understand?" Both children nodded. "Very well, go play quietly for a while. Stay out of my field of vision."

After they left, Walker saw that a couple of drops of his daughter's blood were resting on top of the sand. He kicked at them and they scurried away.

When they'd first checked in, the Crossroads had been practically empty, just a single elderly couple with a camper who'd checked out the very next day. But since then a series of single guests and families had wandered in, almost unnoticeable at first since they mostly came in during the night, but the last couple of days there had been a steady stream, so by week's end the motel was full. Still, more people came into the parking lot, or stopped in the empty land around the building, some on foot with backpacks who set up small tents or lean-tos, others in cars they could sleep in. Despite their numbers these new visitors were relatively quiet, remaining in their rooms or whatever shelter they'd managed, or gathering casually to talk quietly amongst themselves. Many had no particular focus to their activities, but some could not keep their eyes off that horizon far beyond the motel, with its vague suggestion of dunes and mesas shimmering liquidly in the heat.

"Why are they all here?" Angie eventually came around to asking.

"They're part of some traveling church group. They'll be on their way after they rest I'm told."

For the first time she looked doubtful about one of his improvised explanations, but she said nothing.

As more people gathered his son and daughter became steadily more subdued, until eventually they were little more than phantom versions of their former selves, walking slowly through the crowd, looking carefully at every one of them, but not speaking to them, even when some of the newcomers asked them questions.

This continued for a day or two, and although Walker could see a great deal of nervousness, a great many anxious gestures and aimless whispering, and although his sense of the bottled-up energy contained in this one location unexpectedly made his own nerves ragged, there was no explosion, and no outward signs of violence. Some of the people in the crowd actually appeared to be paralyzed. One young, dark-bearded fellow had stood by the outside elbow of the motel for two days, Walker was sure, without moving at all. Parts of the man's cheeks had turned scarlet and begun to blister.

He noticed that the longer the people stayed here, interacting, soaking up one and another's presence, the more they appeared to resemble one another, and him, and his children, as if they had gathered here for some large family reunion. Walker wondered if he were to cut one of them if their blood would also walk, and he was almost sure it would.

He took his morning barefoot walk—why his own feet hadn't burned he had no idea, he didn't really even care to know—by the invisible pool. An old woman crouched there like some sort of ape. At first he thought she was humming, but as he passed her he realized she was speaking low and rapidly, and completely incomprehensibly. She sounded vaguely Germanic, but he suspected her speech wasn't anything but her own spontaneous creation.

He gradually became aware of a rancid stink carried on the dry desert wind. Looking around he saw that those who had sought shelter outside the poor accommodations of the Crossroads were up and about, although moving slowly. When he went toward them, it quickly became obvious that they were the source of the smell.

A tall woman with long dark hair approached him. "You seem familiar," she said weakly, and raised her hand as if to touch his face. He stepped back quickly, and it wasn't because he now saw that a portion of the left cheek of her otherwise beautiful face appeared melted, but because he'd never liked the idea of strangers touching him. He knew this made little sense because he'd always been a lone figure among strangers. Angie, certainly, was a stranger as far as he was concerned, and his children Jack and (what was the girl's name?) little better.

Then an elderly man appeared beside her, and a young boy, all with bubbling, disease-ridden skin. Walker darted past them, and into a crowd of grasping, distorted hands, blisters bursting open on raw, burnt-looking skin. He squirmed his way out, but not without soiling himself with their secretions.

He felt embarrassed to be so squeamish. Was he any different than they? He'd seen the dark familiar shapes swimming in their eyes like the reflections of still-evolving life forms. Clearly, he was no longer alone in the world, because what he had seen in them was both familiar and vaguely familial. But it was an uncomfortable, even an appalling knowledge.

He was some kind of mongrel, a blending of two disparate species, and yet so were they. He doubted any of them had known their fathers. His own children were their blood kin, but at least they knew their father.

The two most familiar children came out of the crowd and gazed at him, their faces running with changes. He felt a kind of unknowable loss, for a kind of kinship that had never been completely his, for the simpler Sunday afternoon picnic world of humanity that would now be forever out of his reach.

Angie came outside for her children then, bellowing the dumb unmelodic scream of a despairing cow, and he struck her down with indifferent blows from both suddenly-so-leaden hands. She had been his last possible door into humanity, and he had slammed her irrevocably closed. Her children looked on as unconcerned as an incursion of sand over an abandoned threshold.

And now they've come out of those distant mesas and deserts, on their astounding black wings, on their thousand-legged spines, their mouths open and humming like the excited blood of ten thousand boiling insects, like the secret longings of the bestial herd, like his blood preparing to leave the confines of vein, like his blood crawling out of the midnight of collective pain, the liquid horizon unfolding.

And out of that shimmering line the fathers come to reclaim their children, the keepers of their dark blood. And Walker must collapse in surrender as these old fathers out of the despairing nights of human frailty, in endless rebellion from the laws of the physical universe, these fathers, these cruel fathers, consume.

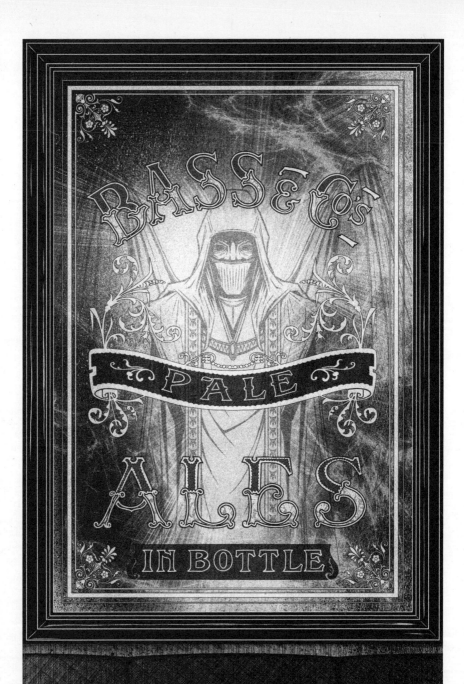

I've Come to Talk with You Again

Karl Edward Wagner

THEY WERE ALL in the Swan. The music box was moaning something about "everybody hurts sometime" or was it "everybody hurts something." Jon Holsten couldn't decide. He wondered, why the country-western sound in London? Maybe it was "everybody hurts somebody." Where were The Beatles when you needed them? One Beatle short, to begin with. Well, yeah, two Beatles. And Pete Best. Whatever.

"Wish they'd turn that bloody thing down." Holsten scowled at the offending speakers. Coins and sound effects clattered from the fruit machine, along with bonks and flippers from the Fish Tales pinball machine. The pub was fusty with mildew from the pissing rain of the past week and the penetrating stench of stale tobacco smoke. Holsten hated the ersatz stuffed trout atop the pinball machine.

Mannering was opening a packet of crisps, offering them around. Foster declined: he had to watch his salt. Carter crunched a handful, then wandered across to the long wooden bar to examine the two chalk-on-slate menus: Quality Fayre was promised. He ordered prime pork sausages with chips and baked beans, not remembering to watch his weight. Stein limped down the treacherous stairs to the Gents. Insulin time. Crosley helped himself to the crisps and worried that his round was coming up. He'd have to duck it. Ten quid left from his dole check, and a week till the next.

There were six of them tonight, where once eight or ten might have foregathered. Over twenty years, it had become an annual tradition: Jon Holsten over from the States for his holiday in London, the usual crowd around for pints and jolly times. Cancer of the kidneys had taken McFerran last year; he who always must have steak and kidney pie. Hiles had decamped to the Kentish coast, where he hoped the sea air would improve his chest. Marlin was somewhere in France, but no one knew where, nor whether he had kicked his drug dependence.

So it went.

"To absent friends," said Holsten, raising his pint. The toast was well received, but added to the gloom of the weather with its memories of those who should have been there.

Jon Holsten was an American writer of modest means but respectable reputation. He got by with a little help from his friends, as it were. Holsten was generally considered to be the finest of the later generation of writers in the Lovecraftian school—a genre mainly out of fashion in these days of chainsaws and flesh-eating zombies, but revered by sufficient devotees to provide for Holsten's annual excursion to London.

Holsten tipped back his pint glass. Over its rim he saw the yellow-robed figure enter the doorway. He continued drinking without hesitation, swallowing perhaps faster now. The pallid mask regarded him as impassively as ever. An American couple entered the pub, walking past. They were arguing in loud New York accents about whether to eat here. For an instant the blue-haired woman shivered as she brushed through the tattered cloak.

Holsten had fine blond hair, brushed straight back. His eyes were blue and troubled. He stood just under six feet, was compactly muscled beneath his blue three-piece suit. Holsten was past the age of sixty.

"Bloody shame about McFerran," said Mannering, finishing the crisps. Carter returned from the bar with his plate. Crosley looked on hungrily. Foster looked at his empty glass. Stein returned from the Gents.

Stein: "What were you saying?"

Mannering: "About McFerran."

"Bloody shame." Stein sat down.

"My round," said Holsten. "Give us a hand, will you, Ted?"

The figure in tattered yellow watched Holsten as he arose. Holsten had already paid for *his* round.

Ted Crosley was a failed writer of horror fiction: some forty stories in twenty years, mostly for nonpaying markets. He was forty and balding and worried about his hacking cough.

Dave Mannering and Steve Carter ran a bookshop and lived above it. Confirmed bachelors adrift from Victorian times. Mannering was thin, dark, well-dressed, scholarly. Carter was red-haired, Irish, rather large, fond of wearing rugby shirts. They were both about forty.

Charles Stein was a book collector and lived in Crouch End. He was showing much grey and was very concerned about his diabetes. He was about forty.

Mike Foster was a tall, rangy book collector from Liverpool. He was wearing a leather jacket and denim jeans. He was concerned about his blood pressure after a near-fatal heart attack last year. He was fading and about forty.

The figure in the pallid mask was seated at their table when Holsten and Crosley returned from the bar with full pints. No need for a seventh pint. Holsten sat down, trying to avoid the eyes that shone from behind the pallid mask. He wasn't quick enough.

The lake was black. The towers were somehow behind the moon. The moons. Beneath the black water. Something rising. A shape. Tentacled. Terror now. The figure in tattered yellow pulling him forward. The pallid mask. Lifted.

"Are you all right?" Mannering was shaking him.

"Sorry?" They were all looking at Holsten. "Jet lag, I suppose."

"You've been over here for a fortnight," Stein pointed out.

"Tired from it all," said Holsten. He took a deep swallow from his pint, smiled reassuringly. "Getting too old for this, I imagine."

"You're in better health than most of us," said Foster. The tattered cloak was trailing over his shoulders. His next heart attack would not be near-fatal. The figure in the pallid mask brushed past, moving on.

Mannering sipped his pint. The next one would have to be a half: he'd been warned about his liver. "You will be sixty-four on November the eighteenth." Mannering had a memory for dates and had recently written a long essay on Jon Holsten for a horror magazine. "How do you manage to stay so fit?"

"I have this portrait in my attic." Holsten had used the joke too many times before, but it always drew a laugh. And he was not going on sixty-four, despite the dates given in his books.

"No. Seriously." Stein would be drinking a Pils next round, worrying about alcohol and insulin.

The tentacles were not really tentacles—only something with which to grasp and feed. To reach out. To gather in those who had foolishly been drawn into its reach. Had deliberately chosen to pass into its reach. The promises.

The vows. The laughter from behind the pallid mask. Was the price worth the gain? Too late.

"Jon? You sure you're feeling all right?" Stein was oblivious to the pallid mask peering over his shoulder.

"Exercise and vitamins," said Holsten. He gave Stein perhaps another two years.

"It must work for you, then," Mannering persisted. "You hardly look any older than when we first met you here in London some ages ago. The rest of us are rapidly crumbling apart."

"Try jogging and only the occasional pint," Holsten improvised.

"I'd rather just jog," said Carter, getting up for another round. He passed by the tattered yellow cloak. Carter would never jog.

"Bought a rather good copy of *The Outsider*," said Foster, to change the subject. "Somewhat foxed, and in the reprint dust jacket, but at a good price." It had been Crosley's copy, sold cheaply to another dealer.

Holsten remembered the afternoon. Too many years ago. New York. Downstairs book shop. Noise of the subway. Cheap shelf. *The King in Yellow*, stuffed with pages from some older book. A bargain. Not cheap, as it turned out. He had never believed in any of this.

The figure in the pallid mask was studying Crosley, knowing he would soon throw himself in front of a tube train. Drained and discarded.

"Well," said Holsten. "I'd best be getting back after this one."

"This early in the day?" said Mannering, who was beginning to feel his pints. "Must be showing your age."

"Not if I can help it." Holsten sank his pint. "It's just that I said I'd meet someone in the hotel residents' bar at half three. He wants to do one of those interviews, or I'd ask you along. Boring, of course. But…"

"Then come round after," Mannering invited. "We'll all be here."

But not for very much longer, thought Holsten; but he said: "See you shortly, then."

Crosley was again coughing badly, a stained handkerchief to his mouth.

Jon Holsten fled.

The kid was named Dave Harvis, he was from Battersea, and he'd been waiting in the hotel lobby of the Bloomsbury Park for an hour in order not to be late. He wore a blue anorak and was clutching a blue nylon bag with a cassette recorder and some books to be signed, and he was just past twenty-one.

Holsten picked him out as he entered the lobby, but the kid stared cluelessly.

"Hello. I'm Jon Holsten." He extended his hand, as on so many such meetings.

"Dave Harvis." He jumped from his seat. "It's a privilege to meet you, sir. Actually, I was expecting a much older...that is..."

"I get by with a little help from my friends." Holsten gave him a firm American handshake. "Delighted to meet you."

The tentacled mouths stroked and fed, promising whatever you wanted to hear. The figure in its tattered yellow cloak lifted its pallid mask. What is said is said. What is done is done. No turning back. Some promises can't be broken.

"Are you all right, sir?" Harvis had heard that Holsten must be up in his years.

"Jet lag, that's all," said Holsten. "Let's go into the bar, and you can buy me a pint for the interview. It's quiet there, I think."

Holsten sat down, troubled.

Harvis carried over two lagers. He worked on his cassette recorder. The residents' bar was deserted but for the barman.

"If you don't mind, sir." Harvis took a gulp of his lager. "I've invited a few mates round this evening to meet up at the Swan. They're great fans of your work. If you wouldn't mind..."

"My pleasure," said Holsten.

The figure in tattered yellow now entered the residents' bar. The pallid mask regarded Harvis and Holsten as Harvis fumbled with a microcassette tape.

Holsten felt a rush of strength.

He mumbled into his pint: "I didn't mean for this to happen this way, but I can't stop it."

Harvis was still fumbling with the tape and didn't hear.

Neither did any gods who cared.

The Bleeding Shadow

Joe R. Lansdale

I was down at the Blue Light Joint that night, finishing off some ribs and listening to some blues, when in walked Alma May. She was looking good too. Had a dress on and it fit her the way a dress ought to fit every woman in the world. She was wearing a little flat hat that leaned to one side, like an unbalanced plate on a waiter's palm. The high heels she had on made her legs look tight and way all right.

The light wasn't all that good in the joint, which is one of its appeals. It sometimes helps a man or woman get along in a way the daylight wouldn't stand, but I knew Alma May enough to know light didn't matter. She'd look good wearing a sack and a paper hat.

There was something about her face that showed me right off she was worried, that things weren't right. She was glancing left and right, like she was in some big city trying to cross a busy street and not get hit by a car.

I got my bottle of beer, left out from my table, and went over to her.

Then I knew why she'd been looking around like that. She said, "I was looking for you, Richard."

"Say you were," I said. "Well you done found me."

The way she stared at me wiped the grin off my face.

"Something wrong, Alma May?"

"Maybe. I don't know. I got to talk, though. Thought you'd be here, and I was wondering you might want to come by my place."

"When?"

"Now."

"All right."

"But don't get no business in mind," she said. "This isn't like the old days. I need your help, and I need to know I can count on you."

"Well, I kind of like the kind of business we used to do, but all right, we're friends. It's cool."

"I hoped you'd say that."

"You got a car?" I said.

She shook her head. "No. I had a friend drop me off."

I thought, friend? Sure.

"All right then," I said, "let's strut on out."

I guess you could say it's a shame Alma May makes her money turning tricks, but when you're the one paying for the tricks, and you are one of her satisfied customers, you feel different. Right then, anyway. Later, you feel guilty. Like maybe you done peed on the *Mona Lisa*. Cause that gal, she was one fine dark-skinned woman who should have got better than a thousand rides and enough money to buy some eats and make some coffee in the morning. She deserved something good. Should have found and married a man with a steady job that could have done all right by her.

But that hadn't happened. Me and her had a bit of something once, and it wasn't just business, money changing hands after she got me feeling good. No, it was more than that, but we couldn't work it out. She was in the life and didn't know how to get out. And as for deserving something better, that wasn't me. What I had were a couple of nice suits, some two-tone shoes, a hat and a gun—.45 caliber automatic, like they'd used in the war a few years back.

Alma May got a little on the dope, too, and though she shook it, it had dropped her down deep. Way I figured, she wasn't never climbing out of that hole, and it didn't have nothing to do with dope now. What it had to do with was time. You get a window open now and again, and if you don't crawl through it, it closes. I know. My window had closed some time back. It made me mad all the time.

We were in my Chevy, a six-year-old car, a forty-eight model. I'd had it reworked a bit at a time: new tires, fresh windshield, nice seat covers and so on. It was shiny and special.

We were driving along, making good time on the highway, the lights racing over the cement, making the recent rain in the ruts shine like the knees of old dress pants.

"What you need me for?" I asked.

"It's a little complicated," she said.

"Why me?"

"I don't know… You've always been good to me, and once we had a thing goin'."

"We did," I said.

"What happened to it?"

I shrugged. "It quit goin'."

"It did, didn't it? Sometimes I wish it hadn't."

"Sometimes I wish a lot of things," I said.

She leaned back in the seat and opened her purse and got out a cigarette and lit it, then rolled down the window. She remembered I didn't like cigarette smoke. I never had got on the tobacco. It took your wind and it stunk and it made your breath bad too. I hated when it got in my clothes.

"You're the only one I could tell this to," she said. "The only one that would listen to me and not think I been with the needle in my arm. You know what I'm sayin'?"

"Sure, baby, I know."

"I sound to you like I been bad?"

"Naw. You sound all right. I mean, you're talkin' a little odd, but not like you're out of your head."

"Drunk?"

"Nope. Just like you had a bad dream and want to tell someone."

"That's closer," she said. "That ain't it, but that's much closer than any needle or whisky or wine."

Alma May's place is on the outskirts of town. It's the one thing she got out of life that ain't bad. It's not a mansion. It's small, but it's tight and bright in the daylight, all painted up canary yellow color with deep blue trim. It didn't look bad in the moonlight.

Alma May didn't work with a pimp. She didn't need one. She was well known around town. She had her clientele. They were all safe, she told me once. About a third of them were white folks from on the other side of the tracks, up there in the proper part of Tyler Town. What she had besides them was a dead mother and a runaway father, and a brother, Tootie, who liked to travel around, play blues and suck that bottle. He was always needing something, and Alma May, in spite of her own demons, had always managed to make sure he got it.

That was another reason me and her had to split the sheets. That brother of hers was a grown-ass man, and he lived with their mother and let her tote his water. When the mama died, he sort of went to pieces. Alma May took mama's part over, keeping Tootie in whisky and biscuits, even bought him a guitar. He lived off her whoring money, and it didn't bother him none. I didn't like him. But I will say this. That boy could play the blues.

When we were inside her house, she unpinned her hat from her hair and sailed it across the room and into a chair.

She said, "You want a drink?"

"I ain't gonna say no, long as it ain't too weak, and be sure to put it in a dirty glass."

She smiled. I watched from the living room doorway as she went and got a bottle out from under the kitchen sink, showing me how tight that dress fit across her bottom when she bent over. She pulled some glasses off a shelf, come back with a stiff one. We drank a little of it, still standing, leaning against the door frame between living room and kitchen. We finally sat on the couch. She sat on the far end, just to make sure I remembered why we were there. She said, "It's Tootie."

I swigged down the drink real quick, said, "I'm gone."

As I went by the couch, she grabbed my hand. "Don't be that way, baby."

"Now I'm baby," I said.

"Hear me out, honey. Please. You don't owe me, but can you pretend you do?"

"Hell," I said and went and sat down on the couch.

She moved, said, "I want you to listen."

"All right," I said.

"First off, I can't pay you. Except maybe in trade."

"Not that way," I said. "You and me, we do this, it ain't trade. Call it a favor."

I do a little detective stuff now and then for folks I knew, folks that recommended me to others. I don't have a license. Black people couldn't get a license to shit broken glass in this town. But I was pretty good at what I did. I learned it the hard way. And not all of it was legal. I guess I'm a kind of private eye. Only I'm really private. I'm so private I might be more of a secret eye.

"Best thing to do is listen to this," she said. "It cuts back on some explanation."

There was a little record player on a table by the window, a stack of records. She went over and opened the player box and turned it on. The record she wanted was already on it. She lifted up the needle and set it right, stepped back and looked it me.

She was oh so fine. I looked at her and thought maybe I should have stuck with her, brother or no brother. She could melt butter from ten feet away, way she looked.

And then the music started to play.

It was Tootie's voice. I recognized that right away. I had heard him plenty. Like I said, he wasn't much as a person, willing to do anything so he could lay back and play that guitar, slide a pocket knife along the strings to squeal out just the right sound, but he was good at the blues, of that, there ain't no denying.

His voice was high and lonesome, and the way he played that guitar, it was hard to imagine how he could get the sounds out of it he got.

"You brought me over here to listen to records?" I said.

She shook her head. She lifted up the needle, stopped the record, and took it off. She had another in a little paper cover, and she took it out and put it on, dropped the needle down.

"Now listen to this."

First lick or two, I could tell right off it was Tootie, but then there came a kind of turn in the music, where it got so strange the hair on the back of my neck stood up. And then Tootie started to sing, and the hair on the back of my hands and arms stood up. The air in the room got thick and the lights got dim, and shadows come out of the corners and sat on the couch with me. I ain't kidding about that part. The room was suddenly full of them, and I could hear what sounded like a bird, trapped at the ceiling, fluttering fast and hard, looking for a way out.

Then the music changed again, and it was like I had been dropped down a well, and it was a long drop, and then it was like those shadows were folding around me in a wash of dirty water. The room stunk of something foul. The guitar no longer sounded like a guitar, and Tootie's voice was no longer like a voice. It was like someone dragging a razor over concrete while trying to yodel with a throat full of glass. There was something inside the music; something that squished and scuttled and honked and raved, something unsettling, like a snake in a satin glove.

"Cut it off," I said.

But Alma May had already done it.

She said, "That's as far as I've ever let it go. It's all I can do to move to cut it off. It feels like it's getting more powerful the more it plays. I don't want to hear the rest of it. I don't know I can take it. How can that be, Richard? How can that be with just sounds?"

I was actually feeling weak, like I'd just come back from a bout with the flu and someone had beat my ass. I said, "More powerful? How do you mean?"

"Ain't that what you think? Ain't that how it sounds? Like it's getting stronger?"

I nodded. "Yeah."

"And the room—"

"The shadows?" I said. "I didn't just imagine it?"

"No," she said, "Only every time I've heard it, it's been a little different. The notes get darker, the guitar licks, they cut something inside me, and each time it's something different and something deeper. I don't know if it makes me feel good or it makes me feel bad, but it sure makes me feel."

"Yeah," I said, because I couldn't find anything else to say.

"Tootie sent me that record. He sent a note that said: Play it when you have to. That's what it said. That's all it said. What's that mean?"

"I don't know, but I got to wonder why Tootie would send it to you in the first place. Why would he want you to hear something makes you almost sick… And how in hell could he do that, make that kind of sound, I mean?"

She shook her head. "I don't know. Someday, I'm gonna play it all the way through."

"I wouldn't," I said.

"Why?"

"You heard it. I figure it only gets worse. I don't understand it, but I know I don't like it."

"Yeah," she said, putting the record back in the paper sleeve. "I know. But it's so strange. I've never heard anything like it."

"And I don't want to hear anything like it again."

"Still, you have to wonder."

"What I wonder is what I was wondering before. Why would he send this shit to you?"

"I think he's proud of it. There's nothing like it. It's…original."

"I'll give it that," I said. "So, what do you want with me?"

"I want you to find Tootie."

"Why?"

"Because I don't think he's right. I think he needs help. I mean, this… It makes me think he's somewhere he shouldn't be."

"But yet, you want to play it all the way through," I said.

"What I know is I don't like that. I don't like Tootie being associated with it, and I don't know why. Richard, I want you to find him."

"Where did the record come from?"

She got the sleeve and brought it to me. I could see through the little doughnut in the sleeve where the label on the record ought to be. Nothing but disk. The package itself was like wrapping paper you put meat in. It was stained.

I said, "I think he paid some place to let him record," I said. "Question is, what place? You have an address where this came from?"

"I do." She went and got a large manila envelope and brought it to me. "It came in this."

I looked at the writing on the front. It had as a return address, The Hotel Champion. She showed me the note. It was on a piece of really cheap stationery that said The Hotel Champion and had a phone number and an address in Dallas. The stationery looked old and it was sun faded.

"I called them," she said, "but they didn't know anything about him. They had never heard of him. I could go look myself, but…I'm a little afraid. Besides, you know, I got clients, and I got to make the house payment."

I didn't like hearing about that, knowing what kind of clients she meant, and how she was going to make that money. I said, "All right. What you want me to do?"

"Find him."

"And then what?"

"Bring him home."

"And if he don't want to come back?"

"I've seen you work, bring him home to me. Just don't lose that temper of yours."

I turned the record around and around in my hands. I said, "I'll go take a look. I won't promise anything more than that. He wants to come, I'll bring him back. He doesn't, I might be inclined to break his leg and bring him back. You know I don't like him."

"I know. But don't hurt him."

"If he comes easy, I'll do that. If he doesn't, I'll let him stay, come back and tell you where he is and how he is. How about that?'

"That's good enough," she said. "Find out what this is all about. It's got me scared, Richard."

"It's just bad sounds," I said. "Tootie was probably high on something when he recorded it, thought it was good at the time, sent it to you because he thought he was the coolest thing since Robert Johnson."

"Who?"

"Never mind. But I figure when he got over his hop, he probably didn't even remember he mailed it."

"Don't try and tell me you've heard anything like this. That listening to it didn't make you feel like your skin was gonna pull off your bones, that some part of it made you want to dip in the dark and learn to like it. Tell me it wasn't like that? Tell me it wasn't like walking out in front of a car and the headlights in your face, and you just wanting to step out there even though it scared hell out of you and you knew it was the devil or something even worse at the wheel. Tell me you didn't feel something like that."

I couldn't. So I didn't say anything. I just sat there and sweated, the sound of that music still shaking down deep in my bones, boiling my blood.

"Here's the thing," I said. "I'll do it, but you got to give me a photograph of Tootie, if you got one, and the record so you don't play it no more."

She studied me a moment. "I hate that thing," she said, nodding at the record in my hands, "but somehow I feel attached to it. Like getting rid of it is getting rid of a piece of me."

"That's the deal."

"All right," she said, "take it, but take it now."

Motoring along by myself in the Chevy, the moon high and bright, all I could think of was that music, or whatever that sound was. It was stuck in my head like an axe. I had the record on the seat beside me, had Tootie's note and envelope, the photograph Alma May had given me.

Part of me wanted to drive back to Alma May and tell her no, and never mind. Here's the record back. But another part of me, the dumb part, wanted to know where and how and why that record had been made. Curiosity, it just about gets us all.

Where I live is a rickety third-floor walk-up. It's got the stairs on the outside, and they stop at each landing. I was at the very top.

I tried not to rest my hand too heavy on the rail as I climbed, because it was about to come off. I unlocked my door and turned on the light and watched the roaches run for cover.

I put the record down, got a cold one out of the ice box. Well, actually it was a plug in. A refrigerator. But I'd grown up with ice boxes, so calling it that was hard to break. I picked up the record again and took a seat.

Sitting in my old armchair with the stuffings leaking out like a busted cotton sack, holding the record again, looking at the dirty brown sleeve, I noticed the grooves were dark and scabby looking, like something had gotten poured in there and had dried tight. I tried to determine if that had something to do with that crazy sound. Could something in the grooves make that kind of noise? Didn't seem likely.

I thought about putting the record on, listening to it again, but I couldn't stomach the thought. The fact that I held it in my hand made me uncomfortable. It was like holding a bomb about to go off.

I had thought of it like a snake once. Alma May had thought of it like a hit-and-run car driven by the devil. And now I had thought of it like a bomb. That was some kind of feeling coming from a grooved up circle of wax.

Early next morning, with the .45 in the glove box, a razor in my coat pocket, and the record up front on the seat beside me, I tooled out toward Dallas, and the Hotel Champion.

I got into Big D around noon, stopped at a café on the outskirts where there was colored, and went in where a big fat mama with a pretty face and a body that smelled real good, made me a hamburger and sat and flirted with me all the while I ate it. That's all right. I like women, and I like them to flirt. They quit doing that, I might as well lay down and die.

While we was flirting, I asked her about the Hotel Champion, if she knew where it was. I had the street number of course, but I needed tighter directions.

"Oh, yeah, honey, I know where it is, and you don't want to stay there. It's deep in the colored section, and not the good part, that's what I'm trying to tell you, and it don't matter you brown as a walnut yourself. There's folks down there will cut you and put your blood in a paper cup and mix it with whisky and drink it. You too good looking to get all cut up and such. There's better places to stay on the far other side."

I let her give me a few hotel names, like I might actually stay at one or the other, but I got the address for the Champion, paid up, giving her a good tip, and left out of there.

The part of town where the Hotel Champion was, was just as nasty as the lady had said. There were people hanging around on the streets, and leaning into corners, and there was trash everywhere. It wasn't exactly a place that fostered a lot of pride.

I found the Hotel Champion and parked out front. There was a couple fellas on the street eyeing my car. One was skinny. One was big. They were dressed up with nice hats and shoes, just like they had jobs. But if they did, they wouldn't have been standing around in the middle of the day eyeing my Chevy.

I pulled the .45 out of the glove box and stuck it in my pants, at the small of my back. My coat would cover it just right.

I got out and gave the hotel the gander. It was nice looking if you were blind in one eye and couldn't see out the other.

There wasn't any doorman, and the door was hanging on a hinge. Inside I saw a dusty stairway to my left, a scarred door to my right.

There was a desk in front of me. It had a glass hooked to it that went to the ceiling. There was a little hole in it low down on the counter that had a wooden stop behind it. There were fly specks on the glass, and there was a man behind the glass, perched on a stool, like a frog on a lily pad. He was fat and colored and his hair had blue blanket wool in it. I didn't take it for decoration. He was just a nasty sonofabitch.

I could smell him when he moved the wooden stop. A stink like armpits and nasty underwear and rotting teeth. Floating in from somewhere in back, I could smell old cooking smells, boiled pigs feet and pigs tails that might have been good about the time the pig lost them, but now all that was left was a rancid stink. There was also a reek like cat piss.

I said, "Hey, man, I'm looking for somebody."

"You want a woman, you got to bring your own," the man said. "But I can give you a number or two. Course, I ain't guaranteeing anything about them being clean."

"Naw. I'm looking for somebody was staying here. His name is Tootie Johnson."

"I don't know no Tootie Johnson."

That was the same story Alma May had got.

"Well, all right, you know this fella?" I pulled out the photograph and pressed it against the glass.

"Well, he might look like someone got a room here. We don't sign in and we don't exchange names much."

"No? A class place like this."

"I said he might look like someone I seen," he said. "I didn't say he definitely did."

"You fishing for money?"

"Fishing ain't very certain," he said.

I sighed and put the photograph back inside my coat and got out my wallet and took out a five dollar bill.

Frog Man saw himself as some kind of greasy high roller. "That's it? Five dollars for prime information?"

I made a slow and careful show of putting my five back in my wallet. "Then you don't get nothing," I said.

He leaned back on his stool and put his stubby fingers together and let them lay on his round belly. "And you don't get nothing neither, jackass."

I went to the door on my right and turned the knob. Locked. I stepped back and kicked it so hard I felt the jar all the way to the top of my head. The door flew back on its hinges, slammed into the wall. It sounded like someone firing a shot.

I went on through and behind the desk, grabbed Frog Man by the shirt and slapped him hard enough he fell off the stool. I kicked him in the leg and he yelled. I picked up the stool and hit him with it across the chest, then threw the stool through a doorway that led into a kitchen. I heard something break in there and a cat made a screeching sound.

"I get mad easy," I said.

"Hell, I see that," he said, and held up a hand for protection. "Take it easy, man. You done hurt me."

"That was the plan."

The look in his eyes made me feel sorry for him. I also felt like an asshole. But that wouldn't keep me from hitting him again if he didn't answer my question. When I get perturbed, I'm not reasonable.

"Where is he?"

"Do I still get the five dollars?"

"No," I said, "now you get my best wishes. You want to lose that?"

"No. No, I don't."

"Then don't play me. Where is he, you toad?"

"He's up in room 52, on the fifth floor."

"Spare key?"

He nodded at a rack of them. The keys were on nails and they all had little wooden pegs on the rings with the keys. Numbers were painted on the pegs. I found one that said 52, took it off the rack.

I said, "You better not be messing with me?"

"I ain't. He's up there. He don't never come down. He's been up there a week. He makes noise up there. I don't like it. I run a respectable place."

"Yeah, it's really nice here. And you better not be jerking me."

"I ain't. I promise."

"Good. And, let me give you a tip. Take a bath. And get that shit out of your hair. And those teeth you got ain't looking too good. Pull them. And shoot that fucking cat, or at least get him some place better than the kitchen to piss. It stinks like a toilet in there."

I walked out from behind the desk, out in the hall, and up the flight of stairs in a hurry.

I rushed along the hallway on the fifth floor. It was covered in white linoleum with a gold pattern in it; it creaked and cracked as I walked along. The end of the hall had a window, and there was a stairwell on that end too. Room 52 was right across from it.

I heard movement on the far end of the stairs. I had an idea what that was all about. About that time, two of the boys I'd seen on the street showed themselves at the top of the stairs, all decked out in their nice hats and such, grinning.

One of them was about the size of a Cadillac, with a gold tooth that shown bright when he smiled. The guy behind him was skinny with his hand in his pocket.

I said, "Well, if it isn't the pimp squad."

"You funny, nigger," said the big man.

"Yeah, well, catch the act now. I'm going to be moving to a new local."

"You bet you are," said the big man.

"Fat ass behind the glass down there, he ain't paying you enough to mess with me," I said.

"Sometimes, cause we're bored, we just like messin'."

"Say you do?"

"Uh huh," said the skinny one.

It was then I seen the skinny guy pull a razor out of his pocket. I had one too, but razor work, it's nasty. He kept it closed.

Big guy with the gold tooth, flexed his fingers, and made a fist. That made me figure he didn't have a gun or a razor; or maybe he just liked hitting people. I know I did.

They come along toward me then, and the skinny one with the razor flicked it open. I pulled the .45 out from under my coat, said, "You ought to put that back in your pocket," I said, "save it for shaving."

"Oh, I'm fixing to do some shaving right now," he said.

I pointed the .45 at him.

The big man said, "That's one gun for two men."

"It is," I said, "but I'm real quick with it. And frankly, I know one of you is gonna end up dead. I just ain't sure which one right yet."

"All right then," said the big man, smiling. "That'll be enough." He looked back at the skinny man with the razor. The skinny man put the razor back in his coat pocket and they turned and started down the stairs.

I went over and stood by the stairway and listened. I could hear them walking down, but then all of a sudden, they stopped on the stairs. That's the way I had it figured.

Then I could hear the morons rushing back up. They weren't near as sneaky as they thought they was. The big one was first out of the chute, so to speak; come rushing out of the stairwell and onto the landing. I brought the butt of the .45 down on the back of his head, right where the skull slopes down. He did a kind of frog hop and bounced across the hall and hit his head on the wall, and went down and laid there like his intent all along had been a quick leap and a nap.

Then the other one was there, and he had the razor. He flicked it, and then he saw the .45 in my hand.

"Where did you think this gun was gonna go?" I said. "On vacation?"

I kicked him in the groin hard enough he dropped the razor, and went to his knees. I put the .45 back where I got it. I said, "You want some, man?"

He got up, and come at me. I hit him with a right and knocked him clean through the window behind him. Glass sprinkled all over the hallway.

I went over and looked out. He was lying on the fire escape, his head, against the railing. He looked right at me.

"You crazy, cocksucker. What if there hadn't been no fire escape?"

"You'd have your ass punched into the bricks. Still might."

He got up quick and clamored down the fire escape like a squirrel. I watched him till he got to the ground and went limping away down the alley between some overturned trash cans and a slinking dog.

I picked up his razor and put it in my pocket with the one I already had, walked over and kicked the big man in the head just because I could.

I knocked on the door. No one answered. I could hear sounds from inside. It was similar to what I had heard on that record, but not quite, and it was faint, as if coming from a distance.

No one answered my knock, so I stuck the key in the door and opened it and went straight inside.

I almost lost my breath when I did.

The air in the room was thick and it stunk of mildew and rot and things long dead. It made those boiled pig feet and that shitting cat and that rotten-tooth bastard downstairs smell like perfume.

Tootie was lying on the bed, on his back. His eyes were closed. He was a guy usually dressed to the top, but his shirt was wrinkled and dirty and sweaty at the neck and arm pits. His pants were nasty too. He had on his shoes, but no socks. He looked like someone had set him on fire and then beat out the flames with a two-by-four. His face was like a skull, he had lost so much flesh, and he was as bony under his clothes as a skeleton.

Where his hands lay on the sheet, there were blood stains. His guitar was next to the bed, and there were stacks and stacks of composition notebooks lying on the floor. A couple of them were open and filled with writing. Hell, I didn't even know Tootie could write.

The wall on the far side was marked up in black and red paint; there were all manner of musical notes drawn on it, along with symbols I had never seen before; swiggles and circles and stick figure drawings. Blood was on the wall too, most likely from Tootie's bleeding fingers. Two open paint cans, the red and the black, were on the floor with brushes stuck up in them. Paint was splattered on the floor and had dried in humped up blisters. The guitar had blood stains all over it.

A record player, plugged in, setting on a nightstand by the bed, was playing that strange music. I went to it right away and picked up the needle and set it aside. And let me tell you, just making my way across the room to get hold of the player was like wading through mud with my ankles tied together. It seemed to me as I got closer to the record, the louder it got, and the more ill I felt. My head throbbed. My heart pounded.

When I had the needle up and the music off, I went over and touched Tootie. He didn't move, but I could see his chest rising and falling. Except for his hands, he didn't seem hurt. He was in a deep sleep. I picked up his right hand and turned it over and looked at it. The fingers were cut deep, like someone had taken a razor to the tips. Right off, I figured that was from playing his guitar. Struck me, that to get the sounds he got out of it, he really had to dig in with those fingers. And from the looks of this room, he had been at it nonstop, until recent.

I shook him. His eyes fluttered and finally opened. They were bloodshot and had dark circles around them.

When he saw me, he startled, and his eyes rolled around in his head like those little games kids get where you try to shake the marbles into holes. After a moment, they got straight, and he said, "Ricky?"

That was another reason I hated him. I didn't like being called Ricky.

I said, "Hello, shithead. You're sister's worried sick."

"The music," he said. "Put back on the music."

"You call that music?" I said.

He took a deep breath, rolled out of the bed, nearly knocking me aside. Then I saw him jerk, like he'd seen a truck coming right at him. I turned. I wished it had been a truck.

Let me try and tell you what I saw. I not only saw it, I felt it. It was in the very air we were breathing, getting inside my chest like mice wearing barbed wire coats. The wall Tootie had painted and drawn all that crap on, shook.

And then the wall wasn't a wall at all. It was a long hallway, dark as original sin. There was something moving in there, something that slithered and slid and made smacking sounds like an anxious old drunk about to take his next drink. Stars popped up; greasy stars that didn't remind me of anything I had ever seen in the night sky; a moon the color of a bleeding fish eye was in the background, and it cast a light on something moving toward us.

"Jesus Christ," I said.

"No," Tootie said. "It's not him."

Tootie jumped to the record player, picked up the needle, and put it on. There came that rotten sound I had heard with Alma May, and I knew what I had heard when I first came into the room was the tail end of that same record playing, the part I hadn't heard before.

The music screeched and howled. I bent over and threw up. I fell back against the bed, tried to get up, but my legs were like old pipe cleaners. That record had taken the juice out of me. And then I saw it.

There's no description that really fits. It was...a thing. All blanket wrapped in shadow with sucker mouths and thrashing tentacles and centipede legs mounted on clicking hooves. A bulblike head plastered all over with red and yellow eyes that seemed to creep. All around it, shadows swirled like water. It had a beak. Well, beaks.

The thing was coming right out of the wall. Tentacles thrashed toward me. One touched me across the cheek. It was like being scalded with hot grease. A shadow come loose of the thing, fell onto the floorboards of the room, turned red and raced across the floor like a gush of blood. Insects and maggots squirmed in the bleeding shadow, and the record hit a high spot so loud and so goddamn strange, I ground my teeth, felt as if my insides were being twisted up like wet wash. And then I passed out.

When I came to, the music was still playing. Tootie was bent over me.

"That sound," I said.

"You get used to it," Tootie said, "but the thing can't. Or maybe it can, but just not yet."

I looked at the wall. There was no alleyway. It was just a wall plastered in paint designs and spots of blood.

"And if the music stops?" I said.

"I fall asleep," Tootie said. "Record quits playing, it starts coming."

For a moment I didn't know anything to say. I finally got off the floor and sat on the bed. I felt my cheek where the tentacle hit me. It throbbed and I could feel blisters. I also had a knot on my head where I had fallen.

"Almost got you," Tootie said. "I think you can leave and it won't come after you. Me, I can't. I leave, it follows. It'll finally find me. I guess here is as good as any place."

I was looking at him, listening, but not understanding a damn thing.

The record quit. Tootie started it again. I looked at the wall. Even that blank moment without sound scared me. I didn't want to see that thing again. I didn't even want to think about it.

"I haven't slept in days, until now," Tootie said, coming to sit on the bed. "You hadn't come in, it would have got me, carried me off, taken my soul. But, you can leave. It's my look out, not yours… I'm always in some kind of shit, ain't I, Ricky?"

"That's the truth."

"This though, it's the corker. I got to stand up and be a man for once. I got to fight this thing back, and all I got is the music. Like I told you, you can go."

I shook my head. "Alma May sent me. I said I'd bring you back."

It was Tootie's turn to shake his head. "Nope. I ain't goin'. I ain't done nothin' but mess up sis's life. I ain't gonna do it."

"First responsible thing I ever heard you say," I said.

"Go on," Tootie said. "Leave me to it. I can take care of myself."

"If you don't die of starvation, or pass out from lack of sleep, or need of water, you'll be just fine."

Tootie smiled at me. "Yeah. That's all I got to worry about. I hope it is one of them other things kills me. Cause if it comes for me… Well, I don't want to think about it."

"Keep the record going, I'll get something to eat and drink, some coffee. You think you can stay awake a half hour or so?"

"I can, but you're coming back?"

"I'm coming back," I said.

Out in the hallway I saw the big guy was gone. I took the stairs.

When I got back, Tootie had cleaned up the vomit, and was looking through the notebooks. He was sitting on the floor and had them stacked all around him. He was maybe six inches away from the record player. Now and again he'd reach up and start it all over.

Soon as I was in the room, and that sound from the record was snugged up around me, I felt sick. I had gone to a greasy spoon down the street, after I changed a flat tire. One of the boys I'd given a hard time had most likely knifed it. My bet was the lucky son-of-a-bitch who had fallen on the fire escape.

Besides the tire, a half-dozen long scratches had been cut into the paint on the passenger's side, and my windshield was knocked in. I got back from the café, I parked what was left of my car behind the hotel, down the street a bit, and walked a block. Car looked so bad now, maybe nobody would want to steal it.

I sat one of the open sacks on the floor by Tootie.

"Both hamburgers are yours," I said. "I got coffee for the both of us here."

I took out a tall, cardboard container of coffee and gave it to him, took the other one for myself. I sat on the bed and sipped. Nothing tasted good in that room with that smell and that sound. But, Tootie, he ate like a wolf. He gulped those burgers and coffee like it was air.

When he finished with the second burger, he started up the record again, leaned his back against the bed.

"Coffee or not," he said, "I don't know how long I can stay awake."

"So what you got to do is keep the record playing?" I said.

"Yeah."

"Lay up in bed, sleep for a few hours. I'll keep the record going. You're rested, you got to explain this thing to me, and then we'll figure something out."

"There's nothing to figure," he said. "But, god, I'll take you up on that sleep."

He crawled up in the bed and was immediately out.

I started the record over.

I got up then, untied Tootie's shoes and pulled them off. Hell, like him or not, he was Alma May's brother. And another thing, I wouldn't wish that thing behind the wall on my worst enemy.

I sat on the floor where Tootie had sat and kept restarting the record as I tried to figure things out, which wasn't easy with that music going. I got up from time to time and walked around the room, and then I'd end up back on the floor by the record player, where I could reach it easy.

Between changes, I looked through the composition notebooks. They were full of musical notes mixed with scribbles like the ones on the wall. It was hard to focus with that horrid sound. It was like the air was full of snakes and razors. Got the feeling the music was pushing at something behind that wall. Got the feeling too, there was something on the other side, pushing back.

It was dark when Tootie woke up. He had slept a good ten hours, and I was exhausted with all that record changing, that horrible sound. I had a headache from looking over those notebooks, and I didn't know anymore about them than when I first started.

I went and bought more coffee, brought it back, and we sat on the bed, him changing the record from time to time, us sipping.

I said, "You sure you can't just walk away?"

I was avoiding the real question for some reason. Like, what in hell is that thing, and what is going on? Maybe I was afraid of the answer.

"You saw that thing. I can walk away, all right. And I can run. But wherever I go, it'll find me. So, at some point, I got to face it. Sometimes I make that same record sound with my guitar, give the record a rest. Thing I fear most is the record wearing out."

I gestured at the notebooks on the floor. "What is all that?"

"My notes. My writings. I come here to write some lyrics, some new blues songs."

"Those aren't lyrics, those are notes."

"I know," he said.

"You don't have a music education. You just play."

"Because of the record, I can read music, and I can write things that don't make any sense to me unless it's when I'm writing them, when I'm listening to that music. All those marks, they are musical notes, and the other marks are other kinds of notes, notes for sounds that I couldn't make until a few days back. I didn't even know those sounds were possible. But now, my head is full of the sounds and those marks and all manner of things, and the only way I can rest is to write them down. I wrote on the wall cause I thought the marks, the notes themselves, might hold that thing back and I could run. Didn't work."

"None of this makes any sense to me," I said.

"All right," Tootie said. "This is the best I can explain something that's got no explanation. I had some blues boys tell me they once come to this place on the south side called Cross Road Records. It's a little record shop where the streets cross. It's got all manner of things in it, and it's got this big colored guy with a big white smile and bloodshot eyes that works the joint. They said they'd seen the place, poked their heads in, and even heard Robert Johnson's sounds coming from a player on the counter. There was a big man sitting behind the counter, and he waved them in, but the place didn't seem right, they said, so they didn't go in.

"But, you know me. That sounded like just the place I wanted to go. So, I went. It's where South Street crosses a street called Way Left.

"I go in there, and I'm the only one in the store. There's records everywhere, in boxes, lying on tables. Some got labels, some don't. I'm looking, trying to figure out how you told about anything, and this big fella with the smile comes over to me and starts to talk. He had breath like an un-wiped butt, and his face didn't seem so much like black skin as it did black rock.

"He said, 'I know what you're looking for.' He reached in a box, and pulled out a record didn't have no label on it. Thing was, that whole box didn't have labels. I think he's just messing with me, trying to make a sale. I'm ready to go, cause he's starting to make my skin crawl. Way he moves ain't natural, you know. It's like he's got something wrong with his feet, but he's still able to move, and quick like. Like he does it between the times you blink your eyes.

"He goes over and puts that record on a player, and it starts up, and it was Robert Johnson. I swear, it was him. Wasn't no one could play like him. It was him. And here's the thing. It wasn't a song I'd ever heard by him. And I thought I'd heard all the music he'd put on wax."

Tootie sipped at his coffee. He looked at the wall a moment, and then changed the player again.

I said, "Swap out spots, and I'll change it. You sip and talk. Tell me all of it."

We did that, and Tootie continued.

"Well, one thing comes to another, and he starts talking me up good, and I finally ask him how much for the record. He looks at me, and he says, 'For you, all you got to give me is a little blue soul. And when you come back, you got to buy something with a bit more of it till it's all gone and I got it. Cause you will be back.'

"I figured he was talking about me playing my guitar for him, cause I'd told him I was a player, you know, while we was talking. I told him I had my guitar in a room I was renting, and I was on foot, and it would take me all day to get my guitar and get back, so I'd have to pass on that deal. Besides, I was about tapped out of money. I had a place I was supposed to play that evening, but until then, I had maybe three dollars and some change in my pocket. I had the rent on this room paid up all week, and I hadn't been there but two days. I tell him all that, and he says, 'Oh, that's all right. I know you can play. I can tell about things like that. What I mean is, you give me a drop of blood and a promise, and you can have that record.' Right then, I started to walk out, cause I'm thinking, this guy is nutty as fruit cake with an extra dose of nuts, but I want that record. So, I tell him, sure, I'll give him a drop of blood. I won't lie none to you, Ricky, I was thinking about nabbing that record and making a run with it. I wanted it that bad. So a drop of blood, that didn't mean nothin.'

"He pulls a record needle out from behind the counter, and he comes over and pokes my finger with it, sudden like, while I'm still trying to figure how he got over to me that fast, and he holds my hand and lets blood drip on—get this—the record. It flows into the grooves.

"He says, 'Now, you promise me your blues playing soul is mine when you die.'

"I thought it was just talk, you know, so I told him he could have it. He says, 'When you hear it, you'll be able to play it. And when you play it, sometime when you're real good on it, it'll start to come, like a rat easing its nose into hot dead meat. It'll start to come.'

"'What will?' I said. 'What are you talking about?'

"He says, 'You'll know.'

"Next thing I know, he's over by the door, got it open and he's smiling at me, and I swear, I thought for a moment I could see right through him. Could see his skull and bones. I've got the record in my hand, and I'm walking out, and as soon as I do, he shuts the door and I hear the lock turn.

"My first thought was, I got to get this blood out of the record grooves, cause that crazy bastard has just given me a lost Robert Johnson song for nothing. I took out a kerchief, pulled the record out of the sleeve, and went to wiping. The blood wouldn't come out. It was in the notches, you know.

"I went back to my room here, and I tried a bit of warm water on the blood in the grooves, but it still wouldn't come out. I was mad as hell, figured the record wouldn't play, way that blood had hardened in the grooves. I put it on and thought maybe the needle would wear the stuff out, but as soon as it was on the player and the needle hit it, it started sounding just the way it had in the store. I sat on the bed and listened to it, three or four times, and then I got my guitar and tried to play what was being played, knowing I couldn't do it, cause though I knew that sound wasn't electrified, it sounded like it was. But, here's the thing. I could do it. I could play it. And I could see the notes in my head, and my head got filled up with them. I went out and bought those notebooks, and I wrote it all down just so my head wouldn't explode, cause every time I heard that record, and tried to play it, them notes would cricket-hop in my skull."

All the while we had been talking, I had been replaying the record.

"I forgot all about the gig that night," Tootie said, "I sat here until morning playing. By noon the next day, I sounded just like that record. By late afternoon, I started to get kind of sick. I can't explain it, but I was feeling that there was something trying to tear through somewhere, and it scared me and my insides knotted up.

"I don't know any better way of saying it than that. It was such a strong feeling. Then, while I was playing, the wall there, it come apart the way you seen it, and I seen that thing. It was just a wink of a look. But there it was. In all it's terrible glory.

"I quit playing, and the wall wobbled back in place and closed up. I thought, Damn, I need to eat or nap, or something. And I did. Then I was back on that guitar. I could play like crazy, and I started going off on that song, adding here and there. It wasn't like it was coming from me, though. It was like I was getting help from somewhere.

"Finally, with my fingers bleeding and cramped and aching, and my voice gone raspy from singing, I quit. Still, I wanted to hear it, so I put on the record. And it wasn't the same no more. It was Johnson, but the words was strange, not English. Sounded like some kind of chant, and I knew then that Johnson was in that record, as sure as I was in this room, and that that chanting and that playing was opening up a hole for that thing in the wall. It was the way that fella had said. It was like a rat working its nose through red hot meat, and now it felt like I was the meat. Next time I played the record, the voice on it wasn't Johnson's. It was mine.

"I had had enough, so I got the record and took it back to that shop. The place was the same as before, and like before, I was the only one in there. He looked at me, and comes over, and says, 'You already want to undo the deal. I can tell. They all do. But that ain't gonna happen.'

"I gave him a look like I was gonna jump on him and beat his ass, but he gave me a look back, and I went weak as kitten.

"He smiled at me, and pulls out another record from that same box, and he takes the one I gave him and puts it back, and says, 'You done made a deal, but for a lick of your soul, I'll let you have this. See, you done opened the path, now that rat's got to work on that meat. It don't take no more record or you playing for that to happen. Rat's gotta to eat now, no matter what you do.'

"When he said that, he picks up my hand and looks at my cut up fingers from playing, and he laughs so loud everything in the store shakes, and he squeezes my fingers until they start to bleed.

"A lick of my soul?" I asked.

"And then he pushed the record in my hand, and if I'm lying, I'm dying, he sticks out his tongue, and it's long as an old rat snake and black as a hole in the ground, and he licks me right around the neck. When he's had a taste, he smiles and shivers, like he's just had something cool to drink."

Tootie paused to unfasten his shirt and peel it down a little. There was a spot halfway around his neck like someone had worked him over with sandpaper.

"'A taste,' he says, 'and then he shoves this record in my hand, which is bleeding from where he squeezed my fingers. Next thing I know, I'm looking at the record, and it's thick, and I touch it, and its two records, back to back. He says, 'I give you that extra one cause you tasted mighty good, and maybe it'll let you get a little more rest that way, if you got a turntable drop. Call me generous and kind in my old age.'

"Wasn't nothing for it but to take the records and come back here. I didn't have no intention of playing it. I almost threw it away. But by then, that thing in the wall, wherever it is, was starting to stick through. Each time the hole was bigger and I could see more of it, and that red shadow was falling out on the floor. I thought about running, but I didn't want to just let it loose, and I knew, deep down, no matter where I went, it would come too.

"I started playing that record in self-defense. Pretty soon, I'm playing it on the guitar. When I got scared enough, got certain enough that thing was coming through, I played hard, and that hole would close, and that thing would go back where it come from. For a while.

"I figured though, I ought to have some insurance. You see, I played both them records, and they was the same thing, and it was my voice, and I hadn't never recorded or even heard them songs before. I knew then, what was on those notes I had written, what had come to me was the counter song to the one I had been playing first. I don't know if that was just some kind of joke that record store fella had played on me, but I knew it was magic of a sort. He had give me a song to let it in and he had give me another song to hold it back. It was amusing to him, I'm sure.

"I thought I had the thing at bay, so I took that other copy, went to the Post Office, mailed it to Alma, case something happened to me. I guess I thought it was self-defense for her, but there was another part was proud of what I had done. What I was able to do. I could play anything now, and I didn't even need to think about it. Regular blues, it was a snap. Anything on that guitar was easy, even things you ought not to be able to play on one. Now, I realize it ain't me. It's something else out there.

"But when I come back from mailing, I brought me some paint and brushes, thought I'd write the notes and such on the wall. I did that, and I was ready to pack and go roaming some more, showing off my new skills, and all of a sudden, the thing, it's pushing through. It had gotten stronger cause I hadn't been playing the sounds, man. I put on the record, and I pretty much been at it ever since.

"It was all that record fella's game, you see. I got to figuring he was the devil, or something like him. He had me playing a game to keep that thing out, and to keep my soul. But it was a three-minute game, six if I'd have kept that second record and put it on the drop. If I was playing on the guitar, I could just work from the end of that record back to the front of it, playing it over and over. But it wore me down. Finally, I started playing the record nonstop. And I have for days.

"The fat man downstairs, he'd come up for the rent, but as soon as he'd use his key and crack that door, hear that music, he'd get gone. So here I am, still playing, with nothing left but to keep on playing, or get my soul sucked up by that thing and delivered to the record store man."

Tootie minded the record, and I went over to where he told me the record store was with an idea to put a boot up the guy's ass, or a .45 slug in his noggin. I found South Street, but not Way Left. The other street that should have been Way Left was called Back Water. There wasn't a store either, just an empty, unlocked building. I opened the door and went inside. There was dust everywhere, and I could see where some tables had been, cause their leg marks was in the dust. But anyone or anything that had been there, was long gone.

I went back to the hotel, and when I got there, Tootie was just about asleep. The record was turning on the turntable without any sound. I looked at the wall, and I could see the beak of that thing, chewing at it. I put the record on, and this time, when it come to the end, the thing was still chewing. I played it another time, and another, and the thing finally went away. It was getting stronger.

I woke Tootie up, said, "You know, we're gonna find out if this thing can out run my souped up Chevy."

"Ain't no use," Tootie said.

"Then we ain't got nothing to lose," I said.

We grabbed up the record and his guitar, and we was downstairs and out on the street faster than you can snap your fingers. As we passed where the toad was, he saw me and got up quick and went into the kitchen and closed the door. If I'd had time, I'd have beat his ass on general principles.

When we walked to where I had parked my car, it was sitting on four flats and the side windows was knocked out and the aerial was snapped off. The record Alma May had given me was still there, lying on the seat. I got it and put it against the other one in my hand. It was all I could do.

As for the car, I was gonna drive that Chevy back to East Texas like I was gonna fly back on a sheet of wet newspaper.

Now, I got to smellin' that smell. One that was in the room. I looked at the sky. The sun was kind of hazy. Green even. The air around us trembled, like it was scared of something. It was heavy, like a blanket. I grabbed Tootie by the arm, pulled him down the street. I spied a car at a curb that I thought could run, a V-8 Ford. I kicked the back side window out, reached through and got the latch.

I slid across the seat and got behind the wheel. Tootie climbed in on the passenger side. I bent down and worked some wires under the dash loose with my fingers and my razor, hot wired the car. The motor throbbed and we was out of there.

It didn't make any kind of sense, but as we was cruising along, behind us it was getting dark. It was like chocolate pudding in a big wad rolling after us. Stars was popping up in it. They seemed more like eyes than stars. There was a bit of a moon, slightly covered over in what looked like a red fungus.

I drove that Ford fast as I could. I was hitting the needle at a hundred and ten. Didn't see a car on the highway. Not a highway cop, not an old lady on the way to the store. Where the hell was everybody? The highway looped up and down like the bottom was trying to fall out from under us.

To make it all short, I drove hard and fast, and stopped once for gas, having the man fill it quick. I gave him a bill that was more than the gas was worth, and he grinned at me as we burned rubber getting away. I don't think he could see what we could see—that dark sky with that thing in it. It was like you had to hear the music to see the thing existed, or for it to have any effect in your life. For him, it was daylight and fine and life was good.

By the time I hit East Texas, there was smoke coming from under that stolen Ford's hood. We came down a hill, and it was daylight in front of us, and behind us the dark was rolling in; it was splittin', making a kind of corridor, and there was that beaked thing, that… Whatever it was. It was bigger than before and it was squirming its way out of the night sky like a weasel working its way under a fence. I tried to convince myself it was all in my head, but I wasn't convinced enough to stop and find out.

I made the bottom of the hill, in sight of the road that turned off to Alma May's. I don't know why I felt going there mattered, but it was something I had in my mind. Make it to Alma May's, and deliver on my agreement, bring her brother into the house. Course, I hadn't really thought that thing would or could follow us.

It was right then the car engine blew in an explosion that made the hood bunch up from the impact of thrown pistons.

The car died and coasted onto the road that led to Alma May's house. We could see the house, standing in daylight. But even that light was fading as the night behind us eased on in.

I jerked open the car door, snatched the records off the back seat, and yelled to Tootie to start running. He nabbed his guitar, and a moment later, we were both making tracks for Alma May's.

Looking back, I saw there was a moon back there, and stars too, but mostly there was that thing, full of eyes and covered in sores and tentacles and legs and things I can't even describe. It was like someone had thrown critters and fish and bugs and beaks and all manner of disease into a bowl and whipped it together with a whipping spoon.

When we got to Alma May's, I beat on the door. She opened it, showing a face that told me she thought I was knocking too hard, but then she looked over my shoulder, and went pale, almost as if her skin was white. She had heard the music, so she could see it too.

Slamming the door behind us, I went straight to the record player. Alma May was asking all kinds of questions, screaming them out, really. First to me, then to Tootie. I told her to shut up. I jerked one of the records out of its sleeve, put it on the turntable, lifted the needle, and—

—the electricity crackled and it went dark. There was no playing anything on that player. Outside the world was lit by that blood-red moon.

The door blew open. Tentacles flicked in, knocked over an end table. Some knickknacks fell and busted on the floor. Big as the monster was, it was squeezing through, causing the door frame to crack; the wood breaking sounded like someone cracking whips with both hands.

Me and Alma May, without even thinking about it, backed up. The red shadow, bright as a camp fire, fled away from the monster and started flowing across the floor, bugs and worms squirming in it.

But not toward us.

It was running smooth as an oil spill toward the opposite side of the room. I got it then. It didn't just want through to this side. It wanted to finish off that deal Tootie had made with the record store owner. Tootie had said it all along, but it really hit me then. It didn't want me and Alma at all.

It had come for Tootie's soul.

There was a sound so sharp I threw my hands over my ears, and Alma May went to the floor. It was Tootie's guitar. He had hit it so hard, it sounded electrified. The pulse of that one hard chord made me weak in the knees. It was a hundred times louder than the record. It was beyond belief, and beyond human ability. But, it was Tootie.

The red shadow stopped, rolled back like a tongue.

The guitar was going through its paces now. The thing at the doorway recoiled slightly, and then Tootie yelled, "Come get me. Come have me. Leave them alone."

I looked, and there in the faint glow of the red moonlight through the window, I saw Tootie's shadow lift that guitar high above his head by the neck, and down it came, smashing hard into the floor with an explosion of wood and a springing of strings.

The bleeding shadow came quickly then. Across the floor and onto Tootie. He screamed. He screamed like someone having the flesh slowly burned off. Then the beast came through the door as if shot out of a cannon.

Tentacles slashed, a million feet scuttled, and those beaks came down, ripping at Tootic like a savage dog tearing apart a rag doll. Blood flew all over the room. It was like a huge strawberry exploded.

Then another thing happened. A blue mist floated up from the floor, from what was left of Tootie, and for just the briefest of moments, I saw Tootie's face in that blue mist; the face smiled a toothless kind of smile, showing nothing but a dark hole where his mouth was. Then, like someone sniffing steam off soup, the blue mist was sucked into the beaks of that thing, and Tootie and his soul were done with.

The thing turned its head and looked at us. I started to pull my .45, but I knew there wasn't any point to it. It made a noise like a thousand rocks and broken automobiles tumbling down a cliff made of gravel and glass, and it began to suck back toward the door. It went out with a snapping sound, like a wet towel being popped. The bleeding shadow ran across the floor after it, eager to catch up; a lap dog hoping for a treat.

The door slammed as the thing and its shadow went out, and then the air got clean and the room got bright.

I looked where Tootie had been.

Nothing.

Not a bone.

Not a drop of blood.

I raised the window and looked out.

It was morning.

No clouds in the sky.

The sun looked like the sun.

Birds were singing.

The air smelled clean as a new born's breath.

I turned back to Alma May. She was slowly getting up from where she had dropped to the floor.

"It just wanted him," I said, having a whole different kind of feeling about Tootie than I had before. "He gave himself to it. To save you, I think."

She ran into my arms and I hugged her tight. After a moment, I let go of her. I got the records and put them together. I was going to snap them across my knee. But I never got the chance. They went wet in my hands, came apart and hit the floor and ran through the floor boards like black water, and that was all she wrote.

That of Which We Speak When We Speak of the Unspeakable

Nick Mamatas

IT WAS AUGUST. Everything was going to change. They could feel it. Jase was a prophet and prophets like to talk, so he did. He was talking about the end of all things and how great it was going to be.

They were sitting—Jase and Melissa and Stephan—near the mouth of a cave, around a rock shaped conveniently like a coffee table. The kerosene lamp flickered and stank up the place a little bit. Stephan could taste it in his whisky.

"And you can forget about love," Jase said. Jase wasn't into love, and really he wasn't even into sex anymore, though he'd had plenty, he told his friends. Even just on the way up to the cave to wait for the end, he'd hired a girl and then later stopped at the bus station. Anything, anytime, anywhere, he said. Stephan thought that Jase was just going on about sex because Melissa was right there, cattycorner to him, on the side of the rock deeper in the mouth of the cave.

"Why do you even bring up love?" Stephan asked. Then Melissa said that she thought the conversation was already about sex, as it would have to be once the Missoula bus station bathroom was brought up as a setting, if not the main topic. She gulped her Teacher's right after that, and Stephan took a sip of his and then reached for the bottle.

"Love is that supposed all-powerful, all-encompassing force. You know, a dog gets lost on vacation with its owners and then four months later shows up on the doorstep, covered in twigs and with its fur all matted up, but in fine shape and with a big panting smile."

"Yeah, I saw that on television," Stephan said. "Dog follows owners home on a 3000-mile beam of love."

"Beam of love, exactly," said Jase.

"So how do you think the dog got home?" asked Melissa. "Luck?" Stephan guessed aloud that Jase didn't believe in luck either, or maybe just bad luck, or that luck was running out for everyone.

"No, not at all. I consider myself very lucky." Jase poured himself another drink. He waved his plastic cup of Teacher's under his chin like he was sniffing at a fine wine or some Italian grandma's Sunday meat sauce. "Lucky to be here for the end. To see the sky when the stars blink out, to watch the seas boil and the Elder Gods crush us all."

"That's him," Melissa said to Stephan. "Jase is all about the tentacles and the worship. He likes the drama. He's a drama king."

Stephan said, "There's a sucker born every minute." He tried to keep it going, extend it into a joke. Suckers and tentacles, something like that, but the whisky took the joke away from him even as it had helped him open his mouth for the windup. "Suckers," he repeated, just like that.

Jase stood up, dusted off his ass and teetered toward the mouth of the cave. Stephan thought Jase might start urinating, sending a stream down into the valley below the cave, into the colorless grass. Instead Jase just threw up his arms and shouted, "Fuck love!" If he was hoping for an echo, he didn't get one—not even a cricket cricketed in response. "I'm lucky," he said, turning back to Stephan and Melissa, "because I've never had a thing to do with love. You know what my childhood was like?"

"Same as anyone else's," Melissa said.

"Exactly, yeah, exactly," Jase said. "Sitting on a couch. Doing stuff, growing up. I catch a ball, my father's proud. I hurt my foot, my mother clucks her tongue and pulls out the splinter with a pair of tweezers."

"Sounds dreadful," said Stephan. He squinted his eyes to keep the flicker of the lamp away, turning Jase into a little buzzing kaleidoscope. "Sounds just like being raped twice a day, every day, for fourteen years or something."

"Well, here's the thing," Jase said. He stomped back up the rock and kicked at it twice, knocking the mud from his heels. "It's boring. Everything gets boring."

"Yeah," said Melissa. "I had a boyfriend once who ended up doing some time in prison." Stephan and Jase both got quiet at that. "Nothing bad…well, nothing that bad. It was just a fight, but he knew some stuff, judo, and the guy he was fighting ended up in a coma. Anyway, he went to prison for ninety days and he was mostly very bored. He said everyone else was eager for their hour of exercise, even if it meant getting shived or raped by three guys because otherwise it was just boring."

Jase snorted. "You probably loved him too, eh? Waited for him to get out of prison."

"It was only three months," Stephan said. Stephan wondered if someone would wait for him for three months if he ended up in prison for accidentally putting some guy into a coma. Not that he knew how to put anyone into anything, not even a headlock. Maybe he could run somebody down with a car. He could go to prison and be bored except for the hour of raping every day.

"Yeah, I guess I did. I loved him more when he wasn't around." She looked a little anxious, or maybe she was just chilly. She was deeper in the cave, where it was wet, on the lip of the dark. "You know, when someone is around you remember the bad breath and the rolls of fat hanging over the elastic of his underwear and that annoying way he winks when he's saying something he isn't sure about. So I broke up with him, but I waited until he was out of prison."

"Because you loved him?" Stephan said.

"Because you were bored?" Jase said.

"Because I didn't know what else to do. It's hard to break up with someone in prison. The phone calls are monitored. You have to wait for certain days to go visit, and it's not a place for a real conversation. You can taste metal on your tongue; it's like being sick or allergic to everything."

"Allergic to everything, yeah," Jase said. "I feel a prophecy coming on." He shook out his hair. There was a leaf in it.

Stephan leaned back, his arms behind him, a finger brushing against Melissa's jeans.

Jase trembled, his arms wide, and started doing his tongue tricks. Melissa scooted forward and shifted on her hips to keep from making contact with Stephan. She reached for the Teacher's and took a pull from the bottle, then put it back on the rock and held her cup to her lips, tilting it backwards to get some last drop she had forgotten before. There was still almost a third left in the bottle so Stephan poured some more into his cup too and said, "What do you think of all the yoobalalala stuff," which was a pretty good impression of Jase right then.

"I don't know."

"Is it real?"

"I don't know if he's real, but it's sure real," Melissa said. "No denying that now. Not after New York and not after the Mississippi River."

"And China." It annoyed Stephan that everyone forgot about China, how they tried to nuke the thing when it appeared, all hungry eyes and inside-out angles, and the bomb wiped out half of Shenzhen and flooded Hong Kong and then the thing just rematerialized in the same spot the next day, but radioactive. One time Jase just laughed and said that in China everyone forgot about New York, but Stephan doubted it.

"You see, that's the thing," said Jase. He was on the ground, arms and legs swaying like he was making a grass and leaf and twig angel. "Everyone thinks love is the answer. You look at someone and say 'I love you' and the cancer gets better, or 'I love you' and they'll love you back, or 'I love you' and the decades they spend in shitty jobs to buy shitty food mean something, or 'I love you' and you're not a fat drunk anymore." Stephan wondered if Jase's mother had been a fat drunk.

"Is this still prophecy?" asked Melissa.

"Can't you tell yet?" asked Stephan. Melissa had been following Jase around for longer than Stephan had, for two months, since the Mississippi started swimming with the carpets of tadpoles with the faces of men. Stephan had just wandered up to the cave with them the night before.

"Not prophecy, baby, reality. That's just a story. My story. My folks said they loved me, and showed it by buying me fishsticks and a Christmas present and then they died after a car wreck. You know, not in one, after one. Months later, in traction, their skin all shriveled and burnt. Nothing but screaming pain for the both of them, the pain of sponges and businesslike nurses with thick shoulders going at them, just to keep them alive and in more pain."

"Sorry," Stephan said.

"Are you really?" Jase said.

Stephan thought about it for a second and decided that he wasn't sorry. He said that mostly he just hoped that saying sorry would get Jase to move on to another topic.

"Yeah, that's what we do, right? We move on. I loved my parents too—they trained me to love them with food and physical contact. My brain developed under the tyranny of love. And you know what? After they died and I cried and all that and I still had to figure out how to keep the lights on and the fridge running and the love didn't matter anymore. And when I took off and hit the road people asked about my parents, but just in general. 'Where are your parents? Why are you out here on the streets?' I was just a broken tooth on an otherwise functional cog in a great big machine. There was no love out there, and I moved on. I don't even love my parents anymore. Love fades, like a rash." That last made Stephan laugh.

"Keep laughin', laughing boy," Jase said. He was up on one elbow now, another arm stretched toward the rock. "Whisky," he said, and Stephan leaned over and gave him the bottle of Teacher's and he took a sip and scowled. "Well, so much for all that, eh? Forget cogs, we got crazy backwards ninth dimensional geometry in the machines now. Can't you see 'em in the sky, when you look up and squint and concentrate on the ajna chakra? The dark tentacles in a sky just as dark—"

"Yeah, the end of the universe and it's a whistling squid. Greeeeat," said Melissa. Stephan looked at her. Her hair was stringy and slick from the road and the woods. She smiled tightly over her teeth and fiddled with her thumbnails. "Ah, here they come," she said, more quietly, to Stephan. She pointed with her chin to the dark patch of woods. If there was something moving or crawling or oozing out there Stephan couldn't see. Stephan often couldn't see much anyway. Jase didn't seem to notice either, because he was still talking about the sky tentacles.

"This is truly, you know…" Stephan said, then he stopped talking. He held out his arms and waved them around a bit. Jase's talk had devolved back into the thrashy gibbering.

"Yeah, it is," said Melissa. The shoggoths oozed into the clearing like an oil slick, filmed and then projected backwards, sliding uphill. It seemed to take them a long time to do. "You know, I got into this sort of thing a long time ago, before the Mississippi, before New York. When it was all just hints and footnotes in history. It felt good, really. I was just a kid. I went to the mall, painted my nails, drank Orange Juliuses." Stephan took the hint and jogged around the rock to pick up the bottle from next to where Jase lay and brought it back into the cave. Melissa had both hands up and fingers outstretched, like she was waiting for a baby to be passed to her. She drank, then said, "It just felt good, that there was something bigger than yourself out there. To think you knew something that other people didn't know. Well, everybody knows now."

"Yeah, and mostly people got used to it. We didn't go insane or anything. Not more crazy than people get in some war or during some epidemic. Well, except for Jase, maybe. Are you in love with him?"

"I dunno. Kinda. He's like looking in the mirror. 'So that's what would have happened,' I think when I look at him, 'if I never really grew up, never got used to the idea of doing the dishes even though they'd just get dirty again—'"

At the last minute, Jase broke. He stopped his twisting around and babbling and tried to run back to the cave. A shoggoth drew itself high and came down on him like a wave. Stephan heard a hard crunch. He looked over to Melissa, who still looked passive. The shoggoths pulled themselves across the little plain on pseudopods, dragging and sliding closer and closer.

"Whisky's gone," Melissa said, but it wasn't, and then Melissa took up the bottle and turned it up into her mouth, puffing up her cheeks. She stood up and took the kerosene lantern and turned the little dial to bring down the wick, leaving only a sliver of orange to glow.

Stephan could hear his heart beating. He could hear Melissa's heart beating too, he thought, even over the wet-shoe squelching noises of the shoggoths. He could hear the human noises he sat there making, not moving at all, as the cave went dark. The shoggoths stretched over the entrance. Then a ball of fire from Melissa's mouth as she spit the Teacher's out and across the burning wick of the lamp. A shoggoth burned and shriveled in retreat, but then a few more came.

Haruspicy

Gemma Files

FOR H. P. LOVECRAFT
(AND CAITLÍN R. KIERNAN)

Under the gallows
you open a hanged man up like a book
for practice—
teach by doing.
Call the cubs forth, even
those halflings cursed
with human faces
and show them:
Here, look here, look.

Madame, Madame;
I know I am not made to dance
to either tune, not with
my light-glazed eyes, my knees
set backwards. Not with
my forefinger longer than its nearest fellow,
black nails with their rim of razor
awaiting just the right
Inquisitor's beckoning.

I give myself away.
I apologize, simply for
existing,

never having chosen
to exist.

Down in the cellar, those faint noises—
my relatives come calling.
Unexpected, yet not
unwelcome.

(I am not as you: True.
And yet, I am still
more as you than either of us
would like to think.)

At least, when the skin is peeled away
we are all flesh, blood, guts—
a red-bone rosary, fit for telling.
Not soundless depth, awful dream,
darkness wave-locked
and waiting.

For when that dream is over—
(and this one, too)—
when cold descends and the sun goes out
we will huddle close
for warmth, amongst the tombs,
our two great cultures reduced
to a tumult of cemeteries.
Awkward, insides steaming,
we will share
a final communion—
meat, as memory.

The only thing left to prove
we ever squatted
on the void's thin skin
together.

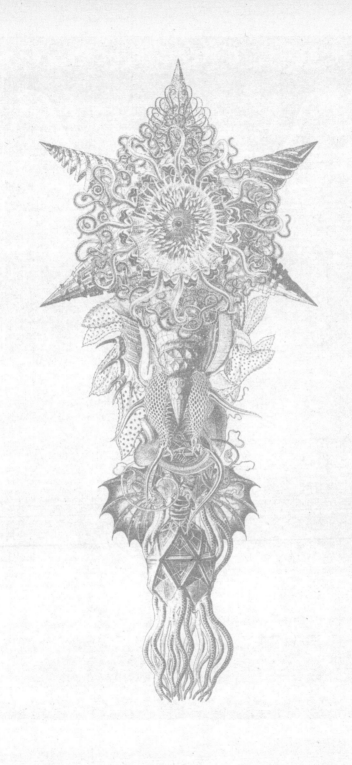

Children of the Fang
John Langan

i. In the Basement (Now): Secret Doors and Mole-Men

THE SMELLS OF the basement: dust, mildew, and the faint, plastic stink of the synthetic rug Grandpa had spread down here two decades ago. The round, astringent odor of mothballs stuffed in the pockets of the clothes hung in the closet. A distant, damp earthiness, the soil on the other side of the cinderblock walls. The barest trace of cinnamon, mixed with vanilla; underneath them, brine.

The sounds of the basement: the furnace, first humming expectantly, then switching on with a dull roar. The rug scraping under her sneakers. What Rachel insisted was the ring of water in the water tank, though her father swore there was no way she could be hearing that. The house above, its timbers creaking as the air in its rooms warmed.

The feel of the basement: openness, as if the space that she knew was not as large as the house overhead was somehow bigger than it. When they were kids, Josh had convinced her that there were secret doors concealed in the walls, through which she might stumble while making her way along one of them. If she did, she would find herself in a huge, black, underground cavern full of mole-men. The prospect of utter darkness had not troubled her as much as her younger brother had intended, but the mole-men and the endless caves to which he promised they would drag her had more than made up for that. Even now, at what she liked to think of as a self-possessed twenty-five, the sensation of spaciousness raised the skin of her arms in gooseflesh.

The look of the basement: the same dark blur that occulted all but the farthest edges of her visual field. Out of habit, she switched her cane from right hand to left and flipped the light switch at the bottom of the stairs. The resulting glow registered as only the slightest lightening in her vision. It didn't matter: she hardly needed the cane to navigate the boxed toys and clothes stacked around the basement floor, to where Grandpa's huge old freezer squatted in the corner opposite her. For what she had come to do, it was probably better that she couldn't see.

2. The Tape (1): Iram

Around her and Josh, the attic, hushed as a church. Off to one side, their grandfather's trunk, whose lack of a lock Josh, bold and nosy at sixteen as he'd ever been, had taken as an invitation to look inside it. Buried beneath old clothes, he'd found the tape recorder and cassettes. Rachel slid her index finger left over three worn, plastic buttons, pressed down on the fourth, and the tape recorder started talking. A snap and a clatter, a hiss like soda fizzing, and a voice, a man—a young man's, someone in his teens, rendered tinny and high by time and the age of the cassette: "Okay," he said, "you were saying, Dad?"

Now a second speaker, Grandpa, the nasal complaint of the accent that had followed him north to New York state from Kentucky accentuated by the recording. "It was Jerry had found the map and figured it showed some place in the Quarter, but it was me worked out where, exactly, we needed to head."

"That's Grandpa," Josh said, "And...Dad?"

"It isn't Dad," Rachel said.

"Then who is it?"

"I'm not sure," she said. "I think it might be Uncle Jim."

"Uncle Jim?"

"James," she said, "Dad's younger brother."

"But he ran away."

"Obviously, this was made before," she said, and shushed him.

"—the company would have been happy to have the two of you just take off," Uncle Jim was saying.

"Well," Grandpa was saying, "there was time between the end of work on one site and the beginning of work on the next. It's true, though: we couldn't wander off for a week. If we said there was a spot we wanted to investigate, the head man was willing to give us a day or two, but that was because he thought we meant something to do with oil."

"Not the Atlantis of the Sands," Jim said.

"Iram," Grandpa said. "Iram of the Pillars, *Iram ḏāt al-ʿimād*."

"Right," Jim said, "Iram. So I guess the sixty-four-thousand-dollar question is, Did you find it?"

Their grandfather did not answer.

"Dad?" Jim said.

"Oh, we found it, all right," Grandpa said, his voice thick.

3. THE FREEZER (1): EARLY INVESTIGATIONS

Enamel-smooth, the surface of the freezer was no colder than anything else in the basement. Once he understood this, at the age of nine, Josh declared it evidence that the appliance was malfunctioning. Rachel corrected him. "If it was cold," she said, "it would mean it wasn't properly insulated." She softened her tone. "I know it sounds weird, but it's supposed to feel like this." She had tested the freezer with her cane, drawing the tip along the side of it and knocking every six inches. "There's something in it," she announced. She set the cane on the floor and pressed her ear to the appliance. She could hear ice sighing and shifting. When the motor clicked to life and she placed her hands on the lid, the metal trembled under her fingertips.

Six feet long by three high by three wide, the freezer served her and Josh as a prop when they were young, and a topic of conversation as they aged. She would lie, first on top of, then beside the metal box with one ear against it, trying to decipher the sounds within, while Josh ran his fingers along the rubber seam that marked the meeting of lid and container. Both of them studied the trio of padlocked latches that guaranteed Grandpa's insistence that the freezer's contents were off-limits. Josh inspected the bolts which fastened the locks to the freezer, the makes of the padlocks, their keyholes; she felt for gaps between the heads of bolts and the latches, between the latches and the freezer, tugged on the padlocks to test the strength of their hold. After speculating about diamonds, or some kind of rare artifact, or a meteor, she and Josh had decided the freezer most likely housed something connected to their grandfather's old job. Grandpa had made his money helping to establish the oil fields in Saudi Arabia, in what was known as the Empty Quarter. As he never tired of reminding them, it was among the most inhospitable places on the planet. It was, however, a desert, whose daily temperature regularly crossed the three-digit mark. What he could have brought back from such a land that would require an industrial freezer remained a mystery.

Interlude: Grandpa (1): The Hippie Wars

The house in which Rachel and her brother were raised was among the largest in Wiltwyck. However, its second storey belonged entirely to their grandfather. Within the house, it was accessed by a staircase which rose from the front hall to a door at which you were required to knock for entry; outside the house, a set of stairs that clung to the southern wall brought you to a small platform and another door on which you were obliged to rap your knuckles. There was no guarantee of entry at either door; even if she and Josh had heard Grandpa clomping across his floor in the heavy workshoes he favored, he might and frequently did choose to ignore their request for admission.

When he opened the door to them, they confronted a gallery of closed rooms against whose doors her cane knocked. Should either of them touch one of the cut-glass doorknobs, Grandpa's "You let that alone" was swift and sharp. To her, Josh complained that Grandpa's part of the house smelled funny, a description with which Rachel did not disagree. It was the odor that weighted the air after their father performed his weekly scrub of the bathroom, the chlorine slap of bleach. Heaviest in the hallways, it was slightly better in the sitting room to which Grandpa led them. There, the couch on which she and Josh positioned themselves was saturated with a sweet scent spiced with traces of nutmeg, residue of the smoke that had spilled from the bowl of Grandpa's pipe for who knew how long. Once he had settled himself opposite them, in a wooden chair whose sharp creaks seemed to give warning of its imminent collapse, he conducted what amounted to a brief interview with each of them. How was school? What had they learned today? What was one thing they'd learned this past week they could explain to him? In general, she and her brother were happy to submit to the process, because it ended with a reward of hard candy, usually lemon-drops that made her cheeks pucker, but sometimes cherry Life Savers or atomic fireballs.

Once in a while, the questioning did not go as smoothly. As time passed, Rachel would understand that this was due to her grandfather's moods—generally neutral if not pleasant—which could take sudden swings in a hostile, and nasty, direction. Should she and Josh find themselves in front of him during one of these shifts, the hard candies would be replaced by a lecture on how the two of them were squandering the opportunities they hadn't deserved in the first place, and were going to end up as nothing but hippies. That last word, he charged with such venom that Rachel assumed it must be among the words she was not permitted to say. If Josh had done something particularly annoying, she might use it on him, and vice-versa. Long after her parents had clarified the term's meaning, it retained something of the opprobrium with which Grandpa had infused it—so much so that, when Josh, aged twelve, answered the old man's use of it by declaring that he didn't get what the big deal about hippies was, Rachel flinched, as if her brother had shouted "Motherfucker!" at him.

Given Grandpa's reaction, he might as well have. Already sour, his voice chilled. "Oh you don't, do you?" he said.

Josh maintained his position. "No," he said. "I mean, they were kind of weird looking, I guess, but the hippies were into peace and love. Isn't that what everyone's always telling us is important, peace and love? So," he concluded, a lawyer finishing his closing argument, "hippies don't sound all that bad, to me."

"I see," Grandpa said, his phrasing given a slight slur as he bit down on the stem of his pipe. "I take it you are an expert on the Hippie Wars."

The name was so ridiculous she almost burst out laughing. Josh managed to channel his amusement into a question. "The Hippie Wars?"

"Didn't think so," Grandpa said. "Happened back in 1968. Damned country was tearing itself apart. Group of hippies decided to leave civilization behind and live off the land, return to the nation's agrarian roots. Bunch of college drop-outs, from New Jersey, New York City. Place they selected for this enterprise was a stretch of back woods belonged to a man named Josiah Sparks. He and his family had shared a fence with our people for nigh on fifty years. Good man, who didn't mind these strangers had settled themselves on his land without so much as a by-your-leave. 'Soil's poor,' he said. 'Snakes in the leaves, bear in the caves. If they can make a go of it, might be they can teach me something.' All through the spring and summer after they arrived, he left them to their own devices. But once fall started to pave the way for winter, Josiah began to speak about his guests. 'Kids'll never make a winter out there,' he said. Good, folks said, it'll send them back where they came from. Josiah, though—it was as if he wanted them to succeed. Not what you would've expected from a marine who'd survived the Chosin Reservoir. One especially cold day, Josiah decided it was past time he went up and introduced himself to his tenants, found out what assistance he could offer them.

"Turned out, they didn't need his help. Could be, they had in the weeks right after they'd arrived. In the time since, they'd figured out a crop they could tend that would keep them in money: marijuana. When Josiah went walking into their camp, that was what he found, row upon row of the plants, set amongst the trees to conceal them. He hadn't spoken two words to them before one fellow ran up from behind and brought a shovel down on Josiah's head. Killed him straight away. Hippies panicked, decided they had to get rid of his body. They had a couple of axes to hand, so they set to chopping Josiah to pieces. Once their butchery was finished, they dumped his remains into a metal barrel along with some kindling, doused the lot with gasoline, and dropped a match on it. Their plan was to mix the ashes in with their fertilizer and spread them over their plants. Anything the fire didn't take, they'd bury.

"Could be their scheme would've worked, but a couple of Josiah's nephews decided their uncle had been gone long enough and went searching for him. They arrived to what smelled like a pork roast. Hippies ambushed them, too, but one of the brothers saw the fellow coming and laid him out. After that, the rest of the camp went for them. They fought their way clear, but it cost an ear and a few fingers between them.

"By the time Josiah's nephews returned with the rest of their menfolk and what friends they could muster, the camp had improved its armament to fire-arms, mostly pistols, a few shotguns. I figure they were supplied by whoever had partnered in their little enterprise. For the next week, your peace and love crew proved they could put a bullet in a man with the best of them. They favored sneak attacks—sent a handful of men to the hospital.

"So you'll appreciate why I do not share your view of the hippie, and you'll understand my views, unlike yours, are based in fact."

Neither Rachel nor Josh questioned that their visit was over. She picked up her cane. As they stood to leave, however, Josh said, "Grandpa?"

"Hmm?"

"Weren't you already living up here with Grandma in 1968?"

"I was."

"Then how did you know about the Hippie Wars?"

Grandpa's chair creaked as he leaned forward. "You think I'm telling stories?"

"No sir," Josh said. "I was just wondering who told you."

"My cousin, Samuel, called me."

"Oh, okay, thank you," Josh said. "Did you go to Kentucky to help them?"

Grandpa paused. "I did," he said. His voice almost light, he added, "Brought those hippies a surprise."

"What?" Josh said. "What was it?"

But their grandfather would say no more.

4. THE TAPE (2): DOWN THE WELL

"—the shore of a dried-up lake," Grandpa was saying. "Looked like an old well, but if you'd dropped a bucket into it, you'd have come up empty. Ventilation shaft, though Jerry thought it might've helped light the place, too. He lowered me down, on account of he was a foot taller and a hundred pounds heavier than I was. Played football at Harvard, was strong as any of the roughnecks. The shaft sunk about fifty feet, then opened out. I switched on my light, and found myself dangling near the roof of a huge cavern. It was another seventy-five feet to the floor, and I couldn't tell how far away the walls were. The rock looked volcanic, which set me to wondering if this wasn't an old volcano, or at least, a series of lava tubes."

"Was it?" Uncle Jim asked.

"Don't know," Grandpa said. "I was so concerned with what we found in that place, I never managed a proper geological survey of it. I'd stake money, though, that it was the remains of a small volcano."

"Okay," Jim said. "Can you talk about what you found there?"

"It was a city," Grandpa said, "or a sizable settlement, anyway. Maybe two-thirds of the cavern had collapsed, but you could see from what was left how the ceiling swept up to openings like the one I'd been lowered through, which gave the impression of enormous tents, rising to their tent poles. Huge pillars that joined ceiling to floor added to the sensation of being under a great, black tent. Iram had also been called the city of the tent poles, and standing there shining my light around it, I could see why."

"But how did you know it was a city, and not just a cave?"

"For one thing, the entrance I'd used. We took that as a pretty clear indication that someone had known about the place and used it for something. Could've been a garbage dump, though—right? We found proof. Around the perimeter of the cavern, smaller caves had been turned into dwelling-places. There were clay jars, metal pots, folded pieces of cloth that fell apart when we touched them. A few of the caves led to even smaller caves, like bedrooms. There was evidence of fires having been kept in all of them. Plus, most of the walls had been written on. I didn't know enough about such things to identify it, but Jerry said it resembled some of what he'd seen on digs down in Dhofar."

"You must have been pretty excited," Jim said. "I mean, this was a historic find."

"It was," Grandpa said, "but we weren't thinking about that. Well, maybe a little bit. May have been some talk about an endowed chair at Columbia for Jerry, a big promotion for me. Mostly, we were interested in the tunnels we saw leading out of the cavern."

5. FAMILY HISTORY

Officially, Grandpa had been retired from the oil company since shortly before Rachel's birth, when a series of shrewd investments had vaulted him several rungs up the economic ladder. His money had covered whatever portion of Rachel's appointments with a succession of retinal specialists her father's teacher's insurance did not, and he had paid for all of the specialized schooling and instruction she had required to navigate life with minimal vision. To Rachel's mother, in particular, her grandfather was a benefactor of whose largesse she was in constant need of reminding. To Rachel, he was a sharp voice which had retained most of the accent it had acquired growing up among the eastern Kentucky knobs, when a talent for math and science had allowed him to escape first to the university, then to the world beyond, working as a geologist for the American oil companies opening the oil fields of Saudi Arabia. The edge with which he spoke matched what he said, which consisted in almost equal parts of complaint and criticism—a rare compliment thrown in, as her father put it, to keep them on their toes.

According to Dad, his father had tended to the dour as far back as he could remember, but the tendency had been locked into place after Uncle Jim had run away from home at the end of his junior year in high school. Jim had been the brains of the brothers, a prodigy in math and science like his father before him. He tried not to show it, Dad said, but Grandpa favored his younger son, seemed genuinely excited by Jim, by his abilities, kept saying that, once Jim was old enough, there were things he was going to show him... When they realized that Jim had left home, and without a note or anything, the family was devastated. The police had conducted a lengthy investigation, which had included multiple interviews with each member of the family, but which had led nowhere. Grandma was heartbroken. Dad had no doubt the pain of Jim's departure lay at the root of the heart attack that killed her the following year. Grandpa was overtaken by bitterness, which his wife's death only deepened.

Dad had already been away at college, and so had missed a lot of the day-to-day pain his parents had suffered, but for a long time, he said, he had been angry at his missing brother. Jim had given no hint of anything in his life so wrong as to require him abandoning it, and them, entirely. Later, especially after he'd met Mom, Dad's anger had softened. Who knew what Jim had been going through? Still waters run deep and all that.

Jim's disappearance, combined with Grandma's death—not to mention, the blossoming of his stock portfolio—had set Grandpa on the path to retirement, a destination he had reached in the months before his first grandchild appeared. As far as Dad could tell, it had been years since the old man had been happy with his job. Every other week, it seemed, he was complaining about the idiots he worked with, their failure to recognize the need for bold action. Dad had never been much interested in his father's problems at work, and while Jim had been more (and genuinely) sympathetic, Grandpa had said that he couldn't explain it to his second son, he was too young. Dad supposed it was a wonder his father had stayed at his job as long as he had, but the pay was good, and he had responsibilities. After his principle obligation shrank from three members to one, however, he was free to play out the scenario he'd probably imagined a thousand times, and tender his resignation.

Grandpa's retirement had been an unusually active one. Several times a year, sometimes as often as once a month, he hired a car to take him and several large cases down to one of the metropolitan airports, JFK or LaGuardia or Newark, from which he boarded flights whose destinations were a survey of global geography: Argentina, China, Iceland, Morocco, Vietnam. Asked the purpose of his latest trip by either of his grandchildren, he would answer that he'd been called on to do a little consulting work, and if they were good while he was gone, he'd bring them back something nice. Any attempts at further questions were met by him shooing them out of whatever room they were in, telling them to go play. He was usually away for a week to ten days; although once, he was gone for a month, on a trip to Antarctica. While he was abroad, Rachel missed his presence in the house, but her missing him had more to do with her sense of a familiar element absent than any strong emotion. Neither her father nor her brother seemed much affected by his absence, and her mother was clearly relieved.

6. THE TAPE (3): THE TUNNELS
"—two kinds," Grandpa was saying. "There were four tunnels leading out of

the main chamber. Big enough for one, maybe two folks to walk along side-by-side. They led off to smaller caves, from which further tunnels branched to more caves. Jerry was for investigating these, trying to map out as much of the place as time would allow."

"But you wanted to look at the other tunnels?" Uncle Jim said.

"There were two of them," Grandpa said, "one next to the other. Each about half as tall as the first set: three and a half, four feet. Much wider: eight, maybe nine feet. More smoothly cut. The walls of the taller tunnels were rough, covered in tool marks. The walls of the shorter tunnels were polished, smooth as glass. To me, that made them all sorts of interesting. While Jerry sketched the layout of the main cavern, I got down on my hands and knees and checked the opening of the short tunnel on my right. Straight away, when I passed my light over it, I saw it was covered in writing. That brought Jerry running. The characters were like nothing either of us had seen before, and Jerry, in particular, had seen a lot. Had the tunnel's surface not been so even, you might have mistaken the writing for the after-effect of a natural process, one of those times Mother Nature tries to fool you into believing there's intent where there isn't. The figures were composed of individual curved lines, each one like a comma, but slightly longer. These curves were put together in combinations that looked halfway between pictures and equations. We checked the tunnel on the left, and it was full of writing, too, the same script—though whatever it spelled out seemed to differ from tunnel to tunnel.

"Thing was," Grandpa went on, "while the shorter tunnels had the appearance of more recent construction, they had the feel of being much older than their counterparts. Sounds strange, I guess, but you do enough of this work, you develop a sense for these things. To Jerry and me, it was obvious that some amount of time had passed between the carving of the two sets of tunnels, and whichever came first, we were sure a long time separated it from the second. What we had was a site that had been occupied by two different—two very different groups of people. We crept into each of the shorter tunnels about ten feet, and right away, felt the floor sloping downwards. The tunnel on the right veered off to the right; the tunnel on the left headed left. I think it was that that decided us on exploring these tunnels, first. The taller tunnels appeared to be carved on approximately the same level. The shorter ones promised a whole new layer, maybe more. We flipped a coin, and decided to start with the one on the right.

"We didn't get very far. No more than fifty feet in, the tunnel had collapsed. If it had been our only option, we might have searched for a way around it. As it was, we had another tunnel to try, so we crawled out the way we'd come and entered the tunnel on the left.

"Our luck with this one was better. We followed the passage down and to the left for a good couple of hundred feet. Wasn't the most pleasant trip either of us had taken. The rock was hard on our hands and knees, and it had been a spell since we'd done much in the way of crawling. We had our lights, but they didn't seem that much in the face of the darkness before and behind us, the rock hanging above us. I'm not usually one for the jitters, but I was happy enough to see the end of the tunnel ahead. Jerry was, too.

"The room we emerged into was round, shaped like a giant cylinder. From one side to the other, it was easily a hundred feet. Dome ceiling, twenty feet overhead. Across from where we'd entered was another tunnel, same dimensions as the one that had brought us here. I was all for finding out where that led, but Jerry stopped to linger a moment. He wanted to have a look at the walls, at the carvings on them."

INTERLUDE: GRANDPA (2): COUSIN JULIUS AND THE CHAROLAIS

As a rule, Grandpa did not interfere with their parents' disciplining of them. Any decision with which he disagreed would be addressed via an incident from his own experience which he would narrate to Rachel and Josh the next time he had them upstairs. For Rachel, the most dramatic instance of this occurred when she was twelve. Seemingly overnight, a trio of neighborhood girls her age, previously friendly to her, decided that her lack of vision merited near-constant mockery. While she had been able to conceal the upset their teasing caused her from her parents, Josh had witnessed an instance of it in front of their house and immediately decided upon revenge. Rather than attacking the girls then and there, he had waited a few days, until he could catch one of them on her own. He had leapt from the bushes in which he'd been concealed and swung his heavy bookbag at the side of her head. The girl had not seen him, which had allowed him to escape and attempt the same tactic with another of the girls the following day. After what had happened to her friend, though, this girl was prepared for Josh. She raised her shoulder to take the brunt of his swing, then pivoted into a punch that dropped him to the sidewalk. As black spots were dancing in front of his vision, the girl seized him by the hair and dragged him into her house, where she turned him over to her shocked mother. During the ensuing rounds of phone calls and parental meetings, the girls' cruelty to Rachel was acknowledged and reprimanded, but the heaviest punishment descended upon Josh, who was grounded for an entire month.

In the aftermath of this incident, the mixture of embarrassment, anger, and gratitude that suffused Rachel received a generous addition of anxiety the next afternoon, when Grandpa descended to the first floor to request her and Josh's presence in his sitting room. The two of them expected a continuation of the lectures they had been on the receiving end of for the last twenty-four hours—as, Rachel guessed, did their parents, who released them into their grandfather's care with grim satisfaction. Despite her belief that Josh hadn't done anything that bad—and that there was no reason at all for her to be involved in any of this—the prospect of a reprimand from Grandpa, who had a talent for finding the words that would wound most acutely, made her stomach hurt. If only she could leave Josh to face the old man himself—but her brother, stupid as he was, had acted on her behalf, and she owed him, however grudgingly, her solidarity. Swinging her cane side-to-side, she followed Josh up the stairs to the second floor and passed along the halls with their faint smell of bleach to Grandpa's sitting room and the smoky couch. She collapsed her cane and sat beside Josh. Maybe Grandpa would finish what he had to say and turn them loose quickly.

She recognized the tinkle of glass on glass that came from one of the six-packs of old-fashioned root beer that their grandfather sometimes shared with them. The pop and sigh of a cap twisting loose confirmed her intuition that he was going to sit in front of them and drink one of the sodas as he lectured. The second pop and sigh, and the third, confused her. Was he planning to consume all three of their root beers? The floor creaked, and cold glass pressed against the fingertips of her right hand. She took the bottle, its treacly sweetness bubbling up to her nostrils, but did not lift it to her mouth, in case this was some sort of test.

Grandpa seated himself, and said, "The two of you are in a heap of trouble. It's your parents' right to raise you as they see fit, and there's naught anyone can say or do about it. It's how I was with my boys, and I won't grant your dad any less with you. Joshua, they don't take too kindly to you walloping this one girl and trying for the other, and Rachel, they're tarring you with some of the same brush in case you had anything to do with putting your brother up to it. These days, folks tend to take a dim view of one youngster raising his hand against another. Especially if it's a girl—your dad would say I'm wrong, times've changed, but rest assured: if those had been two boys you'd gone after, the tone of the recent discussions you've been involved in would have been different.

"I can't intervene with your parents, but there's nothing that says I can't have a few words with you. So. When I was a tad older than the two of you, I went everywhere and did everything with my cousin, Julius Augustus. Some name, I know. It was the smartest thing about him. I expect your folks would call him 'developmentally delayed' or some such. We said he was slow. He was four years older, but he sat through ninth grade with me. It was his third time, after two tries at the grade before. He'd wanted to quit school and find a job, maybe on his uncle's farm, but Julius's dad fancied himself an educated man—which I guess you might have guessed from the names he loaded on his son—and he could not believe a child of his would not possess the same aptitude for learning as himself. Once I'd moved on to tenth grade and Julius had been invited to give ninth another try, his father relented, and allowed him to ask his uncle about that job.

"Julius's dad, Roy, was my uncle by marriage. His family owned a farm a couple of miles up the road from where I lived. Had a big house set atop a knob, from which they looked down on the rest of us. They'd been fairly scandalized when Roy took a liking to Aunt Allison, who was my mom's middle sister, but Roy had proved more stubborn than the rest of his family, and in the end, his father had granted Roy and Allison a piece of land which ran along one bank of the stream that swung around the foot of the hill. Julius Augustus was their only child who lived, and if folks judged it ironic that a man of Roy's intellectual pretensions found himself with a boy who had trouble with the Sunday funnies, none of them denied the sweetness of Julius's temperament. You could say or do nigh-on anything to him, and the most it would provoke was a frown.

"It let him get along at his uncle's, which had been his grandfather's until the old man's heart had burst. The grandfather hadn't been what you'd call kind to his laborers, but he had been fair. His elder son, Roy's brother, Rick, was less consistent. Not long after his father's death, Rick had sunk a fair portion of the farm's money into a project he'd been talking up for years. He bought a small herd of French cattle—Charolais, the breed was called. He'd seen them while he was serving in France, in what we still called the Great War. Bigger cattle, heavier, more meat on them. Cream-colored. Rick had a notion that they would give him an advantage over the local competition, so he returned to France, found some animals he liked and a farmer willing to sell them, and arranged to have his white cattle shipped across the Atlantic. This was no easy task, not least because the Great Depression still had the country in its claws. More than a few palms wanted crossing with silver, and then a couple of the cows sickened and died on the journey. The Charolais that arrived took to the farm well enough, but Rick had imagined that, as soon as they were grazing his fields, everything was going to happen overnight, which, of course, it didn't. The great sea of white cattle he pictured needed time to establish itself. I guess some folks, including Roy, tried telling him this, but Rick would not, maybe could not, accept it. After another pair of the Charolais died their first summer, Rick decided it was because they hadn't been eating the best grass. Anyone could see that the grass all over the farm, and all around the farm, was pretty much the same. But Rick got it in his head that the grazing would make his herd prosper lay on the far side of the stream that snaked around the base of their family's hill—where Roy, Allison, and Julius had their home. Had he asked Roy to allow the cattle to feed on his land, his brother might've agreed. Rick demanded, though, said it was his right as elder son and heir to the farm to do what was best for it. Roy didn't argue his authority over what happened on the farm. But, he said, his property was his property, granted him fair and square by their father, and the first one of those white cows he caught on his side of the stream was going to get shot, as were any subsequent trespassers. As you might expect, this did not go down so well with Rick.

"Despite the bad blood between his father and uncle, Julius was offered and accepted a job on the farm. Consisted mostly of helping with whatever labor needed done, from repairing a fence to painting the barn to baling hay. I suppose I found it unusual that Uncle Roy would permit his son to cross the stream to the farm, but there wasn't much else I could picture Julius doing, except digging coal, which was a prospect none of our parents was eager for us to explore. Anyway, Julius let me tell him how to spend what portion of his wages his parents allowed him to keep. Usually, this was on candy or soda pop; though sometimes, I'd promise him that, if he bought me a certain funnybook I especially wanted, I'd read to him from it. I would, too, at least until I was tired of explaining what all the big words meant. I reckon I wasn't always as kind to my big cousin as I should've been, and I reckon I knew it at the time, too. He was a great, strapping fellow, taller, stronger than me. Long as he was near, the boys who teased and occasionally pushed and tripped me kept their distance. Julius never let on that he didn't like spending time with me, so I didn't worry about the rest of it too much.

"Did I mention that Rick had a daughter? He had three of them, and a pair of sons, besides, but the one I'm speaking of was the second youngest, a girl name of Eileen. Plain, quiet. Don't know that anyone paid her much mind until her daddy showed up at Roy's house with her on one side of him and the Sheriff on the other. Eileen, Rick said, was going to have a baby. Julius, he also said, was the baby's father. I don't know what-all your folks have told you about such matters, but a man can force a baby on a woman. This was what Rick said Julius had done to his Eileen. Julius denied the accusation, but it was Eileen's word against his, and given he wasn't the sharpest knife in the drawer, her yes carried more weight than his no. The charge was a serious one, enough to have brought the Sheriff to the door; though you can be sure Rick's house on top of that knob helped guarantee his presence. The way the Sheriff told it, he already possessed sufficient evidence to put Julius under lock and key, at least until a trial. And, Rick chimed in, did his younger brother know what would happen to Julius once the other prisoners learned what he was awaiting trial for? Messing around with a young girl—it would not go well for him. Julius might not reach his day in court, and that wasn't even mentioning the cost of hiring a lawyer to defend him...

"In a matter of ten, fifteen minutes, Rick and the Sheriff maneuvered Roy and Allison into believing that all they held dear was about to be taken from them. They were frantic. You can be sure Roy had some notion that there was more going on here than his brother was letting on, but he couldn't ignore the situation at hand, either. Rick let Roy and Allison sweat just long enough, then sprung his trap. Of course, he said, there might be another way out of this for all of them. He wasn't saying there was, mind you, only that there might be. Everyone knew that Julius wasn't equipped with the same faculties as those around him. There were places which would take care of such folk, ensure they would not be a danger to anyone else. In fact, there was a fine one outside of Harrodsburg, small, private, where Julius could expect to be well-looked-after. Wasn't cheap, no, though Rick supposed it was less than they might lay out for a decent lawyer, especially if the trial dragged out, or if Julius was convicted and they needed to appeal. Not to mention, it would avoid the talk about

Julius that was sure to spread as a result of his imprisonment. Thing about that kind of talk was, it got folks riled up, thinking they needed to get together and take matters into their own hands. There wasn't much the Sheriff and his boys would be able to do if a mob of angry men marched up to the jail and demanded his prisoner, was there?

"By the end of an hour, Rick had everything he needed. To pay for the asylum to which their son was to be shipped in lieu of criminal charges and time in jail, Roy and Allison agreed to sign over their property to him. Within a couple of days, Julius's bags were packed and he was on his way to Harrodsburg. I saw him before he left, and he wasn't upset—mostly, he seemed confused by everything. Soon after he left, his parents went, too, to be closer to him. A school hired Roy as a janitor, and Allison took in washing.

"I saw Julius once, not long after he'd entered the asylum. Nice enough place, I guess, an old mansion that'd seen better days. But Julius was different. Among the conditions of his entering this place was that he not pose a danger to any of the women who worked or were patients there. Shortly after he arrived, he was given an operation to prevent him forcing babies on anyone else. When I called on him, he hadn't fully healed. They'd dressed him in a white shirt and pants, to make him easy to track down in case he went to leave. There was a patch of damp blood down one leg of his trousers. He couldn't understand what had been done to him, and they had him on some kind of pain medicine that made things worse. He kept asking me to explain what had happened to him, and when I couldn't, tried to show me his wound to help. I don't imagine my visit made things any clearer for him.

"All the ride home, I kept thinking about those white cattle. Our family had talked about the situation. Wasn't anyone doubted it had been a way for Rick to get where he wanted to go. Question was, had the road presented itself to him, or had he paved it, himself? No one could credit the charge that had been brought against Julius. On the other hand, whatever his intelligence, his body was a man's, subject to all a man's urges. With only a boy's understanding to guide him, who could say what he might have done, had his blood been up? The women, in particular, would have liked a word with Eileen, but she was gone, sent off to a cousin in Memphis the day after her daddy had reached his agreement with her uncle.

"I knew. I knew that my cousin was innocent and that a terrible crime had been committed against him and his family. Sitting with him in the asylum had made me certain. For a brief time, I hoped the other members of my family might take action, avenge the wrong done Julius, but the furthest they would go was talking about it. One of my uncles proposed shooting Rick's special cattle, but the rest of the family rejected the plan. Rick would guess who'd done it right away, they said, and he'd already proved beyond any doubt he had the law snug in his pocket. God would take care of Rick in His time, my Aunt Sharon said. We had to be patient.

"While I didn't put much stock in Divine Justice overtaking Rick, I saw that my aunt was right about the necessity of waiting. Such a man as Rick couldn't help making enemies. He collected them the way a long-haired dog does ticks. The secret was to wait until he had gathered so many enemies as to move our name well down a list of potential suspects. This meant another six years, till I was halfway done with the university. Julius was dead—had died not many months after I'd seen him. The wound from his operation had never closed properly. Infection set in, and though he fought it for a good long time, this was in the days before penicillin. I was at his funeral. Rick insisted he have a place in the family plot. As much as anything, what he intended as a magnanimous gesture settled me against him. If a man had done to your daughter what Rick had accused Julius of, there was no way you'd make room for him alongside the rest of your kin. Had he been your patsy, you might try to soothe any twinges of conscience by permitting him the privilege of a burial amongst the elect of your line. I swear to you, it was all I could do not to walk over to where Rick and his wife stood beside Roy and Allison and spit in his face. Not then, though, not then. Years had to pass, Julius's grave received a fancy headstone, the grass grew thick over it. Roy and Allison had to leave for a fresh start in Chicago, where the family lost touch with them.

"At last, the time came around. It was a rainy night, the tail end of a storm that had hung about for a couple of days. I wanted it raining so no one would think twice of my wearing a raincoat and hat, gloves and boots. There was a fellow at the university who owed me a considerable favor. He owned a car. I proposed to him that, should he drive me a couple of hours to a location with which I would provide him, wait there no more than an hour, and return me to campus, we would be square. He agreed. I had him take me to a crossroads a mile or so up the road from Rick's farm, where the stream that circled the bottom of his hill swerved close to the road. The stream was swollen with the rain, but not so much that I couldn't wade it to the spot where Roy and

Allison's house had stood. Rick had torn it down, had a kind of lean-to built for his cattle to shelter under. This was where I found the lot of them, crowded in together. Their huge white bodies glowed in what little light there was. I dug around in my coat pocket, and came out with my buck knife. I didn't know if the cattle would spook, so I opened it slowly. The ones on the open side of the lean-to shifted their feet, but made no move to run. Speaking softly, smoothly, the kind of nonsense you coo to a baby, I approached. I put my free hand on the cow to my right, to steady her. Then I leaned behind and drew my knife across the backs of her knees. She didn't scream, just gave a little grunt as her hamstrings split and her back end collapsed. That knife was sharp as a smile. I doubt she felt much of anything. I did the same to her forelegs, and moved on to the cow in front of her. Once I had the cattle on the open side done, and the way out of the lean-to blocked, I relaxed. The rest of Rick's Charolais put up no more resistance, though a couple called in protest. I was quick and I was thorough, and when I was done, I retraced my steps to the stream and walked it to where my friend sat waiting for me. The rain and the stream had washed most of the blood and mud from me. All the same, he kept his eyes fixed straight ahead. I told him we could go, and we did.

"You can be sure, I spent the next few days wondering what had been reported by the local press. It was all I could do not to rush out and buy them. Problem was, as a rule, I didn't pay much attention to newspapers; plus, I was in the middle of exams. I wasn't sure at what stage the investigation into what I'd done to Rick's cattle was. I didn't want to do anything, however trivial, that might cast suspicion on me, later. I didn't really need to read a reporter's account of what had taken place after I'd left. I could picture it well enough. Early the next morning, whoever Rick had put in charge of tending the cattle would've wandered over to check on them. He'd have discovered the herd under the lean-to, unable to move, blood watering the mud. He'd have run for Rick, who might've sent someone to fetch the veterinarian. The precise details weren't important. What was, was there was nothing could be done for the animals. To a one, they would have to be destroyed, the meat sold for whatever Rick could get for it. I couldn't decide if he'd have what it took to load the rifle and do what had to be done, himself, or if he'd direct a couple of his men to it. I preferred the former scenario, but either possibility would suffice, because whoever's finger was on the trigger, he'd hear the gunshots, each and every one of them.

"For a couple of months afterwards, I half-expected a visit from one lawman or another. Over the Christmas holidays, I kept a low profile. Rumor was, Rick's suspicion had lighted on a fellow out towards Springfield with whom he'd had a dispute about money the man claimed Rick owed him. Naturally, everyone in my family had an opinion as to who was responsible, but none of them so much as glanced in my direction. I was at the university; I was the last person who would commit such an act, and jeopardize his future. The exception was Aunt Sharon, who, as she decreed that God's wrath had descended on His enemy, let her eyes fall on me long enough for me to know it.

"Obviously, what I did on behalf of Julius, I got away with. Even if I hadn't, though—even if the police had broken down my door and dragged me off to prison—it was the right thing to do. Family comes before everything. Someone wrongs one of yours, you do not let that go unanswered. You may have to bide your time, but you always redress an injury to your own. And when you do, you make certain it's in a way that will bring misery to whoever offended. That's what your blood demands of you.

"So anybody who stood up for his big sister to a trio of girls who deserve to have their lips sewn shut, I'd not only give him a bottle of pop, I'd hoist mine in salute to him."

Rachel followed her grandfather's direction and lifted her soda in Josh's direction. The time it had spent in her hand had taken the chill from it, but it was still sweet, and she drank it down eagerly.

7. THE FREEZER (2): OPENED

One time that Grandpa was away, he left the freezer unlocked. As they always did after he was safely gone from the house, Rachel and Josh descended the basement stairs; although she, for one, had done so without much enthusiasm, as if she were going through the motions of a ritual grown stale and meaningless. At least in part, that was due to her being seventeen, and more concerned with college applications and the senior prom than with a riddle whose solution never came any closer, and was probably not all that exciting, anyway. But Josh had insisted she come, the moodiness that had erupted with his fifteenth birthday temporarily calmed by the reappearance of their familiar game. He had been working on his lock-picking skills, he said—for reasons she did not wish to consider—and was eager to exercise them on the freezer's locks. Rachel couldn't remember the last time she'd spared any thought for the freezer, but the change in Josh was welcome and substantial enough for her to want to prolong it, so she had accompanied him.

As it turned out, her brother would have to find another test for his burgeoning criminal skills. For a moment, she thought the trickling she heard as she swept her cane from basement stair to basement stair was water running through the brass pipes concealed by the basement's ceiling tiles. Except no, there was none of the metallic echo that passage made. This was water chuckling into open air. At almost the same time, the smells mixing in the basement reached her. The typically faint odors of cinnamon and vanilla, with the barest trace of brine, flooded her nostrils, the cinnamon filling the end of her nose with its powdery fragrance, the vanilla pushing that aside with its almost oily sweetness, the brine suddenly higher in her nose. There was another smell, too, stale water. In comparison, the basement's usual odors of synthetic carpet, dust, and damp were hardly noticeable.

Josh's "Holy shit" was not a surprise; nor, really, were his next words: "It's open. Grandpa left the fucking thing wide open." The sound, the smells, had told her as much. She said, "He's defrosting it."

He was. He had pushed the freezer a couple of feet to the left, until the spigot that projected from its lower left side was hanging over the edge of the drywell. He unplugged and unlocked the freezer, turned the lever on the spigot, and who knew how many years' worth of ice was trickling down into the ground. Late-afternoon sunlight was warming the basement, but Josh flipped on the light. Rachel would have predicted her brother would run across to inspect the freezer, but he hesitated, and she swatted his leg with her cane. "Hey," she said.

"Sorry," he said.

"What?"

"This is kind of weird."

"No weirder than having the Goddamned thing here in the first place."

"Do you think he knows—you know?"

"That we've been fixated on it since we were kids?" she said. "Yeah, I'm pretty sure he's figured that one out by now."

"Could it be some kind of, I don't know, like a trap or something?"

"A trap? What the fuck are you talking about? This is Grandpa."

"Right," Josh said, "it is. Are you telling me he'd pass up a chance to teach us a lesson, especially about minding our own business?"

"You're being paranoid." She shoved past him and made her way across the basement. Her cane clacked against the freezer. When her hand had closed on the edge of it, she said, "You want to come over here and tell me what's in front of me?"

With the exasperated sigh that had become the trademark of his adolescence, he did. "Move over," he said, pushing her with his hip. She shuffled to her left. Standing over the open freezer, she found the cinnamon-vanilla-brine combination strong enough to make her cough. "I know," Josh said, "pretty intense, huh?"

"What do you see?"

"Ice, mostly. I mean, there's a lot of ice in here, a shitload of it. I'd say that Grandpa had this thing about two-thirds full of ice."

"Well, it is a freezer."

"Ha-fucking-ha."

"The question is, what has he been using it for?"

"Storage."

"Obviously. Any sign of what, exactly, was being stored?"

"I—wait."

She felt him lean forward, heard ice shifting. "What the fuck?" he breathed.

"What is it?"

"I don't know. It's like, paper or something."

"Let me—" she held out her hand.

"Here." He placed a piece of what might have been heavy tissue paper in her palm. She leaned her cane against the freezer and ran her other hand over the substance. Its texture was almost pebbled. It crinkled and bunched under her fingertips. Josh said, "It's translucent—has a kind of greenish tint. At one edge, it's brown—light brown."

"It's skin," she said. "It could be from a plant, I guess, but I think it's a piece of skin." She brought it to her face. The cinnamon-vanilla-brine mix made her temples throb.

"Skin?" Josh said.

"Like from a snake," she said, "or a lizard."

"What the fuck?" Josh said.

Rachel had no answer.

8. THE TAPE (4): THE CARVINGS

"—ten disks," Grandpa was saying, "evenly spaced around the room. Each was a good six feet or so across. They were hung low, only about a foot off the floor. I'm not one for art, but I reckon I could find my way around a museum. The style of these things wasn't like anything I'd run across before. What was pictured tended more in the direction of abstract shapes—cylinders, spheres, cubes, blocks—than of specific details. The scenes had been carved in something like bas-relief, and incised with the same writing we'd found at the tunnel mouths. I couldn't decide if it was vandalism, or part of the original design. The letters seemed too regular, too evenly placed to be graffiti, but I'm hardly the expert in such things.

"Jerry had brought his camera. He'd used up most of his film shooting the main cavern, but had enough left for the disks, so he photographed them."

"What did they show?" Uncle Jim asked.

"Half of them, I couldn't make heads nor tails of. Maybe if I'd had another few hours to study them, I might've been able to decipher them. The hands on our watches were moving on, though, and there was that other tunnel to consider."

"How about the ones you could figure out?"

"There was a picture of a city," Grandpa said, "although no such city as I'd ever seen, in or out of a book. Great buildings that curved to points, nary a straight line amongst them, like fangs of all different sizes. Another showed that same city—I'm pretty sure it was—destroyed, shattered by an enormous sphere crashing down into it. Third was of a long line of what I took for people, crossing a wide plane full of bones. There was one of another catastrophe, a large group of whoever this had been being trampled by a herd of animals— actually, this disk was a bit confusing, too. The animals were at the lead edge of a mass of triangular shapes that I took to be waves, but whether the animals were supposed to represent a flood, or vice-versa, wasn't clear to me.

"The picture that was most interesting was the one set over the tunnel out of the room. At its center, there was a person—or, what was supposed to be a person—and, at all four points of the compass surrounding him, there was another, smaller person, maybe half his size. Seemed to me there was more writing on this disk than the others, concentrated between the fellow in the middle and his four satellites. Jerry said it might be a representation of their gods, or their ancestors, or their caste system—which was to say, just about anything."

"Did you explore the other tunnel?" Jim said. "Of course you did. Did you find anything?"

Grandpa laughed. "I guess you know your old man, don't you? Jerry would've been happy to return, said we'd already found plenty. We had, and I wasn't too sure of our lights, but by God did I want to find out what lay at the end of that other tunnel. Told Jerry I'd go myself, which I would've; though I was betting on him not wanting to be left alone. He didn't, but he made me promise we'd turn around the second our lights started to go.

"The tunnel out of the chamber was the exact copy of the one that brought us to it. For another couple hundred feet, it slanted down and to the left. The darkness wasn't any darker here than it had been at any point since we'd started our descent, but I found myself estimating how far below the surface we'd come, and that number seemed to make the blackness thicker.

"We issued into a room that was pretty much identical in size and shape to the one we'd left. Only difference was the tombs along the walls."

9. A Familiar Debate

"Suppose everything Grandpa told Uncle Jim on that tape—suppose it's true."

"What?" Rachel said. Her bed shifted and complained as Josh lowered himself onto it. She closed the textbook her fingers had been trailing across. "Are you high again? Because if you are, I have the LSAT to prepare for."

"No," Josh said, the pungent, leafy odor he'd brought with him a clear contradiction of his denial. "I mean, I might've had a little grass to chill me out, but this is serious. What if he was telling the truth?"

With a sigh, Rachel placed her book on the bed. "Do I have to do this? Are you really going to make me run through all the problems with what's on that tape?"

"They were in the Empty Quarter," Josh said, "the *Rub' al Khali*. There's all kinds of crazy shit's supposed to be out there."

"Actually," she said, "that point, I can almost believe. Apparently, there are some famous caves not too far from where they were, so why couldn't they have discovered another? And why couldn't it have been inhabited? If there was a cave-in, and the desert came pouring through the ceiling, there's your Atlantis of the sands legend."

"So—"

"But. This would have been an archaeological find of historic significance. It would have made his friend Jerry's career. He would have been famous, too. You don't think two young guys wouldn't have publicized the shit out of something like this?"

"Ah," Josh said, "but you're thinking in twenty-first-century terms. They couldn't snap a picture with their phones and upload it to Facebook, while verifying their coordinates with their personal GPSes. They had to do things the old-fashioned way, which meant returning for additional photos and a survey of the location."

"By which time," she said, "there had been not one, but two week-long sandstorms, and the terrain had been entirely changed."

"It's the desert. There are sandstorms all the time."

"I'm sure there are, which begs the question: How did they find a map to guide them there, in the first place?"

"Maybe it was a star map."

"Then why couldn't they find their way back?"

"Okay, so it was dumb luck they found the place. There's still the pictures they did take."

"Most of which," she said, "were ruined by some kind of mysterious radiation they're supposed to have encountered underground. What could be developed is—apparently—so generic it could be anyplace."

Josh paused. "What about the egg?"

"Seriously?"

"Why not?"

"Why—because extraordinary claims require extraordinary proof."

"There's the freezer," Josh said, "and its locks."

"That's hardly—"

"Remember the piece of skin we found in it?"

"You don't think that was Grandpa fucking with us?"

"We hadn't found Jim's tape in the attic, then. What would have been the point?"

"I said: to fuck with us."

"I don't know," Josh said.

"I do," Rachel said. "Our grandfather is not keeping a pet monster in the freezer in the basement."

"Not a monster," Josh said, "a new species."

"An intelligent dinosaur?"

"It's not—that's like calling us thinking monkeys. It's what the dinosaurs developed into."

"Again—and this is ignoring a ton of other problems with your scenario—what you're describing would have been—I mean, can you imagine? A living example of another, completely different, rational creature? Grandpa and Jerry would have been beyond famous. Yet we're supposed to believe Grandpa raised it, himself?"

"They wanted to study it. They thought it would be better for them to observe and document its development."

"Which neither of them had any training for," Rachel said. "And, once more, where's the data they're supposed to have accumulated?"

"Presumably, Jerry lost it, sometime before his heart attack."

"How incredibly convenient, on both counts."

"Anyway, from what I can figure, it isn't as if the thing is all that smart."

"Does it matter? You do not keep an earth-shaking scientific find on ice in the cellar of your house in upstate New York. Shit," she added, "why are we even having this conversation?"

"It's Uncle Jim," Josh said.

"What about him?"

"I've been thinking about him running away—the timing of it. Near as I can tell, he and Grandpa sat down to record that tape about a month before Jim split."

"And?"

"Well—do they sound like they aren't getting along?"

"No," Rachel said, "but that doesn't mean anything. This could have been the calm before the storm."

"Not according to Dad. The way he tells it, everything was fine between Uncle Jim and Grandpa and Grandma right until he left."

"You have to take what Dad says about Uncle Jim with a chunk of salt. It's safe to say he was a little jealous of his baby brother."

"What I'm getting at," Josh said, "is maybe Uncle Jim saw what was in the freezer. And maybe he didn't like it. Maybe he freaked out."

"So he ran away?"

"Could be. Could also be, he never left the house."

"What—the thing ate him?"

"Maybe it was an accident," Josh said. "He figured out how to unlock the freezer while Grandpa wasn't there. Or Grandpa was there, but Jim got too close. Or—what about this?—Grandpa turned the thing loose on Jim because he was threatening to tell people about it, go public."

"That's pretty fucked-up," Rachel said. "Grandpa's an asshole who's committed some acts that are, to put it mildly, of questionable morality, but that doesn't mean he'd sic his pet monster on his child."

"It would explain why Jim disappeared so completely, why he's never been found."

"As would a less elaborate—and less ridiculous—narrative. Not to mention, weren't you sitting beside me during his family-comes-first lectures? Remember cousin Julius Augustus, the terrible things you do for your kin?"

"Family loyalty cuts both ways. If Jim set himself against the family, then he'd be liable for the consequences."

"Seriously? Are you sure this paranoid fantasy isn't about Grandpa and you?"

"Don't laugh. You honestly believe that, if Grandpa thought I was harming the family, he wouldn't take action?"

"'Take action': Will you listen to yourself? He's an old man."

"With a very powerful weapon at his command. You don't need to be too strong to fire a gun."

"Jesus—okay, this conversation is over. I have to get back to studying." As Josh raised himself from the bed, Rachel added, "Occam's razor, Josh: the simplest answer is generally the right one."

"If I'm right about what's in that freezer," he said, "then this *is* the simplest answer."

INTERLUDE: DAD AND MOM

Neither of Rachel's parents cared to discuss her grandfather at any length. In her father's case, this was the residue of an adolescence complicated by the loss of his brother and mother, and an adulthood spent in a career for which his father showed a bemused tolerance, at best. In her mother's case, it was due to her father-in-law's decades-long refusal to be won over by her efforts to achieve anything more than a tepid formality. Mom had been enough of a hippie in her youth for Rachel to have a sense of the root of Grandpa's coldness to her; on a couple of occasions, however, she had hinted to Rachel that her uneasiness around her husband's father had to do with more than his disdain for her lifestyle. There was something she thought she had seen—but it was probably all her imagination. Rachel wasn't to say anything to her grandfather, or he'd accuse Mom of having had a flashback, or worse, of having been tripping.

Rachel tried to coax her mother into describing what she had seen, but she refused to be drawn.

10. The Tape (5): Visions of the Lost World

"—eight sarcophagi," Grandpa was saying. "That was what it looked like, at first. Huge stone boxes, ten feet long by four high by four deep. Cut from the same stone as the tunnels and the chambers. Six of them set around one side of the room, the remaining two opposite. It appeared the tombs had been turned over, because the front of each was open. Full of what we took for rocks, smooth, oblong stones the length of a man's hand, all a speckled material I didn't recognize. We circled the room, and it seemed every last one of the stones was cracked, most from end to end. I picked up one to inspect. Lighter than its size, almost delicate. Surface was tacky. I aimed my light into the crack, and saw it was hollow. I replaced it, and chose another one. It was empty, too, as were the others I checked. I moved onto the next stone box, and the one after that, and all the stones I examined were the same, fragile shells that stuck to my fingers. Not until I lifted a rock which hadn't split all the way—and which was heavier than the others—and shone my light into it did the penny finally drop. These weren't stones. They were eggs. The stone containers weren't sarcophagi. They were incubators. This wasn't a mausoleum. It was a nursery."

"What?" Uncle Jim said. "What was in there? What did you see?"

"Broke the shell, myself," Grandpa said. "Shouldn't have, wasn't anything like proper procedure, but what was inside that egg…"

"What?" Jim said. "What was it?"

"Conditions in the chamber had preserved the creature it contained well enough for me to make out the pattern on its skin. It was dried out, more like paper than flesh and bone. Guess you could say I found a mummy, after all. Curled up in the half-shell I was holding, it put me in mind of an alligator, or a crocodile. The body and tail did, anyway. Head was something else. For the size of the skull, the eye was huge, round, like what you find in some species of gecko. Its brow, snout, flowed together into a thick horn that jutted beyond the end of its lower jaw. Damnedest looking thing, and when I studied its forelimbs more closely, I noticed the paws were closer to hands, the toes fingers."

"No way," Jim said.

"Boy, have you ever known me to lie to you?" A warning edge sharpened Grandpa's question.

"No sir," Jim said. "So what was it? Some kind of pet lizard?"

"Not by a long shot," Grandpa said. "I was holding in my palm the withered remains of one of the beings who had carved out the very room in which we were standing." During the pause that followed Grandpa's revelation, Rachel could feel her vanished uncle's distant desire to call her grandfather on his bullshit vibrating the silence; apparently, however, Uncle Jim had decided to water his valor with discretion. Grandpa went on, "Of course, I didn't know this at the time. I assumed the thing I'd found was another lizard, if a strange one. There were a couple more mummified creatures in amongst the eggs in this box, and something even more important: a single, unopened egg, its outside sticky with a coat of the gel that had been left on the others. I wrapped the unbroken egg with the utmost care, and placed it in the bottom of the rucksack I'd worn. Beside it, I packed the three dried-out creatures, along with a sampling of a half-dozen empty eggs. Wasn't anything else we could take as proof we'd been here, but I figured this was better than nothing.

"The trip back to the main cavern, then to the surface, then to the camp, was uneventful. Jerry and I talked about what we'd found, what it might portend for us. We agreed not to say anything to anyone until he'd developed the pictures he'd taken and we'd found someone we could trust to examine the things in my rucksack. Neither seemed as if it would take long—a week or two at the outside—and once we were in possession of evidence we could show someone, we didn't think we'd have any difficulty locating a sponsor who would reward us generously for leading a second, larger and better-equipped, expedition to Iram.

"What we didn't count on was the rolls of film Jerry had shot being almost completely ruined, most likely by some variety of radiation we encountered underground. The couple of photos you could distinguish in any detail showed cave structures that could've been anywhere. On top of that, within twelve hours of our return, I developed a rash on my hands that raced up my arms to my chest and head, bringing with it a raging fever and a coma. Camp doctor'd never seen the like, said it was as if I'd had an allergic reaction to some kind of animal bite."

"The eggs," Jim said, "the stuff that was on them. Was it poisonous?"

"Delivery system," Grandpa said, "for a virus—several, each hitched to a cartload of information. Imagine if you could infect someone with knowledge, deliver whatever he needed to know directly to the brain. Was what was supposed to happen to the creatures when they hatched. On the way out of their eggs, they'd contract what learning they required to assume their role in their civilization. I assume the process was more benign than what I, the descendant of a different evolutionary branch, went through. Prior to this, had you asked me what I thought a coma was like, I would have predicted a deep sleep. It's what the word means, right? Not once did it occur to me such a sleep might be filled with dreams—nightmares. Now, I understand what I saw while unconscious as my brain's effort to reckon with the foreign data being inserted into it. At the time, I felt as if I was losing my mind. Even after I came out of the coma, it was weeks till I could manage a day without some pretty strong medicine, or a night in anything close to peace."

"What did you see?" Jim said.

"Lot of it was in fragments," Grandpa said, "whether because the viruses had decayed over time, or my brain chemistry was too different, I'm not sure. Maybe both. I saw a city standing on the shore of a long, low sea. Made up of tall, triangular structures that curved to one side or another, like the teeth of a vast, buried beast. Their surfaces were ridged, like the bark of a plane tree, and I understood this was because they hadn't been built so much as grown. They were of a piece with the forest that surrounded the place. Herds of what looked like a cross between a bird and a lizard, their feet armed with a single, outsized claw, patrolled the forest lanes, chasing off the larger animals that wandered into them from time to time. These bird-lizards had been grown much the same way as the city, what was already there shaped to the ends of the place's inhabitants. That was what the creatures had raised it did, took what the world around them gave and altered it to fit their purposes. They'd done so for an unimaginable length of years, while the stars rearranged into dozens of sets of constellations. They did it to themselves, steering their biology down certain paths, until they'd split into four...you might call them castes, I suppose. They were distinct enough from one another to be almost separate species. Soldier class was at the bottom; next came the farmers, then the scientists, and finally the leaders. They'd fixed it so they developed from infant to adult in about three years.

"Some kind of disaster brought the whole thing tumbling down. I couldn't tell exactly what. I glimpsed a wall of fire reaching all the way to the sky, but that was it. There weren't many of the creatures to begin with. Their civilization had been in decline for tens of thousands of years, pulling back to the location I'd seen, the original city. Had it not been for some of them working underground, the things would've been burned away entirely. As it was, there were only a few thousand survivors, left with a landscape that had been charcoaled, bunched up like a blanket. Overhead, the sky was black clouds. A few of the creatures proposed throwing in the towel, joining their brethren in oblivion, but they were outvoted by the rest of the survivors, who decided to search for a new spot to call home. Dissenters didn't have much choice in the matter: their leaders had the ability to force their actions with their minds. So the lot of them left on a journey which would consume decades. Everywhere they went, things were the same, the earth and pretty much everything that had lived on it seared to ash. Once, they came to an ocean, and it was choked with carcasses out to the horizon. The air chilled. Clouds churned above, spilling dirty snow by the foot. Half the creatures died over the course of their travels. In the end, the leaders decided their best hope was hibernation. There were places—the sites of cities long-abandoned—where they could find sufficient facilities left to put themselves into a long, deep sleep, from which they might awaken when the planet had recovered itself. They found one such location in the far south, on the other side of what would be called Antarctica. As best they could, they secured the site, and settled down to sleep.

"And sleep they did, for fifty thousand, a hundred thousand years at a stretch. The world's wounds scarred over. New plants and trees appeared, spread across the land, were joined by new and strange animals. The creatures had lived during the great age of the dinosaurs—were its crowning achievement. They'd witnessed families of beasts like small mountains ambling across the grasslands; they'd fought feathered monsters with teeth like knives in the forests. Now, when they sent scouts to inspect their surroundings, they heard tales of smaller animals, covered in hair. As they woke from rests that lasted millennia, those animals grew larger, until it was as if the wildlife they'd known in their former existence was being recast in other flesh. Nor was the rise of these beasts the only change in their environment. The continents were shifting, sliding towards the positions we know. Antarctica was cooling, ice and snow spreading across it. Never ones to act in haste when they didn't have to, the creatures chose to wait. Eventually, they did abandon that location. I can't say when, or why.

"The rest was even more fractured. They left Antarctica in search of a spot closer to the equator. That might have been what we called Iram, or it might have been another spot before it. For a little while, they did all right. Population increased, to the point a group set out west, to find another of the old sites. The two settlements kept up contact with one another. After more time than you or I could comprehend, it appeared the creatures might be on the rebound.

"There was one problem for them, one fly doing the backstroke in the ointment: us, humans. They'd been aware of us as we'd risen from four legs to two and started our long climb up the evolutionary staircase, but it was only as another instance of the weird fauna that had overtaken the world. In what must have seemed the blink of an eye, we were on our way to becoming the dominant life-form on the planet. To make matters worse, we were hostile to them from the get-go, aggressively so. If a human encountered one of them, he fled screaming in the other direction. If a group of humans ran into one of them, they would do their level best to kill it. The creatures had the advantage in terms of firepower. Each of their soldiers had been crafted to be all the weapon it would need against foes much worse than a handful of hairless apes. We had the advantage in terms of numbers—not to mention, we had an ability to make leaps in our reasoning that was completely alien to them. We could surprise the creatures in ways they couldn't us. So began a war which spanned a good deal of man's prehistory. By and large, it was fought by small groups from either side, sometimes individual warriors. There was a point when the creatures who'd settled in the west came out in force against the human kingdom that had arisen near them. Fought all the way into its capital city, to have it swept by a mighty wave that drowned both sides alike. Creatures never recovered from that. They ceded more and more of what territory they'd held to humans. In the end, they opted for the only route left open them: another long sleep. As they had before, they fortified their retreat as best they could, and let slumber take them."

There was a moment's pause, Uncle Jim allowing his father to pick up the thread of his narrative. When it was clear that was not about to happen, Jim said, "Then what?"

"That was it," Grandpa said. "Wasn't anything else. Believe you me, what had been stuffed between my ears was more than enough. You know how full your brain feels after you've pulled an all-nighter prepping for a big test? This was like all the cramming you'd ever done for every test you've ever taken, present at the same time. After I'd climbed out of the coma, the doctor and nurses thought I was delirious. Wasn't that. It was a library's worth of new information trying to squeeze itself into my neurons. Gradually, over a span of weeks, I came to terms with the knowledge I'd gained. By the time I was walking out of that room, though, there was more for me to reckon with. For one thing, after sweating whether anyone would blame him for the sickness that had overwhelmed me, Jerry had gone off in search of Iram, alone. But the entire region had been swept by sandstorms that had reconfigured the landscape beyond his ability to accommodate. For another thing, our team had been moved to a new site, fifty miles east of where we'd been. Fortunately, Jerry had kept my rucksack close and unopened. Absent his photographs and unable to retrace the path to Iram, he doubted anyone would credit him with finding anything but a cache of lizard eggs.

"They were more than that—much, much more. I'd an idea we might locate a scientist to show the eggs to. Wasn't sure if we'd be better with a paleontologist, or a zoologist. I also figured a biochemist might be interested in the substance that had coated the eggs, what it contained. Hadn't paid much mind to the single unhatched egg I'd found; guess I assumed its contents would be useful for purposes of comparison. I certainly was not expecting it to hatch."

11. Thanksgiving

Thanksgiving was the kitchen summer-hot, humid with dishes simmering and steaming on the stove. It was the tomato-smell of the ketchup and soy-sauce glaze her mother had applied to the turkey in the oven; the rough skins of the potatoes Mom had set at one end of the table for Rachel to peel, a tradition that reached back seventeen years, to when her seven-year-old self had insisted on being involved in the preparation of the meal, and her mother had sat her down with a peeler and a handful of potatoes and allowed her to feel her way through removing the tubers' skins. Mom usually bought potatoes whose surfaces were covered in ridges and bumps, and there had been moments Rachel fancied she could almost pick out letters and parts of words encoded on them. She had advanced well beyond those first four potatoes; now, she was responsible for peeling and chopping all the necessary vegetables. For a brief time in his late teens, Josh had insisted on helping her; mostly, she had thought, to improve his standing with their parents. The last few years, he had abandoned the kitchen in favor of the living room, where their father and grandfather passed the hours prior to dinner watching whatever football games were on the television. Dad wasn't a big football fan, not in the same way as Grandpa, who took an almost visceral delight in the players' collisions. But he had grown up with his father's passion for the sport, and had learned enough about it to discuss the plays on-screen with the old man. It wasn't something they did that often—the Super Bowl was the only other instance she could think of—but it seemed to fulfill a need both men felt to demonstrate their bond as father and son. Rachel hadn't been surprised when Josh, despite his almost complete ignorance of anything sports-related, had wanted to join their fraternity. She judged it a demonstration of the event's ongoing importance to him that he had raised himself from the bed into which he'd collapsed at who-knew-when this morning, and, still reeking of stale cigarette smoke and watery beer, shuffled in to join them, stopping in the kitchen long enough to pour himself a glass of orange juice. Their father had greeted him with typical irony—"Hail! The conquering hero graces us with his presence!"—their grandfather with his typical grunt.

Afterwards, Rachel would think that she hadn't been expecting any trouble, today. Then she would correct herself, as she realized that she had been anticipating a disruption of the holiday, and had tied it to Josh. What she had been prepared for was her brother disappearing for ten minutes right as they were about to sit down to eat, and returning reeking of pot. Mom would say, "Josh," the tone of her voice a reproach not so much of the act—she and Dad had done (and continued to do, Rachel thought) their share of grass—as of his total lack of discretion. Grandpa wouldn't say anything, but his end of the table would practically crackle with barely suppressed rage. Dad would hurry to ask Rachel, who would be attempting to recall a sufficiently lengthy and distracting anecdote, how Albany Law was going. Scenarios approximating this one had played out over the last several Thanksgiving and Christmas dinners, since Josh had discovered the joys of mood- and mind-altering substances. To the best of her knowledge, his proclivities hadn't interfered with his studies as an undergraduate or graduate student, which Rachel guessed was the reason their parents hadn't come down on him with more force than they had. But it angered Grandpa to no end, which, Rachel increasingly believed, constituted a good part of the reason her brother did it.

But the argument that erupted this day: no way she could have predicted it. It began with something her grandfather said to her father, something that registered as background noise because she was answering her mother's question about where she was planning on going after she passed the bar. Clear as a bell, Josh's voice rang out: "Hey, Grandpa, why don't you give Dad a break, okay?"

"Josh!" their father said.

"All I'm saying is, he should take it easy on you," Josh said.

"That's enough," Dad said. "We're watching the game."

"That were my boy," Grandpa said, "he'd speak to his elders with a bit more respect."

"Dad," their father said.

"That were my son," Josh said, "I wouldn't treat him like a piece of shit all the time, especially after what I did to his brother."

"Josh!" Dad said. "What the hell is wrong with you?"

Grandpa said nothing.

"I'm fine," Josh said. "Not like poor Uncle Jim. Right, Grandpa?"

"What the hell are you going on about?" Dad said. "Are you high?"

"No I am not," Josh said. "If I were, it wouldn't have any bearing on what we're talking about, would it, Grandpa?"

"Stop it," Dad said. "I don't know what you're talking about, but give it a rest, okay?"

"What I can't work out," Josh said, "is whether it was an accident, or deliberate. Did things slip out of control, or did you turn that thing on your son? And if you did loose it on him, what can he possibly have done to drive you to do so? Oh, and one more thing: How can you stand yourself?"

"Leave," Dad said. "Just leave. Get out of here."

"Boy," Grandpa said, "you've gone beyond the thin ice to the open water."

"Which means what? That I can expect a visit from your friend in the freezer?"

"Josh," Dad said, his easy-chair creaking as he sat forward in it, "I'm not kidding. You need to leave."

"All right," Josh said, "I'll go. If there's anything you want to show me, Grandpa, you know where to find me." The couch springs groaned as he stood. Rachel half-expected him to pause in the kitchen on his way to his room, or for her mother to call his name, but neither happened. When his footsteps had finished their tromp along the hall, their father said, "Dad, I am so sorry for that. I don't know what got into him. Are you all right?"

"Game's on," Grandpa said.

12. THE SECOND TAPE

The second tape had been damaged, to the extent that the portion of Uncle Jim's conversation with Grandpa it recorded had been reduced to a stream of garble to whose surface select words and phrases bobbed up. The majority of them ("room," "go," "space") were sufficiently generic to be of little aid in inferring the contents of Grandpa's speech; although a few ("scared," "raw meat," "soldier") seemed to point in a more specific direction. From the first listen, Josh insisted that their Grandfather had been describing how the creature which crawled out of the egg had been frightened, until he had fed it the uncooked flesh of some animal or another, probably winning its trust. Later on, Grandpa had identified the creature as belonging to the soldier class he'd learned about during his coma. While she conceded that Josh's interpretation was reasonable, Rachel refused to commit to it, which Josh claimed was just her being a pain in the ass. Given what they'd already listened to, what better construction did she have to offer?

None, she was forced to admit, nor did the three longer passages they found on the tape provide any help. The first came five minutes in; the babble unsnarled and Grandpa was saying, "—like when you come down with the flu. High temperature, head swimming, every square inch of skin like a mob of angry men beat it with sticks. Maybe it would have had the same effect on the creatures, but I doubt it. Has to do with the difference in biology, is my guess. Doesn't help that the thing fights you. Especially if there's blood in the air, it's like trying to wrestle a strong man to the ground and keep him there. Sometimes, there's no choice but to let it go, a little bit. Why I use the freezer. Long as it's in there, it's dormant. After you take it out, if you're careful and don't overdo things, there's no problem keeping it under control almost the entire time. I—" and his words ran together.

Twenty-four minutes after that passage, long after they had given up hope of encountering another and left the tape playing so they could tell themselves they had listened to all of it, the garble gave way to Grandpa saying, "After that, I received a visit from a couple of fellows whose matching crew cuts, sunglasses, and black suits were as much ID as what they flashed in their wallets. I'd caught sight of such characters before. Every now and again, they would show up at the camp, ask to speak to one of the experts about something. Wasn't too strange, when you thought about it. Here we were, working in a foreign land, where we might notice a detail about the place or people that would be useful for these boys. Cold War was in full swing, and the lessons of the last big one were fresh in everyone's mind, especially the strategic advantage of a plentiful supply of fuel. Our work was tied up with national security, so it wasn't a surprise that the fellows who concerned themselves with it should keep an eye on us. Tell the truth, I was curious to find out what they'd driven all this way to ask me about. Naïve as it sounds, not once did it cross my mind that they might be here to inquire about my other activities. Not that the company would have had any remorse over what they'd had me do to the competition: I just assumed they wouldn't want me revealing such a valuable secret. Never did learn if someone had blabbed, or if the G-men had sweated it out of them. No matter. These boys cut straight to the point. Said they knew I'd been up to some extracurricular activities, and were going to provide me the opportunity to put those activities to work for my country. Which was to say—" a paraphrase that was swallowed in a mess of sound.

Before the third and final section, the tape spat out the phrase, "children of the fang." Three minutes after that, at the very end of the second side of the second tape, the nonsense came to an end and was replaced by silence. As Rachel was running her finger across the tape recorder's buttons, Grandpa's voice said, "What we never could work out was whether the viruses floating around my blood had changed me permanently. Could I pass along my control of the creature to my child, or was it confined to me? How could we know, right? I hadn't met your ma, hadn't settled down and started a family, yet."

Uncle Jim said, "What do you think, now?"

"I think we might find out," Grandpa said, and the tape recorder snapped off.

Interlude: Grandpa (3): Knife Wants to Cut
Whether birthday, Christmas, or other celebration such as graduation, the gift Rachel or her brother could expect from Grandpa was predictable: money, a generous amount of it tucked into a card whose saccharine sentimentality it was difficult to credit their grandfather sharing. When they were younger, the bills that slid out of their cards from Grandpa had been a source of puzzlement and occasional frustration to her and Josh. Why couldn't their grandfather have given them whatever present they'd requested of him, instead of money? In a relatively short time, their complaints were replaced by gratitude, as Grandpa's beneficence enabled Rachel and Josh to afford extravagances their parents had refused them.

The exception to this practice occurred on Josh's thirteenth birthday. After he had unwrapped his gifts from his parents and Rachel, but before he had moved on to their cards, Grandpa said, "Here." A box scratched across the table's surface.

"Grandpa?" Josh said. Whatever was inside the box thwacked against its side as Josh picked it up. Something heavy, Rachel thought, probably metal. A watch? "Buck knife," Josh read. "Really?"

"Open it and find out," Grandpa said.

Rachel could feel the look her father and mother exchanged.

The cardboard made a popping sound as Josh tore into it. "Cooooooooooool," he said. Plastic crinkled against his fingers.

Their father said, "Dad."

Grandpa said, "Boy your age should have a knife—a good one."

The blade snicked as Josh unfolded it into place. "Whoa," he said.

Their father said, "Josh."

Grandpa said, "It's not a toy. It's a tool. A tool's only as good as your control of it, you understand? Your control slips—you get sloppy—and you'll slice your skin wide open. Someone's next to you, you'll slice them open. That is not something you want. Knife wants to cut: it's what it's made for. You keep that in mind every time you reach for it, and you'll be fine."

Their mother said, "Josh, what do you say?"

"Thank you, Grandpa," Josh said, "thank you thank you thank you!"

Within a week, the knife would be gone, confiscated by Josh's homeroom teacher when she caught him showing it off to his friends. After a lengthy conference with Mrs. Kleinbaum, their father retrieved the knife, which he insisted on holding onto until the school year was out, his penalty for Josh's error in judgment. By the time summer arrived, Josh had pretty much forgotten about his grandfather's present, and if he remembered to mention it to their father, it was not in Rachel's hearing.

Before all of this, though, Josh let her hold the gift. The knife was heavy, dense in the way that metal was. Longer than her palm, the handle was smooth on either end, slightly rougher between. "That's where the wood panels are," Josh said. On one side of the handle, a dip near one of the ends exposed the top edge of the blade. By digging her nail into a groove in it, she could lever the blade out. As it clicked into place, a tremor ran up the handle. Rachel slid her finger along the knife's dull spine. About a third of the way from its end, the metal angled down to the tip. "Like a scimitar," Josh said. She dimpled her skin on the point. "Careful," Josh said.

"Shut up," she said, "I am being careful." Ready to part her flesh, the blade's edge passed under her touch. In her best approximation of Grandpa's voice, she said, "Knife wants to cut." She folded the knife closed, and handed it back to Josh.

He laughed. "Knife wants to cut," he said.

13. In the Basement (Now): The Thing in the Ice

Because of Grandpa's stroke Christmas Eve, neither Rachel nor her parents paid much attention to what they assumed at the time was Josh's refusal to appear for Christmas. Granted, it had been a few years since he'd last missed a family holiday, but he had spent most of his Thanksgiving visit complaining about the workload required by his doctoral classes (the stress of which their parents had diagnosed as the cause of his blowup with Grandpa). He had a trio of long papers due immediately before Christmas break—not the most work he'd ever faced, but on a couple of occasions on the day before Thanksgiving, he'd alluded to Rachel about a mid-semester affair with a guy from Maine that had crashed and burned in spectacular fashion, leaving him dramatically behind in all his classes. She had offered his backlog of assignments to her mother as the reason for his abrupt departure Saturday afternoon, while Rachel and her parents were braving the crowds at the Wiltwyck mall. His assignments were probably the reason that none of them had heard from Josh the last few weeks, either.

And if she and her parents were to be honest with one another, it was likely as well that Josh had opted to give Christmas a pass. After Mom heard the thump and crash on the front stairs and went to investigate, and found Grandpa sprawled halfway down, his breathing labored, the left side of his face slack, his left arm and leg so much dead lumber, the focus had shifted from holiday preparations (which included planning for a possible Round Two between Josh and Grandpa) to whether the old man would survive the next twenty-four hours. Even after the doctors had pronounced Grandpa's condition stable, and expressed a cautious optimism that subsequent days would bear out, he remained the center of attention, as Rachel and her parents talked through what needed doing at home to accommodate his changed condition, and set about making the necessary calls to arrange the place for him. She left a couple of messages on Josh's phone, the first telling him to call her, the second, a few days later, informing him of Grandpa's stroke, and though she was annoyed at his failure to respond, especially once he knew the situation, she didn't miss the inevitable torrent of self-reproach with which he would have greeted the news—and which certainly would have been worse had he been there with them.

By Valentine's Day, what Rachel referred to as her brother's radio-silence had become a source of worry for their mother. "Do you think he's still upset about Thanksgiving?" she asked during one of their daily calls. Rachel could not believe that Josh would sulk for this long; although there had been a couple of occasions during his undergraduate years when a particularly intense relationship had caused him to drop off the face of the earth for a couple of months. She phoned his cell, but her, "It's me. Listen: Mom's worried. Call her, okay?" betrayed more pique than she intended. But she could not credit the edge to her voice for Josh's continuing failure to phone their mother. And, despite his assurances that Josh was probably caught up in some project or another, Dad's voice when she spoke with him revealed his own anxiety. Only Grandpa, his speech slowed and distorted by the stroke, seemed untroubled by Josh's silence. Both her parents were desperate to drive up to Josh's apartment, but feared that appearing unannounced would aggravate whatever the situation with him was. Rachel bowed to their none-too-subtle hints, and offered to do so for them.

Before she could take a taxi to the other side of the city, however, one of Josh's fellow students at SUNY Albany called her to ask if everything was okay with her brother, whom, he said, he hadn't seen since he'd left for Thanksgiving vacation the previous semester. He'd left messages on Josh's cell, but had heard nothing in reply. He'd remembered Josh mentioning a sister at Albany Law, so he'd looked up her number, which he'd been meaning to call for a while, now. He didn't want to be intrusive. He just wanted to be sure Josh was okay and knew his friends were asking for him. That conversation was the first of a chain that led to several of Josh's other friends, then their parents, then the police. By the end of the day, her mother had left her father to watch Grandpa and raced up the thruway to pick up Rachel and drive to Josh's apartment, where they were met by Detective Calasso of the Albany PD and a pair of uniform officers. Both Rachel and her mother had keys to the door. Her heart was beating so fast it was painful, not because of what she was afraid they were going to find, but because of what she was certain they were not. The moment the door swung in, the smell that rolled out, dry, cool dust, confirmed her suspicion. During their search of Josh's small living quarters, the detective and his colleagues discovered two bags of pot, a smaller one in the top drawer of the bedroom dresser, and a larger one sunk inside the toilet's cistern. Once they'd found the second bag, the tenor of the detective's questions underwent a distinct change, as Josh went from graduate student in philosophy to small-time drug-dealer. Rachel could hear the narrative Calasso's line of inquiry was assembling, one in which her brother's criminal activities had brought him into jeopardy from a client, competitor, or supplier. Best case, Josh had gone into hiding; worst, he'd never had the chance. From the detective's perspective, she could understand: it was an attractive explanation that had the virtue of neatly accounting for all the evidence confronting him. Her and her mother's protests that this wasn't Josh were to be expected. How often, in such situations, could family members admit that their loved ones were so markedly different from what they'd known? Detective Calasso assured them that the police would do everything in their power to locate Josh, but by the time her mother was dropping her back at her apartment, she was reasonably sure that the detective deemed the case essentially solved.

That she would entertain Josh's claims about Grandpa and what he had locked away in his basement freezer was at first an index of her frustration after four weeks of regular calls to Detective Calasso, during which he never failed to insist that he and his men were working tirelessly to ascertain her brother's whereabouts. Approximately every third conversation, he would inform Rachel that they were pursuing a number of promising leads, but when she asked him what those leads were, he appealed to the sensitivity of the information. She hardly required a lifetime spent mastering the nuances of spoken expression to recognize that he was bullshitting her. She could believe that Calasso had queried what criminal informants he knew for information on her brother, as she could that his failure to turn up anything substantive would have done little to change his theory of the case. Compared to the plot in which her brother had been assassinated by a rival drug dealer and his weighted corpse dumped in the Hudson, the prospect that the accusations he'd lobbed at their grandfather at Thanksgiving had prompted the old man to some terrible act had the benefit of familiarity.

In the space of a week, however, the Grandpa's-monster-theory, as she christened it, went from absurd to slightly less than absurd, which, while not a huge change, was testament to the amount of time she'd spent turning it over in her mind, playing devil's advocate with herself, arguing Josh's position for him. Her dismissal of the story Grandpa had told Uncle Jim was based on her assumption that he and his friend, Jerry, would have been sufficiently competent to take full advantage of the opportunities with which their supposed discoveries presented them. What if they hadn't been? What if they hadn't known how to exploit their findings? After all, why should they have? Especially if they couldn't trace their way back to the place? And say, for the sake of argument, that Grandpa had come into the care of...something, something fantastic. Who was to say he would have turned it over to a zoo, or university? It wouldn't have been the most sensible course of action, but, as her favorite professor did not tire of reminding her, logical, self-consistent behavior was the province of bad fiction. Actual people tended to move in ways which, while in keeping with the peculiarities of their psychology, resembled more the sudden shifts in course typical of the soap opera.

Which meant, of course, that her younger brother could have had a secret life as a drug dealer. And that their grandfather could have been keeping an unimaginable creature in enforced hibernation in the basement. The impossibility of what she was considering did not stop her from making a couple of discrete inquiries among her closer friends as to the possibility of acquiring a set of lock picks and being instructed in their use. This proved remarkably easy. One of those friends had a friend who earned extra cash as a stage magician whose skill set included a facility with opening locks. For the price of a couple of dinners, the magician was happy to procure for Rachel her own set of tools and to teach her how to employ them. She wasn't certain if she was one hundred percent serious about what she appeared to be planning, or if it was a temporary obsession that had to work itself out. The entirety of the bus ride to Wiltwyck, she told herself that she was not yet positive she would descend to the basement. That her parents were away for the afternoon and Grandpa still of limited mobility meant no more than it meant. She managed to keep that train of thought running for the taxi ride from the bus station to her parents' house. But once she had let herself in the front door, hung up her coat, and slid the soft bag with the lock picks in it from her pocketbook, it seemed pointless to continue pretending there was any doubt of her intentions. She listened for Grandpa, his home health aide, and when she was satisfied there was no one else on the first floor, set off sweeping her cane from side to side down the front hall, towards the basement door.

In no time at all, she was resting the cane against the freezer. How many times had she been here, sliding her hands along the appliance's edge until they encountered each of Grandpa's locks? Always with Josh maintaining a steady stream of chatter beside her. Now, the only sound was the low hiss of her palms over the freezer's surface, the click of metal on metal as she found a lock and tilted it up. How long ago had Grandpa switched entirely to padlocks? It made what she was about to do easier. She placed the lockpick bag on top of the freezer, rolled it open, selected her tools, and set to work.

The locks unclasped so easily, it was almost anticlimactic. Half-anticipating an additional security measure she'd missed, Rachel searched the freezer lid. Nothing. She put the opened locks on the floor, returned her tools to their bag and put it beside the locks, and braced her hands against the lid. After all these years, to be… There was no point delaying. She pushed upwards, and with the pop of its rubber seal parting, the lid released.

A cloud of cinnamon, vanilla, and brine enveloped her. She choked, coughed, stepped away from the freezer. Her eyes were streaming, her nose and tongue numb. She bent forward, unable to control the coughs that shook her lungs. So much for secrecy: if Grandpa had been unaware of her presence in the house previously, she'd just advertised it. Still coughing, she returned to the freezer and plunged her hands into it.

Ice cubes heaped almost to its top rattled as her fingers parted their frozen geometry. She moved her hands back and forth, ice chattering and rattling. There was a click, and the freezer's motor whirred to life. When had Grandpa loaded all this ice in here? Funny to think that not once had she and Josh asked that question.

Her fingertips brushed something that wasn't ice. She gasped, overcome with sudden terror that she had found her brother, that Grandpa had flipped out, murdered him, and used the freezer to hide the body. Even as her heart leapt in her chest, her not-completely-numb fingers were telling her that this wasn't Josh. It was an arm, but it was shorter than her brother's, the skin weird, pebbled. She followed it to one end, and found a hand with three thick fingers and a thumb set back towards the wrist. A claw sharp as a fresh razor protruded from each of the fingers.

Nausea roiled her stomach. She withdrew her hands from the ice and sat down hard on the basement floor. Her head was pounding. She pressed her cold palms to either side of it. Somewhere in the recesses of her brain, Josh crowed, "See? I told you!" Her pulse was racing. She felt hot, feverish. The floor seemed to tilt under her, and she was lying on it. She could not draw in enough breath. Her body was light, almost hollow. She was moving away from it, into darkness that gave the sensation of movement, as if passing through a tunnel. She

14. Affiliation

opened her eyes to light. Brilliance flooded her vision. She gasped, and heard it at a distance. She jerked her hands to her face, but found her arms weighted with something that rattled and rustled as she tried to move them. Her entire body was covered in the stuff. Panic surged through her. She thrashed from side to side, up and down, the medium that held her snapping and cracking as it shifted around her. There was something wrong with her arms and legs. They were sluggish, clumsy. The brightness before her eyes resolved into shapes, triangles, diamonds, blocks, jumbling against one another. With a crash, her right arm broke free of its confinement. Her hand flailed on the rough surface of the material. She braced her forearm against it, and pushed her head and shoulders into the air.

She was in a large box, filled, she realized, with ice. That she could see this was no less remarkable than the circumstance itself. Her head had emerged near one side of the container. If she stretched her neck, she could take in more of the space around her. The figure lying beside the box startled her. She gasped again—and heard it from the woman's lips. In a rush, she took in the sweater and faded jeans, the hair in its shoulder-length cut, the round, freckled face, its eyes wide and unfocused (*and the colors, God, was this what color was?*)—

—and she was looking at a dark blur that kept all except the outermost limits of her vision from her. Above, something moved in Grandpa's freezer, shoving ice from side to side, spilling it on the carpet. She went to sit up—

—and was in the box, her head hanging over the side. Her hands clutched the metal of the box. Below her, the woman on the floor shivered. Her face was flushed, her breathing rapid. She reached a hand to her, and what already had registered peripherally—the pebbled skin, patterned with dark swirls, the three fingers, each taloned, the thumb almost too far back to be practical, armed with its own claw, longer and more curved—shouted itself at her, bringing with it a thunderclap of understanding. A fresh wave of nausea swept her, but it was the woman on the floor who coughed and vomited. For a moment, less—

—she was spitting out the remains of a partially digested Danish—

—and then she had heaved herself out of the box (*Grandpa's freezer*) and went stumbling across the basement floor, pieces of ice dropping from her on the way. Her legs were different—out of proportion in a way she couldn't assimilate. Some of the bones had been shortened, some lengthened, the angles of her joints changed. Her balance was shot. If she stood straight, she felt as if she was about to tip over onto her back. Not to mention, the sight of everything around her, which kept tugging her head this way and that, further unbalancing her. She had developed a fair estimate of the basement's appearance, but it was as if, after having encountered water a handful at a time, she had been dropped into the ocean. All of it was so *vivid,* from the swirling grain of the paneling on the walls to the spiky texture of the carpet, from the squat bulk of the freezer to the sharp edges of the cardboard boxes stacked around the floor. On top of that, the rest of her senses were dulled, practically to nonexistence. She struck the wall at the foot of the basement stairs, and realized that she hadn't felt the collision as painfully as she should. *Grandpa,* she thought, and half-pulled herself, half-climbed towards the door at the top of the stairs.

As she pushed through into the kitchen, an image burst across her mind's eye: a man, looking over his shoulder at her, his eyes widening with the shock that had stunned the rest of his face. He appeared to be wearing a gray suit jacket, but there wasn't time for her to be sure, because he was replaced by another man, this one dressed in a white robe and a white headdress, his mouth open in a shout that she heard (*"Ya Allah!"*), his eyes hidden behind sunglasses in the lenses of which something awful was reflected as it bore down on him, claws outstretched. She caromed across the kitchen, slamming into the breakfast bar at its center. The tall, glass cylinders in which Mom kept the cereal toppled onto the floor, where they detonated like so many bombs, spraying glass and corn flakes across the tiles. She stepped away from the breakfast bar, and was staring down at a man whose eyes were rolling up as blood bubbled from his lips, over his scraggly beard, and the claws of her right hand slid deeper into his jaw. The next man she saw was dressed in a tuxedo, the white shirt of which was turning dark from the wave of blood spilling down from the slash to his throat. She lurched out of the kitchen, down the hallway to the stairs to the second floor. The sightless eyes of a fair-haired boy (*Jim?*) whose throat and chest were a ruin of meat and bone stared at her while a man's voice wailed somewhere out of sight (*Grandpa?*). A lab-coated man held out his hands in front of him as he retreated from her. She shouldered aside the door to her grandfather's portion of the house, and saw the terrified expression of a young man whose round, freckled face and curly hair marked him as Josh, while her grandfather's voice screamed something (*"Is this what you wanted? Is it?"*).

The door to Grandpa's bedroom had been left ajar by the home health aide. She shoved it open and crossed the threshold.

Despite the unbridled insanity in which she was caught up, a small part of her thought, *So this is what his room looks like.* It was larger than she would have anticipated, the far corner filled by a king-sized bed draped with a plaid comforter. Next to it, a nightstand held a lamp that could be bent to direct its light. On the other side of it, her grandfather sat dozing in a recliner. A coarsely knitted blanket covered his legs and lap; under it, a thick, heavy robe wrapped his chest and arms. His face was as she'd imagined it: the flesh sparse on the bone, the mouth downturned at the corners, the nose blunt as a hatchet, the eyes sunken, shadowed by the brows. Lines like the beds of dried rivers crossed his skin, which had not lost the tan his years in the sun had burned into it. The stroke's damage was visible in the sag of the left half of his face, which lent it an almost comically morose appearance. The ghost of her and Josh's mocking mimicry of him flitted through her memory. She leaned closer to him.

He opened his eyes, and she leapt back, thumping into a wall as she did. Although his eyelids raised ever-so-slightly, his voice remained level. Nodding, he said, "Wondered if it might be…you." His tongue slid over his lips. "Tried with… Jim." He shook his head. "Couldn't…leave remains. Beast needed…to eat…" He shrugged. "Lost…Joshua…"

Had he attempted the same experiment with Josh? Did it matter? Like a swell of lava rising over the lip of a volcano, anger rolled through her, carrying her deeper into the thing she was inhabiting. She crouched forward to steady herself. She could feel the claws jutting from her fingertips, the fangs filling her mouth. Anger swelled within her, incinerating everything in its path. She drew back her lips, and hissed, a long, sibilant vent of rage that summoned her grandfather's attention from whatever memory had distracted him.

He saw her teeth bared, her claws rising. Something like satisfaction crossed his face. "That's…my girl," he said.

"They have the power of calling snakes, and feel great pleasure in playing with and handling them. Their own bite becomes poisonous to people not inoculated in the same manner. Thus a part of the serpent's nature appears to be transfused into them."
—Nathaniel Hawthorne, *American Notebooks*

For Fiona, and for Ellen Datlow, a most belated birthday present

Monster Index

Azathoth

"Ultimate Chaos, at whose center sprawls the blind idiot god Azathoth, Lord of All Things, encircled by his flopping horde of mindless and amorphous dancers, and lulled by the thin monotonous piping of a demonic flute held in nameless paws."
—H. P. Lovecraft, "The Haunter of the Dark" (*Weird Tales*, Dec. 1935)

Azathoth the "daemon-sultan" is the creator deity of H. P. Lovecraft's mythology and the progenitor of Cthulhu, Nyarlathotep, Yog-Shothoth, Shub-Niggurath, and others. He is described as a bubbling, writhing mass who lies at the very heart of the universe, blind, indifferent, and mad beyond imagining, surrounded by a court of musicians who play loathsome music to entertain and placate him for all eternity.

Azathoth's first published appearance is in "The Whisper in the Darkness" (*Weird Tales*, Aug. 1931), although Lovecraft writes of him earlier in his novella *The Dream Quest of Unknown Kaddath* (Arkham House, 1943), which would go unpublished until after his death.

✳ "The Sect of the Idiot"

"That is not dead which can eternal lie, And with strange aeons even death may die."
—H. P. Lovecraft, "The Call of Cthulhu" (*Weird Tales*, Feb. 1928)

Lovecraft's most beloved eldritch horror, **GREAT CTHULHU**, is a monstrous alien deity who eons ago descended to Earth from weird and distant stars. In his sunken city of R'lyeh, deep in the Pacific Ocean, Cthulhu lies dead and dreaming, waiting for the stars to align so that he may awaken, devour humanity, and conquer the Earth. Even as he slumbers, his malevolent presence can be sensed by sleeping mortals, who may dream of his Cyclopean sunken city, full of strange angles and slimy stone, and find themselves sparked with creativity, or madness, as a result.

Great Cthulhu, High Priest of R'lyeh, is described in "The Call of Cthulhu" as a "monster of vaguely anthropoid outline, but with an octopus-like head whose face was a mass of feelers, a scaly, rubbery-looking body, prodigious claws on hind and fore feet, and long, narrow wings behind."

Cthulhu first appears in Lovecraft's classic tale "The Call of Cthulhu" (*Weird Tales*, Feb. 1928).

✳ "THE SAME DEEP WATERS AS YOU"

"Flopping, hopping, croaking, bleating—surging inhumanly through the spectral moonlight in a grotesque, malignant saraband of fantastic nightmare.... One, who led the way, was clad in a ghoulishly humped black coat and striped trousers, and had a man's felt hat perched on the shapeless thing that answered for a head."
—H. P. Lovecraft, *The Shadow over Innsmouth* (Visionary Publishing Co., 1936)

The Deep Ones are a race of squamous, sea-dwelling grotesqueries, vaguely humanoid but sharing many characteristics with fish and amphibians. They live in deep underwater cities, where they worship Father Dagon, Mother Hydra, and Great Cthulhu. Sometimes, it is said, Deep Ones come ashore to breed with human beings. The unfortunate offspring of such unholy unions often appear to be normal men and women in their youth but grow increasingly ugly and fishlike in appearance as they age, acquiring "the Innsmouth look." Their deformity worsens until their eyes bulge, their skin scales, gills form on their necks, and their hands grow into webbed claws. The offspring begin to dream strange dreams and yearn to join their ancestors in the gloaming depths; once they have fully transformed, they will inexorably do so.

Deep Ones first appear in *The Shadow over Innsmouth* (Visionary Publishing Co., 1936), although their existence is suggested in Lovecraft's much earlier short story "Dagon" (*The Vagrant*, No. 11, Nov. 1919).

✳ "Only the End of the World Again"; "The Same Deep Waters as You"; "A Quarter to Three"; "Inelastic Collisions"; "Love is Forbidden, We Croak and Howl"; "Jar of Salts"

"Six feet end to end, three and five-tenths feet central diameter, tapering to one foot at each end. Like a barrel with five bulging ridges in place of staves. Lateral breakages, as of thinnish stalks, are at equator in middle of these ridges. In furrows between ridges are curious growths—combs or wings that fold up and spread out like fans...which gives almost seven-foot wing spread. Arrangement reminds one of certain monsters of primal myth, especially fabled Elder Things in the Necronomicon."
—H. P. Lovecraft, *At the Mountains of Madness* (*Astounding Stories*, Feb.–Apr. 1936)

THE ELDER THINGS are an ancient and advanced alien race that colonized Earth before the dawn of humanity. They built numerous cities both on land and deep in the sea and bioengineered the race of shoggoths to be their servants and build their cities. This did not work out well for the Elder Things, as the shoggoths eventually rebelled against them and destroyed their civilization, which was already weakened by the climate changes of Earth's ice age.

Elder Things are some of the most peculiar-looking beings in Lovecraft's canon. Human characters who encounter them have sometimes been unable to tell whether they are plants or animals. Elder Things have vaguely football-shaped bodies with starfishlike appendages that serve as feelers, eye-stalks, and legs. They also possess tentacles and delicate, fanlike wings. Despite their bizarre appearance, Elder Things are, surprisingly enough, not particularly malevolent toward humanity, just incredibly *alien*.

Elder Things first appear in H. P. Lovecraft's "The Dreams in the Witch House" (*Weird Tales*, Jul. 1933).

✳ "BLACK AS THE PIT FROM POLE TO POLE"

"It was a colossal and nameless blasphemy with glaring red eyes, and it held in its bony claws a thing that had once been a man, gnawing at the head as a child nibbles at a stick of candy."
—H. P. Lovecraft, "Pickman's Model" (*Weird Tales*, Oct. 1927)

Lovecraft's **GHOULS** are a race of monstrous creatures that dwell in underground labyrinths of catacombs and tombs, feasting on the flesh of corpses. Possessing both humanoid and canine features, ghouls have long bestial muzzles; hunched, hairless, and pallid bodies; and clawed or hooflike feet. They can pass between the Dreamlands and the waking world through magical tunnels in their subterranean worlds and can be either helpful or very dangerous to humans who encounter them. It is implied that these creatures were once, or are descended from, mortal men and women who succumbed to cannibalistic appetites and were hideously transformed.

Ghouls originate from Arabian folklore, where they are a type of flesh-eating Jinn, or demon, that haunts graveyards and ruins. *One Thousand and One Arabian Nights* is the oldest surviving piece of literature to feature ghouls, although many later authors, including Edgar Allen Poe, write of them. Lovecraft had adored Poe and *One Thousand and One Arabian Nights* since his childhood, and so he includes his own version of the macabre creatures in several of his stories.

Ghouls first appear in Lovecraft's work in "Pickman's Model" (*Weird Tales*, Oct. 1927).

✳ "Love Is Forbidden, We Croak and Howl"; "Haruspicy"

"'Beyond life there are'—his face grew ashen with terror—'*things* that I cannot distinguish. They move slowly through angles. They have no bodies and they move slowly through outrageous angles.... I think they have scented me!' He shrieked. 'They are slowly turning toward me.'"
—Frank Belknap Long, "The Hounds of Tindalos" (*Weird Tales*, Mar. 1929)

THE HOUNDS OF TINDALOS are strange and ravenous creatures that exist in the angles of time (while human beings descend from the curves of time). They can move freely through time and can transport themselves anywhere in the physical world where sharp angles meet. Although their bodies have been described as "lean and hungry," little else of their appearance is known, as no one who encounters them survives to record a detailed account. Their moniker, "Hounds," is thought to refer to their hunting capacity rather than anything doglike about their appearance. Human beings who time travel may draw the attention of the Hounds of Tindalos, which, having caught their scent, will relentlessly pursue the unfortunate individuals across dimensions and devour them, leaving behind only their desiccated corpses and a strange bluish ichor.

The Hounds of Tindalos were invented by Frank Belknap Long, a close friend, mentee, and collaborator of Lovecraft's. They were written specifically to be a part of the grim mythology Lovecraft had created, and appear in one of the first Cthulhu Mythos stories written by someone other than Lovecraft. Lovecraft himself incorporates these nasty creatures into some of his later work.

The Hounds of Tindalos first appear in "The Hounds of Tindalos" (*Weird Tales*, Mar. 1929) by Frank Belknap Long and later appear in H. P. Lovecraft's "The Whisper in the Darkness" (*Weird Tales*, Aug. 1931).

✳ "INELASTIC COLLISIONS"

The King in Yellow

"Camilla: You, sir, should unmask.

Stranger: Indeed?

Cassilda: Indeed it's time. We have all laid aside disguise but you.

Stranger: I wear no mask.

Camilla: (Terrified, aside to Cassilda.) No mask? No mask!"

—Robert W. Chambers, "The Mask" (*The King in Yellow*, 1895)

THE KING IN YELLOW is one of the avatars of the alien deity Hastur the Unspeakable. He may appear as a stranger in tattered yellow robes and a pallid mask (or perhaps his face) as a harbinger of calamity and madness.

Originally, *The King in Yellow* was a collection of supernatural tales written by Robert W. Chambers and published in 1895. Several of the short stories in this anthology revolve around a fictional, madness-inducing play, also titled *The King in Yellow*, and its sinister titular figure. Chambers himself makes references in these stories to the fictional god Hastur, first invented by Ambrose Bierce in his short story "Haïta the Shepherd" in 1891.

H. P. Lovecraft was such a fan of Chambers's collection that he references Hastur and other elements from *The King in Yellow* in his own short story "The Whisper in the Darkness" and in his poem "The Elder Pharos."

The figure of the King in Yellow was further developed by August Derleth, a great friend of Lovecraft and contributor to the Cthulhu Mythos. Derleth is the first to depict Hastur as one of the Great Old Ones, kin of Cthulhu and Yog-Shothoth, and depicts the King in Yellow as one of Hastur's avatars.

The King in Yellow first appears in Robert W. Chambers's short-story collection *The King in Yellow* (F. Tennyson Neely, 1895) and later appears in H. P. Lovecraft's "The Whisper in the Darkness" (*Weird Tales*, Aug. 1931).

✷ "I'VE COME TO TALK WITH YOU AGAIN"

"Hideous jaws gaped at him; terrible eyes blazed into his unblinkingly; a frightful fetid scent pervaded the atmosphere—the serpent scent."
—Robert E. Howard, "The Shadow Kingdom" (*Weird Tales*, Aug. 1929)

THE SERPENT MEN, or SERPENT PEOPLE, are a race of reptilian creatures invented by Robert E. Howard. Once rulers of the Earth in a forgotten age, their civilization has waned, forcing them to retreat to subterranean cities beneath the Earth's surface. The Serpent Men share human and reptilian features, having bipedal, humanoid bodies; snakelike heads; and scaly skin. Accomplished magicians, alchemists, and illusionists, Serpent Men can use these arts to disguise themselves as human beings. They worship the "Great Serpent," who is assumed to be Yig, the snake god of the Cthulhu Mythos.

Robert E. Howard, creator of Conan the Barbarian and a dear friend of H. P. Lovecraft, often writes stories in the Cthulhu Mythos and incorporates elements of the mythos into his works. He initially created the Serpent Men as villains for his first Kull the Conqueror story, "The Shadow Kingdom," and Lovecraft later mentions them in his short story "The Haunter of the Dark." Serpent Men have been further incorporated into the Cthulhu Mythos by Clark Ashton Smith and others.

Serpent Men first appear in "The Shadow Kingdom" (*Weird Tales*, Aug. 1929) by Robert E. Howard and are referenced in Lovecraft's "The Haunter of the Dark" (*Weird Tales*, Dec. 1936).

✳ "CHILDREN OF THE FANG"

Shoggoths

"The nightmare, plastic column of fetid, black iridescence oozed tightly onward.... It was a terrible, indescribable thing vaster than any subway train—a shapeless congeries of protoplasmic bubbles, faintly self-luminous, and with myriads of temporary eyes forming and un-forming as pustules of greenish light all over the tunnel-filling front that bore down upon us, crushing the frantic penguins and slithering over the glistening floor.... Still came the eldritch, mocking cry—*'Tekeli-li! Tekeli-li!'*"
—H. P. Lovecraft, *At the Mountains of Madness* (*Astounding Stories*, Feb.–Apr. 1936)

The monstrous SHOGGOTHS were bioengineered to be a race of slaves for the Elder Things. After countless ages of mindless servitude, some of the shoggoths evolved beyond the intentions of their creators, developing independent minds and the ability to survive on land. They rebelled against the Elder Things, and although most of them were eventually brought to heel, their rebellion crippled the Elder Things' civilization on Earth.

These amorphous, bubbling monsters hold no solid form but can manifest eyes, tendrils, and maws at will. They gladly consume anything in their path, terrified human and hapless penguin alike.

Shoggoths are first mentioned in H. P. Lovecraft's poem "Night-Gaunts" (*The Phantagraph*, 1936) and make their first prominent appearance in his novella *At the Mountains of Madness* (*Astounding Stories*, Feb.–Apr. 1936).

✳ "The Dappled Thing"; "Remnants"; "Black as the Pit from Pole to Pole"; "That of Which We Speak When We Speak of the Unspeakable"

"Ever Their praises, and abundance to the Black Goat of the Woods. Iä! Shub-Niggurath! Iä! Shub-Niggurath! The Black Goat of the Woods with a Thousand Young!"
—H. P. Lovecraft, "The Whisper in the Darkness" (*Weird Tales*, Aug. 1931)

SHUB-NIGGURATH is a monstrous deity frequently called upon by cultists performing rituals or sacrifices in H. P. Lovecraft's fiction. In a letter to Willis Conover, Lovecraft notes that Shub-Niggurath is Yog-Shothoth's wife and describes her as a "hellish cloud-like entity...in whose honor nameless cults hold the right of the Goat with a Thousand Young." Although Shub-Niggurath never makes an actual physical appearance in any of H. P. Lovecraft's fiction, many extrapolate from Lovecraft's references that she is some sort of horrible and perverse fertility goddess.

Shub-Niggurath is first referenced in a collaboration between Lovecraft and his friend Adolphe de Castro and is mentioned frequently in Lovecraft's subsequent work. Due to her evocative title, Shub-Niggurath has also captured the imagination of many later authors writing in the Cthulhu Mythos.

Shub-Niggurath is first mentioned in "The Last Test" (*Weird Tales*, Nov. 1928) by Adolphe de Castro and H. P. Lovecraft.

✳ "RED GOAT BLACK GOAT"

Contributors

LAIRD BARRON is the author of several books, including *The Imago Sequence, Occultation, The Croning*, and *The Beautiful Thing That Awaits Us All*. His work has appeared in many magazines and anthologies. An expatriate Alaskan, Barron currently resides in upstate New York.

For more information, go to: LAIRDBARRON.WORDPRESS.COM.

ELIZABETH BEAR was born on the same day as Frodo and Bilbo Baggins, but in a different year. She divides her time between Massachusetts, where she lives in a drafty old house with a giant, ridiculous dog, and Wisconsin, where her partner, fantasy novelist and firefighter Scott Lynch, lives. She enjoys rock climbing and cooking, among other extreme sports.

She is a Hugo and Sturgeon Award winner, and her most recent novel is *Shattered Pillars*, the second book in her Eternal Sky series of Central Asian–inspired epic fantasies.

NADIA BULKIN has a master's degree in International Affairs from American University in Washington, D.C., and pays her rent doing research on Southeast Asia, nationalism, social identity, and political violence.

She also writes fiction about similar subjects, except with (more) monsters. Two of her stories have been nominated for Shirley Jackson Awards, and one won the 2010 ChiZine Short Story Contest.

For more information, visit NADIABULKIN.WORDPRESS.COM.

FRED CHAPPELL is an author and poet. He was an English professor for forty years at the University of North Carolina at Greensboro and was the Poet Laureate of North Carolina from 1997–2002. He is best known in Lovecraftian circles for his 1968 novel, *Dagon*, and has written several fantasy and horror stories, two of which won the World Fantasy Award. He has also won the Aiken Taylor Award for Modern American Poetry, the Prix du Meilleur des Livre Étranger, the Bollingen Prize, and the T. S. Eliot Prize.

ELLEN DATLOW (INTRODUCTION & EDITOR) has been editing science fiction, fantasy, and horror short fiction for more than thirty years. She was the fiction editor of *OMNI* Magazine, *Event Horizon*, and *SCI FICTION* and has edited more than fifty anthologies, including the annual *The Best Horror of the Year* as well as *Naked City: Tales of Urban Fantasy*; *Hauntings*, a reprint anthology of ghost stories and haunted houses; *Telling Tales: The Clarion West 30th Anniversary Anthology*; *Teeth: Vampire Tales* and *After: Nineteen Stories of Apocalypse and Dystopia* (two young adult anthologies with Terri Windling); and *Queen Victoria's Book of Spells: An Anthology of Gaslamp Fantasy* (an adult anthology with Terri Windling). Forthcoming is *Fearful Symmetries*, an unthemed anthology of horror and the supernatural, and *The Cutting Room*, a reprint anthology of movie horror.

The recipient of nine World Fantasy Awards, Datlow has also won multiple Locus, Hugo, Stoker, International Horror Guild, and Shirley Jackson awards and the 2012 Il Posto Nero Black Spot Award for Excellence as Best Foreign Editor. Datlow was named recipient of the 2007 Karl Edward Wagner Award, given at the British Fantasy Convention for "outstanding contributions to the genre," and she was honored with the Life Achievement Award from the Horror Writers Association in acknowledgment of her superior achievement over the course of her career.

Datlow lives in New York and co-hosts the monthly Fantastic Fiction Reading Series at KGB Bar. More information can be found at WWW.DATLOW.COM or at her blog, ELLEN-DATLOW.LIVEJOURNAL.COM. You can also find her on Twitter at @ELLENDATLOW.

STEFAN DZIEMIANOWICZ (FOREWORD) has compiled more than forty anthologies of horror, mystery, and science fiction, and collections of macabre fiction by Louisa May Alcott, Robert Bloch, Joseph Payne Brennan, August Derleth, Henry Kuttner, Jane Rice, Bram Stoker, Henry S. Whitehead, and others. A former editor of *Necrofile: The Review of Horror Fiction* and the Necronomicon Press short fiction series, he co-edited *Supernatural Literature of the World: An Encyclopedia*. He is the author of *Bloody Mary and Other Tales for a Dark Night* and *The Annotated Guide to Unknown and Unknown Worlds*. His reviews have appeared in *Publishers Weekly*, *Locus*, and the *Washington Post Book World*.

GEMMA FILES was born in London, England, but is a Canadian citizen and has lived in Toronto, Ontario, her entire life. She has been a film critic and a teacher of screenwriting and Canadian film history in addition to publishing two collections of short stories (*Kissing Carrion* and *The Worm in Every Heart*) and two chapbooks of poetry.

Five of her short stories were adapted for the U.S./Canadian horror television series *The Hunger*, and she wrote two screenplays for the series.

Her short story "The Emperor's Old Bones" won the International Horror Guild Award for Best Short Story of 1999. Her first novel, *A Book of Tongues: Volume One in the Hexslinger Series*, won the 2010 Black Quill Award for "Best Small Press Chill" (both Editors' and Readers' Choice) and made the 2010 Over the Rainbow Book List. The trilogy has since been completed with *A Rope of Thorns* and *A Tree of Bones*. She has is currently working on her first stand-alone novel.

For more information: MUSICATMIDNIGHT-GFILES.BLOGSPOT.COM.

NEIL GAIMAN is the Newbery Medal–winning author of *The Graveyard Book* and a *New York Times* best-selling author. Several of his books, including *Coraline*, have been made into major motion pictures. He is also famous for writing the *Sandman* graphic novel series and numerous other books and comics for adult, young adult, and younger readers. He has won the Hugo, Nebula, Mythopoeic, and World Fantasy awards, among others. He is also the author of powerful short stories and poems.

For more information: WWW.NEILGAIMAN.COM.

BRIAN HODGE is the award-winning author of eleven novels spanning horror, crime, and history. He's also written more than one hundred short stories, novelettes, and novellas and five full-length collections. His first collection, *The Convulsion Factory*, was ranked by critic Stanley Wiater among the 113 best books of modern horror.

Recent or forthcoming works include *No Law Left Unbroken*, a collection of crime fiction; *The Weight of the Dead* and *Whom the Gods Would Destroy*, both stand-alone novellas; a newly revised hardcover edition of *Dark Advent*, his early post-apocalyptic epic; and his latest novel, *Leaves of Sherwood*.

He lives in Colorado, where more of everything is in the works. He also dabbles in music, sound design, and photography; loves everything about organic gardening except the thieving squirrels; and trains in Krav Maga, grappling, and kickboxing, which are of no use at all against the squirrels.

Connect through his website (BRIANHODGE.NET) or on Facebook (FACEBOOK.COM/ BRIANHODGEWRITER) and follow his blog, *Warrior Poet* (WARRIORPOETBLOG.COM).

The *New York Times* recently called CAITLÍN R. KIERNAN "one of our essential writers of dark fiction." Her novels include *The Red Tree* (nominated for the Shirley Jackson and World Fantasy awards) and *The Drowning Girl: A Memoir* (winner of the James Tiptree, Jr. Award and nominated for the Nebula and Bram Stoker awards).

To date, her short fiction has been collected in thirteen volumes, most recently *Confessions of a Five-Chambered Heart*, *Two Worlds and In Between: The Best of Caitlín R. Kiernan (Volume One)*, and *The Ape's Wife and Other Stories*. Currently, she's writing the graphic novel series *Alabaster* for Dark Horse Comics and working on her next novel, *Red Delicious*.

JOHN LANGAN is the author of the collections *The Wide, Carnivorous Sky and Other Monstrous Geographies* and *Mr. Gaunt and Other Uneasy Encounters* as well as the novel *House of Windows*.

He and Paul Tremblay co-edited *Creatures: Thirty Years of Monsters*. His recent stories have been published in numerous anthologies, including *Supernatural Noir*, *Blood and Other Cravings*, and *Shadows Edge*. He lives in upstate New York with his wife, son, dog, cats, rats, and several tanks of fish.

JOE R. LANSDALE is the author of more than thirty novels and numerous short stories, articles, and scripts for comics and films. His novella *Bubba Ho-Tep* was filmed by Don Coscarelli and starred Bruce Campbell and Ossie Davis.

He has received an Edgar Award for his novel *The Bottoms*, the Grinzane Cavour Prize for Literature, the Inkpot Award for Lifetime Achievement, the Herodotus Award for Best Historical Crime Novel, and nine Bram Stoker Awards, including one for Lifetime Achievement in Horror. He has also been awarded the Grandmaster of Horror Award by the Horror Writers Association.

He is Writer in Residence at Stephen F. Austin State University, a member of the Texas Institute of Letters, and a member of the Texas Literary Hall of Fame. His latest novel is *The Thicket*, from Mulholland Books.

For more information: WWW.JOERLANSDALE.COM.

THOMAS LIGOTTI'S first collection of stories, *Songs of a Dead Dreamer*, was published in 1986, with an expanded version issued three years later. Other collections include *Grimscribe*, *Noctuary*, *My Work Is Not Yet Done*, and *Teatro Grottesco*.

Thomas Ligotti has been honored with the Bram Stoker Award for his collection *The Nightmare Factory* and short novel *My Work Is Not Yet Done*. He has also won the British Fantasy Award and the International Horror Guild Award for his work.

Ligotti's most recent publication is a nonfiction book, *The Conspiracy against the Human Race: A Contrivance of Horror*, which comprises an excursion through the darker byways of literature, philosophy, and psychology.

NICK MAMATAS is the author of several novels, including the Lovecraftian mash-ups *Move under Ground* and *The Damned Highway* (with Brian Keene). His latest novel, *Love Is the Law*, is noir. Nick's short fiction has appeared, or will appear, in *Asimov's Science Fiction*, *Tor.com*, *Future Lovecraft*, and *Best American Mystery Stories*.

For more information: WWW.NICK-MAMATAS.COM.

KIM NEWMAN is a novelist, critic, and broadcaster. His fiction includes *The Night Mayor*, *Bad Dreams*, *Jago*, the Anno Dracula novels and stories, *The Quorum*, *The Original Dr. Shade and Other Stories*, *Life's Lottery*, *Back in the USSA* (with Eugene Byrne), and *The Man from the Diogenes Club* under his own name and *The Vampire Genevieve* and *Orgy of the Blood Parasites* as Jack Yeovil. His nonfiction books include *Ghastly beyond Belief* (with Neil Gaiman), *Horror: 100 Best Books* (with Stephen Jones), *Wild West Movies*, *The BFI Companion to Horror*, *Millennium Movies: End of the World Cinema*, and BFI Classics studies of *Cat People* and *Doctor Who*. He is a contributing editor to *Sight & Sound* and *Empire* magazines, has written and broadcast widely on a range of topics, and has scripted radio and television documentaries. His stories "Week Woman" and "Ubermensch" have been adapted into an episode of the TV series *The Hunger* and an Australian short film, respectively; he has directed and written a tiny film called *Missing Girl*; and he co-wrote the West End play *The Hallowe'en Sessions*.

The URL for his official website is WWW.JOHNNYALUCARD.COM. His most recent publications are expanded reissues of the Anno Dracula series and *The Hound of the d'Urbervilles* and a much-expanded edition of *Nightmare Movies*. *Johnny Alucard*, the fourth Anno Dracula novel, appeared in 2012; his next novel will be *An English Ghost Story*. He is on Twitter as @ANNODRACULA.

WILLIAM BROWNING SPENCER is a novelist and short-story writer living in Austin, Texas. He is the author of the novels *Maybe I'll Call Anna*, *Résumé with Monsters*, *Zod Wallop*, and *Irrational Fears* and the short-story collections *The Return of Count Electric & Other Stories* and *The Ocean and All Its Devices*.

Spencer is also a screenwriter whose screenplays are often under option.

Résumé with Monsters, his novel about bad jobs and Lovecraftian monsters, won the International Horror Critics Award. It will be reprinted by Dover Publications in early 2014. He expects to finish a new short-story collection and a new novel in the near future.

STEVE RASNIC TEM was born in Lee County, Virginia, in the heart of Appalachia. He currently lives in Centennial, Colorado, with his wife, the writer Melanie Tem. He is a past winner of the Bram Stoker, International Horror Guild, British Fantasy, and World Fantasy awards. His latest novel is *Deadfall Hotel*. In 2012 and 2013, four new collections of his short stories appeared: *Ugly Behavior*, *Onion Songs*, *Celestial Inventories*, and *Twember*.

You can visit the Tems on the Web at WWW.M-S-TEM.COM.

STEVEN UTLEY was born in 1948 and lived in Austin, Texas, for much of his life. He was a member of the Turkey City Writers Workshop, which was founded in 1973 and included such writers as Lisa Tuttle, Howard Waldrop, and Bruce Sterling.

He mostly wrote science fiction. His best-known collaboration with Waldrop is *Custer's Last Jump*.

He started his Silurian Tales sequence of time-travel stories in 1993, and several of the individual stories have been reprinted in various Year's Best collections. In 2012, Ticonderoga Publications collected the Silurian stories into two volumes entitled *The 400-Million-Year Itch* and *Invisible Kingdoms*. Utley died in 2012.

KARL EDWARD WAGNER'S first novel, *Darkness Weaves*, was published in 1970. He wrote or edited more than forty books over the course of his career, including his collections *In a Lonely Place*, *Why Not You and I?*, *Exorcisms and Ecstasies*, and *Midnight Sun: The Complete Stories of Kane*; and (as editor) fifteen volumes of the annual Year's Best Horror Stories series from 1980 to 1994. He won three British Fantasy awards and two World Fantasy awards. *Where the Summer Ends: The Best Horror Stories of Karl Edward Wagner, Volume 1*, and *Walk on the Wild Side: The Best Horror Stories of Karl Edward Wagner, Volume 1*, were published in 2012 is a comprehensive retrospective of Wagner's short fiction. He died in 1994.

HOWARD WALDROP has been called "a national treasure" by those who love his multi-award-winning alternate- and secret-history short stories and novellas, such as "The Ugly Chickens," "Flying Saucer Rock and Roll," and *A Dozen Tough Jobs*.